OWLFLIGHT

NOVELS BY MERCEDES LACKEY
available from DAW Books

THE MAGE WARS
(with Larry Dixon)
THE BLACK GRYPHON
THE WHITE GRYPHON
THE SILVER GRYPHON

THE BOOKS OF THE LAST HERALD-MAGE
MAGIC'S PAWN
MAGIC'S PROMISE
MAGIC'S PRICE

VOWS AND HONOR
THE OATHBOUND
OATHBREAKERS

KEROWYN'S TALE
BY THE SWORD

THE HERALDS OF VALDEMAR
ARROWS OF THE QUEEN
ARROW'S FLIGHT
ARROW'S FALL

THE MAGE WINDS
WINDS OF FATE
WINDS OF CHANGE
WINDS OF FURY

THE MAGE STORMS
STORM WARNING
STORM RISING
STORM BREAKING

OWLFLIGHT
(with Larry Dixon)

DARKOVER NOVEL
(with Marion Zimmer Bradley)
REDISCOVERY

THE BLACK SWAN*

PHOENIX AND ASHES*
THE GATES OF SLEEP*
THE SERPENT'S SHADOW*

*forthcoming from DAW Books in Hardcover

Justyn

OWLFLIGHT

MERCEDES LACKEY
& LARRY DIXON

Interior illustrations by Larry Dixon

DAW BOOKS, INC.
DONALD A. WOLLHEIM, FOUNDER
375 Hudson Street, New York, NY 10014
ELIZABETH R. WOLLHEIM
SHEILA E. GILBERT
PUBLISHERS

Jacket art by Jody A. Lee.

For color prints of Jody Lee's paintings, please contact:
The Cerridwen Enterprise
P.O. Box 10161
Kansas City, MO 64111
Phone: 1-800-825-1281

Interior illustrations by Larry Dixon.

All the black & white interior illustrations
in this book are available as 8" × 10" prints,
either in a signed, open edition singly, or in
a signed and numbered portfolio from:

FIREBIRD ARTS & MUSIC, INC.
P.O. Box 14785
Portland, OR 97214-9998
Phone: 1-800-752-0494

Time Line by Pat Tobin.

DAW Books Collectors No. 1069.

DAW Books are distributed by Penguin Putnam Inc.
Book designed by Leonard Telesca

This book is printed on acid-free paper.

ISBN 0-88677-754-2

To Dr. Irene Pepperberg and Alex

OFFICIAL TIMELINE FOR THE

by Mercedes Lackey

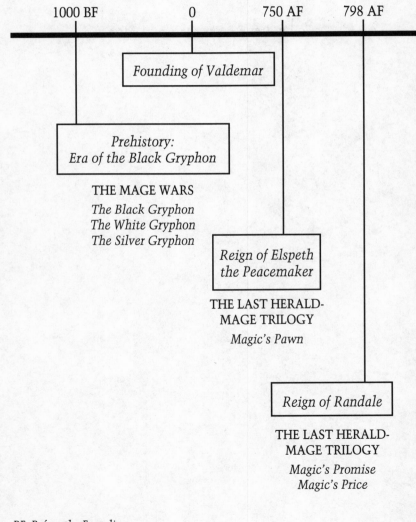

| 1000 BF | 0 | 750 AF | 798 AF |

Founding of Valdemar

Prehistory:
Era of the Black Gryphon

THE MAGE WARS

The Black Gryphon
The White Gryphon
The Silver Gryphon

Reign of Elspeth
the Peacemaker

THE LAST HERALD-
MAGE TRILOGY

Magic's Pawn

Reign of Randale

THE LAST HERALD-
MAGE TRILOGY

Magic's Promise
Magic's Price

BF Before the Founding
AF After the Founding

HERALDS OF VALDEMAR SERIES

Sequence of events by Valdemar reckoning

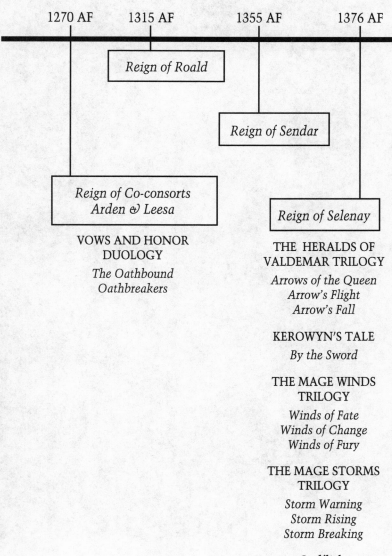

1270 AF   1315 AF   1355 AF   1376 AF

Reign of Roald

Reign of Sendar

Reign of Co-consorts
Arden & Leesa

Reign of Selenay

**VOWS AND HONOR
DUOLOGY**

*The Oathbound
Oathbreakers*

**THE HERALDS OF
VALDEMAR TRILOGY**

*Arrows of the Queen
Arrow's Flight
Arrow's Fall*

KEROWYN'S TALE

By the Sword

**THE MAGE WINDS
TRILOGY**

*Winds of Fate
Winds of Change
Winds of Fury*

**THE MAGE STORMS
TRILOGY**

*Storm Warning
Storm Rising
Storm Breaking*

Owlflight

Snowfire

One

The air was warm, the summer day flawless, and Darian Firkin was stalling, trying to delay the inevitable, and he knew it. He had hopes that if he just lingered enough on this task of wood gathering, his Master might forget about him—or something more urgent than the next lesson might come up before Wizard Justyn got himself organized. It was worth a try anyway, since the very last thing Darian wanted on this fine sunny day was to be cooped up in that musty old cottage. It was worth any amount of physical work to be saved from that fate.

He took a deep breath of the balmy air, laden with the scent of curing hay, damp earth, and growing things, and added another cut quarter-log to his burden of three, the bark and rough wood catching on his shirt and leaving bits of dirt and moss smeared on the sleeve. Would four be enough to qualify as a load? Probably. He headed for the cottage.

Justyn's cottage decayed on the edge of the village, on the side farthest from the bridge and the road, closest to the forest. The village itself was a tight little square of cottages with three finer houses, all arranged in neat rows around the village square; the fields farmed by the inhabitants of Errold's Grove stretched out on either side along the riverbank, but on the back side there was nothing but a single field of corn and a small meadow where goats and sheep were kept in the winter. Behind all of that was the forest. If he paused for a moment and listened, it wasn't at all difficult to hear the voice of the woods from where Darian stood—all the little rustling and murmurings, the birdsong and animal calls. Sometimes that was a torment, on days when Justyn set him some fool task that kept him pent in the cottage from dawn to dusk.

He put down his burden on the pile at the side of the dilapidated cottage and returned for more.

He carefully selected three small pieces of chopped wood from the large communal pile; the woodpile lay at the back of the right-hand side of the village of Errold's Grove. He tucked them under his arm and carried them toward the rick-holder at the side of Wizard Justyn's tiny cottage. Every day that it was possible, the village woodcutter went out with a team of oxen to find and bring back deadfall from the Pelagiris Forest. He never went far, but then, he never had to; the trees in the Pelagiris were enormous, with trunks so big that six men could stretch their arms around one and not have their fingers touch, and one fallen tree would supply enough wood for the whole village for a month. Every time there was a storm, at least one tree or several huge branches would come crashing down. The woodcutter did nothing at all *but* cut wood; no farmwork, no herding. The villagers supplied him in turn with anything he needed, and since he had no wife nor apprentice, the women took it in turn to cook for him, clean his little hut, and sew, wash, and mend his clothing. The woodcutter was not a bright man, nor one given at all to much thought, so he found the arrangement entirely to his satisfaction— and since the villagers never went into the Forest anymore if they didn't have to, it was entirely to theirs as well.

Darian wished they had apprenticed him to the woodcutter instead of the Wizard, but he hadn't had any say in the matter. After all, as an orphan who had been left to the village to care for, he should be grateful that they gave him any sort of care at all. At least that was what they all told him, loudly and often.

The cottage was hardly longer than the wood-rick, built strongly at one time, of weathered, gray river rock with a thatched roof of broomstraw in which birds twittered all spring and summer long. That twittering was the first thing Darian heard every morning when he woke up. It was an adequate enough little cottage by the standards of the village, but it seemed badly cramped to Darian, and always smelled slightly musty, with an undertone of bitter herbs and dust. No one ever cleaned it but Darian, so perhaps that was the reason for the aroma. He didn't really despise the place, since after all, it was shelter, but it didn't really feel like the home the other villagers and his Master tried to convince him it was.

When he reached the cottage and the upright supports that would hold exactly one measured rick of wood between them, he set each piece down on the half-rick already piled there with exacting care, distributing them with all the concentration of a fine lady making a flower arrangement. Only when they were balanced precisely to his liking did he return for another three logs. He listened carefully for any sound of life inside the cottage, for after Justyn had told him to replenish their fuel, Darian had left his Master muttering over a book, and Darian had hopes that Justyn might get so involved that he wouldn't notice that Darian was taking a very long time to fetch wood from a few yards away.

There was no sound from inside the cottage, and Darian ambled off slowly, making as little noise as possible until he was out of easy hearing distance. The village was fairly quiet at this time of day, with most people working in the fields. Only a few crafters had work to keep them in their workshops at this time of year; most of the things that people needed they had to make for themselves these days, or hope that someone else in the village had the skills they lacked. Leather and fur were available in abundance, but the tanner worked hides mostly in the fall, and there was no official cobbler since Old Man Makus died. The blacksmith did all metal work needed, and with forty-odd families to provide for, he generally had enough work to keep him busy all of the time. The miller was also the baker, keeping flour and bread under the same roof, so to speak. He baked almost all of the bread and occasional sweets for the village, so that only one person would have to fire up and tend an oven. Women would often put together a stewpot or a meat pie or set of pasties for the evening dinner, and take it to him to put just inside the oven in the morning. Then they could go out to work the fields, and fetch the cooked meal back when the family returned for dinner. The womenfolk of Errold's Grove did their own spinning, weaving, and sewing, mostly during the long, dark hours of winter, which was when the men made crude shoes and boots, mended or made new harnesses and belts, and carved wooden implements. Once every three or four months, everyone would take a day off work to make pots, plates, storage jars, and cups of clay from the banks of the Londell River, and in a few days when those articles were dry, the baker and the woodcutter would fire them all at once. Those went into a common store from which folk could draw whatever they needed until it was time to replenish the crockery again. The only things that had to be brought in from outside were objects of metal that required more skill than the blacksmith had, such as needles and pins, and bar-stock for the smith. Virtually everything else could be and was made by the people living here. The village was mostly self-sufficient, which was a source of bitter pride, for no one *wanted* to come here anymore.

Errold's Grove could have dropped off the face of the world and no one would miss it.

I certainly wouldn't, Darian thought with bitterness of his own.

He had to pass through one of the busier corners of the village to reach the woodpile, going around both the smithy and the baker. The savory scent of bread coming from the door of the bakery told the boy that Leander was removing loaves from the big brick oven that took up all of the back half of his shop. As for the smith, he was obviously hard at work, as the smithy rang with the blows of hammer on anvil, there was a scent of hot metal and steam on the breeze, and smoke coming from the smokehole in the roof. Leander wouldn't pay any attention to Darian as he passed, but there was a chance that the smith might.

The smithy was a three-sided shed, the forge in the middle, the anvil toward the front. There was a fat old gray plowhorse waiting patiently for his feet to be attended to, tied to the post outside the smithy, and its owner, a man called Backet, watched as the smith hammered out a new shoe for it. Blacksmith Jakem, a huge, balding man with an incongruous paunch beneath his leather apron, paused in his work to watch Darian pass by, his eyes narrowed. Darian ignored him, as he usually ignored the adults of the village when he thought he could get away with it. Jakem didn't think much of Darian, but that was hardly out of the ordinary. Darian didn't think much of Jakem either. As he made the return trip with his three small logs, the smith hawked and spat into the fire.

"Ain't nobody works as hard as a lazy 'un," he said loudly to the farmer sitting on a stump beside the forge.

"That's the plain truth," Old Man Backet agreed, taking off his hat to scratch his head. "Lazy 'un will work twice's hard as anybody else, tryin' to avoid working at all." He cast a sly look at Darian as he replied, to see if his words had struck a nerve.

Darian continued to ignore them; so long as the adults didn't address him directly, there was a certain amount of immunity that being only thirteen gave him. He'd learned some time ago that a retort would only earn him trouble with his Master. Not that Wizard Justyn had ever laid a hand on him—but the reproachful lectures on how much he owed the villagers of Errold's Grove and how little he repaid their care were worse than a beating.

Nobody ever asked me what I wanted, not once. Nobody gave me a choice. If I'd had a choice, I wouldn't be here now, and no one would have had to think about "taking care of me." I'd have offered to work just enough to get a tent and some supplies, and I'd have been off to try on my own. Now I'm stuck here enduring useless blathering from a senile Master and carrying firewood like a dog in harness.

He made three more such trips—ignoring the adults at the forge each time, although it certainly did not escape his notice that the force and frequency of the smith's blows increased each time he passed. If Jakem wanted to wear out his arm trying to impress upon Darian what so-called "industrious labor" looked and sounded like, it wasn't going to bother Darian any.

Besides, if he told the smith *why* he was making such a production out of the simple task of fetching wood, he'd only get another tongue-lashing, and maybe a cuff on the side of the head into the bargain. The smith had a notoriously heavy hand with his own offspring, and if provoked he might well use it on Darian.

As Darian put his scant armload of wood down at the end of the third trip, the voice of doom emerged from the interior of the cottage.

"Darian, leave that for now and get in here. It's time for your lesson."

It was actually a fairly pleasant, masculine voice, a bit tired-sounding and querulous, but not *too* irritated or scolding. Nevertheless, if Darian had been a dog, he would have dropped his head and ears and tucked his tail down. "But the firewood—" he protested, knowing that the protest would do him no good, but making it anyway.

"The wood can wait; I can't. Come in now, Darian."

Darian drew his brows together in a sullen scowl, but obeyed the summons, leaving the sunshine and the fresh air for the closed-in gloom of the cottage. He tried to leave the door open to admit a little breeze, but Justyn frowned and motioned to him to shut it behind him.

He waited with resignation for his eyes to adjust to the dimness. The only light in the cottage came from a trio of very small windows in three of the four walls; even though the shutters stood wide open, they still didn't admit much light. Wizard Justyn waited for him at one end of the scarred and battered table taking up most of the right side of the room, which served as kitchen, dining room, workroom, and study, all in one. At the rear of the room was a set of rungs hammered into the stone of the wall that served as a ladder to the loft where Darian and his Master slept. Most of the rest of the wall-space was taken up with shelves, badly-made bookcases that leaned perilously toward each other, like drunks propping one another up, and several appalling pictures of famous mages. Darian's father, who'd dabbled in painting, had once said that a good engraving or print was worth twenty bad paintings, and Darian could certainly see why. They made his eyes hurt just to look at them, but unfortunately, there was no way that he could avoid looking at them.

Most prominent was the best of the lot, a heroic portrait of a person not even a terrible painter could ruin entirely. His noble features and intelligent eyes made up to a small extent for the stiff daubs of his costume. Shown seated at a table from about the waist up, the great Wizard Kyllian, a Fireflower Mage, looked every inch the powerful sorcerer, right down to his familiar, a sleek and smug-looking striped creature at his elbow that might have been a cat, or might not have been. It was difficult to tell if Grimkin was something other than an ordinary feline, or if the painter had taken the same liberties with cat anatomy that he had with human. Arranged on either side of this portrait were the pictures of Herald-Mage Elspeth, Darkwind Hawk-brother, Quenten of White Winds and the powerful Adept Firesong, all of whom Wizard Justyn had allegedly seen and spoken with before he arrived here to serve Errold's Grove. Darian was more than a little dubious about that claim. For one thing, how could a broken-down fake like old Justyn have ever gotten near enough to the legendary Elspeth and Darkwind to have seen them at close range, much less spoken to them? And if he had, how could he *ever* have thought that the horrible daubs on his wall in any way resembled them? They hardly even resembled portraits of human beings! The picture of El-speth showed her atop her Companion, in an unreasonably heroic pose, both hands upraised with what were supposed to be bolts of lightning coming from her hands. But the "lightning bolts" looked more like sickly pale-green snakes, the Companion looked like a lumpy cow, the face of the Herald-Mage like a blob of dough with two currants stuck in for eyes and a slash of orange carrot for a mouth. She apparently had twisted legs, no neck, and enormous, pil-lowlike breasts. The Herald's uniform and her Companion weren't even white, they were a disgusting muddy-yellow sort of color, as if the painter hadn't been able to afford a pure white pigment. Or maybe he'd used a cheap varnish that had yellowed as it aged. Darkwind at least looked *human*, but the bird on his shoulder had more in common with a fat chicken ready for the pot than any hawk that Darian had ever seen. The rest of the portraits were pretty much on the same level of skill—or lack of it—the firebird posing with the Adept was so ineptly done that most of the villagers thought it was supposed to represent a goose and had wondered aloud out of Justyn's hearing why a mage would have such a silly familiar. As for Firesong's mask—the Adept was never seen without one—it looked like a child's drawing of a sunflower, and if everyone didn't already know that it was a mask, a reasonable person could have thought the painting was of some fabulous monster.

It was painfully obvious that no woman had ever touched this cottage since the day Justyn moved in. Darian had gotten used to it over the last six months, but there was no doubt that it was a worse-than-typical aged bachelor's study. Littering the leaning and badly-made bookcases were an assortment of cheap and flashy "magical" implements, a few tattered old books, a lot of unrecognizable but definitely dead animals which were allegedly "preserved" in some way, several spider webs, a couple of cracked mugs, the upper half of the skull of some largish animal, an apple core, and a great deal of dust. Darian had tried to clean the place up when he'd first been sent here, out of pure self-interest, but being told sharply to leave things alone on numerous occasions, he'd lost interest in cleaning up anything but his own little corner around his pallet in the loft.

Sitting right in front of Wizard Kyllian's portrait on the top of a tipsy-looking bookcase was a beat-up and scruffy old black tomcat currently engaged in cleaning his hind leg, which stuck stiffly straight up into the air as the cat's tongue rasped at the thin fur. This was Justyn's familiar, or so he claimed. It certainly matched its Master, for a less-graceful cat Darian had never seen. It seemed to share the villagers' contempt for its Master and his apprentice, ignoring both of them with a disdain more in keeping with the pampered pet of a princess than of a patchy-furred mongrel of indeterminate age, with a broken tail and chewed-up ears.

Carefully placed in a rack on the wall was a rather plain looking, partially split walking stick with a bit of crystal embedded in the top which Justyn said was his "wizard's staff." That, along with four chairs (none matching) and the thick, warped oak table with a book under one leg keeping it straight, comprised all of the furnishings of the room.

The table was covered with jars and bottles, the remains of last night's dinner in stacked-up plates that had been shoved out of the way, bits of scribbled-on paper, burned-out ends of candles, and one empty wine bottle. Darian glanced with guilt at the stack of dirty dishes; he was supposed to have cleaned them up this morning, but he had been in such a hurry to get up and out before Justyn thought of giving him a lesson that he had neglected that duty entirely. Now he'd have to scrub them with sand to get all the dried-on gravy off them, and he'd have to do so before they could eat or they wouldn't have anything to eat tonight's dinner *on*. At least he'd remembered to take the turnip pasties over to the baker in time for them to go into the oven. It wouldn't have been the first time he'd forgotten and they'd had to make do with bread, raw turnips, onions, and sometimes a little cheese.

But the mess evidently didn't bother Justyn at all; when Darian had first been apprenticed to him, the place had looked much the same. The day he'd moved his things in, Darian had been strictly forbidden to touch anything on any of the bookshelves without specific permission, which frankly led Darian to believe that old Justyn wasn't certain what was on those shelves himself. It had occurred to him that Justyn was afraid that if Darian cleaned and organized things, the boy would ruin the wizard's best excuse for not getting magics done immediately when people asked him for them. Hunting for this or that ingredient or piece of apparatus was a good excuse for stalling, and as Darian knew from his own experience, if you stalled long enough, people sometimes forgot their requests.

"Sit," Justyn ordered. Darian slumped into a seat across from Justyn, taking the chair that wobbled the least. There was a plate with an apple on it right in front of his chair, and sitting where he could watch both the apple and Darian was Justyn. With a resigned sigh, Darian stared at the apple while Justyn stared just as intently at Darian.

He looks like a real rag-bag today, Darian thought critically, looking down at the wrinkled, winter-stored apple. *He looks as if birds were nesting in his beard. Is this part of his act, or is he getting even more senile?* Justyn was about the most ill-kempt male in the village, his only wealth that of his untidy hair and beard. He had three or four shabby and patched robes, all pretty much alike, with badly-made, lopsided, Esoteric Symbols sewn on them by Justyn himself. If you looked closely, you could see little rusty spots where Justyn had stabbed his thumb with the needle and bled on his work. He kept them clean, Darian had to give the old man that much credit, although he was always spilling things on them that made stains that never would come out, rendering the garments into a mosaic of blotches of various faint colors. It was difficult to tell how old the mage was; his hair and beard were gray rather than white, with a few streaks of darker color in them, and his brownish eyes, very sad and tired, were sunken so deeply beneath his shaggy eyebrows that it was difficult to see the wrinkles at the corners. He could have been any age from forty to ninety, and since no one in the village knew anything of his history before he came to Errold's Grove in the company of a Herald on circuit, his true age was anyone's guess.

"Well?" Justyn said, showing a bit of impatience. "Are you going to just sit there wasting time, or are you going to actually do something?"

With another reluctant sigh, Darian stopped merely *staring* at the apple and began concentrating.

He narrowed his focus until the apple filled his vision and his mind, simultaneously relaxing and tensing. He concentrated on the apple *being* above the plate, as if an invisible hand held it there. As he concentrated, the apple began to wobble a little. The movement was so slight that it could have been caused by someone bumping the table itself, except that neither he nor Justyn had moved.

After a long moment of tension, he *felt* something inside himself relax.

Slowly, agonizingly, the apple rose, still wobbling, but now doing so in midair. It hovered about the width of his finger above the plate surface. Sweat broke out all over his forehead in beads, and he felt the pinch of a headache starting just between his eyes. And behind the concentration, he seethed with annoyance and impatience. This was a stupid waste of time; he knew it, and Justyn knew it, but Justyn was never going to admit it, because that would be admitting that he had been wrong about Darian, and Justyn would die before he admitted that. What on earth good would floating an apple about do? Would it bring in more crops? Chase away sickness? Bring prosperity back to the village?

The answer, clearly, was "no" to all three questions.

Behind Justyn, the cat finished his grooming and began coughing, making gagging and strangling sounds. Darian struggled to maintain his concentration, but the wretched creature's noise was more than he could ignore.

The apple wobbled and dipped, as Darian's control over it began to unravel. The cat hacked again, more violently than before, until Darian was certain it was going to cough up a lung this time and not just another wad of hair.

It was too much distraction, and he lost the "spell" completely. The cat spit up a massive, moist hairball with a sound that made Darian's stomach turn, just as the apple thumped down on the plate.

Darian swore furiously under his breath at the cat, the apple, and a fate that conspired to make a mess even of things he despised. The cat sniffed, coughed once more, jumped down, and limped over to the fireplace where it curled up on the ash-strewn hearth.

Darian gave the cat a look that should have set its fur on fire if there had been any justice in the universe, and glowered at the apple. If he'd had half the power Justyn swore he had, the apple should have exploded from the strength of that glare. The fact that it didn't only proved to him that his Master was a fraud and was trying to make him into another fraud. *What is the use of this?* he asked himself angrily. *What's the point? If a stupid cat can break a spell, how is anyone supposed to get anything done by magic? It's stupid, that's all it is, it's just as pointless as everything else in this village!*

"Try again," Justyn ordered him, with a kind of weary disgust that angered Darian even further. What right did *that* old fake have to be disgusted with him? It wasn't *his* fault that he had no magic! And as far as that was concerned, Justyn had no room to find fault with Darian on that score!

How long has it been since he *did anything with real magic? I bet he couldn't have kept that apple in the air any longer than I did!*

Anger and frustration rose to the boiling point, and instead of doing as he was told, he swept his arm across the table in front of him, knocking apple, plate, and anything else in the path of that angry sweep off the table and onto the floor with a crash. The plate didn't shatter, since it was made of pewter, but it made a lot of noise and acquired yet another dent. As Justyn opened his mouth to scold, Darian shoved his chair away from the table, sitting there with his arms folded over his chest, glowering, silently daring Justyn to do his worst.

Justyn visibly pushed down his own temper. "Darian, I want you to try again," the wizard repeated, with mounting impatience. "And since you won't do it properly, you can pick that apple up off the floor and put it back on the table with your mind—yes, and the plate as well! A bit more hard work will teach you to control your temper. A mage can't ever lose his temper, or—"

"Why?" Darian snarled defiantly, interrupting the lecture on self-control that he had heard a hundred times already. "Why should I use my mind to float fruit around? There's no reason to! It's faster and easier to grab it like any normal person would!" And just to prove his point, he bent down and seized apple and plate and banged both down on the wooden tabletop. "There! Now that's what a person with plain common sense does! You don't have to muck around with these stupid tricks to get things done!"

Now, of course, was the moment when Justyn would launch into a lecture on how in magic one must practice on small things before one could expect to succeed in the larger, how he was being immature and childish, and how very ungrateful he was. Next would follow how it was criminal that he refused to obey, that he had such a wonderful gift and was apprenticed to a wizard who would teach him skills, and didn't appreciate his easy circumstances when instead he could have been bound out to a farmer or the blacksmith—

Darian knew it all by heart and could have recited it in his sleep. And it wouldn't make any difference if he protested that he didn't *want* to be a wizard, that he hadn't *asked* for this so-called "wonderful gift," and that he didn't see what was so wonderful about it. Justyn would ignore his protests, just as everyone else had, and did, and always would. For some reason that he did not fathom, every other person in the village was astonished that he didn't appreciate being farmed out to the old fake.

But just at that point, there were sounds of thumping and a grunt of pain outside. Harris and Vere Neshem, a pair of the local farmers, staggered in through the door with Kyle Osterham the woodcutter supported between them, his leg wrapped in rags stained with fresh, red blood. Darian jumped immediately out of his chair and moved aside for them, shoving the chair in their direction.

"He was chopping up a stump and his footing slipped," Vere said, as they lowered Kyle down into the seat Darian had just vacated. "Bit of a mess. Good thing we were close by."

Since Justyn served Errold's Grove in the capacity of a Healer far more often than that of a wizard, Darian had seen men who were worse wounded stagger in through the door, but Kyle's leg *was* a bit of a mess. *Surface cut,* he noted critically. *Ax blade probably hit the shin bone and skinned along the top of it. That'd peel back a lot of skin, but it'll heal quickly as soon as it's stitched, and it won't leave much of a scar. Lucky if he didn't break the shin, though.* It would bleed a lot, and hurt a great deal, but it was hardly life-threatening. He edged out of the way a little more and got nearer the door.

Justyn rummaged through the shelves behind him, grabbing rags, herbs, a needle and fine silk thread, a mortar and pestle.

"Darian, boil some water," he ordered, his back to the room as he hunted for something he needed.

But now Darian was in no mood to comply. This little incident only confirmed what he had been thinking. The people of Errold's Grove didn't need some fool who could suspend apples in the air, they needed a Healer, sometimes a Finder, sometimes a Weatherwatcher, but not a wizard, and they never *had* needed a wizard in all the time Darian had been here. Most especially, they didn't need *him*. It would make more sense for one of the girls to learn everything

Justyn could teach about herbs and simples, distilling and potions, setting bones and stitching skin. So Darian just stood there, ignoring Justyn's order, radiating rebellion and waiting for their reaction.

One of the farmers glanced at him with censure written clearly on his face. "Justyn," he said in an overly loud voice, "is there any help you need?"

Justyn, who had been muttering to himself as he mixed herbs in the mortar, got flustered and distracted at the interruption. He had to dump the lot of what he was grinding out into the tiny fire, and start again. The fire flared up with a roar and a shower of multicolored sparks, and both farmers exclaimed in startled surprise, taking everyone's attention off Darian.

That was all he needed. For once, Darian was not going to stand around and wait for people to give him stupid orders. Taking advantage of the distraction, the boy edged around behind Vere and made good his escape, sliding quickly out of the door before anyone noticed he was gone.

That'll show him! That'll show all of them that I'm not going to be treated like I have no mind of my own! I'm not a slave, and I never agreed to any of the things they've done to me! They don't give me the regard they'd give a rooster; why should I stay and be insulted and made to do things I hate?

He didn't want to be caught, though, so he moved around to the back of the cottage, plastering himself against the wall and ducking under the windows until he reached the side that faced the forest. He was just underneath the open window when he heard Justyn say in an exasperated tone of voice from which all patience had vanished, "Will you *please* boil that water, Darian? Now, not two weeks from now—"

But Darian was out of reach of further orders, and as he paused to listen to find out if either of the farmers was inclined to volunteer to go look for him, evidently Justyn looked around and saw that for himself, for there was a muffled curse.

"Useless brat," the first farmer muttered. "We should have 'prenticed him as a woodcutter to you, Kyle."

Vere gave a snort. "He'd be just as useless there. Lazy is what he is. You oughta beat him now and again, Justyn. You're too soft on him. Them parents of his spoiled him, and you ain't helping by bein' soft on him." There was a clatter of metal as someone put the kettle on the hook over the fire.

Vere's brother seconded that opinion. "Them two was useless to us and *dangerous*, Justyn. It's in his blood, an' you oughta beat it out of him, else he'll bring somethin' out of the woods that none of us'll like.'' Darian, lurking *right* beneath the window, heard every word too clearly to mistake any of it, and his stomach seized up inside of him as both fists clenched in an unconscious echo of the knots in his gut.

They were at it again. In front of him, or behind his back, they never let up, not for a minute! He felt his anger boiling up again, felt his face getting hot and his eyes starting to burn with the misery of loss he had vowed never, ever to show. He *wanted* to storm right back inside and confront both of those miserable old beasts, but what good would it possibly do? They'd only say to his face what they'd just said to Justyn.

With a strangled sob, he wrenched himself around and ran off— not into the village, but into the woods beyond, where the villagers were too cowardly—unlike his Mum and Dad—to go.

His feet knew the path, so he didn't need to be able to see to find his way to one of his many hiding places. That was just as well, since unshed tears of anger and grief kept him from seeing very clearly. Darian wasn't old enough to remember a time when things had been other than hard here at Errold's Grove, but until last year, he had been happy enough. He hadn't spent much time in the village itself, and although he hadn't had any playmates, he hadn't felt the need of them. Solitary by nature, he enjoyed the mostly-silent companionship of his parents.

Errold's Grove lay on the very far western edge of Valdemar; nominally it was part of Valdemar, but the people here seldom saw a Herald more than once a year, and of late it had been longer than that between visits. Not that a Herald would do Darian any good, but the Heralds' absence made the villagers feel neglected and forgotten, and that made them even harder on anyone who didn't conform.

And Darian would never conform. He hated the village, he hated the people who saw no farther than the edges of their fields and wanted nothing more. *He* wanted more; he was stifling for want of freedom, and felt as if he were starving on a diet of confinement and mediocrity. He'd been *out there* where these villagers feared, and he remembered it far more vividly than anything that had happened to him in this dull little huddle of huts. Once he'd traveled the deep forest he was never the same again, and he didn't want to be part of this insular flock of humanity.

He ran like a hare through the field of corn behind the cottage, bare callused feet making little noise on the soft, cultivated earth.

Nobody stopped him; the tall green corn hid him from view, and if they heard his running feet, they probably thought it was one of their own children coming back from an errand. A moment later, Darian burst into the shadows of the forest at the edge of the fields and slowed once he was in the shelter of the undergrowth. He took a moment to orient himself, then twisted his way through the brush and sought refuge in his favorite tree, one of the enormous forest giants that ringed the village and kept it in shade for most of the day. He climbed as swiftly as a squirrel or a tree-hare and as surely; even blinded by tears he had no trouble finding his hiding place where the great trunk split in two, forming a cup that a boy could easily curl up in and still have room for a few possessions. Beneath him lay the village, a cluster of about fifty buildings on the forested side of a bridged ford on the River Londell right on the edge of the Pelagiris Forest.

It went on forever in three directions, climbing hills, plunging into valleys, and crowning the huge bluff that rose above the river downstream of the village, with only the Londell halting its march toward the heart of Valdemar. The hard-won fields carved out of the forest were tended and fertilized with the greatest and tenderest of care, for it took terrible effort to gain a foot of clear ground from the trees, and there was always the chance (so it was said) that the forest would decide to take revenge for trees that were *cut* down rather than falling down naturally. The Forest had always been a fairly uncanny place according to the old granthers and grammers of the village, but since the start of the mage-storms it had gotten very much stranger and far more dangerous.

A Herald had come—the first he had seen—three months after his unwanted apprenticeship to Justyn had been decided for him. The Herald had been light-skinned, with a long blond braid of hair, and looked all the paler because of the white outfit and matching riding coat. With him, of course, had been his Companion, a white horse that was more than a horse—it was more like a dreamer's ideal of everything a horse could be, with lambent blue eyes, a long mane and hide that stayed impossibly clean, and silvery hooves. The Herald had explained that the strange things that were happening were called "mage-storms," and they were caused by the magic of the world being disturbed a very long time ago. They had been told that the greatest mages of the world had united under Valdemaran leadership, and were working to prevent any major catastrophes. The Herald had answered the few questions posed by the villagers, looking to the white horse and then back. Darian had wondered at the time if he was the only one of the group, Justyn included, who felt like the white horse and the Herald were communicating with each other through their looks and subtle gestures. The Herald would have gone on, but several of the older folk of the village hauled him away to explain more, out of Darian's earshot. Since that took Justyn away as well, he was perfectly happy with that, and went off then to spend time alone in this very place of refuge. By the time he'd emerged, the Herald and his Companion had gone, and there hadn't been one through here since.

According to Justyn, the fact that Errold's Grove was relatively near Lake Evendim meant that they got the worst of the mage-storms. Huge circles of land and the creatures in them either changed completely or warped and twisted out of all recognition. Monsters appeared, things worse than the worst nightmare or legend, and unfortunately there were no friendly Hawkbrothers nearby to chase away or kill them—not that the people of Errold's Grove particularly *trusted* the Hawkbrothers. At one time these people had made a good living out of going into the Pelagiris Forest and collecting some of the strange plants and fungi that grew there for use as dye-stuffs, and that business had occasionally brought them into conflict with the Hawkbrothers. Traders had come far out of their way for those dyes, and that had encouraged some people to go in deeper, in search of any other things that traders might find valuable. Of course, the deeper in they went, and the more they looked for ancient treasures instead of mosses and fungi, the more likely it was that they would wander into Hawkbrother lands and be warned off, often at the point of a drawn weapon. Once or twice, outsiders had come hunting treasure as well—and their bound bodies would later be found neatly arranged on the forest edge, without a single copper piece or trinket missing, awaiting discovery and burial. Each such discovery would discourage deeper incursions for a few months, but there were always greedy outsiders ready to dare the Hawkbrothers for the sake of treasures, and their fates were a warning to the dye-traders to stick to their business and leave whatever "treasure" was out there alone.

Nevertheless, there was enough and more than enough of legitimate "quarry" to tempt the people of Errold's Grove out into the Pelagiris until things started getting out of hand. The village had been quite prosperous, with visits from Heralds twice and three times a year, a fine wooden bridge over the Londell built by the order of the Crown, and even a pair of Valdemaran Guards stationed to watch the bridge and keep the peace on the road. There were still two sturdily built guardposts here, one on either side of the bridge, to prove that Errold's Grove had once been considered an important border town.

But war had come, war with Hardorn, and the Guards had been taken away to serve elsewhere, never to return. Now the only way that the people of Errold's Grove could keep the road open was to run their own volunteer patrols over it. Then things had somehow gotten mixed up with magic as well, and so far as the people of Errold's Grove were concerned, order and their old way of life had all but disappeared.

First had come the physical storms, worse than anyone had ever seen before, that washed out the road in places, flooded the village twice, and buried it in yards of snow for most of the last several winters. Then had come the mage-storms to batter them all along with the physical storms, and all anyone from Valdemar could do after the Herald's initial warning was to send a messenger with a map that showed what places were going to change, and when. That was no great help, when all the places were out in the wild forest and no one could *get* out there to chase large animals away from the danger zone. So the animals became monsters, or maybe the monsters were brought in by the magic; no one was really certain. The only thing that everyone in Errold's Grove could agree on was that now it was far too dangerous to leave the village and its fields. You never knew if or when you might disturb something that was canny enough to follow you back home. People stopped going into the Forest, and the dye-traders stopped coming, since there was no longer anything here to trade for, or even worth the peril to investigate.

Cowards! Darian thought, angrily scrubbing the tears from his eyes with his knuckles. *Other people kept going in! Other people weren't so scared of their shadows that they gave up!*

People like his parents, for instance. . . .

Darian's parents had been trappers, as had many generations of his ancestors on either side. But when it became too dangerous to actually live in the Forest, they had made Errold's Grove the base of their operation, carefully working a territory with cautious respect for the Hawkbrothers' claims and the new strangeness that the mage-storms brought with them. Some of the creatures that arrived on the wings of the mage-storms had handsome pelts of unusual colors, and traders would pay a lot for them. Other changes had occurred in the normal species of the Pelagiris, that had made improvements in color or texture of the furs of animals native to the forest, and for these, too, traders would come. Then, although they were not as expert as the villagers had been, they would look for the dye-fungi when time permitted, thus bringing back a bit of the prosperity that had left on the storm-winds.

They were careful! Darian silently told the village. *They knew how to be careful! They would never, ever have let anything follow them here, no matter what* you *think!* They always made certain to use traps that any truly *intelligent* species would spot, just to keep their consciences clean, but even with that caution they had brought in some incredible prizes. Darian had often gone with them, for during the winter they would both be out together for weeks at a time. He loved the Forest, and even at its most dangerous, he had never been as terrified of it as the villagers were now. It was right to be cautious around the Forest, but it was stupid to be afraid of it—after all, it wasn't the *Forest* that was so dangerous, it was the things living in it, and as long as you were careful, there was nothing to worry about! Any fool could see that!

And how could anyone let fear blind him to so much of wonder and beauty?

"Dari, listen," his mother would whisper, and he would cock his head to listen for the new sound that had caught her attention—perhaps the liquid trill of a new bird (or was it a tervardi?*)—or the bell-like tone of a hammer-jay. Whatever it was, once he caught it, he would look to her, and see the pleasure shining in her eyes as she listened, too. Then she would tell him what it was they had just heard, and spin him tales of the little lives of the creatures of the forest, tales far more wonderful than anything in those dusty books the villagers thought so important.*

"Dari, look," his father would say, pointing to something wonderful—a soaring hawk, the sunset light glowing red and orange on a towering cloud, a doe with a fawn only minutes old. And then his father would show him how to follow the hawk and watch it stooping to a kill, what the fiery sunset portended in the way of weather, and how to find the fawn when she hid in the grasses to doze while her mother went off to drink or graze. He would stand an excited witness to the hawk's victory, sit in quiet contentment until the last red rays of the sunset faded into blue dusk, or creep up to whisper to the fearless fawn, being careful not to touch it lest its mother scent him and reject it, even though his hands itched to stroke its soft pelt.

He still loved the Forest, loved the green silences, the huge trees, the sounds of it. He couldn't get anyone else in the village to see what drew him there; when he tried, they looked at him with suspicion and even a little fear, just as they had looked at his parents.

But he could have borne even that, if he still had them.

Dad—Mum—why didn't you come back? Why did you leave me alone? Why did you let the Forest take you away from me?

The pain returned, greater for having been bottled away beneath his anger and rebellion. His eyes flooded with tears, his throat knotted, and he pounded his hand against the bark of the tree until his knuckles were raw and scraped. Loneliness filled him until there was no room for anything else, except for anger at the insular villagers who hadn't even bothered to mount a search party when his parents didn't return. It didn't matter to these fools that the exotic furs his Mum and Dad brought back had been the *only* thing that kept traders coming to the village! Oh, no—because they went *out* into the Forest, everyone was just certain that something would follow them back *into* the village, something too big and monstrous to get rid of! There hadn't been a particle of evidence that something like that had any chance of happening, but it didn't matter; his Mum and Dad had been watched like criminals every time they came back from a trapping run. And they'd felt it; how could they not have? So they would go back out more and more often, spending less and less time in the village. And maybe that *was* taking on too much risk in the middle of the mage-storms. Maybe that was why, after an agony of waiting, he knew that they wouldn't come home this time.

They'd left him behind because there was going to be another mage-storm coming, and Justyn and some of the others had persuaded them not to risk his safety along with their own. He'd protested, but they'd slipped off during the night, leaving him with the innkeeper as they usually did. By the time he woke up the next morning, they were gone, and the wind and snow had obliterated their trail. He'd tried to follow, but had been forced to turn back.

He waited and waited, going out every day to watch for them, sure each dawn that he would see them coming in laden with their prizes.

But this time he had watched in vain, for they didn't return.

Darian was left to the village to care for, and it hadn't taken them long to figure out how to dispose of him. Within a day or two of being certain that Darian's parents were never returning, the village elders had quickly apprenticed him to Justyn. Justyn had long been after his parents to bind Darian over to him as an apprentice; Justyn had told them that he had the Mage-Gift, and that it had to be trained or it would be dangerous. *Mum and Dad only laughed at him and told him he was a silly old fool if he thought a boy could be dangerous to anything or anybody.* But the villagers had been only too ready to believe in the danger, and only too happy to get him disposed of—and more than once there'd been intimations that "disposed of" is exactly what he'd be if they detected any connection between him and these weird times. They told him then, and they continued to tell him frequently, that he should be grateful to them for seeing to his care, and for persuading his parents to leave him behind on that last trapping run. They never stopped telling him how grateful he should be, in fact. There was even a hint behind it all that it was a good thing that his parents had been lost—because now he, Darian, would no longer find his own life at risk in the forest.

The tears welled up again.

Needless to say, he wasn't grateful.

I helped them! They said I did! When they set the traps, I was the one up in a tree, watching and listening for danger—when they needed an extra set of hands, I was right there, and when they were tired, I was the one who was still fresh enough to tend to dinner or build the fire up. Maybe that hadn't been true back when he was just a little boy, but it had been the past couple of years, and there was no denying it. They'd been able to concentrate on the work at hand instead of having to keep one eye on the work and one watching for peril or approaching weather.

And—maybe—that was why they hadn't come back.

That was the stuff his nightmares had been made of for the last year. He kept thinking of times when he'd been *there* when they'd needed him—when they needed a third set of hands on the rope in a blizzard, when he'd spotted large carnivores stalking the camp— even when he'd been up a tree and had seen the signs of a bad storm coming up without warning. Had a pack of some magic-twisted horrors ambushed them, attacking them until finally their defenses were all gone? Had a terrible storm overwhelmed them? Had it been simply accident, the falling branch, the hidden crevice, the slip in the dark that left one or both of them crippled and helpless? Was that why they didn't return? Because they'd counted on his eyes and ears to warn them, his extra hands on a knife or a bow to help fight off danger, and he hadn't been there? He'd never been bad with a knife, and he was even *good* with a short bow . . . could it have made the crucial difference?

Or was it something else? Had they been caught by bandits, eager to steal their precious furs? Had there been an avalanche, or had one or both of them fallen through the ice while crossing a river? Horror of horrors—had they been caught in a Change-Circle and Changed themselves? Were they out there even now, rooted to the spot as half-human trees, or wandering in some shape not even *he* would recognize?

He couldn't shake the conviction that if he had been along, they would have all come back to the village as usual. Somehow, some way, his mere presence would have made the difference. He knew better than to try and tell this to anyone in the village; he'd tried once to tell Justyn, and the old wizard had told him that he was overreacting, that whatever had happened to his parents had nothing to do with him. After that, he had kept his guilt and fears to himself.

But he couldn't help but think that if he had been along, his parents would have had that extra set of hands and eyes that would have kept them safe, and brought them through whatever it was that took them away.

And that was what made it all the more horrible.

Here, in this refuge, away from the fools who didn't understand, he could let his real feelings out.

Why? he cried in silent anguish, face turned up to the canopy of leaves, both fists grinding against the back of the tree, *Why did you leave me? Why didn't you take me with you? Why did you leave me all* alone?

His body shook with silent sobs, and tears coursed down his cheeks, soaking his patched and much-mended shirt. It was too small in the arms for him by far, but he wouldn't let anyone take it from him, nor would he give up the leather vest that went with it. *She* had made him the shirt, and *he* had cut and stitched the vest, and those two articles of clothing were all he had left of them.

Why? he asked them again and again, until there was nothing left in the world but sorrow and guilt. *Why did you leave me alone?*

Finally, his body trembling in every fiber, he collapsed in on himself, curled into a ball, and sobbed, muffling the sound of his weeping in his arms and the bark of the tree. He wept himself dry and exhausted, until there was no more strength left, even for a single tear.

Before Justyn was satisfied that Kyle's injury was no longer life-threatening and was as clean as one herbalist could make it, there was a great deal of blood spilled on the stone floor of his cottage. It wasn't the worst wound he'd ever tended, but it was definitely one of the messiest. Justyn had finally stopped the bleeding with a compression bandage, and after liberally dosing the woodcutter with brandy and poppy-powder, began stitching the wound closed with a curved needle and fine silk thread. Kyle was a stolid enough fellow, and in a way it was a blessing for both of them that he was so very insensitive (and, one might as well say it, *stupid*), for he didn't seem to mind the ugly wound and the stitching half so much as the two farmers who'd brought him in. Vere and Harris grimaced every time Justyn put a stitch in, and Harris, who had no livestock at all but a few chickens, relying on the loan of his brother's oxen to plow his own land, was looking a bit green about the face. Kyle had just sat quietly, as if he were a good plowhorse waiting for a new shoe to be fitted. The brandy and poppy concoction made the muscles of his face go slack and relaxed, and he leaned back in his chair, propped up by Harris and Vere, blinking sleepily whenever the needle went in.

I could be generous, Justyn thought. *I could suppose that he's in shock by now. Except that he hasn't any of the symptoms of being in shock.*

Such stolidity in the face of serious injury had been the hallmark of some of the mercenary soldiers Justyn had tended in the past—the long gone past, so removed from what he was now that it might be the past of another person altogether. There were just some men who never felt much of anything, either physical or emotional. In general, they got along well with their fellows, and they made good enough soldiers, for although they never displayed the least bit of incentive, they always obeyed orders without question. And, if a woman didn't mind being the one to make all the decisions, they made perfectly amiable husbands and fathers. Certainly their phlegmatic temperament never led to beatings or other abuse. There had been times when he envied them that easy acceptance.

Virtually everyone in the village was cast from the same mold, and it wasn't at all difficult to tell that Vere and Harris were Kyle's cousins. All three of them were husky, light-haired, and brown-eyed, but Harris and Vere were darker than Kyle, and Kyle had features that were much more square. Justyn sometimes wondered if the reason he and Darian had never quite been accepted by the villagers was a simple matter of appearance; both he and Darian were thin and dark, in stark contrast to everyone else here. *Or at least,* he amended mentally, *I was dark until my hair started going gray.*

"He's gonna be laid up a couple of days," Vere said with irritation, his thick brows furrowing in a decided frown. "That means we'll have to spare someone from field work to keep an eye on him so he doesn't get into trouble, all juiced up with that poppy like he is. Can't you magic him, 'stead of sewing him up like usual?"

"I've told you before," Justyn said patiently, manipulating the needle through a particularly tough patch of skin, "I'm not a Healer, I'm an herbalist, a surgeon, and a bonesetter. I would have to use a complicated magic spell to do what you suggest. Whatever it was that the Heralds did to end the mage-storms fractured *all* the magic, and left it scattered around like a broken mirror. It takes a long time to gather up enough shards of power to work any spells. It's very tiring, it exhausts all the magic that's nearby, and then, if you really *needed* some magic to be done in the case of an emergency, I wouldn't be able to do it. What if something bad came out of the Pelagiris, and I couldn't protect the village? You wouldn't want that now, would you?''

The farmers both shook their square, shaggy heads, but they also looked skeptical and cynical, and Justyn could hardly blame them. After all, no one in Errold's Grove had ever seen him work anything involving powerful magic, and they had no reason to think he *could* do anything much.

And they have every reason to doubt me, he admitted to himself, taking another careful, tiny stitch and tying it off.

"Besides," he added as an afterthought, "you can get Widow Clay to watch him. She can't work in the fields with that bad leg, but she can still weave baskets, or knit and sew while she keeps an eye on him, and who knows? She might decide that he's better than no husband at all, and then your wives won't have to cook and clean for him anymore.''

Justyn felt a bit badly that he was talking about Kyle as if the woodcutter wasn't there, but in a sense he wasn't. He'd had enough poppy and brandy that he wouldn't recall a thing that had been said once the drugs wore off. And even if he did, Justyn rather doubted that he'd take offense at any of it, since worse things had been said in his presence that he never took offense to. He felt no guilt whatsoever about setting up Widow Clay, however. The good Widow had been setting her cap at *him* of late, and that was something he wanted to put an end to by whatever means it took! The last thing he needed was some meddling woman coming in here and "setting his life to rights.''

Both the farmers brightened at that idea, and they didn't say anything more about magic. Instead, they exchanged the kind of cryptic sentences that almost amount to a code among close kin, and Justyn gathered that their conversation had something to do with a plan to persuade the Widow Clay that her best interests lay in dragging Kyle over the broom. Justyn rather doubted that Kyle would mind if she did; he'd probably accept being married with the good-natured calm with which he accepted having his leg stitched up. As for the Widow—well, she'd have nothing to complain about in Kyle.

Justyn continued to sew the two sticky flaps of skin together with tiny, delicate stitches a woman would have envied, but the meticulous work was not engrossing enough to keep his mind off the past.

The irony was, at one time he *would* have been able to mend a minor wound like this with magic, using magic to bind the layers of skin and muscle together, leaving the leg as sound as it had been before the injury. Granted, his grasp of power had been minor compared to the great mages like Kyllian and Quenten, but at least it had worked reliably—and what was more, it probably would be working better after the end of the Storms than the magics of those who were his superiors in power. He had never used ley-line magic, much less node-magic, and the loss of the ley-lines would have made little difference to him. He had been a hedge-wizard, one of those who practiced earth-magics, with a little touch of mind-magic thrown in for good measure, and he had served in the ranks of Wolfstone's Pack, a mercenary company recruited by Herald-Captain Kerowyn to aid Valdemar and Rethwellan in the war against Hardorn. His had been a minor role in that Company; using the earth-magics to tell him where the enemy was and how many his numbers were, helping patch up the wounded, helping conceal their own men from the enemy and his mages. Kerowyn's Skybolts had worked with the Pack in the past, and they were one of the few mercenary Companies she felt sure enough of to trust in the treacherous times when Ancar still ruled Hardorn. All that had been explained very carefully to the members of the Pack, as had the risks and possible rewards, and the Company had voted unanimously to take the contract. After all, it was *Captain Kero* they were talking about; no one who took the same side as she did ever found himself working for people he would really rather have lost down a mine shaft. And usually no one found himself facing a situation where foreign commanders were spending merc lives like base coin that they couldn't get rid of fast enough.

Justyn had only just hired on with the Pack, and he'd been eager to see some real fighting, to get right into the thick of things. But he had quickly discovered that the place of a junior mage, a mere hedge-wizard, was going to be back with the support-troops.

And foolish me, that wasn't enough excitement for me.

He tried to volunteer every time they called for able bodies, but wisely the commanders kept passing him right over—until they came to the desperate running battles with Ancar's troops that decimated their own ranks and left the commanders little choice but to put a weapon into the hands of anyone they could spare and hope for the best.

Justyn had been a good enough archer, but his mind-magic had given him an edge; as long as he got his arrow going in the right direction, he could *think* it into a target. With a bow in his hands, he impressed even the archery-sergeant, and so they kept him with the archers, and he got more than his share of excitement. Until his first battle, he'd thought that actually *killing* someone might be a very difficult thing, for he would be thinking his arrow into the body of a *man*, not a straw target—but then when he saw what he faced, there was actually a grim and melancholy sort of pleasure in it. "Hell-puppets" were what the other fighters called Ancar's line-troopers; conscripted and controlled entirely by blood-magic, Ancar had depleted the countryside for fighters, and had raised the power for the spells that controlled them by killing their families in cold blood. When Justyn killed one of the troopers, it was actually a longed-for release for the poor clod.

Spell-bound and spell-ridden, for most of them that arrow came as a blessing, taking them out of Ancar's hands and on to a place where their loved ones were probably already waiting. Ancar had not used his people well, to say the least, and Justyn found himself sending prayers along with each arrow.

And as for the officers and mages commanding Ancar's troops— there was *great* pleasure in ridding the world of creatures so depraved and sadistic. And perhaps it was wrong for him to feel pleasure in killing even something as vile as Ancar's toadies, but he couldn't find it in his heart to regret taking even one of them out of the world.

And fighting was a great deal more exciting than grinding herbs, lighting campfires, and sealing wounds. When the archery-sergeant had halfheartedly given him the option to go back with his old group, he'd declined.

And, to be honest, I felt more like a man. I was actually doing something, and other men, other fighters, praised me for it. How could I go back to work among the cooks and the mule-drivers?

It wasn't only the members of the Pack who praised him, either. He'd met several of the Valdemarans in the form of some of the Guard when they'd picked up a stray squad or two along the way, the sadly-depleted remnants of a Valdemaran Company that had been holding the line before the Pack came to reinforce them. *They* thought he was a fine soldier, and said as much as they all shared exhaustion and the rare hot meal between engagements.

Heady stuff for a young fool, I suppose.

"Wonder where the boy went?" Harris said idly, interrupting Justyn's thoughts. Justyn had the needle clamped between his teeth and couldn't answer, but the question was rhetorical, for the man answered it himself. "Probably ran off into the woods. My boy's seen him running off there before. I'm telling you, Justyn, there's bad blood there, and you'd better do something about it before he gets more than himself into trouble."

Justyn really wasn't paying much attention, lost in his own thoughts as he was, and the half-conscious grunt he made in reply seemed to satisfy the man. At the moment, he really didn't want to think about young Darian, though he was getting an increasing number of complaints from the villagers that he wasn't keeping the boy under firm enough discipline.

No, his thoughts were in the past, at the moment, drawn there by the task of stitching up something that could have been a wound made on purpose, rather than accidentally.

If I hadn't been so young, I would have realized from the state of the Valdemaran Guard and the fact that my own commanders were willing to risk a mage in the front lines that something was very, very wrong.

What had gone wrong was that they were all trapped on the wrong side of the enemy lines, and only the fact that they had good commanders had gotten them as far as they had gone. He had learned later that the Guard and Pack Captains had agreed on a last-ditch dash for the Border at a weak spot in the enemy lines, hoping for a combination of surprise and overconfidence to bring them all through. And the ploy worked—

Except that for it to work, someone had to hold the rearguard, and the most logical group was the mixed archery squad guarded by a handful of swordsmen.

They fought their way back toward Valdemar, step by step, until the only barrier between them and safety was a river with a single wooden bridge. One man with a bow could hold the enemy off long enough for everyone else to get across—and by that time, he was considered the best shot in the group.

So, of course, like a young hero who hasn't quite grasped his own mortality, I volunteered.

That was when he learned the great and vital truth about being a bowman.

When you run out of arrows, you can do virtually nothing against a man with an ax.

He had fended off attacks for a few moments with his bow and knife, getting some painful wounds in the process, and the last thing that *he* remembered was watching the flat of the ax blade descending in strangely-slowed time toward his head.

He had awakened in the infirmary tent; after his heroic efforts, there hadn't been a man in the decimated ranks willing to allow him to go down without trying to rescue him.

But his skull had been cracked like a boiled egg, and it had only been good fortune and the fact that Wizard Kyllian was present at that very site that had kept him alive to thank his rescuers.

Kyllian himself was too old by then to take part in any battle-magics; he had confined himself to instructing the new Herald-Mages and to helping the Healers when their own ranks grew too thin, for Fireflower was a School that produced mages who were equally versed in Healing and mage-craft. Reputed to be a great friend of Quenten, the head of the White Winds School at Bolthaven, Justyn really didn't know *why* he'd chosen to come North when the Valdemarans sent out a call for mages through Quenten. Perhaps it was some need of his own that drew him there, or some urge to leave the sheltered confines of the Fireflower Retreat. He didn't confide his reasons to Justyn, who was just one among many of the patients that he pulled back from the soon-to-be-dead and into the land of the living.

It was obvious almost at once that Justyn was not going to be any good for fighting anymore; the blow to his head addled his vision enough that he would never be able to accurately sight an arrow again, and he simply had never had the strength of body to be a swordsman. Nor did he ride well enough for the cavalry.

But there was still magic—the magic he'd despised, that suddenly seemed desirable again.

But like a lover scorned, his magic had left him as well. Much of what he had learned, the blow to his head had driven from his memory; he had trouble Seeing mage-energies with any reliability, and the mind-magic he had was so seriously weakened he could no longer lift anything larger than a needle for more than a few moments.

He had gone in a single instant from hero to a discard. And what would he do with himself outside of the mercenary Companies? He had no skills, no abilities, outside of those of the magic that was now mostly gone from him.

When he was able to get out of bed and care for himself, the Healers turned him loose to complete his recovery on his own, and the Pack gave him his mustering-out pay and their good wishes. The Captain expressed his regret, but pointed out that the Pack couldn't afford anyone who couldn't pull his own weight, and suggested that he might find employment somewhere as a server in an inn, or the like.

A server in an inn? Was *that* what he had come to? All at once, he couldn't bear the idea that he must give up all of his once-promising future to become a menial, a drudge, another cipher with no future and no prospects. That was when he had approached the great wizard, hat in hand, like a beggar, and asked for advice.

He must have fairly radiated despair, for Kyllian had sent away the people he was talking with and took him into his own tent, sitting him down and presenting him with a cup of very strong brandy.

"I suppose you think that your life is over," the great wizard had said, wearily but kindly. "And from your perspective, that's an appropriate response. I understand you put on a fairly brave show out there."

He had flushed. "Brave, but stupid, I suppose—"

"Depends on who you would ask. Your fellow mages, now, *they* would say it was stupid, I'm sure, risking your Gifts as well as your life in physical combat—but the fellows you shot covering fire for would have a different opinion."

He had been rather surprised that Kyllian remembered the details of how he had been injured, but there were more surprises in store for him.

"So, you're brave enough to die," Kyllian had continued, watching him closely. "But are you brave enough to live? Are you brave enough to learn skills that will get you little gratitude, brave enough to practice them among people who will probably despise you and certainly won't believe your tales of battle heroics, but who nevertheless will *need* what you can do?"

What could he answer, except to nod mutely, having no notion of what that nod was going to get him into?

"It wasn't magic that saved you, boy," the old man had told him bluntly. "It was simpler stuff than even *you* are used to practicing. Bonesetting and flesh-stitching, herbs and body-knowledge, patience and persistence and your own damned refusal to be a proper hero and die gloriously. Do you know what's happened, out there in the hinterlands of Valdemar?"

He had shaken his head; obviously, how could *he* have known? He wasn't a native of the place—

"Well, I do, because the Healers come and wail on my shoulder about it at least three times a day. There are *no* Healers out there now; they've all been pulled east to take care of *this* mess. Even the old wisewomen, the herbalists, and the beast-Healers have turned up here; anyone that *could* travel *has* come here, where the need is greatest. That leaves vast stretches of territory without anyone that a sick or injured farmer can turn to—not an earth-witch, not a hedge-wizard, not even a horse-leech. *No one.* And people are going to die of stupid things like coughs and festered wounds unless people like you take the time to acquire a few more skills and go out there to help them.'' Kyllian had eyed Justyn shrewdly. ''And I can virtually guarantee it will be a thankless proposition—but you'll be doing a world of good, even if no one is willing to acknowledge it.''

''Why do you care what happens to the people of Valdemar?'' he'd asked, with equal bluntness. ''And why should I?''

The old wizard had smiled, an unexpectedly sweet smile that charmed Justyn in spite of himself. ''I care—because I *don't* care what land people own allegiance to, so long as they are good people. And I suppose I care because of the philosophies that made me choose the School I chose. Ask any Healer of whatever nation how he feels about Healing a man from another land, even one that is his enemy, and he will look at you as if you were demented for even asking such a foolish question. Healers don't see nations, boy. They see need, and they act on that need. That is why I care.''

''And why should I?'' Justyn had repeated.

''Why did you volunteer to hold the bridge?'' was all Kyllian asked, and although Justyn had not quite understood the question then, discovering the answer had formed a large part of his life from then on.

But at the time, given his utter lack of anything else he thought he could do, and the fact that the great Wizard Kyllian certainly seemed to *want* him to volunteer, that was what he had done.

First, though, he needed to begin a new course of learning. He had apprenticed himself to the leeches and herbalists and wisewomen on the battlefield, absorbing their knowledge of matters other than the injuries of combat when they weren't all up to their elbows in blood and body parts. He acquired herbals and other books, brought what was left of his magic up as far as he could, and when Herald-Mage Elspeth and Hawkbrother Darkwind and Adept Firesong did whatever it was they did to end the war with Hardorn, he was there for the celebration of victory, then volunteered his services to both the Healers and the Heralds. After all, he *was* at least a little bit of a mage, as well as a certified bonesetter and herb-Healer, and Selenay of Valdemar had decreed that Valdemar still needed mages. Kyllian had been right, and he was assured that Valdemar could use anyone with either of those skills, and desperately. Ancar's mages hadn't confined their attentions to killing Valdemaran fighters; they'd made a point of going after the tents of the Healers and other noncombatants, contrary to every accepted convention of war. Far too many of the Healers and leeches who had volunteered were not going back to their homes again.

Those services that he offered were gratefully accepted, and the Healers sent him off so far into the West that he wasn't certain he was still *on* a map of Valdemar. A whole string of folk went, most with about as much magical power as he had, and some with less; a Healer and a Herald went with them and found them towns and villages who wanted and would support folk like himself. The last village on the list was Errold's Grove, and it was here that he found that Kyllian had been only too right. People had already died needlessly of stupid things—a compound fracture gone septic, a winter epidemic of fever, an infected foot. The people here needed him and wanted him, and the Healer and Herald went back to Haven to look for more volunteers to fill all those empty places where Healers had once been.

At first, things hadn't been as bad for the village and the villagers as they were now. Traders still came for the dye-stuffs, and there was both ready money and the goods coming in from outside to spend it on. The villagers had seemed impressed by the little magics he could still do, such as finding lost objects and predicting the weather. He had been given a house and was promised that, like the woodcutter, all his needs would be taken care of. A strange and scruffy black cat had simply appeared one day, a cat that seemed unnaturally intelligent, and he took it as a good omen, that he had gotten himself a proper familiar, that his magic might once again amount to more than the wherewithal for a few parlor games. He set about looking for an apprentice to teach, and saw the light of magery dancing in the eyes of a young child, the son of a pair of fur trappers. He had every confidence that he would one day be able to persuade them that their boy should have a chance at a better life than *they* held, and get young Darian for his apprentice. It seemed as if the gods were finally smiling on him again, and he rechanneled his ambitions into another path. If *he* could not become a great mage, he could train one. It didn't take having the Talent and the Gift to be able to train the person who did. He transmuted his dream into the dream of being the mentor to a powerful magician, and thought that he would be content.

But then the mage-storms began, and his fortune dropped along with that of his village. When one or two monstrous creatures invaded the village, no one wanted to go out into the Pelagiris Forest and encounter more—and since the dye fungus wouldn't grow outside of the Forest, that pretty much put an end to the dye-trade. With no money and no traders coming in, the villagers were forced to become self-sufficient, but self-sufficiency had its cost, in time and hard physical labor. The narrower the lives of his villagers became, the less they in their turn were willing to forgive. The demands on him became greater, and he was less able to meet them. And when Darian was orphaned and was bound over to him by the villagers, the boy reacted in exactly the opposite way he would have expected—not with gratitude, but with rebellion.

That, perhaps, was the worst blow of all. The boy had seemed so tractable with his parents, so bright, and so eager to learn! And with his parents gone and no relatives to teach him a trade or care for him, he should have been relieved and grateful to get so gentle a master as Justyn, who never beat him, never starved him into submission, never really scolded him.

Justyn was nearly finished with Kyle's wound, but the problem presented to him in the shape of young Darian was nowhere near as easy to deal with.

Was it only that the villagers were right, that the boy had bad blood in him? Just how "bad" was the "bad blood," if there was such a thing? Was it insurmountable? Should he give up, and see the boy bound over to the smith, perhaps? Certainly the smith would not tolerate the kind of behavior Darian exhibited now—but how could that be fair to the boy?

Was it only that he was strong-willed and stubborn, unwilling to turn his hand to another path when the one he had been was closed to him? It would have been natural enough for him to plan to follow in his father's footsteps, and certainly there was every indication that he knew quite a bit about the business of trapping and preparing furs. If it was only that, could his stubborn nature be overcome? Surely Justyn could make him see reason—the Forest *was* too dangerous to go out in, now, and the deaths of his parents should prove that to him, if only he could be made to acknowledge the fact. If two people with all the experience and caution *they* displayed could not survive there, Darian had no chance of prospering, and surely Justyn could make him understand that.

Was it that he wanted everything to come to him easily, as magic came to those in children's tales? Was he too lazy to work? If that was the case, Justyn wasn't sure how to remedy it, but that didn't seem right either. The boy wasn't actually lazy, but look at what he'd said this afternoon; that he didn't see any reason to expend a *great* deal of effort to do something much more easily accomplished with normal means, and perhaps it was only that Justyn hadn't been able to persuade him that those little exercises were the only way of building his ability and control to handle anything bigger.

Or was there something else going on, something that Justyn didn't understand?

Justyn could see some things for himself—the boy didn't like being made to feel that he was somehow "different" from the other children in the village. Perhaps part of his rebellion stemmed from the fact that his Talent for mage-craft was bound to set him farther apart from the others. Given the contempt with which the villagers regarded Justyn, he had no reason to assume that they would give him any more respect if and when he became a mage.

And he certainly reacted badly whenever his parents were mentioned. But his parents, too, had been "different," very much so. The entire village had regarded them with suspicion and displeasure, anticipating that they would only bring more trouble than they were worth with them eventually. Some of the villagers had not been entirely certain that Darian's parents were human—the argument was that no *human* would ever choose to go out into the Pelagiris when there were safer ways of making a livelihood. A fallacious argument, to be sure, but the folk of Errold's Grove seemed to have a grasp on logic that was tenuous at best. But was it that Darian wished his parents had been the same as everyone else, and he was angry that they had been "different" and had made him "different" by default? Or was there some other thought going through his mind?

"Bad blood, and reckless, that's what's in that boy," he heard with half an ear, and it occurred to him at that moment that every time anyone in the village so much as mentioned Darian's parents and lineage, it was with scorn and derision, and the certainty that "no good would ever come of those folks." Why, no wonder the boy reacted poorly! Every time the boy heard himself talked about, it was with the almost gleeful certainty that he would come to a bad end, or be nothing but trouble. As reluctant to show any sort of feeling as he was, still, for Darian those words must seem like a blow to the face, or more to the point, to the heart.

Still, one would think that the boy would feel a little proper gratitude. *Justyn* certainly treated him well. He was hardly overworked, he had plenty of free time to himself, enough to eat, proper clothing to wear, and a comfortable place to sleep. There was no telling if he'd had all those things with his parents, but one would think he would be happy enough to have them now.

Wait, think a moment. It is one thing to feel gratitude, it is another to be told over and over again just how grateful you should *be, if only you weren't too much of a little beast to be appreciative. He's only a child, he can't understand how much of a burden one extra mouth to feed is for the people here. Folks with children would have to work that much harder to feed and clothe him, folks whose children are grown expect to be taken care of in their old age, not become caregivers all over again. He hadn't any skills that were useful to the folk here when he was left in their hands, so he wouldn't contribute anything toward his own keep for months or even years—but how is a child supposed to understand that?*

And as a child, his parents were naturally everything to him, the center of his young life, and being told they were idiots and deserved to get swallowed up by the Forest must surely make his blood boil. He must feel impelled to defend them, and yet since he was a mere child, he would be considered impudent and disrespectful if he did.

Another thing that Justyn had noticed about him was that he had a great deal of difficulty in remaining still and concentrating. Perhaps that was characteristic of all young boys, but most were apprenticed to learn skills that involved physical work, not mental work. The boy had a restless heart, and the truth of it was that he was not well-suited to insular village life. He spent most of his free time, not with the three or four boys near his own age, but out in the "forbidden" Forest; whether he was just wandering, or exploring with a purpose, Justyn didn't know, but he certainly seemed to prefer the company of trees and birds to that of his own kind.

And there are certainly times when I don't blame him for that.

Justyn tied off the last of the stitches, and clipped all the threads as short as possible so that they wouldn't catch on something.

"Now," he said to all three of them, although he wasn't at all sanguine about Kyle understanding anything he said. "I know you've heard this before, but it bears repeating. You all three *know* what happens when a wound goes septic. Kyle, please realize that if you let this wound sour, at best, you would be very, very sick and I would have to open up the wound, drain it, and cut or burn out part of the infected tissue. It would hurt a very great deal, both while I was doing it and afterward. You'd have much worse than a scar, then, and it would take much longer to heal. You would probably end up with a limp, or even lame, if the infection grew bad enough."

Kyle grunted and nodded his agreement, his brown hair flopping into his vacant brown eyes. He brushed it away, and although the motion was slow, his hand was steady, arguing for a certain level of sobriety.

"Now pay attention to what I have to tell you," he insisted. "You may have heard this before when someone else was hurt, but chances are you don't remember it as well as you think you do. Harris, Vere, I am counting on you to remind Kyle of all of this."

"All right," Vere agreed, looking as if he felt put upon. Harris just grunted, clearly bored with the entire procedure. Knowing the two as he did, Justyn figured that Vere would try to remember to tell Kyle everything, and Harris would do so only if he happened to think about it.

Justyn sighed, and hoped they wouldn't forget what he was about to tell them. At least Kyle's constitution was so robust that he could take a little neglect. "Once a day, the wound is to be washed in wine, just as I did before I closed it, and allowed to dry in the air."

"Right," Kyle said vaguely. "Wash, and air-dry. Don't bandage it wet."

"After it is dry, *then* put the salve I have given you on it, and put a dressing made of fresh, clean cloth over it. *Don't* put bear fat, or goose grease, or tallow, or river-weed, or anything else your granny used to use for wounds on it. Do you understand that? Forget your granny's and your mother's famous remedies, and stick with mine. Trust me on this, and remember that the Heralds sent me here for just this reason. I've seen and treated more wounds like this than there are people in the village."

"Just the salve you give him," Vere sighed, as Kyle nodded so earnestly that Justyn had some hope that the man might actually remember what he'd been told.

"At night, before you sleep, I want you to change the dressing again, with fresh, clean cloth. I want you to have all the rags you use for dressings washed thoroughly in boiling water and hung to dry in the sun." Sometimes he wondered if they'd pay more attention to the things he told them to do if he gave them some kind of non-sense to say over each task, as a kind of charm against sickness. But no, he was afraid that if he did that, they would trust in the charm and forget cleanliness. How could he get them to believe that there were invisible animals living in filth that made wounds fester, if he couldn't get them to believe in him?

Thank the gods they at least knew the signs of infection and gan-grene. "Examine the wound carefully each time you change the dressing, and if you see anything wrong, come to me at once. Re-member, you're watching for infection, and that can include swelling, red streaks coming up or down your leg from the wound, skin that's hot to touch and more sore than it should be. Understand?"

"Come to you at once," Kyle repeated, nodding vigorously.

"All right," Justyn said, and sagged back in his chair. He waved a hand at them. "You can all go now."

Harris and Vere each took one of Kyle's arms and heaved him up out of his chair. Justyn didn't offer him any more of the precious poppy-powder; he didn't have much, and he had to save it. There was no telling when the next trader would come with the powder he'd ordered almost a year ago.

Rather surprisingly, Kyle made it erect without too much in the way of a wobble, and he didn't lean on the two farmers nearly as much as Justyn thought he would.

The benefits of an iron constitution and a head like a granite boulder, I suppose, he thought dispassionately. *He'd probably have healed up all right without me, which is likely what Vere and Harris will be telling each other.*

He leaned back in his chair and massaged the bridge of his nose between his thumb and forefinger. Kyllian had been right; this was a place where he—and a successor—were desperately needed, and it was a place where they would get little thanks and no credit for what they did. People honored the spectacular, not the everyday. Raise a dead man and bring him back to life, and they would hold you in awe. Keep him from dying in the first place with a little simple hygiene, and they ignored you.

What was he to do? He had known what he was up against when he arrived here. And what was he going to do about a successor? If he couldn't somehow bring the boy around, he would have to find someone willing to do the hard work without any magic at all.

Women tended to be more community minded than men, and in this village at least, they were used to taking on the more objectionable of community tasks; perhaps he ought to check among the girls and see if any of them were willing to learn all he could teach them about bonesetting and herbs and the like. It wouldn't hurt Darian to see that he had a rival for Justyn's tutelage. That might get him interested again when nothing else seemed to.

The only problem with that idea was that it would be hard for a young girl to get a mature man to listen and obey her when it came to following instructions. That had been the idea behind sending a man here in the first place.

If only I could regain my magic! If I could impress the people here, that might bring Darian around. If he just thought that he had a chance of being seen with respect as long as he learned what I have to teach, that might change his attitude.

He turned his attention to the apple sitting on the plate on the end of the table where Harris had put it. He narrowed his focus and concentrated on the fruit, as he had so often and so easily, feeling a now-familiar headache arc across his head, just behind his right eyebrow. He didn't remember the blow that had felled him, but he fancied that it had felt a lot like that stabbing pain.

He willed the apple to rise. This time! Surely this time!

It wobbled a bit on the plate, but did not move.

Still, he continued to concentrate on it, and it rocked faster and faster but still refused to rise, until the pain behind his right eye was enough to blind him. With a sigh, he dropped the apple with his mind, and it stopped moving.

"I'm an old fraud," he said out loud. "I'm a failure and an old fraud, my apprentice hates me and hates magic, and you—" he looked at his cat, which was licking itself again "—probably aren't even a familiar. And even if you are, you're a failure, too. If a whirlwind came out of the sky and swallowed us all up, no one would ever notice, that's how unimportant we are. What do you think of that?"

The cat went on cleaning itself, sticking a scraggly, flea-gnawed leg straight up in the air, arse toward Justyn. He chuckled bitterly, for the cat's silence seemed the only fitting comment.

Mage Starfall

Two

Even grief as profound as Darian's could not be sustained for too long, and after lying exhausted in his hiding place for a time, other feelings began to penetrate his sorrow, all of them maddeningly persistent, and utterly ordinary. It was irritating—which in *itself* was irritating—to have stupid things like a nose that was sore and stuffed up from crying, and an ant crawling up his leg inside his breeches, intrude on something as profound as his grief. But that didn't stop them from intruding. His arms and legs felt cramped, his hands stung where he'd pounded them against the bark and scraped them, and one hip hurt, jammed as it was against the hard bark of the tree. Finally he decided it was time to leave. He sat up, his eyes sore and dry, and peered down through the branches to see if there was anyone about to catch him when he climbed down.

There was no one working in the field below, and from the fact that the long shadows of the trees had crept over the village, he'd been up here a while. He guessed that the women who usually worked in the bean field had probably left their work to go prepare dinner for the men and children. The wind was in the wrong direction for him to catch aromas coming from the village, but it was a good bet that if he could smell anything, it would be the mingled aromas of stews, soups, pies and pasties, same as always.

I wonder why they bother making individual dinners. Surely it would make more sense just to make one big pot of stew for the whole village, he thought, with a touch of contempt. *After all, everyone in the village uses the same half-dozen recipes. I don't think anyone has ever tried to make anything new since I've been here.*

Perhaps it was that, as difficult as things were, there were still some who were more prosperous than the rest, who could afford a little more meat and spices in their food, and who made sure to enjoy that distinction from everyone else whenever the opportunity presented itself.

As if by sharing a bit of spice with everyone else they'd lose the chance to lord it over their neighbors, he thought sourly. The half-dozen "well-to-do" families were the ones who seemed to go out of their way to complain about *his* behavior. *As if they didn't already have the best houses in town, and can even pay somebody else to cook and clean for them!*

Still, if it was mealtime, he'd probably better be getting back to Justyn. There were still dishes to scrub, and the pasties to fetch from the baker, or the old wretch would probably forget to eat, and then Darian would get the blame if Justyn got sick. Sometimes he wondered how Justyn had gotten along before he came—but then he realized that the women had taken care of him, the same way they cared for Kyle. So the villagers had gotten something out of apprenticing him to Justyn; they'd been able to stop cleaning up after and cooking for the Wizard. No wonder they'd been in such a hurry to get him bound over!

I'll have to clean up after Kyle, too, if I don't want to have to eat dinner in a room that looks like someone had butchered a pig there. Justyn is such a slob! How can he be so concerned with keeping wounds clean, and live the way he does? Wrinkling his lip a little with disgust, he stretched his arms and legs until the cramps went away, then climbed slowly down the side of the tree opposite the village. He didn't want anyone to catch sight of him if he could help it; he'd already lost a couple of hiding places by being careless.

Here on the edge of the fields, where there was more sunlight, growth of bushes and vines was especially heavy, giving him cover that allowed him to get into the field without being seen. Already the air was hot and drowsy with midday heat, and hidden insects buzzed and droned on all sides of him. The ground here smelled damp; someone must have opened up the irrigation pipe for this field. He pushed through the dense underbrush until he came to a field of pole beans, and made his way through the rows of tall, tentlike arrangements of poles covered with climbing bean vines. They made a jagged hedge that was difficult to see through, and extended well over the top of his head. Eventually the field ended, and he reached the outskirts of the village on the northern side. He reentered Errold's Grove near the firing pit for pottery and the storage shed where the finished pieces were kept. He didn't see anyone, although the sounds of dinner being served and eaten were coming from every open window.

It must be later than I thought. He still didn't feel much like hurrying, though; his bout of grief had pretty much killed his appetite, and with a bit of pique, he decided that Justyn could wait. If his Master was hungry, his Master could go fetch his own dinner from the baker, and clean a plate or two himself for a change.

He made his way slowly along the paths between the houses, kicking a round rock through the dust, nursing his grievances. The ordinary sounds of people who *liked* each other eating together only made him feel more abused and put upon, because he knew what those people must be thinking and saying about him. Vere and Harris had certainly recounted the tale of his defection to their families by now, and their wives had probably shared the story with others as they brought water from the well, or went to fetch dinner from the baker. So now everyone knew that Darian had shown his "true face" again, and they would be feeling very smug indeed. By suppertime tonight, he'd be the main topic of evening lectures to the family.

They'll be looking at their children, and telling each other, "Thank the gods he isn't like Darian!" or "My boy would never act like Darian." Huh. As if they really had any idea half of what their precious children get into when they aren't watching.

And the very next person he encountered would probably stop him in order to remind him of how ungrateful and unnatural he was. Every time he got into trouble—and "trouble" seemed to have a wide definition for these people—people would go out of their way to give him their own version of the lecture he'd already heard a thousand times or more—the sermon on how kind Justyn was for taking him in and apprenticing him without an apprenticing fee or any kind of familial relationship. Again. And again.

At least Justyn himself usually left that part out, perhaps because he remembered only too well how he had pestered Darian's parents every time they came into Errold's Grove. Darian could recall at least a dozen times that Justyn had come to his Mum and Dad, separately or together, to urge on them a plan of apprenticing him into Justyn's service. There had been a great deal of fuss made about how dangerous it was for someone with Darian's "potential" to remain untrained in his magic. Darian remembered his Dad once telling his Mum that Justyn was trying to frighten them into giving Darian over to him, and that she shouldn't let the old man alarm her.

If Darian could not get away from whoever had decided to deliver the usual lecture, the haranguer would then go through the litany of

Darian's many character flaws and deficiencies, and the only variation was in how much emphasis an individual placed on a particular flaw. This part was actually useful; Darian had noticed over the course of several of these lectures that people tended to stress the flaw that *they* were most prone to themselves. For instance, the rudest man in the village, Old Man Gulian, tended to harp on how rude Darian was, and Erna Dele, who never spoke or showed a thank you for *any* favor and always expected more than she got, would go on at great length on how he didn't appreciate what he was given. He learned a lot by listening to what people thought they saw as deficiencies in him.

Regardless of who was giving the lecture, it always ended with a homily on gratitude, obedience, and humility. That is, how he should daily demonstrate how grateful he was to everyone in Errold's Grove by thanking all and sundry on every occasion for their generosity toward him—how he should show that gratitude by instant obedience to anything anyone wanted of him—and how he should be properly humble and prove that he knew his place in the scheme of things by groveling before everyone he came across.

How I should be so happy to have been permitted to become a bound-over slave that I should demonstrate that gratitude with humble servitude to anyone over the age of fifteen.

"It takes a village to raise a child," was the old proverb, often quoted to Justyn when someone came to complain about Darian, and it certainly seemed as if everyone in the village had his or her own ideas of the proper way for Darian to behave!

Each time he heard the lecture, he was sorely tempted to kick the orator in the shins. He never did, though, because there was always that doubt that they might all be right and that he *was* in the wrong. After all, everyone here seemed to be in agreement on his behavior and worth except he himself, and after all, he was only a boy. What if he was entirely in the wrong? What if he *was* a bad person? What if he *did* deserve to be punished—what if Justyn was too tolerant of his behavior and he really deserved to be disciplined?

What if the reason his parents got swallowed up by the Forest was because *he* was a bad person, and this was how the gods had chosen to punish them for how he turned out?

That was the possibility that gave him a cold lump in the bottom of his stomach, and made him squirm with distress whenever he thought of it.

And that, of course, just made him want to be loud and wild and try some of the magics that Justyn talked about, just to show them all that he was not to be trodden underfoot like a weed and he was not going to take all their lectures and disapproval lying down.

Which, of course, always got him into more trouble. In fact, it seemed as if ever since he'd arrived in this place, he was in trouble to one degree or another—or *thought* to be in trouble.

And it wasn't fair! The other boys pulled as many pranks as he did, or more—they were just slier about it, and they didn't get caught because no one was trying to catch them the way everyone seemed to be trying to catch him.

Hellfires! he thought rebelliously. *When everyone's watching you all the time to catch you doing something wrong, they're going to get you, no matter how hard you're trying to do right!*

And meanwhile, just because everyone in the whole town expected Darian to be the one who made trouble, that meant they weren't going to catch their own boys at it, and Darian would get the blame for things *they* did. It happened all the time, and even when he could *prove* he hadn't had anything to do with the mischief, no one ever apologized to him or made things up to him. They just said that he deserved to get into trouble for all the things he did that he hadn't gotten caught at! Now, there was a prime bit of logic!

And just suppose the beans got pecked a bit by birds, or a deer wandered in and ate some of the young corn, things that he couldn't possibly have any control over—why, *that* was all the fault of his Dad and Mum. It was the Pelagiris-beasts come to take revenge on the village for the terrible trappers who had invaded the Forest. Even the most normal of beast depredations was always blamed on some monster from the Pelagiris that had followed Darian's parents back to Errold's Grove. Though what self-respecting monster would pull up carrots and eat them, or trample down a hill of beans, or pick at ripe strawberries—well, that was beyond him. Must have been a monster with a singularly vegetarian appetite.

Funny how they all forget those coats and rugs and bedcoverings they all have that Dad and Mum traded for food and supplies, he thought sourly, looking up from his rock and noting one of those bedcoverings hanging out on a line to air. A soft shade of subtle cream it was, too, with markings and mottlings of a darker shade of pale brown. Quite a handsome fur, thick and warm, and probably a fine thing to have on the bed in the dead of winter. Darian even remembered what the beast had looked like when they'd caught it—a terribly dangerous beast, it was, completely unable to defend itself, much less attack anyone. It had looked like a huge hassock; with four tiny little legs and a head the size of an apple all stuck on a body easily the size of a fat cow, and certainly much wider. If anything had been born to become a tanned hide, that thing surely had been. It was a wonder it had survived long enough to be trapped in the first place.

Poor Justyn hadn't even gotten the benefit of having furs traded to him in return for taking Darian as an apprentice. He didn't get anything at all, not even other peoples' castoffs, and he was the one who probably deserved some kind of repayment the most. Widow Clay of the bad leg that kept her from hard physical labor had been appointed to make him bedcoverings, which she knitted from odds and ends of yarn that she unraveled from worn-out sweaters or scrounged from leftovers or other projects. She also made quilts of scraps that no one else wanted because they were stained, or faded and threadbare, or too drab to be desirable, even as a patch for a quilt. Poor Justyn! He always got the tag-ends of everything. He was the last person in the village to get a share of meat, of clothing, of anything. Whoever's turn it was to supply him always gave him what they didn't want. Take now, for instance; there was an abundance of turnips, beans, and peas, so their meals featured either turnips, beans, or peas, depending on how the donor herself felt about those vegetables. Mostly, they got turnips, and he was not looking forward to the time when the squash ripened.

Now his mood turned to guilt, as it always did at this point, for the worst part of it was that in his heart he knew he was being treated fairly; well-housed and well-fed, and Justyn, though short-tempered and appallingly sloppy, was fundamentally kind.

He kicked his stone back and forth, from his left foot to his right, making slow progress in the direction of Justyn's cottage. He kept his eyes down on the path and his stone, for it was just possible that if any adult saw him doing this, they would think it was some ridiculous exercise that Justyn had set him, as it certainly would look too tedious to be a game. Justyn had set him tasks that looked sillier in the past, and the one thing they all had in common was that they were tedious.

It's not so bad with Justyn, and I wouldn't mind so much if I was learning something useful. It's just that he keeps insisting that this magic stuff is good *for something. I've heard the stories and I've seen the bad art on his walls. He's talked about great mages and even one or two Hawkbrothers, and told me about their great spells and "weavings." But so far I haven't seen him do anything that couldn't be done easier by plain old ordinary hands.* For that matter, a lot of what Justyn did *was* accomplished by mundane means, and

old Justyn sure didn't get a lot of respect, wealth, or even appreciation. *So why would anyone want to be a wizard in the first place?
What's the point of being a wizard if you get taken for granted and
paid only in what no one else wants? If I was learning something
like being a fighter, a warrior—something that was useful and got
respect—well, things would be different.*

The old man was good at small spells and minor healings; simple
magics that made life better and safer for the villagers. But nobody
really seemed to notice just how much he did for them; they acted
as if he was *supposed* to be at their beck and call for the most minor
of trivialities, and on the whole they treated him very little better than
Lilly, the barmaid at the inn. Justyn just accepted that treatment, as
if it was what he expected and deserved.

*That isn't doing either of us any good, if it comes right down to
it. He doesn't get respect, so I never will either—but he also doesn't
ever do anything to make people think he was important. And any
old wisewoman knows almost as much as he does about healing and
medicines.*

Everything Justyn did or wanted him to do seemed to involve a
great deal of stupid, plodding, repetitive work. So what good was
magic, when all it did was make for more hard, tedious work? He
knew why the villagers didn't respect Justyn's magic—wasn't magic
supposed to be spectacular, instantaneous, and take one's breath
away? Wasn't that the way magic happened in the tales? When the
village was buried in snow, shouldn't Justyn have been able to clear
the snow away from the paths and the doors with a snap of his
fingers? Shouldn't he be able to hold back floodwaters with his will,
or make a well by wishing it there?

Shouldn't he have been able to keep people safe when they went
into the Forest to make a living? After all, that was how the people
of Errold's Grove were *supposed* to make a living—shouldn't a
proper wizard be able to make sure they could still do it, no matter
what those mage-storms brought? That may have been what earned
their scorn—when the monsters came, Justyn wasn't able to do things
that let the village prosper despite their presence.

*If they'd thought that he was going to be able to get rid of any
monsters that came in from the Forest, people wouldn't have been
half as hard on Dad and Mum . . . in fact, they might have helped
them out a bit that last winter, when running the traplines was so
hard.*

And if people had been pleasant to him and his parents, if they'd
been able to prosper on their own, maybe his Dad and Mum wouldn't

have felt as if they had to go out into the Forest as often or for as long. They might still have been here, if they hadn't felt so unwelcome in Errold's Grove.

He shook his head angrily to keep from crying all over again. He had to think hard to be able to get a breath; he felt as if *he* were in a constriction trap, and the trap kept getting smaller every day. *I don't think I can bear too much more of this,* he thought, but this time the thought had more of a feeling of desperation behind it. *I've got to get away; I've got to figure out how I can take care of myself, and get away from here. This place, these people—they're trying to make me just like them, and I don't* want *to be like them! Wanting everything just alike is what's killing them all, they just don't realize it.*

There had to be more to life than the kind of life the villagers were living—a dull, pedestrian, day-to-day existence. When he wasn't being badgered, he was being bored to death.

Every day is exactly like every other day. Only the weather and the seasons change, and even they don't make that much difference, unless there's something like a flood or a blizzard. Or a monster or something they think is a monster. Or maybe a Herald comes along once a year at most. It's always the same food, the same gossip, the same things going wrong or right. Nobody ever does anything just for the sake of doing it, and nobody ever dares try anything new.

There were times when he thought that even the appearance of a monster from the Pelagiris Forest would be preferable to the day-in, day-out sameness. It might wake up some of these people, show them that there were more important things than complaining about one small boy.

No one ever makes songs or tales about people plowing their bean fields. What's the point of living on the edge of a perilous and magical place like the Forest if you don't go looking for adventure in it? Or if not adventure, why not just—life? People used to go looking for adventure—or for mosses and other dye-stuffs, anyway—but now they would rather hide in the village and pretend the Forest wasn't just beyond their carefully cultivated fields. They'd rather do without prosperity than take a chance against danger, and Darian could not understand that.

My folks went out looking for adventure; maybe there is *something in my blood. Only it isn't bad blood, it's just—I don't know. I just know if I don't do something different soon, I'm going to burst. I don't know how these folks stand living like this. Maybe they don't burst because they're hollow.*

He looked back over his shoulder at the Forest with longing. He always felt more contented when he was in there, and the temptation to keep going, to keep on looking to see what was beyond the next stand of trees, behind the next patch of undergrowth, was often overwhelming. It always felt as if there was something exciting out there waiting for him, if he just went far enough in.

And maybe Dad and Mum are still alive in there, somewhere. . . .

His belly wrenched. He was thinking that again, as he had for ages, and he still could not let that hope go. Until someone found proof otherwise, he would always be certain that they weren't dead, that they were trapped or imprisoned somewhere, waiting for someone to find them. As long as he could believe that, he couldn't give up, and he had something to hold onto in the middle of the night, when he woke up and found himself beneath a thick, thatched roof instead of the open sky, or tent canvas, or forest canopy.

That hope faded a little more with each passing day, though. It got harder to believe they were still alive somewhere, when there was never any trace, either of what became of them, or of a force or person that could have imprisoned them.

Maybe when a trader comes, I can get him to take me with him. I could work for him until we get somewhere where there are more people, then I could join the Guard. I bet I'd be a great fighter—in fact, I bet I'd be one of the best fighters there ever was! He was easily one of the best bowmen in the village; more than half the time he'd been apprenticed it was his skill that put meat in Justyn's stew, and not the "gratitude" of the villagers.

Then again, all the wars were supposed to be over now, and maybe they wouldn't need fighters. Well, that was all right. *I could remind people about the furs and the dyes that used to come from here—I could get them to put together an expedition to explore the Forest, that's what I could do! I know all Dad's trapping trails; I could be famous for opening up the Forest!*

Or maybe he could just work for the trader until he had enough put by to buy his own supplies and traps. He could go out into the Forest himself, and become as good a trapper as his Dad was. He remembered his Dad saying more than once that he was doing the villagers a favor by trading those furs for "kind" instead of "cash" and that the traders never gave but a fraction of the worth of the fur. *If I took my furs to a big city myself, I could get a lot of money for them. I could get rich—and I'd probably be famous, too.*

As for the people of Errold's Grove, well, when they saw how he was prospering, maybe they would stop cowering in their houses like rabbits in a burrow, and dare the Forest themselves again.

I haven't seen that many monsters, and most of them weren't dangerous if you kept your wits about you. I've never seen any "forest spirits" or "vapor demons" or anything you could even mistake for something like that. Hellfires, I haven't even seen Hawkbrothers, and I know they're supposed to be out there somewhere—so how dangerous could it be now that the mage-storms are over really? I've probably spent as much time in the Forest as anyone here, and I just don't think that hiding in your house and pretending that the Forest isn't there is going to do anyone any good.

He looked up slyly for a moment, and realized that he had managed to kick his stone up to the back of the inn—or what served as an inn here in the village. It really wasn't much more than another cottage with two rooms, one large room full of benches and tables, one a kitchen, and a loft above the kitchen where the owner slept—it was owned by Hanbil Brason, who brewed the beer and dispensed it to the men who gathered here of an evening, and in earlier years besides selling beer and food, he at times had sold floor space at night to passing traders. Nowadays, when there wasn't much in the way of coined money in the village, Hanbil sold his brew by tally—you brought in a bushel of barley, a bunch of hops, a dozen eggs, some pork or chicken, and he would reckon up how much in "real" money that represented and put it on a tally-stick for you. Then you drank and ate until you used up the tally. Hanbil was the only man with whose tallies no one argued, because he was the only source of beer, and his was the only place in the village where men could gather to complain about their wives in relative peace.

He was aided in his endeavors by Lilly, who served beer and meat pasties, cleaned and washed up, and dispensed some other unspecified services that caused the good wives of Errold's Grove to frown and pronounce her "no better than she should be." Whatever that meant. It might have had something to do with the fact that she wore skirts kilted up above her knee, extremely tight bodices, and blouses that continually fell off one shoulder, showing a great deal more of her than the wives liked. Lilly was no girl; she was older than some of those wives, and really no prettier. The women had no cause to feel any jealousy about *her* looks. But they did, and they took some pleasure in snubbing her at every opportunity. However, like poor old Kyle, folks said she was not especially bright, so she didn't seem to take any notice of being slighted. Or if she noticed, she didn't care; maybe having the approval of the husbands was worth the snubs of the wives.

Darian had some doubts about that; he didn't think it was that

Lilly was stupid at all. He thought it was probably more the case that she was so resigned to her lot and position that she just didn't think about it anymore.

The boys said she was also not quite bright enough to count past ten—anything more than ten was simply "a lot"—and as every child in the village knew, if there were more than ten pasties or fruit pockets cooling on the windowsill, Lilly would never notice one missing. Once again, Darian had doubts, for he'd seen her taking in the plates of cooled baking with a slight smile when one or more was missing. He had the feeling that she knew very well that the baked goods were gone, and that she rather enjoyed the fact that bold children were snitching Hanbil's goods.

And since Hanbil was notoriously parsimonious when it came to his share of the support for Justyn, Darian always considered it his duty to filch something to eat from the inn when he got the chance.

This was his day of golden opportunity. Lilly must have been out berrying on the old road this morning, for there was a line of fine, golden-brown berry-pockets cooling in pans on the windowsill and just beneath it, sitting on upturned buckets so she could reach them from the window. Juice oozed from them enticingly, and there were at least two dozen of them.

Darian sidled up to the window and took a quick glance around to see if anyone was watching, but the area was deserted, and he could hear Lilly talking to Hanbil up in the loft. He snatched, and ran, juggling the pocket from hand to hand to keep from getting burned, while his mouth watered with anticipation.

A moment later he was safe in a spot he often used for strictly temporary hiding, the hollow behind some juniper bushes under the window of what passed for a shop in Errold's Grove. Nandy Lutter and her husband used to buy their goods from traders, but with fewer and fewer coming through, they had to go fetch their own goods. They were the only people in the village who ever went up the road to the outside world. Once every three months, Derrel Lutter would hitch up his horse to his wagon and drive off across the bridge with a wagon full of whatever he and Nandy had traded for over the previous three months. When he came back, he would have the things that the village could not make for itself, and he and Nandy would set them up in the shop, and make trades over the next few months. They brought in things like needles and pins, ribbons and colored thread, sugar-loaves, spices, and salt. They were two of the Errold's Grove elite, and as a result, Nandy had gone to the effort of planting things around their house that were pretty, but impractical, as a means of displaying their wealth. She had beds of spring bulbs, flowering trees that had no real fruit, rose vines, and evergreen-holly and juniper. The latter were planted against the side of the house, and the hollows against the wall where the branches had died back for lack of sunlight made a good hiding place. That was where Darian went when he'd filched a pie; better to get under cover, eat it quickly, and dispose of the evidence at once. They couldn't accuse you for having a blue tongue; you could claim you'd been berrying yourself.

He wriggled into place just below a window, and proceeded to nibble delicately at his treat so as not to waste a single crumb. For such a poorly regarded woman, Lilly was a remarkably good baker, and her efforts certainly surpassed anything Darian could produce. The pastry was flaky and light, perfectly browned and crunchy, the filling sweet and juicy without being too runny. He took a great deal of satisfaction, not only in the fact that he'd cheated Hanbil out of something, but out of the fact that taking it by sleight-of-hand had been a great deal more efficient than trying to get it by levitation or some other daft method Justyn might have suggested. *I don't need his stupid magic to get what I need. I can do anything I have to do with my two hands and my wits.*

The more he thought about it, the more discontented he became. This was no life for anyone with any courage or ideas! This was no place for anyone who wanted something besides a place to sleep and steady meals and—predictability! Errold's Grove was dying, or dead, and no one had noticed it but him. And he had to escape before he died, too.

Nandy and another woman were talking inside, but he didn't pay any heed to them until the tag-end of a sentence caught his attention. "—that old fraud who calls himself a wizard."

"I don't know why we give over anything to support him," the other woman replied querulously. "It's not as if he was like Kyle, and useful."

"I've said as much to my husband," Nandy replied with an air of triumph. "I've said to him that there's nothing that man could do that one of the girls couldn't learn. Take Ida's Saffy—" she chuckled cruelly, "—and the gods know there isn't a boy in Errold's Grove who would."

"Nandy!" her visitor exclaimed in mock shock. "Now how could you say a thing like that?"

"Twenty years old and not married, a face like a horse and a body like a washboard? It's only plain speaking," Nandy retorted, with obvious pleasure. "Now look, my man could take her up when he next goes off to the city and leave her at the Healer there. *He'll* train her for nothing, we've already asked. In a year she comes back, and we can send that good-for-nothing fraud off to swindle some other village. Saffy could go back to living with her parents, just like before, but then she'd go from being a burden to a blessing. The rest of us could pay for her services as we need them, not before, and there won't be that *drain* on everyone, which is purely cruel. And now there's *two* to feed, him and that useless, feckless, bit of bad blood that he calls an apprentice.''

"Well, it isn't fair," the other agreed. "If you're never sick, it doesn't seem fair to have to keep giving over food and clothing and all. Of course, he *does* do Finding, and Weather-watching—''

"And a careful person don't need a Finder, and as for Weather-watching, we got along well enough without it before.'' Nandy pronounced that as the end of the argument. "As for the boy, well, I don't doubt that if he doesn't manage to bring the Forest down on us all as his rootless parents tried to do, he certainly won't amount to anything. He hasn't the intelligence of Kyle and he's as shiftless as Lilly, and the sooner we're rid of both of them, the better off this village will be.''

Nandy and her customer moved away from the window at that point, and Darian couldn't hear anything but the murmur of voices.

He sat where he was, not out of shock, but suddenly struck by a sense of hopelessness so deep he couldn't have moved if his life had depended on it. Now they grudged even the scant food they provided him—they were going to turn him out to fend for himself as soon as they could get away with it. And they were going to do the same to Justyn, too—but of course, Justyn would have a year or so to try to find a new place to go, because they couldn't do without him until Saffy was trained. It sounded as if—supposing Nandy had her way—they were going to just throw Darian out as soon as Nandy could get enough people to agree with her. And Justyn at least had some skills he could barter for a new place somewhere. Darian had nothing except the clothing he'd brought with him, the ability to shoot a bow, and whatever he could convince folks he could do.

So what am I supposed to do? Go live off the Forest, with no supplies and no weapons but my bow and few arrows? It was one thing to plan to become a great hunter and trapper when he was older, and had built up all the things he needed to properly live in the wilds—it was quite another to know that he was going to be cast out to make shift for himself with nothing whatsoever to help him. No

point in asking Justyn for help either—the old wizard would have a
hard enough time finding a new place for himself.

*Maybe I should just run away now, and get it over with. If I go
now, maybe I could steal enough to keep me alive until I get to the
next town. That's Kelmskeep, I think. Isn't it?*

Assuming he could find the next town; he'd never been there, and
he didn't know how far it was, or if he could get there afoot. People
said it was downriver, but how far was it? Could he get there on his
own? And if he could, would anyone want him when he got there?
Assuming he didn't run into something else first, like maybe Hawkbrothers. It used to be that you wouldn't run into them unless you
trespassed in their territory, but that wasn't the case anymore, or so
their yearly Herald had said. Now they could be *anywhere* in the
Forest according to the Herald; they were supposed to be much better
at doing the new kinds of magic than anyone else was, and the Herald
had been rather vague about just what these bands of roaming Hawkbrothers were supposed to be doing. Nor had he been able to tell the
villagers how the Hawkbrothers would react to any strangers they
met in the Forest.

Of course, as long as he stayed on the road, he would probably be
all right, but what if he couldn't? He'd have to eat and drink, and
that would mean going into the Forest to hunt for food and water.

Well, he had warning now. If a trader came by before Nandy got
enough people together to agree to throw him out, maybe he could
get the man to take him along. Or maybe the Herald would come
soon, and he could beg help there—and hopefully, the Herald
wouldn't decide that the best "help" would be to persuade the villagers to give Darian "one more chance." That "chance" would last
only as long as it took for them to get rid of Justyn, and then he'd
be out on his ear, too.

Now so thoroughly depressed that the filched sweet lay like a
leaden lump in his stomach, seeing no future now but a choice between uncertainty and endless drudgery, Darian crawled out of his
hiding place and slunk like a beaten dog back to the dubious protection of his Master.

The short distance to the other end of the village seemed shorter
than usual—and Justyn was waiting for him outside the cottage when
he came into view of the building.

Darian knew by the set of Justyn's chin and the look in his eye
that it would do him no good to tell his Master what he had overheard. At best, Justyn would dismiss it all as idle gossip, betray his
hiding place to Nandy, and hand him over to *her* for punishment. At

worst, Justyn would assume he was making it all up in an effort to avoid punishment.

In either case, nothing would happen until it was too late for Darian.

Justyn had evidently pondered Darian's punishment for some time, and had come up with something both appropriate and suitably quelling.

"It's about time you decided to show yourself," he said, his face set in a fearsome scowl. "I used the last of my mycofoetida on Kyle, as you would know, if you had been here, as you ought to have been. I had to clean up his mess, and then clean up the dishes from last night that you were supposed to have attended to."

Darian just hung his head and looked at his feet, saying nothing. There was nothing much he could say, after all. Justyn was right; he should have been there. If he had been there, Nandy would have less ammunition to use against him. There was little doubt that he had caused all of his misfortunes all by himself.

"So, since you happen to like roaming around in the Forest so much, you can just go out there and collect enough mycofoetida to fill this basket." Justyn dropped the basket contemptuously at his feet, without waiting for him to reach for it.

Darian winced, and picked the basket up without a word. Mycofoetida was a fungus, a particularly noxious shelf-fungus with a perfectly nauseating aroma when fresh-picked. The aroma faded to nothing within a few candlemarks of being gathered, and when dried and packed in a wound, it was a powerful preventive against infection. But for those few hours, it was best that both fungi and picker stayed away from anyone else. It grew best on live tree trunks where there was a fair amount of indirect light, which meant that you didn't have to go far into the Forest to find it. Only Justyn knew how to dry it, prepare it, and use it properly, so only Justyn ever went after it.

It was not a choice task, to say the least. Justyn knew how to gather it without losing the contents of his stomach, but Darian didn't, and he doubted that Justyn was going to impart that information in his current mood.

He was right. Justyn also dropped his bow and quiver of arrows at his feet. "Since you're going to be out there for some time," the wizard continued, "you might as well hunt. Bring back something for our dinner tomorrow. If I have to look at another turnip, I may start breaking plates."

Darian stooped again, gathered up the bow and arrows, and turned, still without saying anything. As he slouched away, he thought he heard Justyn mutter under his breath, *"And it would serve you right if the Hawkbrothers got you."*

That last almost made Darian break into hysterical laughter, it was so incongruous after the things he'd just overheard, for it was a threat that was always being given to naughty children: "You'd better be good, or the Hawkbrothers will get you!" Even Darian's Mum had said it playfully, now and again, when he'd been into harmless mischief. Of all the things to tell him *now!*

As he trudged openly between the rows of corn, heading for the Forest, he sighed and slung his quiver over his shoulder. People always talked about Hawk*brothers*, as if they were all male, and no one had ever said anything about seeing a woman of their kind. Was that why mothers said that Hawkbrothers would *get* a naughty child? Were there no women, and did they kidnap children to replace their numbers?

No, that didn't make any sense—they were supposed to be allies of Valdemar, and your allies didn't go about snatching toddlers. Maybe they might *ask* the Heralds for orphans to adopt; that would be perfectly all right, since the Hawkbrothers were certainly capable of protecting children and caring for them, but it wouldn't make sense for them to out-and-out kidnap little ones. Not that you could convince anyone here of that. After all, the Hawkbrothers were foreign, and as everyone here knew, you couldn't trust foreigners.

Still, given how no one here *wanted* him, maybe it wouldn't be so bad if the Hawkbrothers did carry him off. At least it would be an adventure. Maybe *they* would know something about what had happened to his Mum and Dad—or they would be willing to help him try and find out. After all, they were supposed to know everything there was to know about the Pelagiris, and they actually lived in and off of the Forest itself, never needing any kind of supplies or help from outside. Not even his Mum and Dad had been able to do that. Maybe his best bet *would* be to try and find Hawkbrothers, instead of trying to avoid them.

But given the way my luck has been running, if I run away and try to find them, there won't be any of them for leagues around, he thought dispiritedly while he shuffled toward a copse of trees. *Everything I touch falls apart. Even Justyn would have been better off if he'd never seen me. Hellfires, I bet he really doesn't want me around anymore. He'd probably be grateful if I just disappeared.*

He hunted for the fungus in a rather halfhearted fashion as he tried to formulate plans that didn't fall apart the moment he considered what opposition to them he might encounter. One thing he knew; even if nobody in the village wanted him around, the moment he tried to run off, they'd go after him. It wasn't logical, but it was the way they did things. It didn't matter if the outcome was what they wanted, whatever happened had to be accomplished under their control.

Take the case of Ananda's rooster, for instance. Ananda Pellard had an old rooster that was the most evil-minded, aggressive bird Darian had ever seen. She couldn't catch it to trim off its spurs, and it would attack anything, even grown people, inflicting some painful punctures on children. Ananda always said that she ought to put it down, but it was obvious she was afraid to try and catch it to kill it. One night something plucked it out of the tree it roosted in—Ananda said she heard it squawk, and in the morning there was only a pile of loose feathers with blood on them. Probably it had been an owl, and you would have thought that everyone would be glad that the nasty old bird had been taken care of.

But no. Nothing would do but that the men sat up for the next several nights to try and kill whatever had come in to get the rooster. Darian wouldn't have been surprised if it had only been Ananda who was upset—after all, it was *her* bird, and even a tough old rooster made perfectly good soup—but it seemed as if half the village was annoyed, and all because what had happened hadn't been under their control.

So if he ran away, even though none of them *wanted* him there anymore, they would be angry and upset and sure to send someone after him to catch him and bring him back. So whatever course he took, he had to be somehow certain of being able to elude pursuit.

None of this made any sense, of course, but nothing was making any sense anymore.

He honestly, truly, tried to keep from going too far away, but he couldn't find any of the shelf-fungus growing near at hand, and he really hadn't expected to. The last time he'd hunted for the stuff, he'd had to climb so far up tree trunks that Justyn had been alarmed, and he knew that it wouldn't grow farther up than he'd gone, since there was too *much* light. So, since it needed a great deal of indirect light, and that meant the edge of the Forest, he finally decided to work his way along the riverbank.

It was a slow process; he hunted tree by tree, looking for fungus at ground level, then peering up along the trunk to see if there was any higher growth, then finally climbing to see if what he had spotted was the kind of fungus he wanted, or something else. And that was

probably exactly as Justyn had planned, too, for Justyn knew more
about where things grew on the edge of the Forest than Darian did.
He must have climbed twenty trees before he found a single growth.

By that time, at least, he had worked out something to try to keep
the fetid-smelling juice off his hands when he broke the piece off.
He wrapped several layers of leaves over the place where he held
the fungus to break it off, and immediately discarded them once the
fungus was safely in the basket. Although it still smelled terrible, he
managed not to get any of the smell on himself.

He was up a third tree, when he gradually became aware of a great
deal of noise and shouting from the direction of the village. He craned
his head as far as he could around the tree trunk, and nearly fell off
the limb he was sitting on.

There was smoke rising from the village, and from the road beyond
it—he saw people, made small by the distance, trying frantically to
catch loose horses, or heading toward the river with bundles on their
backs and children stumbling along behind, moving as quickly as
they could.

A moment more, and he saw the red of flame flickering on the
other side of the river, light glancing off something very bright and
metallic, and the shouts turned to screams.

A single thought formed through the shock. Something was *happening*. The village of Errold's Grove—somehow, for some reason—
was under attack!

What am I going to do with this boy? Justyn thought, as he watched
Darian slouch his way through the corn, heading to the edge of the
woods. The boy vanished from sight within moments—and he wasn't
trying to hide, this time. No wonder he could evade virtually any
watcher! Why, he didn't even make the stalks move as he passed
through them—if you didn't know he was in the field, you'd think
it was empty.

Justyn sighed heavily, went back into the cottage, shut the door
firmly behind him to discourage visitors, and sank into his chair. He
didn't want to see anyone else today, unless it was a tearing emergency. All morning he had been receiving visitors eager to give him
their own idea of what he should do about Darian's latest infraction,
and some of the speakers had voiced something stronger than mere
opinion. It was clear that if he couldn't get Darian turned around,
there were those who would take care of the situation for him.

Most of them wanted him to dismiss the boy, and didn't really
care what happened to him after he was dismissed. He wouldn't be

allowed to stay here, that was certain. The villagers didn't like the way their children were reacting to his presence—or, more specifically, his actions. "He's a disruptive influence," was how Derrel Lutter, the shopkeeper, put it. "He doesn't fit, an' every part of a village has to fit."

Widow Clay had dropped by on the pretext of having her bad knee looked at, and had been more to the point. "The other children think he's some kind of hero. Or at least, they think he's somebody to look up to. If he's allowed to sass his elders and get away with it, every young'un in Errold's Grove is gonna start doin' the same," she'd pointed out. "So unless you want to be the reason for a lot of spanked bottoms and soapy mouths, you'd better get that boy to act like something other than a savage. Folks have given him a certain amount of room, on account of losing his parents and all, but they're out of patience."

And the woman was perfectly right. Although he held himself aloof from the other children in the village, Darian was a profound influence on them and even Justyn had noticed it. They envied his freedom, freedom to run off and do what he wanted, and freedom to speak his mind even to an adult. They all wished that their parents had been as adventurous as his, and when he was willing to talk about it (which was not often) they hung on every word of his stories about living in the Forest. Any one of them would happily have traded places with him, even though life with Justyn was hardly one of exalted status. And when they could get away with it, they flat-out imitated him. The most coveted item among the village children at the moment was a tooled leather vest like Darian wore; that was what virtually all of them, of both sexes, had requested as birthing-day presents. Justyn had actually considered that attitude a healthy one, and he had secretly hoped some of it might rub off on the parents. It had been something of a half daydream of his. If their elders got some spine back, and decided to stop fearing the Forest and go back out to do what had brought prosperity to the village in the first place, then the place would stop stagnating. It might even prosper again, and they would discover that there was nothing so terrible in the Pelagiris after all. They would stop denigrating Darian's parents, and might even stoop to consulting him about the Forest, which would raise both his status and Justyn's in the eyes of the village.

Even if Darian's influence had only been on the children, they looked likely to go out and do what their parents feared to. Errold's

Grove would prosper again; perhaps not this year, or the next, but in the future.

That was the *good* influence; in the meantime, the children were as prone to imitate Darian's sins as his virtues. So Darian was likely to cause another uproar when word of this day leaked out to the children. Without a doubt, there would be a brief plague of children sneaking out on their appointed tasks to play truant, and defying their parents when taken to task.

That had *not* been in any of Justyn's half-formed plans.

He sighed, then rested his aching head on his hand. It seemed that nothing he had thought of for Darian was working out in the way he had hoped.

Perhaps if I proved to him what his behavior is doing in setting an example, and a bad one, among the other children? He's not an unreasonable child, and he wouldn't want to get the others in trouble. That might do the trick; perhaps Justyn had been going about this all wrong. Darian had been treated as a sort of miniature adult by his parents; he'd had a great deal of independence with them. He was used to relative freedom and the responsibility of deciding what he was to do for himself, but Justyn had been treating him as a directionless child.

Justyn tapped a little marching rhythm on the arm of his chair with his free hand, and frowned as he thought. *I should sit down with him, I think. Instead of lecturing him, or going on about how much he owes us, I should point out to him—no, that's wrong. That would be treating him as a child again, and although what he is doing is childish, I am no longer certain his motives are entirely those of a child. Instead of telling him anything, perhaps I should begin by listening to him. If I can get him to tell me what has been going through his mind these many months, perhaps we can work out the best way to proceed together. And—perhaps I should tell him my own story, and let him see why I am teaching him the way I am. That might be the way to get through to him.*

Lost in these thoughts, and unexpectedly wearied from the stress of dealing with all those unhappy visitors, Justyn closed his eyes. Just for a moment—just to ease them. One moment turned to two, and two to many, and without intending to permit himself the luxury, he dozed off, dreaming of a repentant apprentice, now willing to be taught and to take on the responsibilities of a proper student . . . then he reached the point in sleep where his dreams themselves faded away.

Justyn was so deep in slumber that it took several moments for the sound of the alarm bell in the village square to penetrate his consciousness. When it did sift through, it brought him awake with a start. It took another few moments for him to collect his thoughts and realize what it was that had awakened him, it had been so long since that particular bell had been rung. The last time had been due to a flood—but what could possibly be amiss this time? A quick glance out the window showed that there was no sign of a storm, and the village had been so quiet that Darian's peccadillo was the worst thing to disturb the dull routine of the day. What had happened to change that?

His heart pounded uncomfortably at the sudden awakening. He struggled up out of his chair, every joint protesting violently at such sudden movement, and got his walking stick down off the wall. He opened his door on pandemonium. Outside beyond the nearest houses in the village square, there was a babble of voices, the noise of many people running to and fro. He heard many people shouting, and there was panic in their tones; he hobbled out his door to see folk streaming toward the center of town from the fields. He joined them, alarm giving him more energy than he'd had for many a day. By the time he reached the square, most of them had beaten him there. Some had already heard the news, which must be terrible indeed to judge from the way they were pelting back to their houses, faces pale and eyes gone panicky and full of fear. Others had already been to their houses and were returning, with hunting bows, boar-spears, and rusty old antique weapons in their hands.

A monster? Bandits? Surely not war—who would we be fighting? The Hawkbrothers? No, that's not possible. Surely there is some other explanation—

Derrel Lutter stood beside Nandy, who was still ringing the bell with wide-eyed determination. Her hair had come undone and flew in wild tendrils all about her face. Beside Derrel was a stranger holding the reins of a tired horse, whose clothing showed the effects of a hard ride, and whose face was pinched with terror he was trying not to let loose.

"Don't try to fight, you fools," the man shouted over the bell and the shouting, his voice cracking with strain. "Run, I tell you, *run!* I tried to tell you before, and you didn't believe me! This isn't some band of brigands, this is an army, and you haven't a chance against it!"

Bewildered, Justyn looked around and saw Vere coming back to the square with a determined scowl on his face and a boar-spear in his hands, and seized his arm. "What in the name of heaven is going on?" he shouted.

Vere thrust his chin at the stranger. "That there's a feller from Riverford Farm, big estate upwater where Derrel does some trading," he shouted back. "Derrel vouches for him. Came riding in 'bout mid-dinner. Says a gang of men and monsters came storming in and massacred everybody in sight; says he was out with the herds and managed to get away on his horse and make a run for it. He wasn't too clear on what he'd seen, not then anyway, so we figured it was bandits, and Tom Kalley rounded up the militia." The man paused when he saw the look of noncomprehension on Justyn's face. "He mounted up, and led 'em out, just like always. Wasn't nothing to frighten the women about, he thought, so nobody told 'em except for the ones whose men hadda go; men'd just go out, turn 'em away from the village, and send a messenger over to Lord Breon. *You* know we ain't never had no trouble before. We figgered Riverford just been caught out, that's all. Too bad for them, but we were ready, see?"

Justyn shook his head, not yet understanding the cause for such a high level of panic. The Errold's Grove militia never *had* experienced any trouble discouraging bandits from coming after the town. It didn't make any sense!

Vere wasn't through yet. "*One* of them—just *one*—came back a short bit ago; his horse was foundering, and it dropped and died right after he tumbled off. The rest—they're gone."

Justyn gaped at him. The militia—twenty men in all—were well armed and quite adequately trained, and their ability to fight on horseback had given them a considerable edge over bandits, who were generally afoot and even when horsed did not know how to fight as a group. When the Guard had been forced to leave to go to the front, the Queen had no intention of leaving them defenseless; she had sent spare horses and arms, and someone to train volunteers from the village in fighting. Their Herald had supervised the training, and had seen to it that the trainer left instructions on drilling and practices, which the militia undertook with religious regularity. One of the duties of their Herald was to make sure that they *stayed* in training, and the occasional bandits only gave them incentive to continue that way. Justyn had watched them, and they weren't bad—and the level of their expertise was obvious in the fact that they had handled every bandit group that they had come up against. How could they have been wiped out so easily?

The stranger grabbed Nandy and took the bell-rope out of her hands by force, so that the clangor finally stopped. "Listen to me—

Listen to me!'' he shouted, and the cries and screams stopped as
abruptly as the cessation of the bell peals. His words fell into the
sudden silence like cold, round stones into a pool.

"You heard the boy—your men are *dead*," he said forcefully, and
a woman's hysterical sob pierced the quiet, only to be muffled by
her neighbor pulling her head into the shelter of her shoulder. The
stranger ignored her. "You can't do anything for them; you can only
save yourselves, and there's not much time to do that. Send someone
downriver to Kelmskeep and Lord Breon, someone on a fast horse
or in a swift boat and do it *now*. The rest of you, grab what you can,
and run, as fast and as far as you can. This is no bandit horde, I'm
telling you, I know because I saw them. This is an army; it's men
and monsters, and it looks like a demon is leading them. They killed
everyone at Riverford that resisted, and they'll do the same here."

Now Justyn saw that young Ado Larsh, barely seventeen and the
youngest member of the militia, was sitting on the platform beside
the stranger; there was a bloody rag acting as a bandage around his
head and one eye, and another binding his arm. He looked white, in
deep shock, but nodded in confirmation of everything the man said.

"What about those who didn't resist?" Widow Clay called out
sharply. "What happened to them?"

Someone else growled, and a few of her neighbors cast her angry
looks, but she gave them back look for look. "There are *some* of
us," she pointed out, "who can't run. Myself and Kyle, for two.
What happened to those who didn't resist?"

The stranger shook his head. "I don't know. I didn't wait around
to see. But I can tell you that from the smoke that rose up behind
me, it looked to me like they put every building on the estate to the
torch, and I can only hope there wasn't anyone in those buildings
when they went up."

"Th-th-they're m-m-moving *f-f-fast*," Ado stammered. "C-c-can't
b-be f-far b-b-behind."

There was silence then, nothing but silence. Clearly, no one knew
what to do next, and if no one took charge, in a moment, there would
be nothing but blind panic. People would be caught between trying
to hide and trying to escape, torn between saving possessions and
getting away quickly, and managing only to confuse matters further.
If someone didn't tell them what to do, nothing would be done at
all, and they would all die stupidly and uselessly.

"Right. I'll take over from here," Justyn heard himself say into
the deathly hush. People turned to see who had spoken, as if they

didn't recognize his voice. Maybe they didn't; this was the first time he had spoken with real authority in years.

He pulled himself up as tall as he could, and pushed through the crowd with the aid of his staff until he got himself up on the platform. Their faces turned up to meet his, all of them white and shocked, all of them looking for an answer from anyone—even him. Well, as it happened, he had one for them. A bit of murmuring started, and he quelled it with three sharp raps of the end of his staff on the boards beneath his feet.

"This is war, and war is what I came out of." He looked around to see if there was any disagreement. "Some of you may not have believed my 'war tales,' as you called them, but they were as true as the fact that I've seen how armies operate. I know what's coming and I know what I'm talking about. The stranger is right—you aren't fighters, anyone who had any real training here is *dead*. You have no experience of anything but dealing with a few bandits, and I tell you now there is no way you can defend yourselves, let alone the village, against an army of trained and organized fighters."

He had their full attention now, and since the majority of those below him were women and children, not men, there were fewer who were disposed to argue with that assessment.

Which is just as well, since it's an honest one.

"Your best bet is to try to escape, or try to hide. Anyone who wants to take a chance on staying—I'd suggest you go to the riverbank as far from the village as you can and stay together," he said briskly. "Don't take anything of value with you; armies like this are paid in loot, and if you stand between them and their loot, they'll kill you. If you have valuables with you, they'll kill you to get at them. Let them have what they want—if you all survive this, you can petition the Crown for relief and get it. If you go hide yourselves beside the river, have nothing they want, and look as harmless as possible, once they're done working out their battle-lust in looting, they'll get around to finding you and they probably won't kill you. *Probably.* That's all I can promise you out of *my* military experience—they might just want loot, and they'll leave you completely alone, never looking for you; or they might decide to make slaves—or something—out of you. If you have young children, take toys and sweets to keep them quiet. When the enemy soldiers find you, grovel, beg, bow your heads to the ground and plead with them and don't stand up until they tell you to. With luck, they won't find you at all, with a little less, they'll let you go, and with a bit less than that, you'll end up serving them."

He didn't say what else might happen; this was not the time to turn the women hysterical. If they hadn't already thought of it themselves, there was no point in bringing the subject up.

"But at least we'll be alive," Widow Clay declared, and began to hobble determinedly toward the river. Justyn gave her credit for good sense; she didn't even look back at her cottage, much less go back to try and save anything. She simply set her sights on the river and in putting as much distance between herself and the approaching trouble as possible.

"The rest of you do as you were told—take boats or horses if you have them, go afoot if you don't, and run, *now*. Don't stop to take anything with you; every moment you waste packing valuables is a moment when you could be putting as much distance between you and here as possible. Don't let your jewelry cost you your life. Go to Kelmskeep; it's fortified, and should be able to hold off a siege."

A few moved to follow the widow, and before anyone else could start, he rapped his staff on the platform again. "As for me," he trumpeted, in a pretty fair imitation of his old sergeant's parade-ground voice, "I'll hold the bridge against them. I've held bridges before, and this one only needs one warrior—or wizard—to hold it long enough for a considerable delay. The rest of you take the time I buy for you and run for Kelmskeep or put some furlongs between you and here. Lord Breon has a real garrison of veteran fighters, and he also has ways of getting word out in a few hours to the Guard. He can protect those of you who reach him long enough for the Guard and the Heralds to get here, relieve a siege, and drive the enemy out of Errold's Grove. If you can spare a moment, set fire to your hay and your outbuildings as you run—the smoke will help hide you and might alert others out there that there's trouble. The fire will confuse the enemy and keep them occupied a little longer. They might stop long enough to try and put it out, or they might run into burning buildings thinking there's loot and get themselves crisped. Whatever you do, if you get caught, *don't fight back.* Fall to the ground and beg for mercy. They're trained, you're not—and there will be many of them for every one of you. Now *move!*" he finished, in a bellow that startled them all out of their poses of shock. *"You haven't much time! Save your lives! Now!"*

As he had expected, they were all so happy that there was someone who could take charge of the situation and tell them clearly what to do that no one argued with him. They simply scattered—some to follow Widow Clay, some to their boats or for their horses, some headed straight for the woods on foot, perhaps planning to take cover there and follow the river road to Lord Breon's estate. He walked slowly and calmly toward the bridge, and as he passed the inn, he saw with a mingled sense of admiration and irony that Lilly had her own strategy for surviving. She had loaded a wheelbarrow with a small keg that could only be brandywine, some mugs, and a mattress, and she was headed obliquely toward the river on the upstream side of the village. It was fairly obvious to Justyn that in this situation at least, Lilly was not as stupid as everyone had thought she was. She had a fair idea what an invading army would do with a woman, and she was going to see that the ones who found *her* had a reason to protect her and keep her out of the hands of their fellows. Able-bodied and used to hard work, she would probably go far enough away from the others that when soldiers found her, there would only be a few of them, and someone who acted like a cooperative, would-be camp follower had good odds of surviving this encounter. She might even find one man strong enough to hold off the others, and willing to act as her protector, which was the best any woman could hope for in a case like this one. He wished her good luck, silently.

As if she had somehow heard his wish, she turned and looked back at him. He couldn't hear her completely over the noise of the fleeing villagers, but he read the words on her lips.

"I know what you mean to do. Gods bless and keep you, Wizard Justyn."

She turned away, but before her face was completely averted, he saw tears starting up in her eyes. *Tears? For me?* With astonishment, he felt a kind of weight lift away from his shoulders and a new strength and dignity enter him; he drew himself up and continued his stately progress to the bridge.

No one else paid him any attention—but no one else even thought to question his plan, to recall that only a few hours before, he had been the unregarded, scorned old fool who couldn't even manage to discipline a young boy. That was just as well, because he *did* have a plan, and he knew it would work. He might not have much magic left, but he had enough for one last trick, and it would delay pursuit long enough . . . long enough.

Long enough for Darian to get deep into the Forest. Thanks to the gods that I sent him off candlemarks ago! He'll see the commotion, and he'll run, like a sensible lad. There's nothing holding him here, after all, and I suspect that he's been tempted to run away more than once. This will just give him the excuse he needs. He has his bow; he knows the woods, it's summer, and he has enough control of magic that his power can help him a little. He knows where Kelmskeep is, if not how to get there. I think he'll be all right.

He went to the middle of the bridge—if the people behind him knew it, a good magic place, suspended among three of the four elements: air, water, and the earth that the wood of the bridge had grown out of and was rooted in. He grounded his staff on the wood of the bridge, and began drawing power out of the world around himself. It was a slow process, but he had time—and besides, all that he gathered was only intended to add to the power within himself. Normally, he would not be able to tap into much of that—

Well, this situation is not exactly "normal."

As he began, the old black tomcat ambled up, and sat down neatly at his feet, just as calmly as if he was sitting down at the hearth, waiting for dinner.

Justyn looked down at the cat, bemusedly. "I wish I knew what you really were," he told the cat. "I wish I knew if you were just an opportunist, or a real Pelagir familiar. It might not make much of a difference to this situation, but—well, it would to me."

Halfheartedly, he tried to shoo the cat away, but it refused to leave his side, and he gave up. Small, aged animals fared poorly in situations like this one; it would be better off with him. The cat looked up at him with one eye, truly a jaundiced look if there ever was one, yawned hugely, and turned his attention toward the road.

Justyn took his cue from the cat, and saw a plume of dust rising above the treetops. The enemy was coming—whoever the enemy was. And as had been warned, it was coming swiftly.

Justyn took a deep breath and closed his eyes for a moment, reaching inside himself for calm and certainty. When he opened them again, a heartbeat later, he was ready.

This will be a very short confrontation.

Darian was out of breath by the time he reached the village; Justyn wasn't in the cottage, the flames he had seen were from haystacks and sheds, and when he saw Vere throw a flaming brand into the thatch of his own cottage, he realized that the villagers themselves had set their property aflame. Everywhere, people were fleeing as if for their lives; in the confusion it seemed as if there were hundreds more folk than actually lived in the village, and he wondered if they had all gone suddenly mad. He coughed in the acrid smoke, and stood poised in the midst of the chaos, searching for someone to tell him what was going on.

Someone seized his arm; he automatically started to wrench away, when as he turned, he saw it was Kyle, the woodcutter. "You gotta run and hide in the woods, boy!" the man shouted over the noise of fire and fleeing people, shaking his arm for emphasis. "There's trouble on the way, big trouble—fighters, an army, more'n we can handle!"

He dropped Darian's arm and hobbled off toward the river, using a stick as a crutch, leaving the boy staring after him, blankly.

Trouble? More than they can handle? What was that supposed to mean?

As Kyle had held him, the last of the villagers had left the confines of the town; nothing impeded him but the refuse of what they'd left behind in their wake, and the fires and smoke. Pigs, goats, chickens, geese, and even cattle milled in the street, evidently turned loose by their owners. He ran up the path toward the bridge, jumping over dropped bundles and dodging the confused and panicky livestock and fowl, certain only that whatever was coming, it would be coming from that direction, since it was away from that direction that everyone was running.

It never occurred to him that Justyn might not have run away with the rest of them until he got around a house and could see the bridge—and Justyn was standing, straight as a post, in the middle of it.

The old cat sat calmly at his side, and Justyn had grounded his "wizard's staff" on the wood of the bridge, for all the world as if it was a real magical staff and not just a glorified walking stick. His back was to the village; all his attention was on the road on the other side of the bridge.

Something was making a very large dust cloud on the road, a dust cloud that approached the river—and it was coming on uncomfortably fast.

Darian stood stock still, and stared. He felt like a fly in amber—feet frozen where he had stopped, able to observe, but unable to move or speak.

The dust cloud neared, approached the bridge; now he saw what made it.

People. People carrying weapons. And *Things*, also with glittering weapons in their hands. A great many of both.

They were arrayed in evenly spaced ranks, armed and armored identically and heavily—or at least, more heavily than anyone in the village militia or the Guard that Darian had ever seen had been. The sun reflected brightly off shiny pike-heads and helms, off shields and axes, all very strong and new-looking. They were led by something much larger than Kyle, and quite clearly not human, who was sitting on an animal that was clearly not a horse. The differences between the humans and the Things weren't subtle; if someone had taken a bear and given it the tusks of a boar, that was what the human-sized Things looked like. They didn't wear much in the way of a helm, but it didn't look as if they really *needed* a helm, which was frightening in and of itself. They had small, red eyes, hairy muzzles, and low brows underneath their helmets. The humans looked—like humans. Only mean, and cold, as if they didn't much care about anything.

The large Thing was something of a different order altogether. Where skin showed under armor, it was a sort of flat, dead, greenish color, like mud with river-algae mixed in. Its face was flat, with a wide nose that had slits instead of nostrils. Its mouth was another slit, lipless, and when it opened its mouth, Darian saw that all of its teeth were pointed. Its eyes were a flat, dull gray, with tiny pinprick pupils, as if it preferred darkness to light. The creature it rode resembled nothing so much as a huge lizard with fat, kneeless legs and a long, fat tail. The mount didn't need armor; it had grown its own.

The leading Thing halted, and the entire army behind it came to a dead stop as it held up its hand. It looked at Justyn, at the cat, and back to Justyn. Darian expected it to laugh at the temerity of one silly old man trying to stop them all from coming across that bridge, but it didn't laugh. Instead, it narrowed its eyes and glared at Justyn, without saying a word.

Justyn simply stood there, calmly, as if he saw such things every day, as if keeping them from crossing the bridge was no great matter.

Darian's heart raced; there was a roaring in his ears, and he had broken into a cold sweat. His stomach was doing flips, his throat was knotted, and he shivered like an aspen leaf. He wanted to run to help Justyn, to drag him away, to shout at least—but he couldn't do anything. Nothing in his body would answer to his will; he could only stand and watch, numb with fear.

Justyn seemed to grow taller for a moment; and his ragged robes gathered around him of themselves like a royal garment. He looked, at that moment, just like a real wizard, the kind they made songs about and painted portraits of. He looked like Wizard Kyllian.

Like a hero—

The Thing lifted the reins of its mount, and the lizard put one ponderous foot after the other onto the bridge, its head swinging from side to side with each pace, and the first lot of bear-things followed until it and the entire first rank of creatures was crowded six-deep behind it on the bridge. Justyn simply stood there, unmoving, until the muzzle of the lizard was barely the length of his staff away from his face.

Justyn bowed his head in a momentary nod.

Then, with no warning, the entire bridge and everything on it vanished into a sheet of flame.

Darian screamed, but his cry of horror and dismay was lost in the sound of the explosion. The concussion of the blast knocked Darian off his feet and stunned him for a moment; when he scrambled back up, there was no sign of Justyn or even of the bridge, just a roaring torrent of fire stretching over the river that reached from one bank to the other.

Darian didn't think, couldn't think—but his body wanted to live, and knew that the only way to make sure that he lived was to run. So it did, and it carried Darian along with it, even though his heart cried to join Justyn in the flames.

He jumped a hedge-row and before he'd hit the ground, the hedge disintegrated and blew past him in pieces. He tumbled onto his left side and cried out, but he couldn't hear himself. Darian's vision narrowed to what was before him, losing his peripheral awareness, his mind obsessed only with being on his feet again and running for all he could gain.

He ran as he had never run before, hardly conscious of anything but picking the path in front of him. Bits of flaming debris from the bridge flew through the air and landed in his path, in the thatch of intact cottages, setting *them* afire. He scattered a flock of chickens before him, as tongues of flame licked at him and smoke blew into his eyes confusing him and making it hard to see as he choked and coughed. He didn't rightly seem to be in control of his body at all; he was carried along, a stunned passenger in a vehicle that had its own ideas about what it was going to do. It wasn't as easy running through the village as it usually was—there were fires everywhere now, and debris and more of the things that the villagers had dropped as they escaped littering the usually orderly pathways. He had to double back and circle around obstacles, so that his path through the village to the safety of the forest took on the twisted quality of a nightmare.

There was a lot of noise behind him, shouting and splashing, and as soon as he broke free of the houses, he turned for an instant and discovered that the enemy had found the ford that the bridge had replaced. They had come up along either side of the burning bridge, flanking the village, and were already running up the riverbank, cutting him off from the woods.

But there weren't many of them yet, they were all human, and they were spaced quite far apart. He was most of the way across a field of waist-high wheat when the first one spotted him and shouted.

The shout acted as an added incentive, not that he had needed one. But somehow he managed to put on another burst of speed and shot past the two men nearest him, bursting through the underbrush and into the woods.

Here he was at an advantage, for he knew the paths, and they did not. It wasn't possible to shoot at anything moving as fast as he was, for the paths twisted and turned, with foliage making it difficult to get off a clear shot. He heard men floundering through the undergrowth for a while, but after a bit, they gave up their pursuit of him.

He continued to run through the thick green forest, pelting headlong down the path, his feet thudding in the dirt. By now his initial burst of energy had worn off; his lungs and legs burned, and he had no choice but to slow his mindless dash. Once he lost his momentum, he woke out of his trance. Strength just ran out of him, he had to slow, and then, finally, to stop.

He bent over double in the middle of the path, hands braced on both his knees to keep them from collapsing, panting and sobbing at one and the same time. He wanted to scream, to weep and never stop, to run until he came to the edge of the world, to run back to the village and fling himself against the entire army.

He hadn't the strength to do anything but take huge, gasping breaths that burned his lungs and brought a stitch to his side.

He could not believe what he had just seen, and yet the scene was etched into his memory as indelibly as if the fires Justyn had called up had scorched the image there.

He still couldn't think clearly; conflicting emotions warred in his mind for the upper hand. Rage grappled with heart-shattering grief and kept him from breaking into helpless tears. Fears warred with confusion and kept him from going on, despair battled with determination and urged him to crawl into the nearest hole to hide. Where was he to go? What was he to do? How was he to get away from these madmen? For madmen they must be; why would anyone in his right mind want to attack an impoverished, dying backwater like Errold's Grove, a place where so few people had even a single copper coin to their names that most of the village transactions were run on barter and tally-sticks?

A single small, sane voice spoke up amidst the confused babble of thoughts in his head. *Get off the path, stupid! If they're still fol- lowing you, that's how they'll come!*

He straightened up with difficulty, trotted a few, stiff paces farther along the wall of underbrush, and wriggled through a set of vines whose springy tendrils would snap back behind him, rather than breaking, leaving no trace of his passage.

Unless, of course, they have some sort of tracking beast, the voice reminded him. *This is no place to hide. Collect your thoughts, and think of something better.*

He wriggled underneath some bushes and huddled there, breathing hard, each breath stabbing the bottom of his lungs like a red-hot poker, and listening. There was plenty of noise behind him, but noth- ing immediately around him.

Where did I get into the woods? Through the wheat-field; that was on the back side of the village, next to the corn and away from the bluff. So I won't be striking the river if I keep on this way, but I also won't have to climb. Will these people have a tracking-beast? Do armies have such things with them? He hadn't seen any dogs, but that didn't mean they weren't there. He tried to remember what, if anything, Justyn had said about the armies he had been with, but he couldn't recollect enough. Now he regretted not listening to the old man's stories; they'd seemed so irrelevant at the time, but now—!

Now I only hope I have more time to regret not listening to him!

His next thought was to climb a tree, but he dismissed it imme- diately as a bad idea. If the enemy had a tracker, he'd be trapped. No, he had to get as far away from the village as possible.

And then what?

One thing at a time; get away first, worry about what comes next after you've gotten away.

He stayed where he was until his sides and legs didn't hurt as much, listening cautiously for sounds that meant pursuit. That didn't just mean the sounds of someone coming down the path behind him; it meant the *lack* of normal sounds from the small birds and animals nearby, and the warning calls of birds that had been disturbed by intruders, cries that would come from higher up in the trees.

There was nothing immediately around him but silence broken only by a few faint rustles and mutters, and he decided with some reluctance that he ought to go back to the path. It was true that anyone hunting him would have to use it, but it was equally true that he would make much better time if he didn't have to fight his way through the undergrowth. His passage would be quieter, too.

I can wait until I'm deeper into the Forest before I get off the path.

A bit farther on, the undergrowth thins, and I can move through the trees a great deal easier.

That would make for another danger, though. Thinner undergrowth would mean a better chance of being spotted if the enemy had also gone off the path. Just because he knew the Forest, it didn't follow that the enemy was ignorant of it.

Nevertheless, sitting here only made being caught more likely. He shook off his doubts, wriggled out of his cover as branches and twigs caught at his hair and clothing, and found his way back to the path he had abandoned, trying to make a minimum of disturbance to the underbrush.

His tough, bare feet made no more sound on the path than the falling of a leaf, and he trotted along with an arrow nocked to his bow, all senses alert, for what seemed like an eternity. His nerves strained to the breaking point, so much that he shivered, like a nervous hare, and started each time a birdcall broke the silence. Every deeper shadow seemed to hide an enemy, and every cracking twig might be the sound of a heavy foot.

What's ahead of me in this direction? He thought about the path for a while, and decided that one of his storm-shelters was—a pile of rock slabs in the middle of a rock-strewn clearing, with enough room under three of them piled together for him to squeeze himself and a small fire beneath. According to the villagers, at some point— farther than any of them had ever cared to go and farther than he had been able to penetrate—it became Hawkbrother territory. Well, weren't they supposed to be Valdemar's allies? Shouldn't *they* do something about these invaders? If he could get away, maybe he ought to try to find them.

If he could get away from the invaders in the first place. A posthumous revenge was not going to be very satisfactory from his point of view.

The undergrowth thinned, as he knew from past explorations that it would, and he put his arrow back in the quiver, fastened the cover over it, and unstrung his bow, slinging it over his shoulder. Now that he could see for some distance, he knew that he no longer had much of an advantage with his bow—if he saw an enemy now, it would not be a case of surprise at short range, and the enemies were armored. He might be the best shot in the village, but a small-game bow had no chance against armor. His only chance of felling one of these men would lie in a lucky shot through the helm-slit, and today did not seem a good day to trust his luck.

He picked up his pace into the lope his father had taught him for covering the greatest amount of ground with the least effort. Now it was possible to see for some distance under the trees; what growth there was here was composed of thin, delicate bushes with slender leaves, a few sparsely-leaved vines with stems as thick as his leg, and some pale-green weeds liberally festooned with prickles. There wasn't a great deal of cover, and it was the huge tree trunks themselves that blocked vision. He got off the path, and under the trees, hoping that he would be able to see trouble before it saw him.

A few furlongs farther on, he ran into the enemy's second line. He literally *ran* into it; a patrol of three mounted men—he rounded a huge tree trunk and suddenly there they were, their horses shying away from the unexpected intruder.

That was all that allowed him to escape them. As they fought their startled horses, he dodged between two of them, and ran, darting in and around the trees, feeling the place between his shoulder blades crawl as he expected an arrow to hit there at any moment.

After the initial surprise, they seemed to treat his appearance as something of a joke. He couldn't understand their language, but their laughter was plain enough—cruel though it sounded. Evidently they thought that hunting him was going to be an entertaining way to pass the time. As he ran and dodged, hoping to get to his rockpile and hide, they pursued him without putting their horses into a lather, and before too many moments had passed, it was obvious to him that they were making a game out of herding him before them.

He glanced back once or twice and saw that they'd taken off their helms and gorgets and both were dangling from the pommels of their saddles by the straps. That only allowed him to see their faces more clearly, and what he saw in those brief glances chilled him. These were cold and hardened men, who were getting a great deal of cruel amusement from playing with him as a cat plays with a terrified mouse. They clearly thought he was as soft as one of the villagers and wouldn't last long before tiring—and they had every reason to believe that. He was skinny and looked younger than he was, and they were on horseback. If they could get him running in a straight line, they could easily tire him out and run him down.

So he wouldn't run in a straight line, and he would try to get to his rock pile, where horses couldn't go without breaking an ankle. Once he got wedged into his hole, he could draw his knife and keep them at bay.

And then what?

Well, maybe they'd get tired of trying to pry him out. At the moment, this was his only hope, faint though it was.

He dodged around a tree, waited until they thundered past him with his back pressed against the bark, and then made a dash for another temporary obstacle in the form of a patch of vines. He dove into those, rolled beneath them and came out the other side while they were still hacking their way through the stems with their swords. Now he saw the sign that he was nearer his goal than he'd thought—a tall, standing stone, shaped like a finger pointing straight upward. He dashed for that, ducked around it, dove and scrambled beneath a bush as one of the men charged him with an incomprehensible shout. He made it through to the other side of the bush, and scrabbled to his feet again to make the last dash for the rock pile.

The men bellowed laughter as they chased him; he threw himself flat as they charged down at him, then picked himself up and made a scramble over the last couple of furlongs. They overshot him and had to pull their horses around in a wide circle to avoid riding them into the treacherous footing of the rocks. His heart was pounding so hard it rivaled the sound of the horses' hooves, and all he could think about was that narrow triangle of dark that meant his hiding place. If he could get in there, he'd be hard to get out—

He scuttled over the rocks, the stones shifting under his feet and making him slip and fall, bruising palms and knees. The crevice was close, almost within reach—

A shadow fell over him as his hand actually touched the first of the great stone slabs that formed his shelter. He flinched away, tried to throw himself to the side, but it was too late.

His heart literally stopped, and a dark film passed over his vision.

A hand seized the collar of his shirt and hauled him upright, dangling him in the air in front of the cruelest face he had ever seen in his life. The man's greasy hair was braided back in a tail and bound around the forehead with a dirty, red scarf. He had cold, flat brown eyes, like dead pebbles, his right eyebrow was split by a scar that continued on down his cheek. His teeth were broken and discolored, his beard untrimmed and full of tiny bits of straw. He held Darian up and shook him, roaring laughter.

Darian stopped breathing.

He was the biggest man Darian had ever seen, bigger than Kyle, and every muscle of his arms and legs under the sweat-damp, dirty skin was rock hard. And a great deal of those arms and legs showed beneath the metal corselet and thigh guards—the armor was very nearly too small to protect him adequately. He said something to his two companions, and chortled, shaking Darian again. He smelled, too; bad breath and rank sweat, and rancid grease all combined to make him stink like a sick and unclean animal.

Darian's mind went blank. He hung limply in the man's grasp, waiting for whatever the man was going to do to him. Whatever it was, it would probably be very bad.

The other two remained on the horses at the edge of the rockfield, shouting encouragement to their fellow. Whatever he planned to do, they obviously approved of.

Darian wondered if it would hurt for very long.

Please, he pleaded silently, hoping some god would listen. *Let it be over quickly.*

At that instant, the shaft of a white-feathered arrow appeared in the man's throat, as if conjured up by his prayer. The man's eyes bulged, blood sputtered from his lips, and his hand came up to claw at the arrow that Darian hadn't even heard pass over his own shoulder.

Trondi'irn Nightwind

Three

Snowfire k'Vala, a Hawkbrother of the k'Vala clan, had only twice or three times before this mission ever been inside the border of the land called Valdemar. He considered himself only passably, and imperfectly, acquainted with the customs of these Valdemarans. He thought of himself as a good scout, an excellent hunter, and an indifferent Mage of no better than Master level, but not any kind of an expert on their affable foreign allies.

But he did know this much: law-abiding mounted Valdemaran fighters of whatever ilk did not chase young boys afoot without a very good reason. They certainly did not chase such boys in the manner of a cruel game, taking pleasure from the child's obvious fear, nor would they do so with clear intent to harm him.

Therefore, when Hweel, his bondbird, came flying silently out of the treetops, projecting urgent images of just that into his mind, Snowfire did not need to ponder diplomatic contingencies to make a decision.

Hweel made one of his rare calls, warning him that he was coming down. The bird's call was a long, profound bass note like a thunderous breath, deeper by far than that of a more common hoot of an owl of normal size and breeding. Snowfire held up his arm with the heavy, wrist-to-shoulder leather gauntlet on it, and prepared for Hweel's landing. As Hweel dropped out of the canopy with his wings spread wide to slow his glide, Snowfire braced himself. He had to; Hweel was easily three or four times the size and mass of most bondbirds, and twice the size and mass of a normal eagle-owl. Even with no intent to harm, simply *landing* came as something of a shock to the one Hweel was landing *on*.

Feet the size of Snowfire's hand closed relatively gently on his arm upon impact, and through a triple-thickness of leather, he still felt their potentially lethal strength. Snowfire endured the buffeting of Hweel's wings for a moment as the bird steadied himself; then Hweel folded his massive pinions and settled on Snowfire's arm. Snowfire stared into the round, golden eyes and opened his mind fully to his bondbird.

Hweel showed him images from above, of course, but every detail was unnervingly sharp. There were three well-armed but ill-kempt fighters on horseback, apparently patrolling through the tall trees. Through Hweel's memory, Snowfire saw a thin boy with a bow, and not much else, suddenly blunder in among them. The boy ran, the fighters followed, making a game of letting him stay just far enough in front to make him think he might escape, taking pleasure in herding him.

:Guide me,: he told his bird, and with an effort that drove a short grunt from him, he cast Hweel up into the air. The bird spread his wings, and with powerful downstrokes, drove himself upward.

:What passes?: his mount asked, tossing his long, curved horns and tilting his head so that the intelligent eyes faced Snowfire.

:Nothing good,: Snowfire replied, dismounting. He told the *dyheli* stag who was his partner to go back to the others with a message that he had been detained and why, then got his bow and quiver down from the roll tied to the *dyheli*'s cream-colored saddle pad that nearly matched the stag's creamy coat.

:Are you certain you wish to do this afoot?: the stag asked, flicking his ears with aloof interest.

:No point in making it obvious that I'm not of k'Valdemar,: he replied, stringing his bow with a little effort. *:Besides, if these ruffians see you, they'll probably shoot you for meat.:*

The stag snorted with affront and disgust. *:Barbarians, then, and ignorant,:* the stag replied. *:I will tell the others.:* And with that, the stag leaped easily and gracefully away, heading unerringly for the encampment. He made scarcely a sound as he ran; the *dyheli* were masters of their environment, the deep forest.

Snowfire followed Hweel, nocking an arrow to his bow, making even less sound than the stag. Like the *dyheli*, the Tayledras were masters of the forest.

The others were expecting him to return to their base camp with game soon; dealing with this situation would probably not take long to resolve. But having sent the *dyheli* Sifyra back with word of what he was doing, if he did not return within a reasonable time, some of the others would come after him, and Sifyra could lead them to the right place.

Half of being clever is making certain you are not being stupid. That was a Shin'a'in proverb, and one of his favorites. He might not be one for swift thinking, but he seldom put a foot wrong. Perhaps Nightwind, his lady love, preferred *Most battle plans do not survive the initial encounter with the enemy,* but she had associated with the gryphons for too long for some of their cavalier and devil-may-care attitude not to have rubbed off.

Snowfire kept every sense alert, now that he was afoot and alone on the ground. He noted every deeper shadow beneath the canopy of the enormous trees here, noted the tenor of birdsong up in the canopy itself, drank in the scents of forest litter, searching for the aroma of newly-bruised greenery. Hweel did not see everything; it was perfectly possible that there was an ambush waiting here somewhere.

Hweel flew silently up through the lower branches of the canopy; Hweel *could* fly silently, because he, unlike every other bondbird in the *ye'dorkandan k'shulah* was a short-eared eagle-owl. Owls flew with no betraying sound at all unless very close, thanks to their soft-edged feathers. And unlike most owls, the eagle-owls were equally adept at day or night flying, making them ideal bondbirds for a scout or hunter who might find himself moving by day *or* night. Yet there were few of them among the Tayledras of k'Vala, for there were only four breeding pairs in the entire Vale at the moment. Snowfire considered himself incredibly fortunate that Hweel had chosen him as his bondmate.

In such a circumstance as this, he felt even greater gratitude. No one would see Hweel unless Hweel chose it to be so—and that would be a bad thing for the one making the sighting, as it would probably be the last thing he saw. The talons of a Tayledras-bred eagle-owl could pierce the skull of a goat, so great was the pressure behind them, and what they could do to a goat, could easily be done to a man. Unlike his lesser kindred, Hweel was intelligent enough to pick distinct targets for his talons—such as vulnerable eye sockets. Although Snowfire had not yet needed to put such killing power to the test against a man, Hweel had already proven himself valiant and valuable against the Changebeasts loosed by the mage-storms.

:Hurry!: Hweel Sent urgently, and filled Snowfire's mind with the image of a brute of a man pursuing the boy across a pile of rocks, laughing. The man was afoot now, having left his horse at the edge of the rockfield.

Snowfire broke into a swift but cautious run. He did not want to betray his presence by either noise or movement, so he dashed from the cover of one giant tree trunk to the next, keeping himself well out of sight.

He reached the edge of the clearing just in time to see the man in question catch the boy and haul him up by the collar. Howling with laughter, he held the boy limply from his hand; he was big enough that the boy's feet dangled some distance off the ground. The boy was as pale as ice, clearly terror-stricken. There were two other men very nearby, mounted on horses, also laughing. Even from here, Snowfire caught an unpleasant scent of rancid grease and stale sweat.

Snowfire eased into the cover of a brush-covered boulder held in place by the massive roots of a nearby tree. Between the mottled shadows at the edge of the clearing and the camouflaging effect of his scout gear, that was quite enough cover to keep him invisible.

One of the mounted men called to the one with the boy; they did not speak Valdemaran, but one of the mountain dialects of the north.

"You caught your rabbit, Cor, now what are you going to do with him?" called the first one.

Snowfire held down his anger; the boy wasn't hurt yet, although he clearly expected something terrible to happen to him. *A mountain barbarian doesn't normally kill an unarmed captive; they do take slaves, though.*

"He's too small for a work-slave, but he's pretty enough," said the other mounted man. "You gonna keep him for a body-slave?"

A body-slave? Do they mean what I think they mean?

"Maybe, if there ain't enough women to go around—" the one holding the boy called back, laughing even harder.

That was all he ever said again; filled with fury at his words, Snowfire acted on impulse as he rarely did, rose out of the shadow of the trunk he hid behind, and fired. The arrow, fletched with owl feathers, flew as silently as Hweel, and as surely, burying itself in the soft tissue of the man's throat.

Even as it was still in the air, Snowfire had pulled a second arrow from the quiver at his belt and was sighting it. The man made a gurgling sound, and reached frantically up, pawing at his throat with his free hand, as the second arrow sped to join the first.

A second arrow appeared beside the first one, and the enemy fighter lost all interest in Darian, letting him go to claw at his throat with both hands. Fortunately, when his captor dropped Darian and began staggering back a little, making hideous noises, Darian was still limp.

The boy made a "soft" fall on the hard slabs of rock and somehow his body acted for him again, and he quickly rolled out of the way of the toppling soldier.

Get up! he screamed at himself. *Get up and run, while you have the chance!*

As Darian scrambled to his feet, scraping himself on the rough surface of the rocks, he instinctively turned to look in the direction from which the arrows had come.

For just an instant, and no longer, he saw a strange-looking man in the shadows of the forest on the other side of the rock pile. He was dressed in mottled green-and-brown clothing, and although he didn't *look* old, and certainly didn't *act* old, his long, oddly-cut hair that was braided in a few places and dyed, had stark silver-white roots.

He had an arrow nocked at full draw on his bow, and he loosed it, just as Darian heard something whistle past his ear from somewhere behind him. He ducked to the side, instinctively. One of his tormentors had returned an attack to the bowman from the woods.

The stranger uttered a brief exclamation as a fighting knife buried itself to the hilt in his arm. He dropped out of sight; vanishing, so far as Darian saw, and behind him Darian heard a harsh cry, a startled snort, and the sound of something heavy falling.

He turned again to see that the second enemy fighter, who had still been mounted, had fallen off his horse, an arrow through one eye. The soldier lay on the ground twitching his hands. His head jerked once as he died, then the body was still. The horse shied, but moved only far enough to join the other dead fighter's horse. Both of them paused a moment, then started cropping the thin grass, as if there was nothing whatsoever the matter.

What are you doing, standing in the open? Hide, stupid, hide!

Darian scuttled into hiding, behind a boulder, in shock at the sudden reversal of his fortunes. Where had this strange man come from? Who was he? And why was he helping him? This was all happening much too fast—

Never mind that, scolded that sensible voice in the back of his head. *There were three, there's still at least one alive. Where there were three of those brutes, there are probably more. Do something!*

Prodded into action, Darian picked up his dropped bow—by some miracle it hadn't been broken in all of the tumbling and rolling—and quickly strung it. Opening his quiver and getting an arrow of his own nocked, he peered cautiously around the boulder.

From where he was, he could see two more of the enemy coming cautiously on foot along the side of the rockpile. Where had the second one come from? He took a quick glance around the other side of his boulder toward the last place where he had seen the stranger, and making a quick estimate, figured that his rescuer could not see these two new foes from where he was now. Injured as he was, he might not be able to defend himself.

So I guess it's up to me.

Suddenly, he felt strangely calm. His stomach stopped flipping about, his hands stopped trembling, and everything took on a crystalline clarity around him, the colors deep, the edges sharp and defined.

Taking a deep breath, he stepped around the side of the boulder, and pulled his arrow back as far as he could, sighting carefully on the head of the man in the lead.

Snowfire cursed aloud with sudden pain as a flat knife, thrown by one of the two still mounted, buried itself in his biceps. He dropped, glad he had already loosed the arrow. The blade had penetrated deep, but by luck had gone in more or less with the grain of the muscle. As he pulled the knife from his arm and discarded it, he was rewarded by the sound of the man's body hitting the ground.

So much for being able to pull my bow for a while. I'd better get the boy and myself out of here before it comes to hand-to-hand. My climbing stick is still with Sifyra, and a match between a war ax or sword and a hunting knife is usually a short one.

He pulled a pressure bandage from the emergency pouch at his belt and wrapped it tightly around his arm, temporarily sealing the injury. A brief caress of power melded the end of the bandage into the wrap; the large magics were difficult these days, but the very smallest still worked reliably, making him often glad that he was of no higher power than a Master. *He* had always depended on the use of small magics, not large, and the loss of the ley-lines and the nodes was of no great import to him.

But he didn't have much time. There was at least one fighter still alert and active out there, perhaps more, and he himself was now wounded and not capable of drawing a bow without breaking the wound open and making it more serious than it already was. And, also to the point, he had just dispatched two of the enemy with arrows that shouted *Tayledras*, as clear to read as if he had branded the corpses with the sigil of k'Vala.

So he had three things to do now. Rescue the boy, take care of the betraying arrows, and get both himself and the boy out of there before any more enemies appeared.

:Two come,: Hweel said, showing him where and how fast they were moving. Both had abandoned their horses, and were creeping toward him, afoot, and separated. *:Two more, but from farther. They heard the pursuit of the boy, maybe. They do not hurry, but will come soon.:*

:Can you protect me while I move toward the boy?: Snowfire asked in return.

The reply was not so much in words as in feelings, a sense of contempt that he had asked so simple a thing. Content in knowing that Hweel would swoop on anyone who got within striking distance of his bondmate, while he in turn worked his way toward the boy, Snowfire began easing his way to the other side of the rockpile. His wounded arm kept sending lances of fire up his shoulder, but he had hunted and fought with worse, and since it wasn't bleeding badly now, he knew he could afford to ignore it until he was in a safer position.

He kept himself as much under cover as he could, but through Hweel's eyes he saw that the boy had gotten himself under the concealment of a boulder and was in the process of stringing and readying his own bow.

Good, he thought with some satisfaction. *So he's not helpless, and he's no coward—and he can think and plan for himself. He isn't counting on me to come to his rescue beyond what I've already done.*

Nevertheless, he couldn't be allowed to take a shot. At the moment he was being ignored as insignificant while the fighters concentrated on Snowfire as the real enemy. That puny little small-game bow didn't have enough power behind it to do much damage, unless the boy got a lucky eye shot. All that would happen was that the two fighters still within striking distance would stop ignoring him and count him as an enemy, and there was no doubt that they would not hesitate for a moment to kill him. While he was unarmed and only trying to flee, their customs counted him a noncombatant. The moment he raised an arm against them, he was a fighter, since their own boys entered a warrior-society when no older than this boy.

Snowfire got to the boy just as he stepped out of cover and prepared to fire. He reached out and grabbed the boy by the collar with his good hand and yanked him down into cover.

Again, poor lad—he must feel like a kitten being mauled by now.

Quick as a thought, before the boy could cry out, he muffled the boy's mouth with his other hand for a moment, and put his finger to his lips, miming a message of ''silence'' the way Valdemarans did. The boy's eyes were as wide and round as a pair of fat plums, and for a moment, as blank as mirrors with the shock of so rude an ''introduction.'' But he recovered quickly, obviously guessed at what Snowfire wanted, and nodded vigorously. Satisfied, Snowfire let him go, and he quickly got his feet and hands beneath him, and backed into hiding beside the Tayledras.

:Hweel, where are they?: he silently asked his bird.

The owl showed him; the two nearest enemy were crouched under cover of a bush, at nearly the opposite side of this rocky clearing. The other two had left their horses—which pleased Snowfire—and were making their way on their bellies to join the first two. None of them had bows, which pleased Snowfire even more.

They must be planning to jump on me all at once, he decided. *The only problem for them is, I'm not where they think I am.*

He thought for a moment, measured distances in his mind, and formulated a plan.

:When we run, spook the farther horses,: he told the owl, and motioned to the boy to stay where he was. He took three arrows from the boy's quiver and wriggled his way to the first body, where he replaced the two Tayledras arrows with the boy's.

Then he worked backward to the second body, and did the same with the last arrow.

It was a good thing that he'd picked barbless game-arrows when he blindly drew in the heat of the moment; they had broad heads, but tapered back to the shaft and were in fact meant to be easy to draw out. Barbed, man-killing arrows, on the other hand, were meant to be difficult to remove from a wound. His hunting arrows came out with very little trouble, and he inserted the boy's arrows with no problem. With such optimal targets, someone with his level of skill would have been just as lethal with the light Valdemaran arrows as his own. The fact that the boy's bow wasn't heavy enough to have given the arrows the power to penetrate as far as they did was of no significance, for the enemy had seen him and knew that *he* had made the shots, not the boy. He only wanted them to think that he was Valdemaran, not Tayledras.

The closer view confirmed his guess that these were northern barbarians, wearing bear-tokens, and surely smelling much worse than even the filthiest of animals. *You would think that they would emulate the cleanliness of their totems—but no.*

Satisfied now that he had removed all the traces of Tayledras activity that a likely-uneducated soldier would recognize, he carefully worked his way to within sprinting distance of the horses belonging to the two men he'd killed, and took a deep breath.

This would be their only chance of getting out of there without having to get into hand-to-hand combat with at least one of the enemy. He would have one opportunity for surprise, so his plan had better work right the first time. He made another survey of the area through Hweel's eyes, waited for his moment—and sprang.

Darian had been so taken by surprise by the stranger's appearance that for a moment he had just stared blankly at his rescuer while the man held one hand firmly over his mouth. The man held a finger against his own lips while staring penetratingly into Darian's eyes. Darian had never seen eyes quite so intensely blue before. Meeting their gaze was like falling into an icy pool, and it took his breath away just as surely. After a moment, Darian realized that he was miming for Darian to be quiet.

He nodded vigorously; after all, the *last* thing he wanted was to draw attention to both of them! Satisfied, the man released him, and Darian got his arms and legs underneath him and scuttled his way back into deeper cover, with the stranger between him and the enemy.

The stranger had already bandaged his knife wound, which astonished Darian. But after a moment, it was obvious why he had done so; he hadn't wanted to leave a blood-trail, and the binding would make his arm at least partially usable for a while.

Now what? he wondered, as the stranger mimed for him to stay where he was, and keep very still.

He nodded again to show that he understood, and to his continued surprise, the stranger took three of his arrows out of Darian's quiver, and began working his way, very flat to the ground and snakelike, through the rocks. He kept going until he came to the body of the man who'd first grabbed Darian.

Darian couldn't see what he did there, but a few moments later, he came back into view and slithered his way to the body of the man who'd thrown the knife at him. Now Darian had the advantage of elevation, for the rocks where he was hiding were a bit taller than the forest verge where the man had fallen from his horse, and he was able to see what the stranger did. Fortunately, those same rocks blocked the view of the enemy across the clearing.

To his puzzlement, Darian saw him carefully work his own arrow out of the wound that had killed the enemy, and insert Darian's arrow in its place.

Now—why is he doing that?

He didn't have long to puzzle over the question, for as soon as the stranger had finished his odd task, he tucked his own bloodied arrows sideways into his belt, gathered himself, and leaped like some great cat for the reins of the nearest horse.

The second horse shied and bolted, pounding off into the forest, but the stranger had the first one caught by the reins. The horse reared and danced, but the stranger held him firmly, and as soon as the beast had all four hooves on the ground, he swung himself up into the saddle before Darian could blink. Without thinking, Darian stood up as the stranger wheeled the horse around on its hindquarters and dug his heels into its sides.

It surged forward toward Darian, and the stranger leaned over its neck, stretching a hand out for him. Darian instinctively reached toward the stranger, who grabbed his arm, hand firmly around Darian's elbow, as they plunged past. With a grunt and a gasp of pain, the man pulled Darian over the front of his saddle, and sent the horse racing off into the deeper forest. This was by far the least comfortable way to ride that ever existed. The saddle-bow drove into his stomach, pounding breath out of him in grunting gasps, and Darian could not see much, but he glimpsed enough between bruisings to know that he was heading deeper into the Pelagiris than he had ever dared go alone.

The boy had good instincts; he could not have reacted better if Snowfire had outlined the plan in advance for him. He stood up automatically when Snowfire leaped for the horse; Snowfire managed to get the reins in his good hand, not his bad one, so when the horse reared and tried to bolt like its mate, he was able to hold onto it. The moment the horse had all four hooves back down on the ground, Snowfire flung himself into the saddle.

Since the boy was perfectly positioned for a pickup, even to the point of having one arm extended, Snowfire dug his heels into the horse's side and urged it into a leaping run. The boy was close enough that the horse had not gotten any kind of speed up before it reached the lad; Snowfire leaned down from the saddle, seized the extended arm, caught the boy's arm at the elbow (ignoring the pain from his wounded arm) and hauled him up over the front of the saddle like a sack of meal. It was a good thing that the boy was so small and thin, or Snowfire wouldn't have been able to manage the feat; as it was, he felt his wound break open under the bandage and tear, and a surge of warm wetness saturated the bandage just after the searing of renewed pain.

Two more strides, and the horse was in full gallop; meanwhile the pounding of hooves told Snowfire that Hweel had managed to spook the other two horses into panicked flight, hopefully without being seen by the distracted soldiers. That should delay pursuit nicely.

Good. By the time those brutes manage to catch their mounts, we'll be long gone and the other horses will be too lathered to follow at any kind of pace.

Nevertheless, Snowfire was not about to slacken *his* pace, especially not here, where the ground cover was so thin and sparse that the horse could gallop safely through it. Snowfire guided the running horse in among the trees, allowing it to set its own speed. At the moment, it was so spooked by his appearance and his cavalier handling, that it just wanted to run, and he was disposed to let it. He simply used reins and weight to control where it was going, weaving his way in and out among the massive, columnar trunks, his main effort bent toward herding it in the direction of the stream he and Sifyra had passed on his way here. As soon as he thought they were well out of reach, he planned to slow the beast and take it into the streambed to break their trail.

Gradually, at about the moment when he was ready to slacken their pace, and he was quite certain the boy was long past ready, the horse slowed of its own will. Hweel had been trailing behind them, keeping watch on their backtrail, and had reported no followers. Now he sent the owl back to see if the barbarians had managed to organize themselves. He hoped not; he hoped they'd cut their losses and report to whomever was in charge of them that a huge force of Valdemaran warriors had used a child to lure them into an ambush. He rather doubted that they'd tell the truth, not with two dead and their horses run to exhaustion and nothing to show for their efforts.

By the time they reached the stream, the energy and excitement that had sustained him had worn off, and his wound was bleeding freely. It had soaked right through the bandage and was going to make a right *mess* of his tunic if he didn't do something about it soon. Hweel reported no pursuit at all—the horses were evidently not at all fond of their masters, and were nicely evading capture. The men didn't have anything with them to tempt the horses into allowing them near enough to grab the reins either, which was certainly a mistake on their part.

That argued further for their being barbarians out of the northern mountains. They weren't used to horses or riding up there, and wouldn't have figured out that if your horse didn't *like* you, he wasn't disposed to coming back to you once he'd gotten rid of you, and if that happened, your only chance of catching him was to have something the horse wanted on your person.

The horse he was on didn't much want to wade into the slippery streambed, but Snowfire used a little Mindtouch to persuade it, muttering to it absently, reminding it with images and feelings how good the cool water would feel on its hot legs. Finally, it stepped gingerly down into the water, and Snowfire allowed it to pick its way carefully among the rocks.

Interestingly, the boy hadn't so much as uttered a sound in all that time, and he didn't squirm or show any sign of discomfort, though he had to have been beaten raw by now. Snowfire hoped that his Valdemaran was equal to dealing with the child; he *had* picked it up mind-to-mind from one of the Guards at the next-to-last site his group had worked, but until he tried to talk to the boy, he wouldn't know if it was equal to communicating with a possibly terrified child.

Of course, if the boy allowed, he could rectify that quickly enough with another mind-magic session. That was how he knew some of the dialects of the northern barbarians; he'd picked *them* up from a bold fellow who actually went up there to trade for furs. Snowfire had gotten a great deal of information from that hardy soul; he'd learned, for one thing, that once the barbarians accepted a person as a *bona fide* trader, he had near-immunity among them. "It's an extension of their traditional immunity granted to tale-spinners and history-singers," Shan had told him, and laughed. "But I suspect that it stems more from their greed for pretty baubles and fine fabrics than it does from any real interest in news of the outside world. At least they're bright enough to know that if they *kill* the trader who brought the goods, there won't be any more to follow him."

The question in Snowfire's mind was, what brought northern barbarians down into Valdemar? He hoped that there were only a few of them, and not an army. There had been trouble on the northern borders before, and that was when they knew that it was guarded by the Forest of Sorrows. If they had learned that Sorrows was no longer tenanted. . . .

Well, he would concentrate for now on the immediate problem; what to do with the boy, stopping his bleeding, and getting back safely to his base camp.

Snowfire pulled the horse to a halt after they had ridden for several furlongs through the streambed itself. By now the horse was cool enough that he could allow it to drink, and he really needed to rebandage that wound before the blood loss became a serious impediment to his performance. He got them all over to the stream bank, coaxed the horse up onto solid ground, let the boy get off, then dropped off the horse's back himself.

What he *really* wanted to do was to lie down, but he wouldn't be able to do that for a while. His arm hurt like fury, and besides needing to get the bleeding stopped, he wanted to get some cool water on it to ease some of the pain. There was only so much pain-dampening he could do, after all, on limited endurance. Tayledras scouts were durable, but he *had* just been through a fight, and the aftermath of a fight could leave anyone feeling as if they'd run the length of the Pelagirs.

He looped the horse's reins around a branch with his good hand, and tied them off, giving the beast just enough slack that it could get a drink and snatch at a few bites of grass. Poor thing—it looked at him with astonishment (perhaps because he'd given it that freedom, or perhaps only because he hadn't beaten it yet) and then buried its nose deep in the cool water. Then he knelt beside the streambed and carefully unwrapped the bandage from around his upper arm.

He let the wound bleed a little more while he put one end of the bandage under a rock in the sparkling clear stream, letting the swiftly flowing, chill water wash it out for him. Then he splashed water on the wound, giving it a little rudimentary cleaning, and made certain that it wasn't any more serious than he had thought.

It wasn't; it was just a very simple penetration wound, and not a nasty-looking one as deep wounds go. There didn't seem to be anything left in it, no signs of poisons visible, and as he had recalled, the knife had not seemed dirty or rusty. He reached into the water for the bandage to redo the job one-handed. It never even occurred to him to ask the boy to help.

Before he could do anything else, the boy was already at his elbow and had taken the bandage out of his hands. In a moment, he had wrung it as dry as possible and seized his arm.

"Please hold still, good sir," the boy said, carefully forming the Valdemaran words as he looked directly into Snowfire's eyes, as if he thought he could give the sense of what he said if he simply spoke slowly and clearly, and locked gazes with his rescuer. Then again, if he had a touch of mind-magic, that might work; Snowfire had not lowered his own shields, so he couldn't have told whether the boy possessed such a thing.

"Yes. Surely—" Snowfire said, too much taken aback to argue. Was the boy in training to be a Healer? It certainly seemed as if he might be. But if that were the case, why was he not in the pale green of a Healer-student?

Using some clean, dry moss picked from a rock beside the stream as a pad, the boy rewrapped the bandage with the deft hands of an expert, putting exactly the right kind of pressure at the proper angles on the wound to hold it closed again. When he came to the end of the bandage and looked at it for a moment in puzzlement, Snowfire took over, and sealed the end of the bandage down again with magic.

And to his surprise, he felt the boy following what he had done with his own mind.

"Oh!" the lad said, sounding surprised. The next words were blurted, as if he spoke before he thought. "So magic *is* good for something—"

Then he clapped his hand over his mouth, his face a comic mask of dismay.

"The littlest magics are usually the most practical," Snowfire said mildly, in accented Valdemaran. He cleared his throat carefully. "I am Snowfire k'Vala, Scout of the Tayledras—or as you say, Hawk-brothers. I return now to my own people, in a place we have made for ourselves."

The boy ducked his head awkwardly, but his eyes were alive with mingled curiosity and apprehension. "My name is Darian," he said simply. "Darian Firkin. And—ah—thank you. I thought they were going to—kill me."

"I do not think that what they had in mind for you would have been pleasant," Snowfire said carefully, unsure of how much or little to tell the lad. He might well be much older than he looked; he had very old eyes for such a young face, and the face itself was a mask of politeness behind which something else was hidden. "Have you any place you need to go, or a place of safety that I may take you to? Or would you care to come with me to a safe haven?"

The boy held his breath, and slowly the polite mask shattered and fell. He crumpled, sobbing, apparently completely overcome by sudden, overwhelming grief.

Snowfire did not need to be an Empath to read that there was something dreadfully wrong, something triggered by mention of safety, or a safe place to go. He decided on his own that the best place for both of them was back with his little band. Whatever had gone wrong had evidently been horrible, terrifying; it likely had a great deal to do with those barbarians, and was probably something that he and his people urgently needed to know about.

But there was a more immediate need: to soothe the child enough so that he could ride without falling apart. The sooner he got back to camp, the better.

Snowfire had never had a little brother, but he had played the role of confidante and helper a time or two in the past, to warriors, mages, and younger scouts. "Hush, now," he soothed, putting his good, though leather layered, arm about the boy's shoulder—close enough to give emotional support, not so close as to be intrusive. He knew before the boy did, by the imperceptible tensing of the lad's muscles, when he was coming *too* close, and backed off a bit. "Here, you may come with me, and we will go to my people. I promise, you will be quite safe enough with us. Eh? Then, when you are rested, you will talk to us, tell us what happened. Perhaps we can help. Even if we cannot, we will see to it that you are safe. Warm and safe and well-fed."

The boy only nodded, and Snowfire mounted, lending the boy a hand so that he could swing up to sit behind the saddle instead of being carried like so much baggage. The boy must have ridden this way before; he put his foot carefully on top of Snowfire's, trusted his weight to Snowfire's arm, and got himself up behind the Tayle-dras with a minimum of awkwardness. And there he sat, his arms around Snowfire's waist to hold him in place. His sobs had ended, but as he held tightly to Snowfire's waist, the Tayledras felt him shivering, and not with cold, but with suppressed emotion and shock. He was very near a breaking point, and Snowfire wanted him to be safely in the hands of someone who could deal with his trauma before he came to that breaking point. Nightwind was an Empath as well as a *trondi'irn*, and she would be the best person for the child at this moment.

Snowfire clucked to the horse, which lengthened its stride readily into a slow canter. Evidently it already preferred Snowfire over its previous masters.

It seemed as if this was something more serious than a single boy and a few sadistic barbarians. Perhaps this situation was more than his little group could deal with; after all, they already had quite a bit on their plate.

After the danger from the mage-storms had ended, magic had been shattered like a broken crystal; the matrixed patterns of ley-lines and nodes was gone as if it had never been, and the energies that had once flowed in them were spread evenly across the face of the land. This had left the more powerful mages at something of a loss, but the Tayledras already had a plan in place to deal with such a contingency. They were a long-sighted and patient people when it came to making and fulfilling plans. They would move with urgency when speed was called for, or could wait for generations to lay something in place.

Magic flowed, like water, and like water it would not remain spread out over the land for long. If left to itself, it would form its own rivers and pools—or ley-lines and nodes—or it could be guided into paths that could be carved for it. The sooner those paths were established, the sooner it could be persuaded to follow those paths, and would flow as it had before—and the less likely it would be that stagnant pools would form, warping creatures and plants as had happened before, in the Pelagirs, after the Mage Wars were ended. There were many more Tayledras now than there had been then, with a great deal more experience, and now that there was no *geas* laid upon them by the Star-Eyed to cleanse the land, they were free to go out into it and rectify the situation before it became necessary to do those cleansings.

More to the point, since no creature ever acts against its own best interest (even though they may act in enlightened self-interest) if it was the Tayledras mages who reestablished the ley-lines and nodes in a matrix, they would be able to arrange and key them so that it did themselves and their allies the most good. But, conversely, if they left an area unmanaged, it would be altogether likely for other mages to come in and arrange things to *their* liking.

This was the reason for the groups of Tayledras traveling about now, dealing with Changebeasts, working to link the local magics up with the greater systems already established. The Crown of Valdemar had not only given its blessing to the massive venture, but had funded their needs and ordered support to be given by Guard, Herald, and citizen, with free passage papers and more. That the now-legendary Tayledras Adept Darkwind had the ear of the Queen in the matter had not hurt a bit. Altruistically, the Hawkbrothers and their chosen allies were able to rid the land of some very unpleasant creatures. Realistically, they were creating a matrix that better supported their own Heartstones than even the original had. In the future, it would assure them of more than adequate power for virtually anything they wished to do.

Could it be that some other, rival mages had decided on the same plan?

Of course it could, he told himself. *In this case, it wouldn't take an Adept to see what the advantage in it would be. It would only take a perceptive Master, in fact, or someone very educated in the nature of types of magical energy and its tendencies, to plan out a local scale version of—gahhh. Snowfire, you need help, your mind is wandering. Deal with the situation in the here and now, and discuss the implications of your speculations over a good meal by the fire later on.*

Well, the best thing he could do now would be to get the boy to a place where he could feel safe. Perhaps after some food and calming, this young Darian could bring himself to reveal what had happened. Surely in Nightwind's hands that would not be long in coming.

Whatever it was, Snowfire was certain, there was going to be a great deal more to it than appeared on the surface.

Snowfire was so deep in his own thoughts that it startled him when the boy spoke. "Who are you? What are you doing here?" came the muffled voice from behind his back.

He considered the language carefully before he replied. He did not want to answer the wrong question and give the boy the impression that he was being uncooperative. "Myself, specifically?" he asked. "Or my people? There are more of us here, not far from here, as I told you."

"Your people," Darian answered, and Snowfire felt him take one hand off of Snowfire's waist; he sniffed, and Snowfire fished in a pouch at his belt to give the lad a bit of unused bandage to wipe his nose with. "Th–thank you," the boy said carefully.

Interesting that his own thoughts had just been on that very subject, of why the Tayledras were here.

"We are a very special group of Tayledras—your people call us Hawkbrothers, usually—and we are here for a number of reasons which all mesh together. What know you of the mage-storms?" he asked. "I ask this, because it is relevant to why we are here."

He felt the boy shrug. "Not much," Darian admitted. "They upset the weather a bunch, made things bad around here, turned monsters loose. I guess they made it hard for mages to work."

Snowfire thought for a moment, and decided that the most complete, if abbreviated, explanation would certainly not be amiss, and would fill up the time until the moment they arrived at the camp. And besides, it might help keep his mind off how his arm hurt. "I will go back to the *very* beginning, then—to the cause of it all. Once, so many hundreds of years ago that most of that time is lost even as a legend, there were many of what we know as the Great Mages. These were Adepts so powerful that they had the ability to actually create new creatures that had never existed before, to change the weather, or to make the rocks run like water."

"Was that where the monsters came from?" Darian asked, as Snowfire paused.

"Some of them created creatures that you would take to be monsters, I am sure," Snowfire told him, craning his head around to smile at the boy with encouragement. "But I think that the monsters you speak of were all created later—and I am coming to that. One of these Great Mages was very evil, and he made war on the rest. In the end, there was only one left to oppose him. That one invented a kind of weapon that was *so* terrible that he swore he would only use it if he himself were dying. He made two of these—and when the time came that he was, indeed, dying, killed by a slow poison delivered by an assassin loyal to the evil mage, he sent one into the hands of the evil mage himself, and triggered the other in his own place."

"Why?" Darian asked. Snowfire suppressed a smile at that oldest of childrens' questions.

"Because," he said patiently, "The way that this weapon worked was to release *all* of the magic contained within every object within a certain area. It released all of the magic in the good mage's Tower, at the same time as the other released all of the magic in the evil mage's stronghold. Now, think for a moment about how powerful these two men were, and think how much magic must have been released. Why, in the case of the good mage, his very Tower had been built with and relied upon thousands of magic devices. Then think what must have been contained *in* that Tower, and around it."

The boy pondered that for a moment, then shuddered convulsively. "That—must have been big. And awful," he said, in a subdued voice. "Worse than a forest fire."

"Much worse," Snowfire assured him. "Where the good mage once lived is now the Dhorisha Plains; where the evil one lived is now Lake Evendim; since both those places *were* strongholds among hills, that should give you an idea how dreadful it was. I assure you, *nothing* that was caught inside where the bounds of the Plains and the Lake are now survived. That Cataclysm completely reshaped the world, it was so powerful. And the effects of *two* of the weapons being triggered simultaneously were worse and more complicated than the good mage had ever dreamed possible. Having two of them go off created the *first* mage-storms, and those, in their turn, created the Pelagir Hills and the Pelagiris Forest."

"Huh." The boy digested that. "I thought they—just were. I thought the Forest had always been like that."

"They were created by the cataclysm and the mage-storms that followed," Snowfire replied. "And it was longer ago than I think you would dream possible, and the Pelagirs extended far out beyond what is now Valdemar. Now, the Tayledras were given a duty, and that was to set things to rights in the Pelagirs, and in return were given the secrets of how to control and confine very powerful magic. And the odd thing is that we were very nearly done with that task, when the mage-storms returned, and they returned because not only did they reshape the world, they made an echo of themselves back across time, exactly like the waves of a stone tossed into a quiet pool will reach the shore and reflect back again." He paused. "Do you see what I am saying?"

Thousands of years of history compressed into a few sentences, but if he is really interested, there are plenty who will teach him the tale in its fullest.

"Not really, altogether," Darian admitted honestly, "but enough so I *think* I'm following the story right. So the mage-storms we had were the . . . echoes of the ancient ones? That would be why they made monsters like the first ones did?"

"Exactly," Snowfire said with encouragement in his voice, thinking as he did so, that this was a good thing to be talking of, for it gave the boy something to engross his mind. Snowfire had a growing suspicion that the barbarians had attacked his home, and that he was the only one to escape, if not indeed the only one to survive. He would figure that out as soon as he had time to think about the attack at all, and he would need to grieve eventually, but it would be better if he did so in a safe place.

For now, I will keep his mind on the strange Hawkbrother, so that he does not think too much about what has happened to him. I cannot afford to cope with a hysterical child right now.

"The new Storms were bad in effect, but worse in potential," he continued. "And they were building up to a second Cataclysm, because they were a *reflection* of the originals, which was why they grew stronger instead of weaker. We are not precisely certain what that new Cataclysm would have done, but several folk determined to prevent it, and succeeded."

"That would be Herald-Mage Elspeth, Adept Darkwind, and Adept Firesong, right?" the boy asked, as if he had suddenly made a connection for himself.

"Yes! Yes, and some others as well." *Not all of them human, or even by common standards, alive,* he thought with a little amusement. *But he can learn that for himself later. No point in piling strangeness upon strangeness. I am impressed, that he would know those names.* "I must continue to shorten the story a great deal more, but if you wish to know all of it, you have only to ask. I will say only now that they *did* prevent it, they *did* stop the Storms and have made it so that they will not reecho at some later time, and that the result of this was to change all the magic as we knew it.''

''They—broke it, didn't they?'' the boy responded, surprising him. ''They broke magic like breaking a plate, so it shattered into pieces.''

''In a sense.'' He tried to think of another water analogy. ''If you could imagine magic as all the streams, and rivers, and lakes in the world, and suddenly all the water has been sucked out of them, and has rained down evenly everywhere. You could walk on what used to be the bottom of a lake that would have drowned you, just after it happens, or you can divert the rainwater to a new place you want filled, but the rain continues to fall. That is what has happened, and that is one of the two things that brings us here at this time. We are cutting new rivers, if you will, and making new lakes. And we are once again putting things to rights, getting rid of the Changebeasts that the Storms created.''

''And when you're done—magic will be where *you* want it to be, and work the way *you* want it to, won't it?'' the boy asked shrewdly. ''That's what you get out of it. Your special magic will work again.''

Such an unexpectedly clever observation startled a laugh out of Snowfire. ''I must admit,'' he replied, with reluctant admiration, ''you are quite correct. Not that this is a secret, you understand. And not that this means that no other mages will be able to use their powers. Things will simply work the way that everyone was used to them working, and everyone who has the ability will be able to use them as of old. Except, some people theorize, more efficiently.''

The horse had slowed to a brisk walk, but Snowfire could tell that it was tired, and its pace was quick enough to suit him. He let it set its own speed without correcting it, poor thing. It was probably used to being ridden to within a breath of foundering, and a little decent treatment would work wonders with it.

''So why are *you* doing this—the Hawkbrothers, I mean,'' Darian asked. ''Couldn't anybody do this—like the Herald-Mages or the Fireflower mages or something?''

''They could,'' Snowfire admitted. ''And in some places, they probably are. We are doing it here because we know how, because there are very few Herald-Mages and even fewer who are at all powerful enough to do these things, and because there are also Changebeasts and other Changes in these same areas that need attending to. So we are paid by you, our allies of Valdemar, to do work that we are used to doing, and we are serving our own purposes at the same time. *We,* in our turn, are getting much-needed goods and foodstuffs for our people for our payment, so we are well content.''

No point in explaining too much more. That there were still Vales was something of a miracle, and was due entirely to the superhuman efforts of Tayledras mages to shield their Heartstones during those final Storms. But without the ley-lines to feed the Heartstones, there was much less power coming in than going out, and the Tayledras back in the Vales were having to be very conservative, even frugal, about what they did and did not do with the power contained in the Stones.

That was the main reason why these parties had been sent out; to make certain that as many of the "old" ley-lines as possible were reestablished—and to see to it that an "adequate" amount of power was sent back to the Stones. That was the request of the First Council of Elders—that it be "adequate." Just what "adequate" meant was being left up to the discretion of the Adepts leading each team.

It means, "don't be selfish," I suppose. And if there really aren't that many mages in the area who would need node-energy, then what's the point of allowing it to pool in nodes for Adepts who don't exist?

"I suppose a bad mage could divert a lot of that power away for himself right now, couldn't he?" the boy asked aloud. "Like a selfish farmer damming a stream so that only he can use the water for his crops."

"I must say, Darian—I am impressed. You are very perceptive. Yes. That's another reason why we are here," Snowfire conceded. "If *we* establish the ley-lines—the rivers—we can make sure that it will be available to anyone who needs to use it. But if a selfish or bad mage got to a place first, he could lock all that power away for all time. So we aren't just working for our own sake." He chuckled gently. "After all, eventually there will be mages in Valdemar who will need to use that power, and they would be rightfully annoyed if we had arranged things so that they could not get at it."

"I 'spose they would," the boy acknowledged. "Would things have gone back to the way they had been if you left them alone?"

"That, we don't know," Snowfire admitted.

"But they went that way the first time, so why wouldn't they go back?" Darian persisted. "I mean, it's *really* hard to change the course of a river; I heard of people who tried, and each time it went right back the way it had been, in its old bed. So, wouldn't things be the same if you left them alone?"

"Even if they would, there are still the Changebeasts that need dealing with,'' Snowfire reminded him. ''And the one thing that still *could* happen if we don't interfere is that a bad mage could lock the power away from everyone else. We can't leave that to chance.''

''I 'spose not.'' Darian sighed, and didn't ask any more questions.

Snowfire made a note to tell Adept Starfall what the boy had said about it being difficult to change the natural course of a river, and how that might apply to the ley-lines. It was something he doubted that the Adept had wanted to consider deeply, and it could spell trouble at some point in the future.

:Any problems?: he asked Hweel, who was still wafting along in their wake, branch to branch every thirty or so horse-lengths, keeping a wary eye on things behind them.

:All quiet,: the bird replied. *:Hungry.:*

He considered how far they were from the clearing, how many times he had undertaken to break the trail, and how long it might take the barbarians to catch their horses. He concluded it was safe enough for Hweel to take the time to go catch something.

:Hunt,: he suggested to the bondbird, who needed no second invitation. Hweel had heard the call of a covey of quail some little distance back, and was eager to see what he could do about helping to control the population.

Owls often seemed more purposeful about their hunting than hawks, or more especially, the falcons. It was no great amount of time later that Snowfire sensed the burst of visceral bloodlust that meant Hweel had gone in for a kill, followed swiftly by triumph and accomplishment. A little longer, and Hweel was back in the air and catching up, now with a full stomach, radiating satisfaction. For a bird Hweel's size, a single quail was a reasonable meal, but not a full day's ration; the owl would probably go out again at night to hunt if Snowfire didn't provide him with something.

The horse was not nearly as swift as a *dyheli*, especially not with a double burden, and the light coming through the trees had taken on a distinctly red hue when Snowfire reached the outskirts of the encampment. He whistled the recognition call for the outermost sentry, and a moment later, spotted the flash of a suntail hawk-eagle's creamy breast in the branches above him. Three of the scouts were bonded to suntails, so it could have been any one of the three who were standing watch, but he thought it was Eere, Skyshadow's second-year bird.

:Go in ahead,: he told Hweel, wearily glad that it was a suntail and not one of the forestgyres, who were fond of teasing the big owl. Not that they would ever harm Hweel, nor would Hweel ever retaliate

with anything more than an irritated beak snap, but Hweel was a ponderously serious bird in many ways, and being teased put him in a bad mood. Just at the moment, having his bondbird grumbling and hunched in a tree was a situation Snowfire didn't want to be forced to endure on top of his other pains.

His arm hurt more and more as they rode, and given a choice, he wanted most to see Nightwind and have it tended to, then drink his weight in pain-killing tea and sleep for about a day. The last of his energy ran out shortly before they reached camp. Fortunately, the boy had been cooperative and quiet during most of that time, and his questions and conversation had been polite and subdued the rest of the time. Perhaps he had sensed that Snowfire was not feeling up to conversation.

The horse took them through some truly spectacular territory, and he wished vaguely that he was feeling good enough to appreciate it. Ancient trees with trunks the size of entire houses stretched toward the sky, their roots firmly embedded in the sides of steep, boulder-strewn hills; rocks thrust themselves out of the soil in fantastic and baroque formations. Tiny, threadlike streams sparkled and danced over rocks in the valleys, or threw themselves headlong down the rocky cliffs and hillsides in exuberant waterfalls that were more spray than stream. Anywhere that the dense foliage overhead allowed a ray of sunlight to penetrate to the ground, other plants flourished—a patch of luxuriant grass studded with flowers, a gnarled bush with glossy leaves, or a graceful young scion of one of the giants that loomed overhead. This was the season of birdsong, and their calls fluted through the shadows from every direction. A fresh, warm breeze carried the faint scent of forest flowers and evergreen on its wings. The only problem, so far as Snowfire was concerned, was that his throbbing arm got in the way of being able to enjoy his surroundings. At the moment, they were something to be endured rather than enjoyed, until landmarks would tell him that he was nearing the camp.

Finally, with grateful relief, he saw just the landmarks he was looking for, and soon he was riding down a long rift that would open up into the valley that his group had turned into as near a Vale as was possible for so temporary an encampment. Nature had provided a fine little valley with tiny springs trickling out of the hillside at the back, which the current dwellers had diverted into a series of three pools; what nature had not provided, the Tayledras had fashioned, constructing temporary, ground-built *ekeles* with stone, spools of cord, windfallen tree trunks, carefully tended vines, and the canvas of their tents as roofs. When Adept Starfall found this place to be nearly ideal for *his* purposes, a bit of extra work made the camp into a place of more comfort and more security than mere tents would have permitted. It made more sense that way; with strong, secure walls about them and a few creature comforts, they all rested better, had more privacy, and felt healthier and happier for both, which allowed them to do their work without missing the comforts of the Vale too much. The spring-fed pools gave them one for drinking water, one for washing, and one that could be heated with dozens of fire-warmed stones (or, for those with the Gift, with magic) for soaking weary bodies. They would be *here* for as long as it took Starfall to impose his will on the newly forming magic-matrices, and for as long as it took to find and deal with any Changebeasts that were still in the area—probably into fall.

Snowfire was very glad for those creature comforts waiting for him, especially the hot pool. He certainly felt that he had earned them.

A fellow called Sunleaf, who was bonded to a forestgyre, had an interesting sort of magic with plants that allowed him to bend them to his purposes and accelerate their growth in a way that was quite remarkable. Outside the encampment, he had coaxed bushes and vines into a thickness and luxuriance that hid the camp from sight, and within it, he had made vines grow in screens that divided the area up and gave a remarkable amount of privacy, and got vines to grow over each *ekele*, shrouding them in cool green that hid the structures beneath an avalanche of leaves. It looked, in fact, as if they had moved into a place that had been abandoned to the forest for decades, instead of one that they had just built.

Snowfire sensed the boy's interest as they rode into the valley and toward the little welcoming party of three that awaited them. It was a *small* welcoming party, and Snowfire blessed the Adept's good sense, as it was composed of only Tayledras who would not alarm the boy—the Adept himself, the gentle *trondi'irn* Nightwind, and the youngest of the scouts, Wintersky, who was something of a protégè of Snowfire's, and shared his *ekele*. Of course, Wintersky mostly had the *ekele* to himself, since Snowfire spent a great deal of time with Nightwind. None of the three could possibly frighten the boy, who'd had enough fright for one day, though Starfall looked very imposing, and probably more like the boy had imagined a Tayledras to look than Snowfire did. Wintersky wore the same scouting-garb that Snowfire did, but Nightwind and Starfall showed the other faces of Tayledras life in their dress. Starfall wore the trailing robes, jewelry, and embroideries of someone who does not expect to be covering a great deal of territory in wild forest, and Nightwind the comfortable, colorful, loose garments of someone who *does* expect to be doing a great deal of physical and practical labor, but who does not have to worry about fading into the landscape. Starfall's waist-length hair hung loose, with a minimum of ornaments braided into it, Wintersky's hair was dyed in leaf patterns and confined in a single tail, and Nightwind's was still dark, for she practiced little magic and had never lived in a Vale with a Heartstone to bleach her hair. She was, in fact, not k'Vala at all, but k'Leshya, the "Lost Clan" of the ancient days, come up out of the farthest West.

But at the moment, all Snowfire could think of was how glad he was to see them all. He slid down off the horse and found his legs unexpectedly wobbly; he managed to save himself from embarrassment by holding for a moment to the pommel of the saddle, and offered the boy his good hand as an aid to get down.

Darian smiled at him wanly. "You don't look so good," he said, with that blunt frankness of a child who hasn't yet figured out that one doesn't always have to voice what one observes. "I can manage to get down myself."

And he did, but his legs were just as wobbly as Snowfire's when he slid off the horse's rump and landed on the ground—though in his case, it was probably from a mixture of fatigue and unaccustomed riding than from pain.

"This is Darian k'Valdemar," Snowfire told the others, in Valdemaran. "He's never seen Tayledras before, and he knows nothing of us. Darian, this is Adept Starfall, who is our Elder and the leader of this group. This is *trondi'irn* Nightwind, who is going to patch up the tears in your hide as she does for the rest of us who have the misfortune to run through brambles."

Darian rubbed some of his scratches with a bit of self-conscious embarrassment, even though some of them were deep and he had many bruises as well.

"And this is Wintersky—" He looked askance at the younger man, who grinned at Darian and finished the sentence.

"Wintersky, who will share his quarters with you and Snowfire, unless you prefer to camp alone in a tent, or have us make some other arrangements." The young man winked. "I pledge you I do not snore. My Valdemaran is the best of all of us save the mighty hunter Snowfire, so I thought I'd volunteer our *ekele*. It's always better to have people about who know your tongue fairly well. Snowfire *does* snore, though."

Darian was clearly getting overwhelmed; his eyes looked a trifle glazed, his face was pale, and his expression bewildered. "I don't mind, I mean, that would be good—whatever you like—"

"Whatever it is that *I* like is that you are to come and be tended, and be eating and drinking, and be then sleeping," Nightwind said firmly, taking the boy in charge with maternal authority. The boy yielded to her with relief and gratitude, and she ushered him off.

"I'll report in brief, and then *I* need to be tended, eating, drinking, and then sleeping after you've gotten the full report," Snowfire told the Adept, as Wintersky took the horse and led it away to be watched by the *dyheli* herd. "Hweel saw the boy being chased by northern barbarians. Bearclan would be my guess, but they were all wearing identical armor, and I don't much care for what that implies."

"Neither do I," Starfall said, his brows furrowing.

"Their tattoos would have told me more, but things were rather impolite at the time, and I didn't stay around to request a viewing from those remaining." Snowfire noted Starfall's lips twitch as he tried not to smile at the understated and offhand manner Snowfire was taking with the tale.

"How impolite?" Starfall asked.

"Only two casualties. Not even a minor quarrel by Bear-clan standards. Hardly more than an ordinary drunken brawl—though I did make sure to substitute the boy's arrows for mine; I didn't want to alert them to our presence. Still—one of them had caught the boy by the time I got there, and he and his colleagues were exchanging pleasantries that implied they had been . . . improving some Valdemaran settlements." He dropped his tone of levity. "I think that the boy belonged to the latest one, though I have not yet questioned him at all. I wished an Empath to be present when I did."

Starfall lost all trace of humor at that. "So, you have barbarians in identical armor, what amounts to something more serious than a little banditry, and all this a good bit farther south than we should expect to see mountain tribes. I shall check my maps, but. . . ." Starfall shook his head. "I do not like this, Snowfire."

"Neither do I, since the barbarians don't move in groups larger than a dozen without having a shaman-mage along with them." Snowfire had been letting what he knew about the northern tribes dig itself out of his memories during the last part of the journey; he was better at recollection when he allowed the memories to surface on their own. "And they don't use horses as a rule, yet all of the barbarians I saw were mounted."

"This isn't sounding very promising." Starfall bit his lip for a moment. "Well, the best thing that *I* can do is to move the progress I was making on ahead. It won't take more than a day or so, and I'll have the matrices set up and completely in my control; I'd like to see the mage that can get it out of my hands *then*."

"I wouldn't," Snowfire replied. "But if there was someone able to do that, he'd have challenged you already, so the worst we'll have to deal with is someone your equal. I think we can do that."

"And I think you'd better have someone look at that arm while you get some hot food inside you," Starfall pointed out. "Your stoicism is respected, but not required. Go, you can make a more detailed report after you've rested and gotten properly patched up—and by then, the boy will be rested, too, and we can find out why barbarians on horses were chasing him."

Now that his initial report had been made, he had the relief of the discharge of duty, and a great weariness descended on him. He decided that the best place for him was in his shared *ekele*. Fortunately, it was one of the nearer structures; he rounded two vine screens, and there it was, looking like nothing so much as a leafy hummock. He parted the vines with his good hand, and found that Nightwind had already preceded him there.

He had taken weather-felled limbs and constructed a fine log home, octagonal in shape, with a roof of sod held up by logs and willow withes woven into fine mats. The snug dwelling would probably serve as well in winter as in summer, except that he would have to fill in the bottom rank with sod; he had left off the bottom rank of logs on four of the eight sides so as to allow the movement of air through the place. A cool breeze came in at the level of the floor and went out at the smoke hole in the middle. It had been a great deal of extra work to make this *ekele*, but he reckoned it had been worth the work. A lantern with a mage-light in it hung from one of the ceiling logs. His sleeping place and Hweel's perch were on the far right as one came in the door, and Wintersky's sleeping pad and Tiec's perch were on the left. That left a cooking place in the middle, and any gear they shared near the door. Now there was a third sleeping place at the rear, with the boy sitting sleepily on it and Nightwind beside him.

Snowfire saw at once that someone had left a young rabbit on Hweel's perch, which meant Hweel would not have to hunt tonight. Pleased by the courtesy, he slipped back out before Nightwind noticed he was there and called Hweel to the fist.

The owl dropped down on his arm with customary aplomb, and ducked his head as Snowfire brought him in. This time, the boy, who did not seem to be noticing much, reacted very strongly and positively to Hweel.

His mouth formed a silent "Oh!" and his eyes went round, but there was no sign of fear in him. Nightwind noticed the lad's reaction, and smiled over her shoulder at Snowfire.

Snowfire took that as an invitation to come closer. Darian stared at the huge owl with intense interest. "Is that your bird?" he whispered, as if he was afraid that he might startle the owl. "I heard Hawkbrothers had birds, but I didn't know they were that *big!* He's— he's amazing!"

Snowfire flushed a little with pleasure; he was not proud of much, but he did take a certain pleasure in having so magnificent a partner as Hweel. "Yes, he is, isn't he?" he agreed. "His name is Hweel, and he was watching out for us, flying behind us in the trees, all the way back. Would you like to touch him?"

"Can I? He won't mind?" Darian looked quite as if Snowfire had given him permission to shake the Queen of Valdemar's hand.

"Hweel is excessively vain, and extremely fond of scratches, and if you are going to offer him plenty of admiration and caressing, he will be your friend for life," Nightwind said with mock severity.

Hweel clacked his beak at her, then softened the rebuke with the soft "huuur" an adult would give a nestling.

"Go ahead," Snowfire urged.

Darian reached hesitantly to touch Hweel's breast-feathers, but the owl had other ideas. Quick as thought, he leaned down and butted his head against the outstretched hand, and before he knew it, Darian was scratching the top of the owl's round, densely-feathered head.

"He's so soft!" the boy exclaimed with delight.

"Don't be afraid to give him a good scratching," Snowfire told him, as Hweel stepped down off the gauntlet to the floor, and made his odd little sideways sidle up to the boy. "You'll have to work to get through all the feathers on his head."

The owl closed his huge eyes in bliss as Darian scratched with more vigor, and shoved his head practically into Darian's chest. Snowfire was delighted, both with the boy's reaction and with Hweel's, and for the first time he entertained the thought that if the boy had nowhere else to go, he might wish to join k'Vala.

Well, it is enough for now that he is not terrified of the bondbirds, and that the bondbirds take to him. Either would be amazing enough, but having both is wonderful. We can worry about what is to become of him when we have a better idea of what he has involved us in.

Nightwind allowed the boy some time to caress Hweel, and before either of them tired of the sport, she Mindspoke to the bird, :*Enough.* *He will still be here in the morning, and so will you. Right now, he needs to sleep.*:

As Hweel heaved a great sigh of regret, she said virtually the same thing to the boy. "Sleep, it is time for; you and Hweel will be here both when sun rises."

Reluctantly, the owl raised his head and the boy took his hand away, but before he could take it entirely out of range, the owl reached out with his powerful beak and gently nibbled Darian's fingertips.

"That is a high compliment," Snowfire told him, as the boy glanced at the Tayledras for an explanation. "He doesn't offer that particular sort of 'thank you' to just anyone."

Darian looked dazzled, and as Hweel waddled toward his perch with an owl's awkward and ungainly ground gait, Snowfire got one of the larger body-feathers, about the size of the boy's hand, from a little basket he had woven of pine needles and tacked to the logs on his side to hold molted feathers. He lifted Hweel up to the perch— given the owl's huge wingspan, he preferred that Hweel not use his wings inside the *ekele*—then gave the feather to Darian. The boy took it with shy thanks, and occupied himself with stroking and examining it.

"That was neatly done," Nightwind complimented him. "I was having trouble getting him to relax enough for the drug I gave him in his tea to work. I want him to be drowsy when you and Starfall question him."

"Thank Hweel for cooperating so nicely," Snowfire replied, as she pushed him over to his own sleeping pad and began unwrapping the bandage on his arm.

"I already have," came the calm reply, and then Snowfire endured a few bad moments as she examined the wound and gave it a thorough cleansing. Once it was clean, however, she was quick to put a numbing salve on it, so that when she stitched it up for him, he scarcely felt the prick of the needle. The boy watched them intently, but with a detachment that Snowfire thought was probably thanks to the drug.

"I am very concerned by the little I have sensed from this boy," Nightwind told him. "He is quite traumatized, and on the whole, I am concerned about what will happen to him when he allows himself to feel the emotions he is holding inside."

"I got the impression that he doesn't show half of what he is feeling,'' Snowfire confirmed, as Starfall tapped the doorframe lightly, then entered.

"He keeps things to himself, I think,'' she told Snowfire. "His griefs are many, and not all concerned with whatever led him to us; once he allows one to be free, the others may come flying out. That will be good for him, but it will be a hard time as well.'' She looked troubled. "I cannot tell you if your questions will trigger this release. They may, or they may not.''

"Whether they do or not, we need to know why Snowfire found him in the predicament that he was in,'' Starfall pointed out. "And the sooner we know, the better.''

"Darian, now that you have eaten and rested, we would like you to tell us what happened to you,'' Snowfire said in his best Valdemaran.

The boy nodded; he looked awake, but not entirely alert. "Those men that were chasing me—there were fighters like them that attacked Errold's Grove,'' he said plaintively. "I guess the militia went to stop them, but they probably didn't have a chance.''

"How many men?'' Starfall asked quickly. "What were they like?''

"It wasn't just men, it was some kind of monster, too, and—I didn't actually *count* how many there were, but they were in ranks of five, and I saw ten times five ranks and I *know* I didn't see all of them,'' Darian said, growing agitated, as Nightwind put a steadying hand on his arm. "There were just a *lot*—an awful lot. I was out in the woods, getting some tree-fungus that Juh—that we needed, and I saw smoke and fire and came running back. When I got there, everybody was running away, and this whole *army* was on the road to the bridge. They had lots of armor, and all kinds of pikes and swords and things, and not all of them were *men*, they were kind of half bear and half man! And there was another thing, a monster or a demon or something, that wasn't anything like a man at all, and it was leading them—it was riding on this big lizard. J—'' A spasm of pain swept over the boy's face, and Snowfire made a mental note to find out who or what began with "J'' that the boy avoided talking about so carefully. That might be the key to releasing some of that pent-up grief. "The bridge got—destroyed—set afire to keep them off, but they came across the river anyway. That's when I ran, and I got away from the first lot, but those others were deeper in the forest and came after me when they saw me.''

Starfall and Snowfire exchanged looks. This did not sound very good.

"Did the others of your village get away from this army?" Snow-fire asked. "Did they have somewhere to go for help?"

The boy frowned for a moment, then shrugged. "I didn't see any-body get caught," he said finally. "And I guess they must have run to Kelmskeep. Lord Breon has got a whole garrison of his own, and Kelmskeep's fortified, they say. He has messengers and things he could send for the Guard, so that's probably where everybody went."

"Now, what about the men who chased you?" Snowfire asked. "How did that happen?"

The boy winced with chagrin. "I ran into them," he admitted. "I didn't think there was any way they could have got ahead of me, and I ran into them, 'cause I wasn't looking for anyone. They came after me, and I headed for that clearing 'cause there's places in there I could've hid, and they couldn't have brought their horses over those loose rocks. But one of them caught me, and that's where you showed up, and that's all."

"That will do; I'll have the others gather, and we can discuss this when you are ready," Starfall said, as he got to his feet and headed for the door of the *ekele*.

"I'll be there as soon as the boy is asleep," Snowfire promised, and turned his attention back to Darian.

"Hweel won't have to hunt for himself tonight, so even though Wintersky and I will be gone for a little, Hweel will be with you," Snowfire told him, then asked the one question that was still puzzling him. "Darian, did you really intend to go after those two barbarians with your rabbit-bow?"

"I had to," Darian replied sleepily. "I knew you were hurt, and I didn't think you'd seen them. I knew I couldn't do much unless I got a lucky shot, but maybe I'd distract them, and for sure they'd make a noise, so you would know that they were there."

"Well, that was good planning," Snowfire told him, and was re-warded with a sleepy smile that faded into drugged slumber. He waited until he was certain that Darian's sleep was too deep to be easily broken, then got up to go outside, leaving Hweel to keep a vigilant eye on the boy.

:Watch and guard,: he told the bondbird, keeping things simple. People had been known to have odd reactions to drugs, and children in particular were prone to sleepwalking after a severe trauma. Snow-fire was not in the least deceived by the boy's apparent calm; Night-wind said that there was great emotion ready to burst out at any moment, and he believed her. *:Find me if something happens.:*

Hweel roused his feathers and *huured* his agreement. Now that he was full of rabbit, he was quite content to stay in one place with a foot tucked up beneath his breast-feathers.

Snowfire joined the rest of the group around the small fire that Nightwind kept feeding with herbs to keep the insects away. He accepted a mug of cool water from the spring from Wintersky with a nod of thanks, and took his place in the council session that had formed.

"I've told the others what the boy told us," Starfall explained, as firelight flickered and cast odd shadows on his face. "And the very first question I can think of is whether we should involve ourselves at all."

"I don't think we can, to tell you the truth," replied Wintersky regretfully. "I mean, this sounds like an army! And we have *how* many? Not quite twenty humans, twice that in the *dyheli* herd, a couple of *hertasi* and a gryphon. We aren't exactly equipped to be fighting battles either."

The fire popped and hissed, blending with the sound of movement of something large, like the sussuration of canvas across canvas.

"I would sssay that one grrryphon isss worrrth an arrrmy, but I rrreluctantly concurrr," a deep voice rumbled from the shadows behind Nightwind. "It only takesss a sssingle arrrow."

"It isn't just an army of men, but of Changechildren as well, and that means a mage is deep in it somewhere," Starfall put in. "Unless what the boy saw were just costumes or disguises, and I can't imagine why barbarians would bother wearing disguises."

"It sounds to me as if someone managed to reconcile a great many Bearclan septs," Snowfire mused. "Maybe—well, this is a wild surmise, but from what *I* know about the northern tribes, they attach heavy religious and emotional significance to their totems, and a lot of emphasis is put on taking on the attributes of those totems. Now, what would happen if a mage came along, perhaps in the guise of a shaman, who could give them *physical* attributes of their totems?"

"He'd own the clan to the point of being able to reconcile all the feuds between the septs," Starfall said flatly. "And there was someone who managed that, once."

"Yesssss." The shadow behind Nightwind rose, and loomed up over her head. "Yessss, therrre wassss. And we all know hisss currrsssed name." The shadow resolved itself into a shape, and the shape into a creature, a creature with the mantling wings and head of a raptor, but a raptor of enormous size, and with four limbs instead of two. "He wasss called *Ma'arrrr*."

"I don't think we're in any danger of seeing another Ma'ar, Kelvren," Nightwind soothed. "It's all right."

But Starfall frowned. "Perhaps. And perhaps *not*. I can't help but think that this is a rather nasty coincidence, these barbarians, presumably led or backed by a mage, suddenly moving into territory where no one has yet established a matrix for magic. The difference between a Ma'ar and a petty tyrant is largely a matter of power."

"All the more reason for you to form and hold the matrix," Snowfire replied firmly. "That will *have* to be our first priority, it seems to me. If the boy is correct, most—if not all—of his people escaped. Surely one will reach Lord Breon, and *he* can take care of the military problem from there."

"That would be best," Starfall replied, but with a little reluctance. "We are hardly the group best suited to taking on an army."

"But think of what it would have meant if sssomeone had ssstopped Ma'arrr when he wasss gatherrring the trrribesss," Kelvren urged, his eyes glinting in the firelight. "Would it not have been worrrth everrry sssacrrrificssse to do sssso?"

"We can stop any mage just as easily by holding the magic energy of this area away from him," Snowfire replied. "I think we should concentrate on getting *that* done first. By then, we should know if the Valdemarans have taken care of the military situation themselves."

"And if they have not?" Kelvren persisted.

"We'll deal with that when we come to it," Starfall said firmly, ending the debate.

The gryphon folded his wings, feathers making a cloth-on-cloth sound as they slid across each other into precise order. "Verrry well. I will be—rrready. And if they *do* rrrememberrr Ma'arrr and hisss waysss—" Kelvren reached for a log of firewood and purposefully splintered it into several pieces merely by squeezing it. "—then I will ensurrre that they rrrememberrr grrryphonsss asss well."

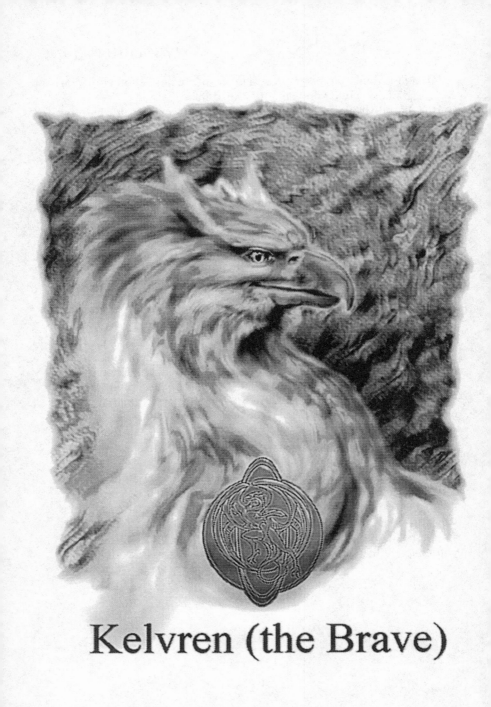

Kelvren (the Brave)

Four

Darian woke in the morning feeling as if his head weren't working quite right. It was difficult to put his thoughts together; he seemed to be taking a very long time to get even a single thought to form. He stared for a long time at the wall that was a hand's breadth or two past his nose, and wondered why the rough texture didn't look the way it should. Why did each rough-sawn plank look rounded? And why wasn't the wall itself slanting toward him as it formed the peak of the roof? His mind moved slowly and his thoughts felt fuzzy around the edges. And what was wrong with the light? It was green-ish, and it was much darker in the loft than it should have been.

It couldn't be just turning dawn, because he *never* woke up that early. *Maybe it's going to rain?* Justyn hadn't ForeSeen any rains, though, and that was one thing that he *could* do right; his weather-watching was always accurate.

He'd had the strangest dream, too—that the village had been at-tacked by a whole army. There was fire, a lot of fire in the dream, the whole town had been on fire. It had been more of a nightmare. Darian shivered and tried to remember more. There was a lot of him running, and monsters chasing him, then more running through the forest, then horrible men on horseback chasing him—getting rescued by a Hawkbrother and an owl, a huge owl—

A pretty strange dream, too. When would I ever see a Hawk-brother? Never in a thousand years. And who would ever bother to attack Errold's Grove with an army? What could they possibly want? Beans and turnips? Or maybe chickens— He had to shake his head at the way he was trying to make sense of a dream. *Anything can happen in a dream, of course—one of Widow Clay's chickens must have started laying silver eggs with golden yolks. Or maybe Justyn's spells finally worked and everyone was suddenly rich, and that was why an army came.*

Then he rolled over, and saw that he wasn't in the loft, but in a strange, octagonal hut made of rough logs—windowless, and with vines over the door. There *was* a huge owl, the same one he thought he'd only "dreamed" about, blinking sleepily on a perch to one side. At that moment, he realized with a plummeting heart that it hadn't been a dream at all. It had all been real, horribly real. Errold's Grove was gone—or if not gone, it was in the hands of an army of violent strangers, and everyone he knew had fled in fear of losing their lives.

In one moment, he went from sleepy and laughing at himself to despair. His insides became cold; a lump rose in his throat that was half grief and half fear, and his thoughts spun dizzily with nowhere to go. He still couldn't quite remember all that had happened, and the way his thoughts kept spinning didn't help. There was something about Justyn—and his mind shied away from the thought, as if he didn't *want* to remember, as if remembering would be the most horrible thing that had happened to him.

The village had been taken—but why? What could anyone possibly want with a little town that was on the verge of drying up and blowing away? If there were a single gold coin in the place, *he* would be surprised. A few of the women had jewelry, silver and silver-gilt, but he was sure there was not enough in the whole village to fill a hat. The women depended on their needlework to brighten their apparel. Most ornaments were made of carved and painted wood, plaited straw, beads and beadwork, copper, and bronze, and not a single *precious* stone in the lot, just turquoise, agate, and colored quartz. There simply was nothing worth looting—and even if you cleaned out every bit of beer and liquor in the place, by the time you parceled it out among all the soldiers, there wouldn't even be enough to get them mildly intoxicated!

This is insane; nothing is making any sense. I should be home, I should be in the loft, not here. Wherever "here" is. . . .

But if he wasn't in the loft in Justyn's house, where was he?

I'm with the Hawkbrothers— he remembered. This house belonged to them. What were they going to do with him now? He remembered, with a dreamlike vagueness, that they had asked him questions about what had happened, but they hadn't given him any idea what they planned to do. Where was he going to go if they didn't want him to stay? Could he get them to take him to Kelmskeep? But *then* what would he do?

Thoughts of Kelmskeep led him back to the village. Kelmskeep must have been where all the villagers were trying to escape to, and that was why they were running without trying to take anything. They could make Lord Breon's lands in a few days or a week or so—it would be a hardship, but this was summer, and no one would die of exposure or thirst. But what had actually happened to the rest of the villagers? How well-planned had that attack been? Had those horrible fighters caught anyone else? How could they *not* have? If there had been four men on horseback ranging out that far from the village to catch those who tried to escape, mightn't there be more?

No matter what the town did to me—they never hurt me on purpose, they just wanted me to be like them. They never did anything to anybody, they don't deserve to have those awful men get hold of them!

What would happen to them? The man who caught *him* hadn't killed him right off, but what would he have done when he learned that Darian didn't have any money and didn't know where any was? Darian had only vague notions of what enemy soldiers wanted, based on what bandits wanted. If you didn't have money for them, what would soldiers do? How could you satisfy them if you didn't have what they had come for?

Now Darian's vivid imagination portrayed all manner of terrible things that could have befallen the folk of Errold's Grove, and he grew more and more agitated as he thought about their possible fates.

The owl turned his head then, as if it sensed something was wrong. It opened a pair of enormous eyes completely and fastened its gaze on him. He found himself locking eyes with it. It clearly was not afraid of him, and strangely enough, he was not afraid of it, although it was easily large enough to hurt him quite seriously, if not kill him, if it took the notion to attack him. In fact, the more he looked into its huge, golden eyes, the calmer and quieter he felt. It was so strange, and warm-feeling, and it made every thought seem to slow down. It was almost as if the owl was putting its wing over him and sheltering him, and telling him that everything would be all right. . . .

Then the owl blinked, and the spell was broken. The bird yawned hugely, snapping his beak shut with a loud *click*. Darian yawned along with the owl, then watched as the bird shook its tufted head so fast it blurred, and felt as if he had to laugh a little at the sight.

The curtain of vines over the door to the hut parted, and a shadow blocked out the light for a moment. By the long, braided hair and the odd clothing, the newcomer had to be a Hawkbrother. As the Hawkbrother came into the light, he saw that it was the one who had rescued him yesterday. He was very tall, with long hair that had white roots, and was dyed all over in patterns of pale and dark brown, golden brown, and bark-gray. His square, chiseled face was very friendly, with many smile-creases at the corners of his mouth. His blue eyes contrasted oddly with his weathered, golden skin. He wore clothing in many shades of brown leather and closely-woven fabric, and his left arm and shoulder were completely encased in a sleeve of padded leather.

Snowfire. His name is Snowfire. And his owl is Hweel.

That was when Darian remembered a calm and friendly voice telling him that this hut was Snowfire's, and someone else's too, and as he took another quick glance around he saw two sleeping pads like the one he was still on, and a scattering of other belongings. There was a second perch on the other side of the room across from Hweel's—although no one had actually said anything about a second bird—but there wasn't a bird on it. From the size of the perch, the bird must be half the size of Hweel, and he wondered what kind it was.

"Well and good," said the Hawkbrother, standing just inside the door and looking at him in the friendliest possible fashion. "It seems that you are awake at last, though I am certain you needed to sleep. It is difficult to tell what time it is in this *ekele*, I know. You have slept entirely through breakfast, and it is now time for lunch. Would you care to eat anything?"

The Hawkbrother had a very odd accent and his phrasing was a little strange, but Darian had no trouble understanding him. *I thought they had their own language; didn't Justyn tell me that?* Somehow Snowfire must have learned Valdemaran from someone, but Darian thought he remembered him talking with—a woman?—in some other tongue.

"Thank you. I'm—not sure if I'm hungry," he replied vaguely, knowing he should say something in reply, but unable to come up with anything appropriate. What *did* you say to someone who'd saved your life? How many times were you supposed to thank them for it? Did the Hawkbrothers have some special significance attached to saving someone's life? It wasn't the sort of thing covered in *The Booke of Manners* that Widow Clay insisted he read—

For that matter, *The Booke of Manners* seemed to give the impression that everyone in the world was Valdemaran.

The Hawkbrother—Snowfire, yes, that *was* right, he was sure now—came up and sat down beside him on a folded-up blanket. Snowfire's arm was bandaged, and obviously stiff and sore from the way he held it, and Darian felt very guilty all at once. After all, if he hadn't gotten into trouble, Snowfire wouldn't have gotten hurt rescuing him. "I'm sorry about your arm," he said awkwardly, blushing. Should he beg Snowfire's forgiveness for getting him into difficulties?

"My arm?" Snowfire looked surprised, then shrugged, as if it meant nothing to him. "I wouldn't worry about it if I were you. It's hardly a serious injury."

"It doesn't look good," he persisted. "I mean, it must hurt an awful lot, and you won't be able to use a bow until it heals up some."

"Oh, I have had worse insect bites," Snowfire said nonchalantly. "Truly, it is nothing for you to concern yourself about. It does give me an excuse to laze about the camp while others go out and do my hunting for me!"

"It's just, if I hadn't been there, you wouldn't have gotten hurt rescuing me—" he began. "But I was so scared, I couldn't think, and after Justyn—"

And then, as if those words had been a trigger, he suddenly *remembered* everything that had happened yesterday—the fight with Justyn, running off, returning and being sent out as punishment—coming back in time to see Justyn—see Justyn on the bridge—

—see Justyn sacrifice himself—one moment, standing there, facing down that *Thing*, the next moment, seeing nothing of the bridge except a sheet of flame.

Some barrier he had not even been aware of let go at that moment, and there was nothing he could do to stop what happened next. Darian felt all the blood draining from his face, leaving him cold and empty; he trembled, then simply fell apart. A thousand unformed regrets triggered the avalanche, and they tumbled together with self-recrimination, simple grief, guilt, and mourning. They held him so paralyzed that he could not even move, he could only shake and stare at Snowfire with a sea of unbearable sorrow flooding him and choking his throat—

Snowfire somehow saw it, or part of it, for he murmured, "Ah, poor fledgling! Let it go, let it out—" and put his arm around Darian's shoulders in a gesture completely natural and fraternal. And that was enough, just enough, to release the flood entirely.

He flung himself into Snowfire's shoulder, and howled. And Snowfire held him, firmly and comfortingly, and let him cry himself out. There was nothing awkward and self-conscious about it; the Hawkbrother just let him cry until he had no more tears left, as if he let total strangers cry on his shoulder all the time. For the first time since his parents disappeared, Darian had someone to cry *with*, someone to share his grief with. It helped. It was amazing how much it helped.

Finally, after what seemed like days, the torrent of tears turned to a stream, the stream to a trickle, and the tears at last stopped altogether. It left him with an ache still in his heart, a burden of guilt pressing down his soul, and a void of loss he could never have expressed in words, but he was too tired for the moment to continue his mourning.

"So, who was Justyn?" Snowfire asked with careful gentleness. "Besides the one who held the bridge so your people could escape."

"Justyn was—was the wizard," Darian managed, as Snowfire let him sit up and handed him a real handkerchief. "I was—he was my Master, and he was teaching me, or he was supposed to be." He flushed a painful crimson, even to the tip of his ears, which burned as if he had gotten frostbite. "I wasn't a good apprentice," he admitted with profound shame and grief. "I kept running off, and I didn't want to practice the way he wanted me to." But there was a tinge of resentment, too, and he couldn't help voicing it in his own defense. "But, Snowfire, no one ever asked *me* if I wanted to be a wizard! They just said I had the Gift, so I *had* to be one! I wanted to be a hunter and a trapper, like—like my parents—" He would have said more, but his throat closed again.

Snowfire was silent for a moment. "I do not know you *well*, Darian," he said after a moment. "But I think that you must have had a reason for running off and not practicing those magics."

Darian shook his head, still flushing, and took refuge in one of the phrases the adults of Errold's Grove had always seemed to hate. "I dunno," he mumbled. Every time he said that, the adult he was talking to always replied with, "What do you mean, you don't know? How can you not know why you've done something? You did it, didn't you? Then *why* did you do it?" The reply of "I dunno," always seemed to trigger an angry interrogation which only got angrier as he retreated farther into himself.

Snowfire, however, did not challenge that phrase. "Perhaps someday you will know how to say what you felt, what your reasons were," he murmured encouragingly. "I would like to know, when you can tell me. It is just hard to say with words. Sometimes, one can *feel* a reason without being able to say what the reason is. We all feel that." He sighed. "So—Wizard Justyn is the one who blocked the bridge against the army. Then he set the bridge afire, and perished in the flame?"

"I think—" Darian began, then stared at Snowfire with his mouth dropping open. "I didn't say anything! How did you know what happened to Justyn?" For a moment, wild tales of how Hawkbrothers could read one's thoughts swept through his mind.

"I am a mage, too," Snowfire reminded him. "If I had been in his place, and brave enough, and desperate enough, it is something that I would have done. It is something that all those who have that Gift know that they may someday need to do, if the situation is hopeless and the need great enough. And those who have given of themselves in that way—are much honored for their bravery and nobility of spirit."

Darian swallowed and took a deep breath, while Snowfire nodded, to reinforce his words. Someone as strong and exotic as a Hawkbrother, honoring Justyn? If only Justyn could have heard it when he was alive. "He was trying to keep those fighters back," Darian said, grief clenching his stomach as he once again found himself holding back tears. Justyn—this Hawkbrother was saying that Justyn had been brave and noble! "I think he must've told everybody to run while he held them back. I think that's why no one was fighting. I think he told them not to fight, because he knew they couldn't fight an army, and he was buying time for them to get away."

"He probably was, and that was the wisest course for everyone." Snowfire put a finger under Darian's chin and lifted it, so that Darian was looking straight into his eyes. "I want you to listen to me and believe me, Darian. What you described to us last night was definitely a very large and organized group, and perhaps as you thought, an entire *army*, of well-trained fighters. If Justyn determined that the best course was for people to run, he was right. There is absolutely nothing your people could have done against them, except be killed. That is the way armies are. It is what they do, it is why they are armies. They are made so that all that can stand against them is another army. Running was not only the best option for your people, it was the *only* option for them. They were not being cowardly; they were accepting the gift that Justyn offered to them. And I will tell you something else; I think that if they had known in advance that the gift included his life, they would *not* have accepted it, and they would have insisted that he escape with them."

"But—I'm supposed to be a mage—*I* should have been there, helping him—" Darian was overwhelmed with shame and guilt, so much so that he was not certain he had spoken aloud until Snowfire shook his head.

"Darian, you will not come into the full potential of your ability for at least another two, perhaps three years," the Hawkbrother replied. "Maybe more. And even then, you could not use that potential without several years of training, study, and practice. Even if you had begun training seriously three years ago, you would not have been ready to help Justyn now. You would have been of no more use to him than—than if you were *going to be* a fighter, and he was an older warrior. Your strength as a mage is something that you must grow into, as you would grow into your strength as a fighter. There is a perfectly good reason why armies do not field ranks full of younglings your age—and it is the same reason why you would have been of little help to Justyn *even if you had been training to your utmost.*"

"Yes, but—" Darian began, then stopped, unable to articulate why he was so certain that if he had been there helping Justyn, the old wizard would still be alive, only sure that it *was* so.

"You feel differently, and I cannot convince you otherwise." Snowfire shrugged a little. "There is no arguing with a feeling; I wish that there was. But Darian, you cannot take on guilt for every bad thing that has happened! Put the guilt where it rightly belongs, at least—for if *someone* had not decided that it is easier to steal from innocents instead of earning their desires, that army would not have appeared on the road to Errold's Grove in the first place! If there is blame to be placed, then place it squarely on the back of the aggressor who is leading these fighters, whomever he is! It is he who deserves to be punished, not your people, and not you!"

Darian was struck by the good common sense of that, and felt a little of the burden he was carrying inside ease. "I—I guess you're right."

"I know I am," Snowfire said firmly. "And I know that you are feeling very strange and worn. But now, I have something difficult that I must ask of you. Adept Starfall and I asked questions of you last night, when you were very tired, but we need to ask more of you now that you are well awake and thinking. And the sooner we can ask you these things, the fresher they will be in your mind. Do you think that you can manage such a thing for us, when you are clean and fed?"

Darian's heart sank. He *really* did not want to go over all of yesterday's horrible events, but he knew that he really needed to say "Yes."

"I—yes," he replied, in a small voice.

"Good, and you are being quite brave to face what you will have to remember," Snowfire told him, so earnestly that he did not doubt that Snowfire actually meant the words, and wondered at Snowfire calling *him* brave. "Now, I will explain to you why we are going to need to know very many tiny details. My people are allies of your people, and we have taken on certain responsibilities. We are, all of us, mages—some with less power than you have at this moment, and some, like Starfall, with a very, very great deal more—but *all* of us are mages. That makes my people very different, and it makes us very desirable to other mages." Snowfire bit his lip as he looked down at Darian for a moment, as if he were debating something, and then his expression settled, as if he had decided to let Darian hear more confidences. "There are—ways—that a mage can use another mage, even if that other is an unwilling prisoner. That is why we must be careful that we do not fall into the hands of mages who are working evil."

Darian shivered all over. Was *that* why that huge fighter who'd caught him hadn't killed him? Vague and ill-defined pictures flitted through his mind, all of them ugly.

"We are only a very *small* party of Tayledras," Snowfire continued. "We must know as much about this enemy as possible. We need to know if we can and should attack him ourselves, if we should merely interfere with him but let your Valdemaran fighters deal with him, or if we should actually *hide* from him. Do you see why we must do that?"

Perhaps one of the other boys from Errold's Grove would not have, but Darian did. He nodded. "I can see it wouldn't make any difference if you waited, so long as everybody got away," he replied. "I mean, what's the point of risking yourself for a bunch of old houses? Right? It isn't as if the people couldn't rebuild, or even move." He bit his lip. "Maybe *now* they'll be willing to settle somewhere else. They surely weren't prospering there."

"That is correct," Snowfire said, looking relieved. "Your Queen once said something both wise and profound when she ordered the evacuation of the Eastern Border—that it was not the *land* that was Valdemar, it was the *people*. It is not the houses that were your village, it was your people. If the people have survived, then the village has, regardless of whether or not the houses are still there."

Darian nodded solemnly. "They could even still call themselves 'Errold's Grove' if they wanted to." He toyed with a bit of fringe on the blanket that had covered him last night. "I would understand if you decided not to fight—them—right away. I mean, as long as everybody got away all right. And if there's a mage with these fighters, you probably shouldn't let him know that there are more mages here—"

"There is *certainly* a mage behind them somewhere," Snowfire interrupted. "Perhaps more than one. Those bear-men you saw could not have been made that way without a mage. And Darian, quite frankly, if there are no people who are in need of rescue, the *very best* thing that we can do is to stay away from those fighters."

"Why?" Darian asked, a little surprised at his vehemence.

"Do you recall what I told you about what the Tayledras are doing in your land? How we are making the channels for magic to flow in?" Snowfire waited expectantly, his head tilted a little to one side.

Darian closed his eyes for a moment, then nodded as memory-fog cleared. "And . . . you said that you were doing that so that a bad mage couldn't get the magic locked away from everybody else and. . . ." He suddenly felt a number of things fall into place in his mind. "Oh! Since there's a mage there, *he* might try and lock the magic away!"

"I am almost positive that is *exactly* why he is here," Snowfire said grimly. "I frankly cannot imagine why the enemy would attack your little village except for that purpose; if a special place for gathering magic is nearby, he would have a ready-built headquarters from which to work, and a food supply already gathered. And that is why it is our first and best duty to prevent him from accomplishing that task."

Darian sighed. He could certainly see Snowfire's point, and as long as everyone was safe, what would the Hawkbrothers accomplish by fighting? Hadn't he just been thinking that there wasn't anything worth bothering about in Errold's Grove? Hadn't he just told Snowfire that it might even be better if the people went somewhere better to resettle?

Still, the idea of a bunch of fur-covered bullies just coming in and taking everything and not being made to pay for it made him angry. And after what Justyn did—

No, Justyn couldn't have thought he was saving the village, just the people. He must have known that there wasn't a chance of saving anything else. So I shouldn't get all worked up over them taking the village.

"Darian, are you ready to help us?" Snowfire asked, interrupting him midway through his attempt to sort out his feelings.

"I guess so," he began vaguely, and before he could have second thoughts, Snowfire had gotten him out of the hut, through a little maze of vine-covered barriers, and he was suddenly confronting, not one or two, but ten or twelve of the Hawkbrothers, each of them with his or her own bird perched on a shoulder or arm. They sat together in a sunny, circular clearing with a tiny stream running along one side. They'd taken their seats either on the ground, or on natural objects such as boulders or pieces of log. All of them were clearly waiting for him, and as Snowfire sat him down in the middle of this half-circle of people, and stood discreetly aside, Darian felt himself to be the uncomfortable focus of their interest.

Although all of the people here had the same sort of green-and-brown clothing that Snowfire wore, no two costumes were alike, and although many had heavy leather gloves on one or both hands, none of them wore the same shoulder-to-wrist gauntlet that he did. All of the birds were enormous, and of the breeds that Darian recognized, these individuals were twice and three times bigger than the ones Darian knew. There were three people with large hawks with vivid rusty-orange and golden-yellow tails, two with thin and nervous hawks with yellow-orange eyes and pale, almost pinkish breasts, three with falcons that looked just like forestgyres, two with ones that looked like peregrines, one with a slate-gray bird with aggressive, reddish eyes that *must* have been a goshawk of some sort, and one with a huge, clever-looking crow. No one else had an owl of any kind. The birds all watched Darian with interest and intelligence, and Darian had the peculiar feeling that they heard and understood every word that was being said.

Another person came around a screen of vines, a most impressive and exotically-dressed man with waist-length white hair, who had a white falcon with pale brown markings perched on a pad on his shoulder. This person's robes were so elaborately cut and layered that it was obvious he could never have gone scouting about through the forest as the others did—so this must be the Adept that Snowfire had been talking about. Something about him seemed very familiar, and as the Adept spoke quietly with Snowfire and one or two of the others, Darian finally remembered why. He'd met this man last night, and the man had questioned him with Snowfire's assistance, because his Valdemaran hadn't been anywhere near as good as Snowfire's. This was Starfall, who must be a very powerful mage indeed, if the deference the other Hawkbrothers showed him was any indication.

As Darian found himself to be the focus of all those eyes, avian as well as human, he began to recall how often he managed to get himself into trouble—and that was with people he *knew!* How could he hope to do anything other than get himself into worse trouble with these folk? And what must they think of him for running away the way he had? Surely they must think he was a dreadful coward at best, and at worst—

At worst, they must think he was good for nothing except to get *them* into more trouble. His heart sank, and he began to feel utterly worthless. What good was he? What good had he ever been? Surely these people could only wish him gone out of their lives.

He began to be a little bit afraid of them, too. Oh, Snowfire seemed approachable and normal enough, but the rest of these folk—well, they *were* the mysterious and dangerous guardians of the forest. Who knew what strange customs they had? What if they decided to make him disappear? After all, if he disappeared, there would be less trouble all the way around.

Snowfire and the Adept finished their conversation and came over to Darian, and took seats beside him with him placed between the two of them. That took him aback; he'd expected to be sitting alone, surrounded by strangers, all of them interrogating him. But it seemed as if Starfall and Snowfire had made themselves his advocates, of a sort.

"We'd like to begin now, if you are ready?" Snowfire said, phrasing the words as a question.

"I guess I am," Darian replied, a bit shaken.

"Some of our scouts do not know your tongue at all, and most do not know it as well as I do," Snowfire told him, by way of explanation. "So. They will ask the question, and I will act as translator— or I will clarify what they are asking. I would like you to think back to just before you saw the signs of the attack. Had you seen or heard *anything* in the past few weeks to make you think that there might be such an attack?"

Darian shook his head. "No," he said truthfully, then added, "but the people don't go out of the village much, and especially not into the Forest. So they might not see anything. Justyn—" his voice quavered, "—Justyn wasn't much good at ForeSight. He could see the weather all right, but never anything on the ground. That was how we got caught by a flood last fall—the rain that caused it was way up north, he didn't ForeSee it, and of course he didn't ForeSee the way it would make the river rise." He shook his head. "Everybody was so afraid of the Forest that they wouldn't stir past the fields if they could help it, and nobody was due to go over to one of the other towns for trading for a while."

Snowfire translated, and some of the scouts discussed what he had said among themselves. "Are towns there, to your north?" called out one.

Darian had to think hard about that one—Justyn had been making him memorize maps, but he had a poor head for it. He had much better luck in remembering things by means of landmarks than by arbitrary marks on a piece of paper. "I don't think so," he said, trying to be honest. "That is, I think that the ones north of us are all a lot farther east as well. I think—" He closed his eyes, and tried to visualize the map he'd been studying. "I think that the border here kind of sticks out in a bump pointing west, and we're at the tip of the bump."

There was more discussion, and some sketching in the sand. "Let us go forward then, to the time of the attack," Starfall said carefully. "When did you first know that there was something wrong?"

"I was up in a tree, looking for *mycofoetida* fungus," he replied. "I was pretty high, because we'd kind of harvested everything that was near the ground and near the town. So the first thing I saw was that there were big fires in town."

One of the Hawkbrothers with a forestgyre said something to Snowfire, who relayed the question. "So the attack had already begun?"

Darian shook his head. "No—no, not yet. *I* didn't know what was happening, but I knew something had to be wrong, so I left the basket and ran back to town, and what was burning, mostly, was haystacks and sheds, and just a few of them. And I saw Vere—that was one of the farmers—setting a fire himself. I guess they were burning things to keep the bad people from getting them."

Now discussion among the scouts lasted for some time, before another called out a question that Snowfire translated. "What did the army look like? Exactly? Can you remember any numbers?"

He shuddered at that one, but he had expected that it would be coming, and he closed his eyes and tried to picture the scene at the bridge. "There was Justyn on the bridge," he said slowly. "Then there was the big monster with the little monster riding on it. Then there were some of the bear-men—they were five across the road, and I think four lines of five—then behind them was a bunch of human people with tall spears—" He tried so hard to visualize the scene that he began to get a headache. "I couldn't see behind them very far, but there were a lot of them. They were lined up on the road five across, and—I remember so many spears sticking up in the air that it looked like a burned forest was on the road, for as far back as I could see."

He opened his eyes at the murmur of surprise, but now attention was completely off him for the moment, as the Hawkbrothers discussed possible numbers represented by what he remembered. From their worried faces, he gathered that the implications weren't good.

"Were all the bear-men on the bridge?" Starfall asked him quietly.

"I think so," he said, just as quietly. "But I don't know for sure, because I ran. Some of them might have jumped into the river, and some of them might have gotten out of the way."

"And some might have been farther back in the ranks," Snowfire pointed out.

Starfall sighed and nodded agreement. "Did you see anyone that—" He groped for words for a moment, then said something incomprehensible to Snowfire.

"Did you see anyone who looked like a mage?" Snowfire asked, then raised one eyebrow as if aware of the uselessness of such a question.

"I didn't see anyone wearing fancy robes, or who looked like he was doing any magic," Darian replied, trying to be as exact as possible. "The thing on the lizard acted more like—like—somebody who was in charge of things, but not really in charge of *everything*, if you get my meaning. He acted like somebody who had to answer to somebody else. And when he got caught in the fire, the rest of 'em acted like it was no great thing that he wasn't there. Like maybe they were getting orders from somebody behind them."

Darian was doing his best to answer the questions to the fullest, but the more he had to think about Justyn, to see the scene in his mind, the worse he felt. He was doing his best to hold back tears, but it wasn't easy.

And it didn't get any easier. "Where were the rest of your people at the time the bridge was destroyed?" Starfall asked.

"Gone," Darian told him glumly. "They were all running *away* from the village when I was running toward it."

"And you turned to run when the bridge was destroyed?" That was one of the scouts, a very young man whose face Darian remembered from last night.

He hung his head, not liking to think what they must believe of him for running. "Yes," he admitted, flushing hotly, from the top of his head on down.

"And where were the enemy then?" the young man persisted. "Still on the other side of the river?"

Darian looked up, surprised to see that there was no open scorn in their faces. "No—" he told them. "No, some of them were on the other side when I got out to the fields. I guess they must have forded the river, or something, but they were working their way through the fields, I guess to keep people from escaping."

"And you eluded them?" came the question.

"Well," he admitted, "there weren't many of them. And I—ran away." Admitting that to all of those people was one of the most difficult things he'd ever had to do, and he felt tension build up suddenly inside him. "I had to!" he cried out, the words forced out by the tension, "I had to! I couldn't help Justyn. I didn't know what else to do!"

And then, unexpectedly, he lost control of himself and burst into tears again, and felt another overwhelming wave of shame for losing control of himself, which ironically only made him cry harder.

Starfall patted his shoulder sympathetically, but evidently was not prepared to leave him alone. "I am sorry that we must ask these questions, Dar'ian, but we need the answers. Now, do you remember how *many* men you saw on your side of the river, and if they were entirely human? An accurate number?"

The questioning went on despite his distress, becoming more and more detailed. Several times he lost control again and began to cry; each time the Hawkbrothers waited politely for him to regain control of himself, then continued from where they had left off.

Finally, though, they had exhausted everything he could tell them about the enemy army—for such, they were all agreed, it was. The questioning turned to another subject, one even more trying for him to face, because the subject was himself. Some of the scouts had gone off, leaving only Starfall, Snowfire, Wintersky, and two others, but the five of them were inexorable in their questions. If all the villagers were afraid to go into the Forest, why was *he* out there? Why was he not afraid of the Forest? What had happened to his parents? Why had he been signed over to Justyn's care by the rest of the villagers? Why did the villagers have any say in what was to happen to Darian? Why didn't Darian want to be a mage? Did he think there was something wrong with being a mage? Did he often run off? What did Justyn do when he disobeyed? Was he thinking of running away at the time of the attack? How did he feel about what Justyn did on the bridge?

It was the last question that undid him. It was bad enough having to admit how often he had gotten into trouble, and worse admitting that the reason he'd been sent out of the village was as a punishment for running away from a duty, but to be asked how he *felt* about seeing Justyn sacrifice himself—

Again, he started to cry, but this time he couldn't get control of himself once he started. Snowfire even tried to soothe him, saying that he wasn't at fault—but he knew that he *was*, and he was certain that, in some strange way, he should have been able to do something. But all he had done was to run away, like the coward he was.

"You weren't *there*, you don't *know*, you didn't see what I did!" he wailed, his voice breaking with hysteria. "You don't understand! I'm a coward, I'm a rotten, lying coward, and it's all my fault!"

And with that, he ran, stumbling and half blinded with tears, out of the clearing, in the direction he'd been led from.

He couldn't think of what to do, but when he found himself back in front of Snowfire's hut, the darkness inside seemed a good place to hide himself in, and he blundered in. The owl was gone, it was very quiet, and he crumpled into a miserable heap on the sleeping pallet, crying so hard that he thought he would never be able to stop.

"Now *I* feel guilty," Starfall murmured to Snowfire, as the child stumbled out of the gathering space, choking on his sobs.

Snowfire sighed. Nightwind had warned him last night that scenes like this would occur, and probably several times. "Nightwind thinks there are emotional hurts that he has not dealt with, except by avoiding them," he told the Adept. "She said last night that he was suffering from other troubles, things that perhaps occurred some time ago. She was quite sure he would not even mention them unless he was prodded into it."

"Well, it seems that one of those hurts was the loss of his parents," Starfall said, and ran his hand through his silver hair. "Poor child. I would feel terrible if something happened to mine—he must feel dreadful."

"It seems obvious to me that he has not been allowed to properly mourn for them," Snowfire pointed out. "These people who took him in seemed to want to make him ashamed of them. Children may be resilient, but—"

"But not *that* resilient," Starfall interrupted, his mouth set grimly. "And although these Valdemarans may have meant well, it is said by our cousins that 'The road to disaster is ordered by the righteous, planned by the well-meaning, and paved with their good intentions.' I think that, although Dar'ian has many faults, as do most younglings, they were viewed in an exaggerated manner. On the whole, they were in a fair way to ruining a fundamentally good child."

Snowfire could only nod, for he was in perfect agreement. *How can good people manage to so mishandle a boy?* he wondered. *Was it only that they refused to see he did not fit in their constrained lives? Or were they only trying to be "cruel to be kind," never realizing they were only being cruel, and their kindness missed the mark altogether?* "I will see if Nightwind thinks she should come help with this latest outbreak," he sighed. "I hate to press the boy, but even if we are going to do nothing more than avoid any contact with these barbarians, we still need his knowledge of the area, and we need to know everything he has seen."

Starfall frowned at that; Snowfire reflected that in many ways, he was made of sterner stuff than the Adept. Well, Starfall might be the heart of the expedition, but Snowfire was its hands—and it was his job to keep the heart safe. Finally Starfall could contain himself no more.

"I don't want to destroy the child just to extract information!" Starfall protested, then colored. "He—I apologize; I know you would never countenance any such thing. It is just that I am not used to having children flee my presence in tears."

Snowfire smiled wanly. "Dar'ian's fragility has an unnerving effect on all of us, and that effect is redoubled by the burden of what he has told us. Two days ago, we were engaged in simple duty; something routine, not unmixed with pleasure, I think, and a duty we were completely prepared to handle. Now, suddenly we have a mysterious enemy of unknown ability appearing to threaten us, without prior warning of any sort. It is quite enough to make anyone feel tempted to indulge in a fit of strong hysterics. I know *I* am tempted."

Starfall stood up, shook out his robes, and tossed back his hair. "I hope you will not think badly of me if I leave the boy in the hands of you and Nightwind—" he ventured. "I feel as if I am playing the coward myself by doing so, but—"

"But *you* have other things to do that involve the welfare of more than one boy," Snowfire reminded him. "And you may think *me* ruthless in some ways, but if it meant preventing the rise of another Ma'ar, or even another Falconsbane, I would not hesitate to sacrifice myself, the boy, and anyone else I could get to volunteer."

"I think you would have a surprising number of volunteers," Starfall replied. "And you are right; I do have a task to complete that cannot wait, regardless of my personal feelings. I am going to leave things in your hands, as usual. Now, more than ever, I need to get those matrices established."

"You might consider locking the power to yourself," Snowfire suggested, and as Starfall looked surprised, even shocked, he added, "there are no other Alliance mages living here to require access to it, you can key the rest of us into it if you really think it is necessary. This may prevent trouble. What can be locked securely can always be unlocked—but it cannot be stolen. That is one way to make *sure* this new mage cannot get at it, and one way to make sure that, if worst comes to worst, he must keep you alive. That would give time for help to come, should disaster befall and you come into captivity."

"You have a point," Starfall acknowledged, looking troubled and just a little queasy. Starfall had never had to face a situation like this before, and Snowfire felt very sorry for him. For all that Tayledras were sturdy folk, not all had grown up prepared to face an enemy in life-or-death struggle, and Adepts especially tended to stay toward the power management side of magic. "I'll consider it. I would not have thought it possible for a mage to work Changes on humans under our current conditions; if he can do that, he may be able to do other unpleasant and unexpected things. That being so—he may be able to bypass anything but a true personal lock."

As Starfall walked off in the direction of his "workplace," Snowfire was left to contemplate the smaller problem of Darian.

He's going to have to cry himself out again, and he hasn't yet gotten to the point where he's going to consider my failure to appear at his side as an act of desertion. In fact, he may just be grateful to be left alone. Better to consult with Nightwind first—and possibly, with Kelvren. The gryphon had managed to get himself wrought up to a high pitch of excitement at the notion that *he* might be the one to confront a second Ma'ar—as unlikely as that was—and it might do Kel some good to have something else to think about. Something like one small boy, parentless and friendless, with an apparent affinity for winged things.

So, the next obvious place to go was the rock at the rear of the valley where the gryphon liked to sun himself between scouting forays. And since he'd already been out once this morning, making certain that the barbarians had not gotten *too* close to the Tayledras' perimeter, he would definitely be there.

The spring that watered this valley had been made to serve many creative purposes; its water had been divided into several channels that gave everyone access to a thread of stream at the very least. Tayledras liked the sound of running or falling water, and preferred to live in the midst of it. Lacking the lovely, secluded spaces of a Vale, everyone in the team had made up for—or *hertasi* had made up for—that lack by creating a scrap of water garden for him- or herself. Some had constructed tiny pools with a single water lily or a stand of reeds and a tiny singing-frog, some preferred miniature waterfalls and gurgling brooks filled with stones, and Nightwind had made a clever little aqueduct and water wheel that powered an ever-changing series of frivolous and colorful whirligigs. But the greater part of the water could be diverted to fill two pools, one to be used only for washing, the other for swimming. The former was emptied when the water was dirty into a sand-filter so that the water that sank into the earth was cleansed. Since there was no natural hot spring here, the Tayledras were making do with a steambath. Kelvren, being a fastidious gryphon, made use of the swimming or washing pool on a daily basis, but could not be persuaded into the steam-hut.

Kelvren's daily bath was an occasion of much splashing and generally emptied the pool. When every feather on his body was soaked, he would shake himself out, thus ensuring that anyone and anything near by that was not already drenched would receive a fair share of the spray. Then he would flap laboriously to a smooth rock high above the pool, one of the few places in the valley that received sun for most of the day. There he would sit and preen until he considered every feather to be perfectly groomed, at least in a serviceable manner; after that his *trondi'irn* could do decorative and restorative tendings in the evening.

By checking the angle of the sun, Snowfire reckoned that Kelvren would be about halfway through the grooming process and damp, but not wet. Gryphons, being more complicated and imperfect creatures than the bondbirds, occasionally suffered some deficiencies, and one of the more common was a tail gland that produced an insufficient quantity of oil to keep the feathers healthy and weatherproof. That was Kelvren's problem, and it was one of Nightwind's duties as his *trondi'irn* to make up for that lack. So she would be with him, adding touches of very light, fragrant oil to the shafts of his larger feathers with a small artist's paintbrush. After that, it was his job to preen it into the barbs. An odd task, but then, caring for gryphons evidently involved a great many odd tasks.

Snowfire walked down the winding paths that threaded the encampment with a lengthened stride that allowed him to move quickly without appearing to hurry. He soon reached the end of the valley and as he came around the last vine curtain and out into the full sunlight beyond the trees, he saw Nightwind sitting beside Kelvren on the gryphon's favored perch. She was the only person in the entire group who had the same raven-wing-black hair as their Shin'a'in cousins, along with the golden complexion and intense blue eyes. She was not tall, but she held herself so well that she gave the impression of being taller than she was. Her finely-sculptured face reminded him a little of a vixen. She did indeed have a tiny paintbrush in one hand, and a pot in the other, all her attention concentrated on the primaries and secondaries of the wings he had stretched out over her lap like a great, feathered blanket. It looked for all the world as if she were gilding or painting the great bird.

In fact, she *could* have been painting him; for special occasions, besides wearing body- and leg-jewelry, the gryphons often had their feathers bleached, then dyed or painted, and sometimes strings of beads or bells were attached to the base of the tail-covert feathers or along the shafts of the crest-feathers or primaries. She had told Snowfire that this, too, was one of her skills—an uncommon one among *trondi'irn*. Kelvren was excessively proud of the fact that *his* attendant was so skillful a feather-painter. Snowfire himself had never seen a gryphon so decorated, and frankly, could not imagine it. The whole idea seemed very bizarre to him, as if Hweel should suddenly express a desire to be transformed with colors, like a firebird or a scarlet jay. But gryphons, being highly intelligent, had an appreciation for artistry and a particular eye for ornament. Since they were in a very real sense living sculptures by a long-lost master artist, Urtho, they felt rightly that they were canvasses for beauty to be worked upon. Snowfire wondered wryly if Urtho had bred them for vanity, or if this trait had been an "accidental" feature of these created creatures.

He hailed them both; Nightwind responded with a wave of her brush, and Kel with fanning the opposite wing from the one being tended to. He rounded the pool—as he had expected, Kel had pretty much emptied it, and it was now refilling from the spring—and climbed up the path to their rock.

"I take it from your expression that the situation is not exactly a good one?" Nightwind asked, as he sat down beside her with his back to the sun.

"In a word, correct," he said, as Kel cocked an ear-tuft at him. He quickly summed up the most salient points of the questioning, and Kel snapped his beak and flattened his head-feathers.

"Not good," the gryphon surmised. "It appearrsss that this trrruly isss an arrrmy, and not jussst a child'sss exagerrration. An arrrmy of rrreasssonable quality, asss well. Well arrrmed, well trrrained."

"And there is a high probability of a mage among them or leading them," he reminded the gryphon. "My guess would be that he is leading them. And to be honest, we don't have the strength to risk a direct or even indirect confrontation."

Kelvren growled, but nodded reluctantly. "I do not like it, but you arrre, unforrrtunately, corrrect. But I sssshould like to venturrre a sorrrtie orrr two, ssstrrrictly ssspy misssssionsss. At night, perrrrhapsss? With Hweel to guide, I am a good night-flyerrr."

Snowfire gazed at the gryphon with surprise and admiration. "Now *that* is one of the better ideas I have heard today," he replied, very pleased with the idea. "Hweel needs a certain amount of mental guidance, and *you* should have a backup, so that could be my role. I think I could manage that without needing to use a weapon."

"That's good, because until that wound is healed, you won't be doing anything like shooting a bow," Nightwind said, rather pointedly.

"I think," Snowfire replied, with a bit of impatience, "that I am perfectly capable of figuring that out for myself."

"And what about the time you went climbing right after a concussion, last year?" she asked.

He ignored her, which appeared to cause her a great deal of amusement. "Hweel and I could go in together as far as that clearing where I rescued the boy," he said to Kelvren. "Then you and Hweel could go on alone. We can get some idea from the boy how near the trees grow to the village, but my impression was that you could easily use them as cover quite close in."

Kel nodded, clearly satisfied by having *something* constructive to do.

"Now that you mention the boy," Nightwind put in, "how badly did he take to being questioned?"

Snowfire winced. "Well, he left the meeting in tears, if that tells you anything."

"No more than I expected," she replied with a shrug. "Did he happen to let anything out that would give you a hint to those other emotional burdens he's carrying?"

"Some of his background. His parents were trappers, and apparently disappeared a year or so ago. The people of his village were afraid of the Forest and have been since the mage-storms brewed up some nasty creatures out there. Evidently the encounters they had with the monsters gave them some severe shocks. So the villagers disapproved of anyone who would go into the Forest on a regular basis, claiming that the Storm-Changed monsters would track such people back to the village to attack *them*."

"So what happened when the parents didn't come back?" Nightwind asked. "What made the villagers take him in?"

"Guilt, maybe," Snowfire hazarded. "He was apprenticed to the village mage, who evidently was not very good, and didn't get much respect. Dar'ian did not really want to be a mage himself. And the villagers did their best to persuade him that his parents brought their fate on themselves." He assumed that Nightwind could make her own assessment from those rather bald facts, probably much more accurately than he could.

"Oh, no—" she said, looking at him with all traces of amusement gone. "No wonder he's a tangle of unhappiness inside! I hardly dare think of what he must be going through."

"I do need your insight," he reminded her. "You *are* the only Empath among us, you know."

"I'm *not* trained in sorting out human emotions," she protested, then made a face. "I know, I'm making excuses. Emotions are emotions."

"But among my peoplesss, ourrr emotional sssolutionsss arrre much morrre dirrrect," Kel pointed out with a chuckle.

"And your emotions were modeled on your maker's, which were quite human. Point taken. Now, let me think a moment." She pressed her fingers to her temples. "I'm going to assume that he had a strong and positive bond with his parents, so we have the obvious trauma of losing them, and the not-so-obvious trauma of not knowing what really happened to them. He could even be coping with the loss by inventing reasons why they might still be alive, which is only delaying the mourning period."

"That sounds reasonable," he agreed. "The people of his village strongly disapproved of his parents themselves as well as their profession. I don't imagine too many days went by without Dar'ian hearing how reckless and dangerous his parents were."

"Which made it imperative to him to defend them, except that defending them would be disrespectful of the adults in the village, who would in turn punish him in some way, never thinking that this was telling him that he either had to disassociate himself from his parents—"

"Not likely. Hrrrr," Kel rumbled.

"Or take on the same disapproval. It also told him that it was inappropriate to mourn them, since presumably he was now in the care of much 'worthier' people." She shook her head fretfully. "I wish people would *think* before they do things like this to children! All right, so before he has lived a single day with these people, he has been given the message that they disapprove of him, it is wrong to care deeply about the parents he loved because they didn't deserve it, and he is to be grateful to people whose ways are utterly at odds with his. That's a fine way to begin a new life, isn't it?"

Snowfire coughed, and scratched his head. "There isn't a great deal I can add to that statement," he said awkwardly. "Nightwind, pardon me for saying this, but you seem very—direct—for an Empath. The k'Vala Empath was more—how should I put this?—dip-lomatic.''

''The k'Vala Empath is one of your Elders,'' she chuckled. ''Be-sides, you aren't the one whose emotional turmoil is under discussion. I *might* be more diplomatic with you.''

''Get back to the sssubject,'' Kel grumbled, ''orrr the two of you will begin courrrting behaviorrr again, and I will have to sssprrread thisss oil myssself while you arrre posssturrring.''

''Oh, *excuse* me,'' she mocked him, dabbing a bit of oil on the tip of his beak in a lightning-quick stroke of her brush. ''Since you insist—now, you say he has Mage-Gift and was apprenticed to a rather ineffective village mage, but did not actually want to *be* a mage?'' At his nod, she pursed her lips. ''Again, I am going to assume that he *liked* his Master. So, his Master is of low status and meager ability. He has been bound to this man, regardless of his own preferences. And he has, no doubt, been told how grateful he should be for having been so bound. So—the message he has been given is that he is so worthless he is now forcibly associated with a low-status individual. Because they believe he obviously is incapable of making a logical decision, his own preferences are of no bearing on the sit-uation. Because they tell him he is too ignorant to make his own choices, his future has been determined for him whether or not he likes it, and because he cannot understand why he should be pleased and gratified with the situation, he is obviously morally and mentally deficient.''

''Starfall quoted the Shin'a'in about the road to disaster,'' he ob-served.

She massaged her temples with her fingers, looking pained. ''I know that one. You know, it is a very good thing that there are none of them available for me to strangle, for I would be very tempted to do so. I am also very tempted to suggest that what happened to that village seems very like a proper retribution for what they loaded upon this poor child! But, of course, that would be making a moral judg-ment based on limited information, about another culture.''

''And that would be wrrrong,'' Kel said, with an ironic tilt to his head. ''Ssso of courrrsse you could not posssssibly do that, unlesss it werrre sufficiently enterrrtaining.'' The gryphon half-rumbled, half-burbled a laugh, and received a poke in the side in return.

''Well, now I have some clearer idea of what I will probably be walking into when I go root him out of my *ekele*,'' Snowfire sighed. ''Mind you, I have no doubt that the boy is as full of mischief as a gryphlet, is *quite* convinced that he knows better than any adult born, and is stubborn, willful, and rebellious. Just exactly as any other boy his age would be. Nevertheless, it seems to me that if these folk intended to create a situation designed to bring out the worst in him, they could not have been more effective.''

"That would be my conclusion, Snowfire," Nightwind agreed, and dropped a thistledown-soft kiss on his forehead. "Now, go and see what you can do to turn the child around. You have a knack for that which astonishes me. For someone who claims to have no ability as an Empath, you certainly handle young creatures well."

"Let's hope it *is* a knack, and not just a streak of good luck," he replied, and stood up. "And as for you, old bird," he continued, looking to the gryphon, "I should think a distraction would do him some good, and you are the most distracting creature I can think of. Would you care to help me out with him?"

"Why not?" the gryphon agreed genially. "But—not immediately. I think he isss likely to indulge in morrre weeping, and I have only now gotten my featherrrsss drry."

"Vain bird," Snowfire told him with mock severity, and took himself back down the path to his *ekele*, leaving Nightwind and Kel together on the sunning rock.

He had no doubt that Kel was waiting to get Nightwind's advice about how the gryphon should handle the boy, and not for any specious reason about drying feathers. That was fine; they should, ideally, have different approaches. After all, they couldn't *both* play "elder brother." *Let me see; Starfall obviously is better suited to the role of "respected elder"—and when Darian sees that a mage is the* highest *statused person in our group, that might make him change his mind about magic. Nightwind may be waiting to see if he accepts her as "mother surrogate"—it would be better if he made that choice. I think he is a little too clever to accept her if she puts herself forward in that role, and I* know *she knows it could be trouble if she tried to force it on him. The gryphon being the gryphon, he will no doubt take the role of "mysterious wonder" or "entrancing enigma" and play his appearance for all he can, to work in advice we could not give.*

As he continued to plan out several possible approaches to take, he reached the door of his hut and carefully parted the curtain of vines. The boy was huddled up on his pallet with his face to the wall—and somewhat to Snowfire's surprise, the owl, who was normally rather aloof, had come down off his perch and was on the ground beside the boy with one wing stretched over him as if Hweel was sheltering a nestling.

The owl turned his head and fastened his great golden eyes on Snowfire as the Tayledras entered. Instead of words, Hweel Sent emotion, a complicated flavor of distress and protectiveness.

:Boy hurts. Inside, loss. Shelter lost, caring lost. Pain, but no blood.: Hweel finally articulated.

:I know,: Snowfire replied simply. *:I'll do the best I can for him.:*

Hweel relaxed immediately, as if certain, now that Snowfire understood and had promised to help, that Snowfire could solve all of the boy's complicated problems. Sometimes Hweel's absolute trust in his bondmate's ability to solve any problem was as irritating as it was touching, but Snowfire took great care never to convey that irritation.

Hweel relinquished his place on the boy's pallet, waddling over to be lifted up to his perch, and once the owl was back where he belonged, Snowfire took up the place Hweel had vacated. He touched Darian's shoulder carefully.

"Dar'ian," he said, quite calmly. "I came to see if you were feeling any better."

His immediate answer was a sniff, but Darian at least sat up. "N–no," the boy replied, his voice hoarse.

Snowfire suppressed a chuckle, which would have been taken amiss. *At least the lad is honest!* "I'm sorry to hear that; no one wanted to upset you, least of all Starfall. He is quite personally distressed that you were made so unhappy by our questions; his last words to me were that he is not accustomed to having children run from him in tears."

Darian rubbed his reddened eyes and sniffed again, but looked up at Snowfire with mingled surprise and disbelief. "Why should he care? It doesn't matter how I feel—"

"But it does," Snowfire interrupted. "It matters a great deal. Adept Starfall is a great favorite among the children of our Vale; he is accustomed to being liked for his kindness as well as respected for his wisdom, and it makes him feel badly if someone is hurt by his actions or words."

"I'm not worth worrying about," Darian mumbled, looking down at the ground. "There's no reason why he should think about me. There's no reason why any of you should think about me, you're all important people. You're all these amazing warriors and mages, you can do things that nobody back in Errold's Grove would believe, and I'm—I'm just the worthless troublemaker nobody else wants."

Snowfire nodded to himself mentally as the boy's words echoed what Nightwind had already surmised.

"I'm sorry to hear you say that, since I don't in the least agree with you. I truly hate to spoil a friendship by beginning it with a quarrel," he replied lightly, and was rewarded once again with Darian's glance of dumbfounded astonishment.

"How can you say that?" the boy asked, incredulously. "There isn't anybody in Errold's Grove who'd believe their ears if they heard you say that!"

"Why, what would *they* say?" Snowfire asked, ingenuously.

"That—that I'm ungrateful, disrespectful, and I don't know my place," Darian said, in what was very nearly a growl, turning his gaze away from Snowfire's face and back down to the ground.

Snowfire made a noncommittal sound. "And why would they say that you're ungrateful?"

"Because after all the effort they've gone to in order to make sure I had someone to take care of me, and have food and shelter, and the trouble they've gone to in order to see that I was going to learn a useful trade, I'm not grateful, and I don't know my place," Darian muttered, his voice full of resentment.

Snowfire shifted his weight, and took a more comfortable pose, giving himself time to think out his answer. "It seems to me," he said carefully, "that you already *had* the grounding in a very good trade, that being the one that your parents followed. It seems to me that—provided you *liked* that trade, of course—you could, with a little effort, have found someone else in that trade to take you as half-trained apprentice, and thus you would have supplied your own food, shelter, and Master. So I fail to see why they should think you should consider yourself beholden to them for what they did. After all, the choice of caretaker, lodging, and trade was *theirs*, not yours, and you had never asked them to undertake it on your behalf. If someone cooks food I do not care for and offers it to me when they know I am not hungry, should I be grateful to them?"

"Some people would think so," Darian replied, but his spirits seemed a little higher.

He shrugged. "Then some people are foolish, and that is their problem, not mine, nor should it be yours. However, there is this to consider; would any of their children, at your age, have been able to do as you would have done had they waited to let you try?"

"No," he admitted. "They'd have been pretty helpless. They'd have had to get a relative to take care of 'em and sort things out for them."

"Then wouldn't it be reasonable to say that they were taking care

of things for you as their own children would have needed care?''
Snowfire waited for Darian to make the next leap of logic.

"I guess so.'' Darian didn't say anything else, but Snowfire could
tell he was thinking about something. *I hope it's that he can see why
they would* expect *him to be grateful, even though he wasn't obliged
to feel gratitude.* Poor lad. He was a *tervardi* being brought up by
hertasi, who didn't understand why he wanted to live at the tops of
trees instead of a nice, safe burrow deep in the ground. And *he* didn't
understand why he should be grateful that they kept giving him the
room farthest from the exit!

"Well,'' Snowfire said at last. "Why would they say you were
disrespectful?''

"Because I pretty much told them what you just did,'' Darian said
with some wonderment, so surprised to hear his own thoughts echoing from Snowfire's mouth that he was hard put to keep his eyes
down on the ground.

"Well, if you told them in approximately the same words that I
used, I can understand being called disrespectful,'' Snowfire chuckled. "You might consider cultivating a more diplomatic approach to
avoid conflict in the future. But what is this about 'knowing your
place'?''

Darian looked up at him from beneath a pair of fiercely knitted
eyebrows. "I guess I wasn't humble enough,'' he replied. "Old Justyn, he just let everybody treat him like the whole village's servant,
and I guess I was supposed to act the same.''

"Really?'' Snowfire did not let his expression of friendly interest
slip. "Perhaps, though, it wasn't that they treated Justyn as if he were
a servant, but as if they had become so accustomed to his services
that they took him for granted?''

"Maybe.'' Darian's fierce expression eased a little. "I suppose that
was it. I guess when you do things for people and they get used to
you being there, it's natural to kind of get taken for granted.''

"Exactly true.'' Snowfire nodded calmly. "That is why, from time
to time, our Vale Healer goes out into the deep forest to meditate
and refresh his spirit. When we have to do without him for a while,
we notice again how much he does. Of course, if any of us were to
have a genuine emergency, he would return, but that rarely happens.
When he comes back, he is invigorated by his rest, and we are properly appreciative of all he does. Now, that your Master did not do
this is as much his own fault as the villagers'. Our Shin'a'in cousins
have a saying, 'To treat a person like a carpet, it is necessary that
one do the walking, and one allow himself to be walked on.' ''

Darian actually smiled a little, and rubbed his reddened nose with the back of his hand. "That's a funny saying. But I guess I see the point."

"It seems to me," Snowfire continued, with perfect calm, "that the people of your village could have used a deal more exposure to the wider world, and were stubborn and loud in their refusal to change their ways."

Now Darian laughed out loud. "That's a funny thing for a Hawk-brother to say!" he replied. "Hellfires, you people never even came *out* of the Forest till just a little bit ago! Most people thought you had feathers instead of hair!"

"That would be the *tervardi*, not the Tayledras," Snowfire chuckled. "And again, the cousins say, 'It takes a mule to repeat a mule's bray,' which is to say, the one most likely to recognize a fault is the one who suffers from the same fault. Hmm?"

"I guess so." Darian grew quiet and thoughtful, and Snowfire wondered if he had caught the second lesson—that a great deal of the trouble between himself and his guardians lay in the fact that neither of them cared to compromise the vision they had for Darian's future. A clue that he just might have came a moment later, when he asked plaintively, "Do I *have* to be a mage?"

"That is a good question, Dar'ian. Well, you have the Gift, and it seems reasonable to train it, so that it is at least under your control," Snowfire replied judiciously. "Having a Gift is a bit like having a very large and active dog. Think about the large dogs you have been around in your life, from pups to adults. If you do not train a dog to obey you—what happens?"

"He jumps all over people, steals what he wants, maybe bites someone." Darian nodded, as if the analogy made sense to him.

"But if he is trained, even if you do not go to the extent of training him for—say—pulling a cart, or searching for lost children, he will stay out of trouble. That is why you should at least train your Gift. Otherwise, like the dog, it is likely to break loose and do something unanticipated, usually at a bad moment."

Darian sighed and propped his chin on his hand. "It's just that, before you did that stuff with the bandage, I couldn't see much you could do with magic that you couldn't do with a pair of hands."

Snowfire stretched and thought quickly. He needed to find something that would convince Darian to undertake real training, which would mean a great deal of hard work. "Well, in the long run, you are correct. If I wish to know something happening at a distance, I could work the magic to find it out, or I could go there and find it out for myself. If I needed to hide myself, I could work the magic to do so, or I could wear the correct clothing and learn to move without making a sound. Now—I could not call lightning by myself, for instance, but the Artificers of Valdemar have a powder that will certainly leave a large hole and make one *think* that lightning was called. So you are in the right of it. But—the black powder does not work in the rain, sometimes the right clothing still would not conceal a watcher, and it is not always convenient to go off on a journey to learn what is going on somewhere." He spread his hands wide. "You see? It is good to know *how* to do things without magic, but it is good to know how to do them with magic as well. It gives you more options than just one or the other."

"Justyn couldn't do much," Darian said meditatively. "Magic, I mean. Something was wrong with his head, he said, and he couldn't do magic like he used to. I don't know."

"That may have been as much the result of the mage-storms as anything else," Snowfire replied. "With the way that magic was scattered, he may not have had the *power* to do the things he used to—and that may be why he lost some of the respect that he had in the past. And also—we do not know why, but a small number of mages were affected by the Storms. Some lost ability, some gained it. He may have been one of those who lost it, and that is hardly his fault. Do you fault a man for no longer chopping wood when he has lost a hand?"

"But he figured out ways of doing things that needed getting done, without magic!" Darian protested.

"And that is certainly to his vast credit, I have no argument with you. It is too bad that your villagers were so certain that something done by magical means is intrinsically more valuable than something done any other way that they forgot that the value lies in the accomplishment, not how it was done." Snowfire decided enough had been said on that issue. "Well, that, after all, is how it is said that carnival sharpsters manage to separate the gullible from their earnings, by accomplishing the ordinary with so much flash and tinsel that their victims forget that they are seeing nothing but a gaudy illusion overlaid on the absolutely commonplace."

Darian looked so puzzled by that last remark that Snowfire reminded himself sharply that he was only dealing with a young lad, no matter how clever the boy sounded.

"I don't know what that means," the boy admitted honestly, impressing the Hawkbrother even more.

"It matters not, Dar'ian, we can talk about it another time. We have time to be friends. But for now—'' He led Darian, gently and by careful questions, to talk about his parents.

He discovered that Nightwind had been correct about Darian's close and affectionate relationship with his parents. He also learned that, as she had surmised, he still held to the hope that they were still alive somewhere.

He saw no reason to disabuse the boy of that hope. Certainly his guardians had made that attempt, and failed, and after all, what harm did it do him? That hope had probably sustained him, rather than harming him in any way, and had helped him to keep his spirit intact. That was hardly a bad thing.

Finally he persuaded Darian to come out of the *ekele*, get something to eat, and continue answering questions.

''You will feel better with a meal inside you,'' Snowfire assured him, as he led Darian to the central cooking area. ''I know that I always do. I would also like you to meet the rest of us one at a time, rather than facing all of us in a group. That cannot have been comfortable.''

Darian averted his eyes for a moment. ''It felt like—like I was in trouble again, and you—you people are pretty scary,'' he murmured uncomfortably.

Snowfire mentally berated himself for not seeing that beforehand. ''I apologize, Darian, but that is how we always conduct our information-meetings. When people must know some crucial intelligence, we all come together to hear it and ask questions, then folk go off to think about the situation, then return some time later to discuss possible strategies. You were not in trouble—but you were the focus and the most important part of the meeting.''

Darian flushed, and Snowfire decided that the subject had better be changed. ''Never mind,'' he said. ''Let's get food.'' By that time they had reached the cook shelter, which had clay ovens constructed on the spot for baking, open fires with tripods for pots and spits for roasting small beasts and birds whole, and grills over coals for fish. Snowfire spotted the *hertasi* Ayshen taking fresh, hot bread from one of the ovens, and headed straight in that direction, for there was nothing he loved so much as hot bread. It was only when he noticed that Darian was no longer beside him that he turned to see the boy staring at the little *hertasi* with an expression of horrified surprise.

''Dar'ian?'' he asked, puzzled. ''Is something wrong?''

Darian's face was as pale as a cloud. ''What—is—that?'' he whispered, as if he was afraid to make a sound lest the *hertasi* suddenly leap at him and rend him with claw and fang.

"That is Ayshen, a good friend of mine, and a wonderful baker," Snowfire said, deciding that the best approach would be to be completely matter-of-fact about the *hertasi*. Did the Valdemarans have no *hertasi* in their land? Evidently not, judging by Darian's pinched expression. "His mate Drusi makes a better stew, but no one can rival his bread, and his meat pies are worth suffering any hardship to earn! Come, I'll introduce you."

Darian could hardly hang back after that, and he trailed along after Snowfire with wide eyes and a set look of determination on his face. "Ayshen!" Snowfire hailed. "I am about to perish of famine, and our young friend Dar'ian k'Valdemar has not even had breakfast. Surely you can take pity on us and feed us!"

Darian obviously understood none of this—probably not even his name, given that Snowfire had given it the Tayledras pronunciation— but he could not misunderstand the tone of friend-to-friend that Snowfire used. Nor could he misunderstand the similar tone with which Ayshen replied to this sally.

"Shame on you, Snowfire. I thought the hatchling was in your charge! You are supposed to *feed* hatchlings, don't you know that? Are you trying to stunt his growth through starvation so that you will no longer be the runt of this pack of humans?" Ayshen swiftly tore one of the steaming loaves in half, then tore each half in half, lengthwise. Onto two of the quarters he laid juicy slices of venison he carved from a roast over one of the fires, knife flashing in his blinding speed. He topped the meat with some mouth-watering concoction of his own, made of finely chopped herbs, wild garlic, and watercress from a set of nested simmering pots. Then he restored the top quarters of each, and handed one to each of them. Darian took his gingerly, unable to take his eyes from the hertasi's lizardlike face.

Ayshen was a k'Leshya *hertasi*, and did not suffer from the painful shyness shared by all of the Pelagirs *hertasi*, including his mate. So he was neither offended nor alarmed by Darian's reaction.

"The boy has never seen one of us, eh?" Ayshen chuckled. "No worries. I mind me the time I saw my first Haighlei; I thought my eyes would pop out of my head. To me, the idea that you humans had hide colors that wildly different just set my brain afire." He turned to Darian, and cleared his throat. "To hearth, bed, and bread, be welcome," he said in slow and uncertain Valdemaran.

Darian jumped, but held onto his meal with both hands, and made an awkward little bow. "Thanks be to the keeper of the house; my hand is at his service," he replied in the formal manner.

Ayshen chuckled. "Tell him he shouldn't have said *that*—I need a dishwasher today! You were on the roster, but with that bad arm, you can't lift pots. It's probably why you got the wound, as an excuse."

Snowfire obediently translated, and a slow smile crept across Darian's face. "I wouldn't mind—if he really needs the help," the boy said shyly. "I used to do all the dishwashing for Justyn—and—I could pay you back a little by taking your place."

The glance he gave Snowfire had more than a shadow of hero worship to it, but Snowfire knew how to deal with that. "If you have no problem in taking my place, I would be grateful," he replied and made a face. "On the whole, I don't mind washing dishes; it's preferable to a lot of other camp chores that I *won't* escape because of my bad arm. And I will miss out on the special treats Ayshen keeps for his helpers."

The ploy worked; he not only established that he was grateful to Darian for volunteering, but that the job of dishwasher brought with it some extra rewards.

It was arranged that Darian would report to Ayshen after the evening meal; with a bit of trial, they determined to both of their satisfaction that Ayshen could direct the boy with a bit of mime and a great deal of pointing.

That certainly went well, Snowfire thought with satisfaction, as he led Darian off in the direction of the *dyheli* grazing grounds. *He is resilient, I must give him credit for that. Now that he has the concept of nonhuman partners planted in his mind, I'll show him the next set.*

Darian had hardly known what to think when he first saw the *hertasi* cook, Ayshen. The creature had looked—at least at first—so very much like the horrible Thing that had been leading the enemy fighters!

But Snowfire hadn't been afraid of Ayshen, and the *hertasi* himself had been very kind—as Ayshen had put together a lunch for the two of them, and as Darian had gotten over his fright enough to look closely at him, it was obvious that he wasn't very much like the enemy Thing at all. Darian found himself volunteering to act as a dishwasher, and even more surprising, found himself looking forward to the task. At least now he would be able to accomplish something useful here!

It was so odd, though—feeling an urgent *need* to be useful.

"So—what's a *hertasi*, anyway?" he asked Snowfire around a mouthful of bread.

"They are, so we believe, one of the creations of that same great mage who ended the Mage Wars,'' Snowfire replied. ''As you saw, they are descended from lizards, and they share many characteristics with lizards. Cold sends them into a stupor, and extreme cold could kill or injure them very badly. They act, more or less, as our helpers; they cook and clean for us, make clothing, act as the assistants for artisans—when they are not, themselves, artisans as well. In return, we give them the protection of our Vales and scouts and things that they need. They tend to live in colonies, although they take single mates. They are one of the five nonhuman races that we Tayledras associate and work with.''

''Five?'' Darian could hardly believe it. ''There are five kinds of— of—*things* that you have around your Vales?''

''As equal partners and helpers and not always *in* the Vales. The *tervardi*, or Bird-people, the *kyree*, or Fur-brothers, and the *dyheli*, or Straight-horns, usually live outside our Vales. The *hertasi* and the gryphons in our Vales entwine their lives with ours; the others live entirely separate lives from ours, and only become partners with us where there are specific tasks that are better done with all our peoples.'' Snowfire was so matter-of-fact about this—as if he were telling Darian how the Hawkbrothers arranged to get things from traders, or worked with the Valdemaran Guard! Darian found his head swimming. First, two-legged, intelligent lizards, and now this!

''In fact,'' Snowfire was continuing, ''we have *dyheli* with us as well as *hertasi* on this journey. They have volunteered, in token of their separate alliance with Valdemar, to act as our mounts and burden bearers. Selenay has offered, in light of the fact that they are grazers and most of the Pelagirs are forested, to sponsor colonies of *dyheli* into some of the unused grazing lands on the western border, and our *dyheli* are also along as scouts to investigate this possibility. We could say that, as grazers, they wish to find if the lands and available grasses and plants suit their tastes.''

Darian giggled at the word play. ''What—what do these *dyheli* look like?'' Darian asked. ''I mean, I've heard stories, about some of the things in Hawkbrother lands, but I've never seen any.''

Snowfire smiled. ''That, my friend, you are about to see for yourself. Look there—''

He pointed as they came around another of the ubiquitous vine curtains—and there, in a sunny meadow, was a small herd of something vaguely like deer with ghostlike coloration of pale beige and cream.

At least, they had four legs, hooves, and two delicately curved, unbranching horns on their heads. But the heads themselves were much larger than that of a deer, the enormous brown eyes looked more forward than a deer's did. But the biggest difference was in the shape of the skull; a small and delicate muzzle, comparatively speaking, but an elongated cranium, something that could easily contain a brain the size of a man's.

As he and Snowfire stood at the edge of the clearing, every *dyheli* head came up, the humans were examined closely, but swiftly, and then every *dyheli* head came down again, back to the important business of grazing.

Darian blinked at them in awe; he was no stranger to the concept of an intelligent, four-legged creature. After all, he was a native of Valdemar, and you'd have to have the brains of a wheel of cheese not to know all about Companions. But these creatures were so— different.

"Do they talk?" he asked in a whisper.

"Not like the *hertasi* do," came the reply. "The *dyheli* speak mind-to-mind. Some of us find it difficult to speak to them, as some of us are better at Mindspeech with nonhumans than others." Snowfire smiled down at him. "I happen to be one of the lucky ones; I find it as easy to speak with them as I do with you. Easier, in fact, for I am not translating into a foreign tongue."

Darian turned his attention back to the *dyheli*. "I wonder if I could learn to talk to them," he mused out loud.

:Why not simply try?:

"Because I don't know if I can—" he began, then realized that Snowfire had not spoken aloud.

In fact, the voice he had heard had been entirely in his mind—and had *not* been Snowfire's.

One of the *dyheli* had raised his head again, and was walking toward them, his eyes centered on Darian. The delicate creature had no expression to read, but the voice in Darian's head was warm and amused. *:It is a great advantage to speak this way, little brother,:* the *dyheli* stag said to him. *:It requires no translators, and it is very, very difficult to lie or be lied to. It tends to make all things level, as it were.:*

Darian stared up into the stag's huge, brown eyes, and didn't realize that he was holding his breath until his lungs began to ache. Belatedly, he took a gasping breath of air, as Snowfire chuckled at his expression.

"Tyrsell tends to be a bit more direct than I do," he told Darian. "I would have waited to test you for Mindspeech, but his approach

is to simply try it and see if you can Hear him. Well—I suppose this
means that now I shall have to teach you to use that Gift—''

:Oh, not immediately; his natural shields are good enough to hold
for now,: the stag replied lazily. :And if it comes to that, I'm as good
a teacher as you are. Better, maybe—I've had more practice at it.:

"Are you volunteering?" Snowfire asked, as Darian felt his mind
reeling under this latest revelation.

:Why not? The boy could use a competent teacher,: the stag replied
teasingly. :Actually, and more honestly, young Darian, you need a
teacher with a little less to attend to than our friend Snowfire. I have
more time to spare than he.: The stag lifted his head to look up into
Snowfire's face. :But, I think, Snowfire, that it would be a good thing
if you let me give Darian your language now. It would be better for
him if he did not require a translator.:

Then, for several moments, the stag and Snowfire looked into each
others' eyes, and Darian sensed that they were exchanging words that
he couldn't "hear." Snowfire was frowning, as if he didn't agree
with what was being said. Finally, though, the Hawkbrother sighed
and nodded.

"Dar'ian," he said carefully, "I *was* going to work a very small
magic that would allow you to understand our tongue—but as my
friend and herd leader has just reminded me, he can do the same
thing without magic, and with fewer problems. But—there are some
things that will also happen that you might *consider* problems."

"Like what?" Darian asked immediately. Having people talking
over his head and not being able to understand them had been making
him very frustrated, although he had been too polite to say anything.

"It might hurt a little. It will definitely be a shock to your system.
You might get some of his memories as well, or mine, since he will
be taking the language of the Tayledras from my mind. They'd probably crop up in your dreams, and they might be disturbing. You
already know that I am used to fighting. My friend is also a warrior—
he has to be, or he couldn't lead the herd—and he knows how to
use his weapons." Snowfire glanced at the *dyheli*'s horns signifi-
cantly.

"I don't care—I mean, I'd really like it if he could do that,"
Darian said quickly. Just at the moment, the idea that he might finally
be able to understand all the people chattering around him made him
almost sick with longing.

:Then look into my eyes, young one,: the *dyheli* commanded, and
without another thought, Darian obeyed.

Time slowed, then stopped.

He came to himself lying flat on the grass, gazing up at the blue sky, feeling very much as if someone had kicked his feet out from underneath him.

"I did warn you," Snowfire said, holding out a hand to help him up—and as Darian took it and clambered clumsily to his feet, lightning flashes and glitter dancing in his eyes, he suddenly realized that the language had *not* been Valdemaran.

"So you did," he agreed, and to his delight, he realized a moment later that he had replied in the Hawkbrother tongue without thinking about it. He felt the back of his head gingerly, but the ground had been nicely cushioned with grass, and there was no knot on his skull, which was a good thing. He did have a headache, though, which felt as if someone had taken the top off his skull, looked inside, stirred the contents up a bit, and then replaced the skull top and left him lying in the grass.

"Are you quite all right?" Snowfire asked him, with concern.

"I think so, but I've got a headache," he admitted as he rubbed his temples. "It doesn't seem to want to go away." Then he realized that he had not yet thanked Tyrsell, and he flushed.

"Thank you *very* much, sir," he said, turning hastily to the waiting *dyheli*, and bowing a little. "I hope I don't sound as if I'm complaining, because I'm not! Being able to understand people—" He groped for words.

:Being able to understand people will prevent you from feeling like such an outsider,: the stag said smoothly. *:You have quite enough troubles without that added to your burden. Being able to understand their words will help you to understand them. And you are quite welcome; be sure to come to me when you have time for a lesson in Mindspeech. Until then, I hope you learn to enjoy being among us. It is the way of a herd to encompass and support.:*

Darian said that he would, reflecting that at least a *dyheli* would not be able to smack his fingers with a rod like the Widow Clay who had taught him his letters had. The stag nodded and moved back toward his herd, flowing over the grass in a way that hardly resembled walking.

Darian steadied himself against Snowfire for a few long minutes. His head felt compressed, twisted, and then expanded again to a size larger than his skin could hold. There were words for things he had never *seen* inside his mind now, and images associated with rituals and crafts, and trees and plants, and women and men, and clothing and tools, and names for all of them. There were even some images of things he did not *want* to understand, and a few that he didn't think he was quite old enough for. There were even names for tastes he had never tasted, and feelings his body had never known. Darian would have felt disassociated and frightened enough to scream, if it weren't for the effect of hopeful wonderment these new words were having upon him. So many great things had now *touched* him, and were a part of him, and there was a spark inside him—now that he had names, he wanted to learn the meanings.

"Well, if you have a headache," Snowfire said gently after a few minutes, "then this will be a good excuse to go find Nightwind and introduce you to the third species that is with us on this expedition." Snowfire patted him on the shoulder and rubbed at Darian's back a bit, companionably. "Nightwind can get you a soothing-potion, and you can meet Kelvren."

"Who's Kelvren?" Darian asked, both curious and a little apprehensive. His headache had subsided from the worst disorientation, and he tried to remember what the other nonhuman races were that Snowfire had mentioned. One was *kyree*, and one was *tervardi*—

"Oh, I think you'll like him a great deal," Snowfire said with a chuckle. "Though you mustn't let him intimidate you. He won't *try* to intimidate you, it is simply that sometimes, his people do, just by being themselves. Kelvren is—a gryphon."

Snowfire

Five

Snowfire had been struck speechless when Tyrsell offered to "give" Darian the Tayledras language. *Just what is he planning, here?* he asked himself—not with any suspicion that Tyrsell intended any kind of wrong, but because of what that "gift" would entail. For one thing, Snowfire certainly hadn't expected the *dyheli* to make any such offer, and for another, it was definitely an offer of far more than appeared on the surface.

:*What do you think you're doing?*: he asked the stag. :*Not that this isn't a great deal more expedient, but the boy has* no *idea what this is going to mean to him!*:

:*That is precisely why I suggested it,*: Tyrsell replied calmly, blinking as lazily as if he had suggested a change of grazing spots. :*In this case, it is quite true that although what he does not know about what we'll have to do is not going to hurt him, what he doesn't know about the Mind-Gifts* is, *and if by taking a few shortcuts we can keep his own budding abilities from harming him—and, not so incidentally,* us—*where's the wrong?*:

:*The wrong is in the deception,*: Snowfire told him severely. :*You're deceiving him into thinking this is something very simple.*:

:*What deception? He won't care about what we have to do to put the knowledge in his mind, he's only interested in the results.*: Tyrsell, as was the case with most of the *dyheli*, had a slightly different perspective on morality than humans did. To Snowfire's mind, this was one of the two-edged swords of being allies with nonhumans. *Dyheli* focused on expediency, *hertasi* saw no harm in meddling in private affairs because *hertasi* had no such thing as a "private affair," and gryphons were downright bloody-minded at times.

:*And he is rightly concerned only with results, too,*: Tyrsell continued. *:We know that the fact is that we'll have to establish links and shields in order to get that knowledge into him, but that's of no concern to him. He could care less, and since those links and shields are not only not going to harm him, but are actually going to help him, I think that the fact that we'll have to put them in place without his actual consent is irrelevant.:*

Snowfire couldn't put into words why he objected to the *dyheli's* high-handed assumption that mucking about with someone else's mind didn't matter as long as the results were good—but he Sent his feelings about it as forcefully as he could.

Tyrsell remained calm, switching his tail to ward off some troublesome flies as he continued to bombard Snowfire with impersonal logic, his eyes warm and serene above the dark cheek-stripes that made his face look like a painted mask. *:Let's look at this from the position of efficiency. Can you really afford the time, effort, and energy it would take to give him the language magically? Of course not. Can you keep shepherding him around and translating for him? That's equally absurd. Can you explain to him what links and shields are in a way he'll understand right now, given that you are not only working with someone who doesn't have the understanding of Mind-Gifts, but are having to translate from your language to his? Not a chance. So, by doing this, you free yourself for other work, you give him some much-needed autonomy, and you keep him from being overwhelmed if his Gift of Mindspeech suddenly decides to develop. What would you, what could you do if it decided to flower overnight at a time when you were off on a scouting sortie or trying to fend off those barbarians? Expect Wintersky to take care of it? He's barely into controlling his own Mindspeech as it is! Leave it to Starfall? And just how is he supposed to hold the matrices at the same time? Nightwind's Mindspeech is rudimentary; she hasn't the tools to teach a beginner. And who else is there he will trust?:*

Snowfire frowned, but he had to admit that Tyrsell was right. *:You come perilously close to amorality,:* he told the *dyheli.*

:Never. My morality is just that of the herd, that the herd is more important than a single member; and when it comes to it, your morals are the same. Didn't you just say that if it would save the world from another Ma'ar, you wouldn't hesitate to sacrifice yourself and the boy and anyone else?: Tyrsell held his head up and looked Snowfire right in the eyes, challenging him stallion to stallion, daring him to deny what he had told Starfall not more than a few moments ago.

:I said, I'd sacrifice volunteers—: he replied weakly, but Tyrsell had him, and they both knew it. *:You win,:* he admitted. *:This time.:*

:And next time, you may.: Now that the challenge was over, Tyrsell was perfectly amiable again. *:Don't worry so much about winning arguments, my friend. Concentrate on keeping the herd intact and in good health.:*

Darian was pathetically eager to have the ability to understand those around him, and from the little Snowfire could sense from him, he would have been willing to get it at almost any cost. That soothed his raw conscience a little. After he'd given his immediate consent, the boy waited expectantly, eyes focused on Tyrsell's, for the magic to happen.

:Get ready to catch him,: the *dyheli* warned, and reached out to seize the boy's mind. This was the greatest Gift the herd leaders had; the ability to overwhelm any mind not heavily shielded—and many that were—without any damage to that mind whatsoever. This was how a herd leader could guide his frightened followers to safety when they were hysterical with terror and unable to think or reason. He could seize as many as a dozen minds at once or even more, and use those he controlled to guide the rest of the herd behind him. *Dyheli* never seemed to resent this, perhaps because herd morality was as deeply a part of them as individuality was for Tayledras. This was how the herd leaders were chosen. Instead of grappling horn-to-horn as their distant ancestors had, they fought mind-to-mind, and the strongest mind, or the one with the most endurance, won the right to father the next generation and guide this one.

A moment later, Snowfire caught the child as he collapsed, all his joints suddenly gone loose, every muscle limp. He laid Darian down carefully in a spot of sun on the grass, and lowered all his own shields, joining his mind as intimately to Tyrsell's as he ever had to Hweel's. More so, perhaps, since that melding was so natural a part of a *dyheli*'s mind.

With the two of them working as one, the speed with which they built temporary shields around Darian's mind was literally that of thought. Then Snowfire formed a deep link to Darian below the level of thought itself, so deep that the boy would never know it was there, and never detect any difference in the way he felt. While he held that link wide open, Tyrsell went to work on Snowfire's memories. The herd leader extracted, not only the language of the Tayledras, but the *knowledge* of the language, and placed it carefully into the boy's own memories, building it up from the level just above instinct, the way that a baby learns. Now Darian would not have to think to translate— he would have the Tayledras tongue as if he had been bilingual from his very first word.

In this fashion, Tyrsell's way was infinitely better than the spell and Mindtouch that Snowfire had used to learn Valdemaran. Snowfire made a mental note to one day ask Darian—once the boy really knew what he was consenting to—to allow Tyrsell to reverse the process, and give Snowfire such a sure knowledge of the language of Valdemar.

Tyrsell was swift and certain; there was something about the way that a *dyheli*'s mind worked that (when they had Tyrsell's particular Gifts) made them instinctive geniuses at laying in language-paths. In the time it took Snowfire's heart to take three, slow beats, Tyrsell was done. He withdrew his mind first, leaving Snowfire to close all but the deep-link path behind him, and setting the shields he had laid in place to fade as the boy took over his own shielding needs. Darian would hear and understand any deliberate Mindtouch on the part of any *dyheli* or Tayledras, but no one could force his mind open, or really do anything other than *talk* with him. And Darian would never hear unwanted thoughts intruding on him if his ability to Mindhear suddenly became more than the close-range, rudimentary ability he had now.

As Snowfire withdrew and made some swift observations of the boy's potential Gifts, he realized that such a thing was far more likely than he had thought when Tyrsell first proposed this operation. Perhaps it was the sheer number of traumas that the boy had passed through, but—well, going abruptly from "normal" to wide open was a very real possibility.

And it was a good thing that Snowfire had the deep-link in place. At that level, he would not eavesdrop on the boy's private thoughts, but he *would* know if Darian was in distress, he would know if any of the boy's potentials suddenly opened up, and he would be able to track Darian if he somehow got separated from the Tayledras encampment.

Tyrsell had certainly noticed the same things, and very diplomatically did not say "I told you so." *:A neat piece of work,:* was all he said, and about that moment, the boy awoke—probably with a splitting headache. *Still,* Snowfire thought, not without sympathy, *the spell would have given him as bad a headache, and maybe worse.*

Darian's words and actions confirmed that diagnosis, but he still remained polite enough despite the pain to thank Tyrsell for his efforts. Snowfire noted with pleasure that he spoke Tayledras with the unconscious ease of a native.

Tyrsell lost all interest in the boy now that the work was complete; that, too, was typical of *dyheli*, and because Snowfire was used to it, he wasn't at all offended. Darian was too preoccupied with his headache to notice what could have been considered very rude behavior, but was really only more *dyheli* "expediency."

But the boy all but forgot the pounding in his skull when Snowfire told him that he was about to meet a gryphon.

"A gryphon?" Darian asked incredulously, his eyes lighting up with absolute delight. "A real gryphon? Here?"

"A real gryphon," Snowfire told him, smiling a little at his wide eyes. "Nightwind is only incidentally acting as our Healer; her main job is to be Kelvren's *trondi'irn*." Since that word was *not* Tayledras, but Kaled'a'in, and not part of the language as Darian had "learned" it, Snowfire explained it. "A *trondi'irn* is a special attendant for nonhuman creatures, although usually it is only the gryphons who need such help. They do all the things that the gryphons cannot—it is very difficult for gryphons to manage fine manipulations with talons, for instance—and they take care of the little ailments that nonhumans fall prey to. Because they understand these things so well, if they are attending to only one nonhuman, they often double as the Healers for small expeditions such as ours. Back in the times of long ago, a *trondi'irn* would often manage the needs of a very large group of gryphons or other nonhumans, but that is no longer the case."

Darian nodded earnestly, but it was very obvious that his mind was not on Nightwind and her duties. "Is he really as big as they say?" he asked eagerly. "Is he really as big as a house? Can he really *fly*? Does he eat whole horses in a bite?"

Snowfire chuckled. "Oh, gryphons are not as large as all that, but if they spread their wings wide, I think it is safe to say that their wingspan is easily as big or bigger than a house. And although they do not eat whole horses in one bite, they do eat quite a lot. Kelvren has to do a great deal of hunting to keep himself supplied with meat."

"Can he talk?" Darian asked next, practically skipping in eagerness to see the marvel. "Will I hear him thinking at me like Tyrsell?"

"No, he speaks Tayledras very well, although he tends to have what we call a 'gryphonic accent.' You'll see what that means in a little." Snowfire patted the boy's shoulder. "He really is looking forward to meeting you."

By this time they had wound their way back to the clearing, and as Snowfire made that last statement, a deep voice spoke from the shelter of a shadowy bower immediately ahead of them.

"Ah, but isss the young gentleman *quite* prrreparrred to meet *me?*"

A deeper shadow rose out of the rest, and strolled forward into the sunlight, then posed perfectly in the best possible light. Kelvren looked truly magnificent, and knew it.

Darian's eyes widened, and he stared at Kelvren with all the fascination of a Kaled'a'in messenger-bird with a shiny new toy.

Darian had not yet gotten used to the wonder of being able to talk to Snowfire in the Hawkbrother tongue without having to *think* about it, when a deep, resonant voice speaking out of the shadows just ahead of them captured all of his attention. He and Snowfire were standing in a rare patch of brilliant sun in the middle of the clearing that he had been taken to for the meeting; ahead of them, the shadows were so deep and black by contrast that he might have been peering into a well. When he tried to make out who or what was speaking, the contrast defeated him.

"Ah," said the voice, a rumbling bass with odd overtones, "but isss the young gentleman *quite* prrreparrred to meet *me*?"

A moment later, part of the darkest shadow detached itself from the rest, and moved forward into the sun. And although it was not as big as a house, it was entirely large enough to satisfy Darian.

The creature that moved into the sunlight was a glistening golden brown with a hint of metallic gold at the edges of each of his perfectly-defined feathers. His head, broad and handsome, with jaunty ear-tufts, had a definite eagle look about it, and at a guess, the folded wings would easily span the length of a house, if not more. Both front and rear feet ended in formidable talons, each as long as Darian's hand. He sported a wide leather collar adorned with delicate scrollwork attached to an equally handsome body-harness with a chest-plaque, the front yoke of which had a matching leather pouch attached. As he stared down at Darian, looking every bit as haughty and regal as Darian could have wished, he took the boy's breath away. He was, in every way, a wonder, and Darian could not have taken his eyes off of him if the earth had fallen away beneath the boy's feet.

Once he had come fully into the sun, the gryphon didn't move, which was probably just as well. Darian's heart was pounding with excitement, and he had a shivery feeling as he looked at that huge beak and those cruel talons that his excitement could easily turn to fear.

"I think you've made a conquest, Kel," Snowfire laughed, his eyes crinkling at the corners with merriment.

"Asss it ssshould be," the gryphon replied, raising his head a bit higher with such unconcealed vanity that Darian, too, was startled into a laugh. And the gryphon joined in their laughter, proving that he was not unaware of his vanity and the absurdity of it.

"Darian, this is Kelvren Skothkae, who is an unranked gryphon-scout of the full k'Vala gryphon-wing," Snowfire told him, his eyes sparkling. "Kel, this is Dar'ian Firkin k'Valdemar."

"Unranked?" Kelvren replied, cocking his head to one side speculatively. "Perrrhapsss now—but I think ourrr wingleaderrr had bessst look to hisss posssition, or think about rrretirrring. I intend to make a grrreat name forrr myssself on thisss expedition."

"You've certainly said so often enough," Snowfire teased, and Kelvren snapped playfully in his direction, then turned his head pointedly toward Darian, pretending to ignore Snowfire.

The boy found himself the focus of those huge, piercing eyes, and suddenly understood why rabbits froze when hawks caught sight of them.

"And what think you of ourrr little family?" the gryphon asked. "Arrre we all you had thought we would be, when you thought of Tayledrrrasss?"

"More," Darian was able to say honestly, and with unfeigned enthusiasm. "I—I think that you're all just—just—unbelievable!" He shook his head carefully, to avoid making the headache any worse. "And you, sir, you're just like seeing an amazing tale come right to life in front of me! I *never* thought I'd ever get to see a real gryphon in my whole life, and I never, ever, thought a gryphon would be as—as—as wonderful as you are!"

"Rrreally?" the gryphon purred, and Darian could tell that he was very pleased. He even preened a little. "Well. Thank you! I hope I can jussstify that impressssssion."

"You could prove how great a tracker you are by finding Nightwind," Snowfire suggested, with a twitch of his mouth that showed he was trying hard to keep from laughing.

"Pah, that takesss no trrracking," Kelvren replied dismissively. "You will find herrr at the pool, wherrre I left herrr. I believe ssshe is waiting forrr you and wissshesss to sssee thisss obssserrrvant young brrrancherrr."

"And you? Are you coming with us?" Snowfire asked.

"I am sssstarrrved, and if we arrre to underrrtake that sorrrtie tonight, I musssst eat now ssso I am crrrop-light but enerrrgizsssed." With that, the gryphon spread his wings, which were even larger than Darian had imagined; as Snowfire took Darian's shoulder and pulled the boy back to the edge of the clearing, Kelvren made one or two experimental wingbeats that sent wind whipping around both of them.

Then, leaping grandly into the air with a thrust of his wings that was vastly more powerful than his trial, the gryphon took off, creating a veritable whirlwind within the confines of the clearing, and sending dust and stray leaves surging into the sky in his wake.

Darian stared after him with his mouth dropping open in amazement. Wings pumping rhythmically, the gryphon surged up above the treetops, then vanished above the foliage.

Snowfire laughed, then patted him on the shoulder. "He did that for your benefit, you know," the Hawkbrother said with amusement. "He could very easily have gone to the mouth of the valley and taken off from there. In fact, it would have taken him a lot less effort—but gryphons seem to love to impress an audience, and you are the only one of us who isn't used to seeing him take off and land. I wouldn't be the least bit surprised if he tries to find out where you are before he comes in for a landing, and arranges to make a dramatic entrance in front of you."

"Are all gryphons like that?" Darian asked, still dazzled.

"Most of them; endlessly cheerful, considerably vain, but able to make fun of themselves. Oh, and beautiful, of course, but we try not to say that too often in front of them; they're conceited enough as it is," Snowfire chuckled, his shoulders shaking a little.

Darian's eyes began to water from staring so long into the bright blue of the sky, and his head throbbed in protest. He moved quickly back into the shadows, and Snowfire must have noticed the grimace of pain he couldn't repress, for the Hawkbrother gestured him to take a particular path leading out of the clearing and set off down it himself. Darian followed him willingly now, recalling that Snowfire had said something about Nightwind having some way of getting rid of that pounding ache.

The way that the paths here twisted and turned around little groves and vine-covered huts and tiny water gardens made him very confused, and made this place seem much larger than it probably actually was. It was very bewildering, and Darian had quite lost his way when they came out into sunlight again, at the side of the smaller of two pools of water. This was clearly the end of the valley; a short, cliff cut out of the rocks of the hills rose before them, with steep, tree-covered slopes on either side. A spring emerged from the rock at the base of the cliff, feeding the two pools and a stream which led from them into the tangle of the Tayledras encampment. One of the pools was considerably smaller than the other, being just large enough for—say—a gryphon to bathe in.

"This is where you will bathe," Snowfire said, pointing to the smaller pool. "You see the sluice there? Lift the lever when you are done, and the dirty water will drain away—then drop it, and lift *that* lever, and new water will flow into the pool from that larger one. Don't worry about trying to find bathing things. Just come here and start to undress; a *hertasi* will see you and there will be soap and towels beside you before you are finished disrobing. Your clothing will disappear as if by magic, and clean clothes will be waiting for you when you are done bathing." Snowfire smiled at his expression of surprise. "Now you see why we hate to travel without our *hertasi* friends."

"I dunno," Darian said dubiously, looking down at the pool and then out at the spring that fed it. "It looks awfully cold." Of all the things he hated most, he hated cold baths—which was mostly all he got, since everybody else in the village had precedence over him at the bathhouse.

"Ah, I forget you cannot heat your water with magic—or can you?" Snowfire looked at him quizzically.

He shook his head, and regretted doing so almost at once, as his head protested. "Not that Justyn ever taught me," he replied.

"Well, can you call fire?" the Hawkbrother persisted. At Darian's cautious nod, he looked satisfied. "It is the same, only spread out over the water and not concentrated on the kindling. I would ask you to try it, but I think you had better wait until I find where Nightwind has gone."

He peered around the clearing, and then left Darian to nurse his head beside the pool while he went off to investigate some of the places at this end of the valley that were not immediately visible. Darian stared at the surface of the pool and wondered why on earth Justyn had never taught *him* how to heat water. It would have made a great many winter baths more bearable.

But maybe he didn't know how, Darian told himself, trying to be fair. *I mean, it could be that only the Hawkbrothers know about this sort of thing. It isn't all that logical to think you can use the same magic that calls fire to heat up water—fire and water are opposites, right? So maybe it wasn't his fault he didn't know.*

Just then, Snowfire appeared, parting the trailing branches of a huge willow, and holding them aside to let Nightwind pass through them. Of all of the Hawkbrothers that Darian had seen thus far, she was the only one who didn't have snow-white hair, or hair dyed in patterns of pale cream and various shades of brown. Her hair was as black as a raven's feather, and she wore it in a heavy knot at the nape of her neck, with little wisps escaping from it. Her eyes, set under a pair of brows as curved as a falcon's wings, were a darker blue than the others, and her skin was just a few shades duskier. Her clothing was a bit different, too; nothing he could put a finger on, since he hardly cared what he wore from one day to the next, but something he definitely noticed—and on the breast of her tunic was a peculiar silver badge, rather like the wings and head of a bird of prey. He thought perhaps he had seen it before, and then he realized that he *had*—in the center of the chest-piece of Kelvren's harness. Perhaps it signified that they weren't actually Hawkbrothers, but were—his new memories supplied the word—*Kaled'a'in*.

She had a basket over one arm, and a friendly smile on her lips, and held out one hand to him which he took in reflex. "I don't know if you recall me from last night," she said, her speech betraying a faint accent, as opposed to the way his new memories told him that Tayledras *should* sound. "I'm Nightwind, in case you've forgotten or this ruffian forgot to mention my name, and I understand you have one demon-rending headache."

"Well," he said, feeling suddenly shy. "It does hurt."

"I can certainly understand that," she replied, and put her basket down to take his face in both hands, turning his eyes into the light and examining them. "Yes, indeed, I can certainly understand that. However, I think I have a remedy for you; it'll taste vile, but it will work."

She let go of him to rummage in her basket, as he had to laugh a little at her honest directness. "I like your claim better than Justyn's; he always said that his potions wouldn't taste *that* bad, and the more he said that, the worse they'd taste."

"You can do that to younglings a few times before they stop believing you, and then you'll *never* get them to take their medicine," she replied, holding up a stoppered clay bottle with a little frown. "I always say things will taste worse than they do, and then they're always surprised; follow that up with a honey-candy or a bit of other sweet, and they take their doses without much of a fuss." She paused to uncork the bottle and sniff. "This is what I want." She looked at him and smiled. "Are you going to need a sweet after *your* dose?"

"Not unless that stuff is going to linger in my mouth all day," he replied, as manfully as he could.

"Not after a good drink of cold water." She handed him the bottle. "Take a good stout mouthful and swallow it fast."

He held his breath, braced himself, and did as he was told. The stuff wasn't as *bad* as some of Justyn's potions, many of which seemed to contain mycofoetida, but it was very strong-tasting, more sour than bitter, with an astringent bite. He swallowed it before he had a chance to gag, and found she was holding out a cup full of water, ready to exchange it for her bottle. He drained it, and passed it back to her; she tucked it and her bottle back into her basket.

"Well?" she asked. "How bad was it?"

"Not as bad as I thought, but—gleah! Nothing I'd drink for pleasure." He shuddered. "How did you make that stuff, anyway? Justyn always brewed teas and tisanes."

"This is tea—concentrated, so one swig is as good as a cupful," she told him. "These concentrated versions have to be pretty fresh, but things like the headache potion are needed often enough that they're used up before they go weak. I also make some preparations—distillations as well as decoctions—with spirits of wine as the carrier, but those tend to be very powerful."

"And," Snowfire added helpfully, "they taste so much worse that none of us ever want to drink them unless we absolutely have to."

"I—I think I'd like to learn how you make them," Darian said, a little surprised at himself, and feeling his ears heat up as they reddened with embarrassment. "Maybe I can help."

"Then I'd be happy to show you," Nightwind promised, looking a bit surprised at him herself. "I always like to have extra medicine on hand, and I never have enough time to make all that I want. Now, I want you to sit down for a moment until that medicine takes effect. I don't think you'll have an unusual reaction, but it's better to wait a moment and see."

Darian obeyed, although he didn't expect to feel anything more than he did with Justyn's medicines. He just hoped this potion *would* make some of the pain go away quickly, without slowing him down too much. Justyn's potions generally didn't do too much unless he drank so much he went from "sick" to "asleep" without much warning. At the moment, it felt as if someone inside his skull was trying to pound his way out.

"Look—" Snowfire said, pointing up at the sky. "There's a gyre; it must be one of ours, it's too big to be one of the wild ones around here."

Darian followed his pointing finger, squinting, until he made out the gray-and-white bird against the gray-and-white clouds, a dot moving so fast that Darian wondered how Snowfire could tell it was a forestgyre, much less that it was bigger than the wild ones. "Are the wild ones around your Vale as big as the bondbirds?" he asked with surprise.

"Most of them *are* bondbirds—or of bondbird stock, anyway,"

Snowfire replied, still watching the bird, shading his eyes with his hand. "There are usually far more birds around the Vales than there are people to bond with, because we need a large breeding pool of each species to keep the stock healthy. The adult birds are polite to us, though rather standoffish, unless as adults they decide that they want to bond rather than continuing to be wild. Sometimes that happens, especially in the larger species, like eagle-owls and hawk-eagles—" He winced. "And, Goddess help us, bondbird eagles themselves. We have two species of eagles that are bondbirds, the Black and the Golden, and a color-morph of the Golden that looks red—they almost never bleach out white, since I've never known an Adept-class mage to fly one. Not too many people of any sort fly eagles for that matter; not too many can carry one. They aren't as *greatly* oversized, proportionately, as the smaller species—bondbird merlins are about the size of wild tiercel peregrines, just as an example—but they are very, very big and heavy. There is *one*, and I mean *one* k'Vala Tayledras who flies a Black eagle, and he's the blacksmith. That should tell you something."

Darian thought about the shoulders on the smith at Errold's Grove, and how much he could carry and lift, and nodded solemnly. He tried to picture carrying a bird bigger than Hweel, and couldn't. *It must be like carrying a barrel of flour on your shoulder,* he thought. "How does someone get a bondbird, then?" he asked curiously. Not that he thought he'd ever get one, but it was more likely than being Chosen by a Companion.

"Either an adult picks you out, or, more often, the adult parents pick you as the bondmate for one of their offspring. If the adults are bonded to someone, they let that person know who the eyas is going to, and if that person has experience with downy baby birds, very often they co-parent with the eyas's new bondmate. If not, they wait until the little one is fledged, and lead him to you." Snowfire turned his attention from the sky to smile at Darian. "That's how I got Hweel; he blundered down out of a tree behind his parents, landed tail over head, fluffed all his feathers, and told me with the solemnity of a Kal'enedral that he was ready for me."

"Does anybody have more than one bondbird?" Darian asked, wishing he could have seen that moment.

"Sometimes. One of us has an owl and a merlin for day and night scouting, I know of someone with a whole flock of ravens, and there are others. And sometimes your bondbird's mate may decide she wants to bond with you, too." Snowfire raised an eyebrow. "Hweel says his mate is considering it, bonding with me, that is."

"Hweel has a mate?" Darian replied, feeling oddly excited at the idea, though he didn't know why. "Where is she?"

"Back at the Vale, teaching the youngster to hunt. I wouldn't have left if there were still young in the nest, but by the time we were ready to go, the young one was fledged. Eagle-owls lay their eggs in deep winter; they're hatched and fledged by the time most birds are going to nest, and once they're no longer in the nest, they don't need their father unless there's more than one to teach to hunt." Snowfire crossed his arms over his chest, and gave Darian a measuring look. "Now, you've spent plenty of time in the forest, can you guess why they'd do things that way?"

"Uh—" Darian thought hard. "They build up for egg-laying in fall, when there's a lot of dumb young animals on their own for the first time. Then they sit the eggs in winter, when there isn't quite as much to eat but they also aren't going to have to eat as much, then they have babies to feed in deep winter when there starts to be winter-kills and cold-kills lying around?"

"Good!" Snowfire applauded. "Then, obviously, it's a good time to teach the youngsters to hunt when there are litters of very young and *extremely* stupid young rats, rabbits and squirrels about—not to mention the odd snake or duckling."

"Do you have a bondbird?" Darian asked Nightwind, curiously.

She broke into peals of laughter. "Mercy, no!" she managed after a moment. "Trust me, the gryphons are more than enough for any poor *trondi'irn* to keep up with! Besides, with my temperament, I'd likely end up with something like a raven or a crow, and a bird with that much mischief in him would never be able to resist snatching at gryphon ear-tufts and jewelry, and there would *never* be any peace! How is your head?"

"It's—fine!" he said in surprise, realizing that his headache had vanished without his noticing.

"That's good, because you promised to help Ayshen with wash-ing-up, and he'll be expecting you about now," Snowfire reminded him. "Now you'll be able to talk to him—you might just go up and remind him of your promise and surprise him. There isn't anything about the Tayledras that Ayshen doesn't know—"

"—and there isn't anything that he isn't *dying* to gossip about—" Nightwind interjected wryly, with a tilt of her head.

"—so if there is anything you want to know, and you feel awk-ward about asking one of us, go ahead and ask him," Snowfire con-cluded, with a wink.

Darian gave a sigh of relief at that; there *were* things he wanted to know, but he'd felt uncomfortable about talking to Snowfire about them. It wasn't that Snowfire wasn't kind, and it wasn't as if the things he wanted to know were at all personal, it was just—well— they felt like stupid questions, and he was embarrassed to ask them of Snowfire. *I look bad enough, with him having to rescue me and all,* he thought. *I don't want him thinking I'm so dumb that I'm going to be nothing but a bother to him.*

"If you want to get back to Ayshen right now, just follow the path and only take right-hand turns," Nightwind added helpfully. "When you're done, well—by then, the rest of the scouts will have thought over what you've already told them, and I suspect someone will come fetch you for another round of questions. And *this* time, you won't feel as if they're talking over your head!"

Darian beamed at her. "Thank you!" he told her, both for the directions to Ayshen's kitchen, and for understanding how *horrid* it had been to hear all those people chattering away, being certain they were talking about him, and not being able to understand a word of it. Suddenly eager to find the gossip-hungry *hertasi* and barrage him with a deluge of questions, he shyly took his leave of both the adults. Feeling as if he had been freed from a leash, he sped off down the path, always taking the right-hand turns, until he found himself at his goal, only a little winded. The *hertasi*, who was mixing something in a large bowl, looked up at him in some surprise—probably because very few people ever ran anywhere in this tranquil-seeming place.

"Hello, Ayshen!" he said cheerfully, taking great pleasure in the way the *hertasi*'s eyes widened with surprise at his perfect Tayledras. "Here I am, just like I promised!"

"You and Tyrsell are in a conspiracy over the boy, I know it. The two of you agreed to do something with him," Snowfire said—trying not to sound *too* accusing—as soon as the boy had run off. "Just what have you two done to him? And don't try to play the innocent with me; no child who's just had his teacher go up in flames before his eyes and his entire village overrun by bloodthirsty barbarians can go running happily off to wash dishes!"

Darian had become cheerful—*too* cheerful—right after Tyrsell laid in the Tayledras language on his memory. Tyrsell was quite good enough to have meddled further with the boy's memory without Snowfire noticing. Snowfire had seen the change in the boy's behavior at once; he lost the haunted look that was in his eyes and started acting like a child on an adventure.

"Tyrsell has put a little 'forgetfulness loop' in his mind at my suggestion,'' Nightwind told him with her usual forthrightness. "Whenever he starts to get frightened, anxious or stressed, he will forget what he was getting upset about. He'll know that his mentor is dead, objectively, but when the memory of that fact starts to make him upset, he'll get distracted and then temporarily forget the fact. It's strictly a palliative, and it will go away in a few days, but we can't have a hysterical boy upsetting Starfall, you, and other key people while you're deciding what to do about this situation. Furthermore, as an Empath and the only Healer you have, *I* can't devote all my time to him.'' She looked him straight in the eye, as challenging as the *dyheli* had been. "I went to Tyrsell this morning before you saw him and suggested it. That was why he was so eager to volunteer his services.''

"I'd wondered,'' Snowfire growled, not at all happy with the way his opinions had been subverted.

"I didn't see a choice,'' she told him flatly, with what Wintersky called her "take no prisoners'' expression. "My only other course of action was to keep him sedated, and that would be very bad for him. This way, he has a chance to absorb the situation without thinking about it for a few days, *then* try and come to terms with it—gradually, instead of all at once. And by then, you all should know more about what's going on; you'll be able to tell him where his people are and what Valdemar is going to do about the attack. He'll be able to make some choices for himself with a reasonable amount of information, and we'll see how he's fitting in and what we're going to do with him.''

Snowfire knew he was going to have to accept whatever she told him she'd done—not only because it was already an accomplished fact, but because *he* was not a Healer and an Empath, and his opinions really didn't matter. However, having Nightwind make the decision was a bit more palatable than Tyrsell; Nightwind might primarily *treat* nonhumans, but she herself was human, and her reasoning came out of her human experience.

"All right,'' he said with resignation. "I can see why you decided the way you did, and this *is* better than keeping him drugged. And I know why you didn't ask me first, because I would have argued with you.''

"And last night, I was in no mood to *argue* with you; my intentions were in the other direction entirely.'' She grinned at him and fluttered her eyelashes coyly in a way that drew an unwilling laugh out of him. "As for the headache potion, that was all it was. Now, if you need to question him more about the attack—''

Snowfire interrupted her with a shake of his head. "I don't think so. What we'll need are descriptions of the village, where things are, at least for now. Kel and Hweel and I are going to do a little scouting there tonight, just to see who and what's still there."

She nodded. "Then there should be no problem; his memories of the village before the attack are going to be perfectly clear, just don't be surprised if he blanks out in describing the things he thinks are damaged. He'll probably completely forget the fact that the bridge was burned, for instance." She licked her lips and twisted a strand of hair around her index finger as she paused for a thought. "In fact, he's very likely to act and talk as if the whole town is *still* intact, so don't correct him."

"I won't. You say in his deeper thoughts he's still going to be aware of what happened, though?" At her nod, he sighed, and gazed out over the pool for a moment, collecting his thoughts. *If he's got it in his deeper memories, those are what usually come out in dreams.* "Well, we could be looking at some interrupted nights, if he starts having nightmares."

"If he does, we'll move him into the Bower, and I'll deal with it. He'll very likely have them, and in some ways that would be good; if he does, they will mean he's absorbing and coming to terms with the experience on the deeper level." She didn't seem at all adverse to having the boy in the "Bower," the half-cave in the rocky cliff where she had built isolated facilities for those who were sick or injured. Well, if she didn't mind having *her* sleep disturbed, Snowfire was not going to try to argue her out of it.

So he shrugged. "Once again—you are the expert; I am not. And much as I enjoy your company, I have a scout's meeting to gather—"

"So go gather it." She paused, resting a hand against the side of his face and making him look deeply into her eyes so he could not miss her sincerity and her regret. "*Kechara,* if I didn't have to balance a potentially dangerous, even explosive situation against this boy's needs, I wouldn't have made the decisions I have. But if I didn't also have his welfare in mind, I would have told you to pack him up and send him off with Wintersky and a couple of *dyheli* to the nearest large settlement. I think that for now at least, he will be better treated among us. Now, *I* must be off, too, so go find your scouts."

They parted, with Snowfire feeling a little better about Darian's welfare than he had been. When it came right down to it, the boy could not be in better hands.

*   *   *

It's been a long day, Snowfire thought, as he laced up his climbing boots by the light of the fire. *And it's going to be a long night.*

Darian was safely asleep, and so, most probably, were the current inhabitants of Errold's Grove. It was time for that little scouting run. *Little? Not so little. I've never run a sortie against an army before. But it's not as if I don't have the experience to carry it off.* Snowfire had been an active scout since he was a mere fourteen winters old, although he hadn't been permitted in the field against human intruders for the first four years. *So how much different can they be, I wonder, than a large bandit gang?*

Across the fire from him, Nightwind was getting Kelvren ready. Kelvren's eyes pinned with excitement, the pupils contracting to a mere nothing, then widening until there was nothing showing *but* pupil, then contracting again. In the firelight, the effect was particularly striking; his eyes looked as if they were flashing with a gilded light as his golden irises appeared and disappeared. Nightwind calmly tightened his harness at all points, checking his gear, making certain that the amplifying metal lacework-headband of the teleson set was properly in place under the feathers on his head, and that it wasn't going to distract him in any way. Kelvren's Mindspeech wasn't particularly strong, and this little bit of metal filigree that looked so much like one of his favorite ornaments would help him reach Snowfire without effort.

Snowfire was already outfitted for a nighttime sortie; his costume of soft blacks and grays was much like his daylight scouting gear except for color—or rather, lack of it. He had streaked his face with random stripes of black-and-gray paint, and before he braided it, he had dusted his hair with a charcoal-colored powder that would cling until washed out. He wore black gloves and soft, black boots made for climbing; his climbing staff was in its sheath on his back and his throwing-darts in a bandoleer across his chest. There was a knife at his belt and another in each boot, thin and incredibly strong rope with a grappling hook coiled in one pouch at his side, a strangling-wire in another, and a darker version of his leather arm-guard strapped in place over his clothing for Hweel to land on in case he needed to. He probably wouldn't; Snowfire intended to be up in the treetops, and there should be plenty of places for Hweel to land without choosing his arm.

A small herd of three *dyheli* waiting patiently at his elbow would carry him as far as the clearing where he'd discovered Darian, or farther if it seemed safe; that way he would leave no footprints. A herd of animals would leave tracks that were much less suspicious than a single animal. The plan called for the *dyheli* to wait for him at the clearing until he returned. Kel, of course, would fly, leaving no tracks at all.

"Think you're ready for this?" Nightwind whispered as she passed him, crossing to Kel's left side to continue her checks. He winked; he knew what she meant. *He* had made night sorties as a scout countless times, but this was Kelvren's first "offensive act of war." That was why the young gryphon was so excited; he was about to prove his mettle, and he could hardly wait to get into the air. Hweel, by contrast, was so utterly calm he seemed bored.

Kel was as well-trained as any Silver Gryphon ever turned out by the Kaled'a'in, and since Nightwind seemed completely confident in his abilities, Snowfire was prepared to be just as confident. After all, *she* had been a Silver for several years before Kel even began his training; she'd seen a great many gryphons wear that stylized badge, and she had once said that the Silver Gryphons had ways of weeding out the unsuitable a long time before they ever put on the badge and harness of a full Silver.

Nevertheless, Snowfire hoped that Kelvren wouldn't wear himself out with excitement before they ever got to Errold's Grove.

Snowfire gave his own equipment one last check, swung himself up onto the back of Sifyra, and turned to Kel. "Ready, partner?" he asked.

The gryphon gave a quick, eager nod. "Rrrready!" he replied. Waiting none too patiently for Snowfire's hand signal, he launched himself skyward, followed a moment later by Hweel. Snowfire's little group of Sifyra and two mares followed at a careful trot. *Dyheli* had much better night-vision than horses, but the dark shadows beneath the trees could easily hold unpleasant surprises; there was no point in risking broken legs or ankles.

There was another reason for a more leisurely pace—Snowfire rode bareback. Since Sifyra and the mares would pretend to be a set of wild grazers, it would not do to have something as obviously unnatural as a saddlepad strapped to his back. Not for the first time, Snowfire wished silently that *dyheli* could manage the same smooth gaits as Companions allegedly could. Like all *dyheli*, Sifyra had a prominent spine, and Snowfire expected to know the position and size of every vertebra in intimate detail before the ride was over. One of his fellow scouts had once described the *dyheli* as "backbones covered with hair, balanced on four springs," which was about as succinct a description as Snowfire had ever heard.

If they'd been able to travel at a walk instead of a trot, and if they hadn't been going into dangerous territory, the ride would have been stunningly beautiful. As impressive as these woods were by day, at night they were far lovelier, at least in Snowfire's opinion. Of course, he could have been biased in that direction by flying an owl.

The moon was at its full and well up, so soft, silvery shafts of light pierced the canopy and illuminated patches of ground all around him. The night was anything but still; insects and frogs called or sang, and an occasional bird pierced the forest with its call, harsh or sweet. Other birds high overhead called complainingly as their sleep was disturbed, and bats flitted like bits of the darkness itself in and out of the shafts of moonlight, chasing the moths drawn to dance there.

Snowfire was also aware of two other minds linked with his own— the ever-present dignity of Hweel, and the unfamiliar exuberance of Kel.

:We're waiting for you at the clearing,: Kel Sent back, and Snow-fire sensed that he and Hweel were perched side by side in the concealing boughs of a great tree on the farther side. :There's no sign of any trouble, or any guards.:

Hweel confirmed Kel's observation without words, turning his head and peering through the darkness so that Snowfire could see for himself. It was very strange to look through the owl's eyes; from Hweel's point of view the place was as brightly-lit as daylight, although the colors were very faded. The bondbird's eyes were so much keener than a human's that Hweel had no trouble focusing on tiny details far below him on the ground. The barbarians had packed up their two dead and left no real traces of the fight behind, except for a bit of disturbed rock and scuffed earth.

Hweel's keen sight and hearing alerted him to the smallest movements and faintest of sounds, even so small as a rat or a mouse would make, so if there had been anyone left as a sentry out here, Hweel would have spotted him without any trouble. So, the barbarians had not posted watchers out this far from the village. Did that mean they had simply looted it and left?

I don't think so; there wasn't enough there to loot. I think they had some other purpose in coming there, and that Starfall is right about what that purpose is. They're here for power, and perhaps to establish a stronghold here on the border of Valdemar.

Motive was irrelevant right now, though; he was out here to learn facts, not speculate on motive. :Go farther in,: he told Hweel. :Go in until you've spotted a sentry, then come back.: Here was another advantage of flying an owl; sentries would neither hear nor see him, and that meant Hweel was never a target in night-stalks. That gave him a degree of security that those who flew other birds didn't have.

Hweel took off obediently. Snowfire stopped Kel before he could follow. *:Wait for Hweel to come back; I want to get as near as I safely can before I take to the trees. It might be easy for you two to flit about, but I'm going to have to work to get in as far as the first sentry.:*

Hweel returned in fairly short order, and as Sifyra paced swiftly through the trees, Snowfire let the *dyheli* set their own path as he concentrated on what Hweel had seen.

He directed Hweel and Kel to move nearer to the village, and gave Sifyra the landmarks to look for just as they came to the edge of the rock-strewn clearing. It seemed to his impatient soul to take forever to reach the tree where Hweel and Kel waited, and he knew it seemed like twice that to them. *They* were ready to go, and Kel probably felt that they hardly needed him.

Well, that's where those who are inexperienced differ from old hands. I'm Kel's backup, whether or not he thinks he needs one.

He pulled out his climbing staff as Sifyra approached the giant trunk, and swung the bark-hook at the body of the trunk with his left hand as Sifyra actually came alongside. The hook bit solidly into the bark of the trunk, and he pulled himself up and off Sifyra's back and onto the rough bark of the tree with his one good arm. As his feet cleared Sifyra's back, he sank his right palm-cleat into the bark and used the rough soles of his climbing boots to further brace himself in place. As soon as he had a palm grip and secure footing, he swung the bark-hook up for his next step, and worked his way up the trunk like a tree-hare, and nearly as fast. Because he had chosen a tree with rough bark, he was able to keep most of his weight on his legs rather than his arms, but by the time he got to where the others were perched, his hair was damp with sweat and his muscles burning with fatigue.

Kel and Hweel were a pair of oddly-shaped shadows crouched together amid the warm semidarkness here in the boughs. The other two were not *too* impatient when he reached their bough, a branch as broad as a highway and as easy to walk on. By that time, Sifyra and the mares had found a patch of grass and were pretending to graze on it, with one wary eye out for hunters. "Take me to where the first sentry is, and I'll stop there," he told the other two. "Then you can go on; if something goes wrong for you and you can't fly, I can take out the sentry before he knows there's anything going on, and leave a hole in the line."

Kel nodded. "That isss a good plan," he acknowledged, with a little surprise in his voice. "I had not thought of having to passs ssssentrrriesss on the grrrround." Hweel just roused his feathers, ready to be off. This time Kel dropped off the bough first, but Hweel, being smaller and more maneuverable among the branches, was leading the gryphon before the latter had taken more than two wing-strokes.

Hweel was actually guiding his bondmate as much as the gryphon. Now Snowfire followed them by "walking the tree-road," balancing along the branches, and moving from tree to tree by following Hweel to the intersections of branches and jumping from one to the next with the aid of either his grappling hook and rope, or his climbing staff. It was easy enough to follow the boughs, and when he needed a better look at a crossing, he examined it through Hweel's eyes. This, in many ways, was the part of his duties that Snowfire lived for. There was something about doing all this in near-darkness, with the scent of bark and leaves all about him, the sounds of insects and frogs far below, that made all of his senses come alive. He felt as if he could see with his skin, and as he concentrated on the placement of each footstep, it seemed as if he and the forest were a single living entity.

He had been doing this since he was old enough to walk, as had most Tayledras, and he didn't even think about the risks anymore, though occasionally Kel would pause and perch to watch him, the gryphon's mind fairly radiating pleasure and surprise. This was just something Tayledras *did*, and it was largely how they were able to travel undetected through the forest. It was hard work, certainly, and required a great deal of planning and concentration, more so since he had only one "good" arm, but he was never afraid, any more than he was when walking on the ground. At this level in the canopy, branches tended to intersect when they were about as big around as his waist; they were still broad and easy to walk on, with very little sway. Higher up—well, things would have been more of a challenge.

He was pleased that he detected the movement of a sentry on the ground below only a little later than Hweel did; he slowed at that moment, and crept forward, making no noise at all, until he reached the trunk of the tree he was in. Then he settled down with his back to the trunk to wait, concealed from detection from below by the bulk of the branch.

Not that any barbarian would think to watch the tree canopy, even if he heard a noise above him.

Now Hweel and Kel went on; as soon as Snowfire was settled in place, he closed his eyes and opened his senses to the owl, concentrating most of his attention on what the bondbird heard and saw.

For a little while, that consisted mostly of branches going past, with occasional backward glimpses to make certain Kel was following. But then, the growth up ahead vanished, and Hweel swooped up to land on a branch overhanging open fields. A moment later, Kel landed beside him, and the two of them looked down at the village of Errold's Grove.

There seemed to be very little damage; only a single house, a couple of barns, and a handful of sheds were burned, although those had been allowed to burn to the ground and there was nothing left of them but piles of blackened rubble with a timber or two sticking out of the ashes. The bridge, amazingly enough, was still there—at a single place in the middle, the timbers of the floor had been replaced with a patch of newer wood, obvious because it shone whitely in the moonlight. Evidently the fire that Justyn had called had been put out before the bridge suffered much permanent damage. There was no other sign of conflict.

Hweel could not smell the remnants of smoke from the burned-out buildings, for owls had no sense of smell, but he could taste it in the back of his throat, and he sneezed as it irritated his nostrils. Snowfire felt his own nose itch in sympathy.

There were a *lot* of horses in makeshift enclosures at one side of the town. The houses were dark, not a single light showing anywhere, and from the chimneys, a little smoke trailed out, showing that the fires were banked until morning. There were no tents, no sleeping forms in bedrolls out in the open. However, there were more of those makeshift enclosures everywhere, and they were full of livestock. Evidently the barbarians were all sleeping in houses, barns, and sheds, displacing the animals into the open. Obviously they didn't care if the livestock broke loose or strayed during the night, probably because those animals were all destined for the cookpot sooner or later. To the conquerers of Errold's Grove, those animals represented a resource for the present, not the future.

The house nearest them looked as if it might have been Justyn's cottage. Unlike the rest, it had no cottage-garden, and it seemed to match what Darian had told them about the place.

:There's something odd over there—: Kel swooped ahead of Hweel, intent on getting a closer look at whatever it was that he'd spotted.

That was when the two—*things*—crawled out from an airspace

beneath the very house at the edge of the village that Snowfire had been examining through Hweel's eyes.

:Wyrsa!: Snowfire warned Kel—but they weren't *wyrsa*, or not exactly. They had a similar look to them—as if someone had crossed a dog with a serpent, getting something with a hound-shaped body, scaled skin, with the head a melding of viper and canine with sulfur-yellow eyes and fangs. But the *wyrsa* Snowfire knew had the look of emaciated greyhounds, whereas these two—

Well, the big one was the size of a pony and had the blocky, muscular look of a mastiff, and the little one was the size and general configuration of a terrier. Whatever they were, they didn't match the *wyrsa* that Snowfire was familiar with.

Furthermore, they seemed to know exactly where Kel was.

The little one started to make a kind of high-pitched keening sound as it followed Kel's flight, eyes gazing intently. It trotted after the gryphon, the bigger creature trailing behind, the smaller continuing to emit the whining keen. With every passing moment the sound grew louder, and it would not be too long before the creature's masters heard it and came to see what the matter was.

Kel looked down at the two creatures with some alarm, and ducked into the forest canopy to try and lose them. *:If I hide from them, they'll probably lose interest in me and go away,:* he told Snowfire, coming to a soft landing on a massive branch screened from view from below by foliage. Hweel swerved to follow them, coming down from above Kel's perch. *:They can't possibly smell me, the wind's not in their favor, it's in mine. Can* wyrsa *follow a scent?:*

Snowfire watched them trotting along, with the little one still making that annoying, whiny noise. *:Evidently no one told them that they're not supposed to be able to find you,:* he suggested, as the two creatures broke into a lope and wound up directly beneath Kel, looking up at him. *:And yes,* wyrsa *can follow a scent trail very well indeed.:*

Kel suddenly slammed his shields up, locking Snowfire out of his mind with no warning whatsoever, and flung himself off the branch in a steep dive.

Snowfire slipped quickly into Hweel's head, acutely aware of how helpless he was to stop the gryphon—and he didn't even know what Kel planned to do!

Assuming he even had a plan—

Through Hweel's eyes, he saw the gryphon burst through the foliage at an angle so steep it looked as if Kel was falling. It took the two creatures below him completely by surprise, too—they both froze where they were for an instant, and that was an instant too long.

At the last possible second, the little one broke and ran, leaving the bigger one to stand its ground. That was the worst thing it could have done; it gave Kel the chance for a tail-chase, and the gryphon snapped open his wings so abruptly that Snowfire winced, knowing how much the move would hurt. Kel had made the classic aerial maneuver of trading height for speed; fast as the little monster was (and it was greyhound-quick), Kel was faster.

He hit it with outstretched talons and bound to it, bringing it to the ground and pulling it to his beak; before it could turn its own teeth or claws on him, Kel had snapped its neck, and just to make sure it was dead, gave it a doglike shake.

By now the bigger creature was charging Kel from behind, but this time Snowfire *could* do something; he had already directed Hweel to attack the bigger creature's head and eyes. Even if those scales armored it, the eyes would still be vulnerable, and it would stop to protect them.

Hweel went into a dive of his own, intending to make a raking pass from behind. He hit the creature's head just as it had covered about half the distance between the tree and Kel. Hweel's talons scraped across the scales without penetrating, but the silent and unexpected attack from behind disoriented the creature and it stopped, whirling, to face whatever had struck it.

But of course, Hweel was already out of reach, and his attack had given Kel a chance to recover. The gryphon launched into the air, dangling the body of the smaller creature from his foreclaws, pumping his wings laboriously for a few moments, then going into a relatively shallow glide beneath the branches.

The larger creature snarled with rage, and followed; Hweel followed it, flying just above the lower branches.

Kel glanced back over his shoulder to make sure the monster was still following him. When it began to lag a little, he dropped lower and slowed a bit, dangling the body of the little creature tauntingly just out of reach. That seemed to drive the big one insane with fury, and it would redouble its efforts to reach him.

Now Kel opened his shields just a little, and Snowfire seized the advantage. :*Just what do you think you're doing?*: he demanded, trying *not* to project the thought with the edge of incipient hysteria that he certainly *felt*.

:*Leading the Big Dog away so I can kill it quietly,*: Kel replied, sounding amazingly cool.

:I don't suppose anyone told you that wyrsa *have poisonous fangs and claws, did they?:* he asked, just before Kel slammed his shields shut again, locking him out. He tried not to curse with frustration.

At least I got the warning in, he consoled himself, and continued to watch through Hweel's eyes. He figured that Kel would repeat the same dive and tail chase he'd used to kill the "Little Dog"; he didn't expect what Kel actually did, and neither did the "Big Dog."

Kel suddenly slowed and went for height again, but at the top of his upward-reaching arc, he flung the body of the "Little Dog" at the "Big Dog" with all of his strength.

Snowfire had forgotten that the structure of the gryphon's forelegs actually allowed him to throw things if he chose, and certainly the "Big Dog" hadn't anticipated any such thing. The carcass hit the larger animal dead-on, and sent it tumbling end-over-end, and *then* Kel went into a dive.

If he'd stayed on the ground to meet it, the fight would have been equal, with Kel having the advantage of size, but the "Big Dog" having the advantage of speed and poison. But Kel had no intention of getting within reach of those fangs and claws; he made dive after raking dive, pounding the thing with fisted talons that sent its head into the forest floor, and raking it with open talons with enough speed behind him to penetrate even the tough scales that protected it.

Dive after dive he made, choosing to rake or strike based on what the monster itself was doing and how well it had recovered from the previous hit. Snowfire held his breath and even the normally stoic Hweel was excited, gripping the bough he had chosen with enough power to drive the talons through the bark and deep into the wood.

It began to seem as if the thing was indestructible; it had taken a dozen blows that would have shattered the skull of a lesser creature, and as many raking strikes that left furrows along its head and back. *Wyrsa* were known to be tough, but this monster was tougher than any *wyrsa* that Snowfire had ever fought. Now Snowfire saw the wisdom of leading it away; had this combat taken place anywhere near the village, Kel would have had an unwelcome audience in very short order.

What's he doing? Snowfire wondered, fretting. It was obvious to him that Kel had a plan, but what was it? Surely the gryphon could see for himself that his worst blows just weren't having the effect he wanted!

In fact, the monster had worked itself into the partial shelter of a bush, and in a moment, Kel wouldn't be able to reach it at all.

Abruptly Kel did a wingover and another steep dive, heading deliberately *into* the bush! Snowfire flung out a hand and stifled a cry of dismay.

Kel crashed into the bush—and brought it down *on top of* the creature, pinning it completely to the ground with so many branches that it was unable to move at all!

Kel stood up, still atop the bush, holding it and the creature pinned beneath it to the ground. Then, in a manner that was almost insulting, it was so casual, he began breaking twigs and branches with his beak until he exposed the nape of the creature's neck. He contemplated it for a moment, as if choosing exactly the right place. Then his head darted forward savagely, and he bit through scales, hide, and ultimately, spine, sawing with his beak until the spine was completely severed.

He stood atop the beast still, until its final convulsions were over. It took a very long time.

Finally the body went flaccid, and Kel cautiously opened his shields again.

:I'm sorry,: he said apologetically, but behind the veneer of apology was a seething cauldron of satisfied bloodlust, the euphoria of conquest, the thrill of victory. *:There is an old lesson of Tadrith Wyrsabane's first combat with a litter of Changed* wyrsa, *that could sense and eat magic. When these followed me, I suspected that they were following the "scent" of magic, and I didn't want to give them a chance to get any farther than just the scent.:*

:Apology accepted,: Snowfire replied immediately. *:And congratulations; you were truly magnificent!:*

:I was, wasn't I?: The reply was made with as much wonder as pride, and Snowfire chuckled under his breath. *:Well, if Hweel could come help carry the body of the Little Dog, I can take the Big Dog, and we can drop them somewhere that they'll never be found. Is* wyrsa *meat poisonous?:*

:Not that I know of,: Snowfire told him after a moment of thought. *:I never saw dead scavengers around the carcasses, anyway.:*

:Then we'll dump them in a crotch up in the canopy,: Kel decided immediately. *:Their masters will never find even a bone, then, and it will give the scavenger-birds a good meal or two.:*

So that was what they did, he and Hweel laboring heavily up into the canopy until they were well screened from the ground, leaving the two bodies wedged tightly into forks in neighboring trees. Perhaps eventually bones would fall down, but not until every scrap of flesh had been picked away or eaten by insects and larvae, and by then the matter of their masters should have been settled.

Afterward, both owl and gryphon rested while they conferred with Snowfire.

:I honestly didn't see anything that would make me think there were still any villagers there,: Kel told the Tayledras, as he cleaned the monsters' blood fastidiously from beak and talons. *:I will grant you, we weren't overhead long, but I can't imagine where they would put the villagers if there were as many fighters as the boy thought.:*

Snowfire thought back on the brief look that he'd had through Hweel's eyes, and tended to agree. *:We know they've fixed the bridge, and that most of the buildings are still intact; we know that the enemy is still in possession of the place because of all the horses we saw. That's really what we came to find out. If you want to go back, I'm certainly ready.:*

Kel sighed, and spread wings which were probably starting to ache. He'd put his flying muscles through a great deal of abuse, and just about now was when they would start to complain. *:I think we ought,:* he replied, trying to sound reluctant. *:I hate to admit it, but I'm not good for much more.:*

:Oh, I think you could rise to the occasion if you had to,: Snowfire said encouragingly. *:But I see no reason why you should have to. You were mighty enough tonight. Let's go home.:*

Very well,: Kel replied, and took off—carefully—gaining altitude until he was above the treetops.

Snowfire began the slower process of making his way toward the clearing where the *dyheli* waited.

But Kelvren could not contain his pleasure in silence. *:You know, I really was* good *tonight. Wasn't I?:*

Snowfire sensed a certain wonder behind the boast, and smiled. *:Definitely,:* he replied with warmth, too busy picking his way through the canopy to give a more elaborate reply.

But Kel didn't seem to mind; he was still intoxicated with success—and mostly talking to himself. *:I was,:* Kel sighed with content. *:I really was. . . . :*

The Invaders' Mage

Six

Snowfire kept having to hide his smile the next day when he encountered Kel; the young gryphon was *so* pleased with himself—not in any truly vain way, but simply full of joy and astonishment at his own daring deeds. He had probably been a great deal less sure of himself at the time than he had pretended. In fact, he reminded Snowfire of a certain young Tayledras after *his* first successful mission, some few years ago. It was odd how certain things transcended the boundaries of species.

Nightwind, of course, had made a great fuss over Kel; over both of them, actually, but she was more demonstrative with Kel. So when, after greeting the gryphon, he'd gone to her to ask her to make sure he hadn't done any damage to himself, he also asked her why she'd been so effusive.

"I was beginning to think you were being a little too enthusiastic," he told her. "You know, the way doting mothers make a great fuss over a child who's done something perfectly ordinary? I don't mean to try to teach you your job, but Kel's old enough to see through that sort of thing."

"Gryphons, especially young ones like Kel, are a lot more fragile than you'd think," she told Snowfire, as she checked his arm wound and rewrapped it. "They need a great deal of encouragement before they become secure in making their own judgments. It's a fledging sort of thing; they really go through several stages of fledging, and the most critical is in learning to trust their training and make their own decisions instead of waiting for orders from someone else." She sealed down the end of the bandage with a firm finger. "He really *was* very clever to remember Tadrith Wyrsabane, and the Changed creatures he encountered. I can promise you that not one in a dozen of the gryphons I've tended would remember a tale that old. Tadrith is ancient history, and the young ones tend to dismiss history out of hand.''

Snowfire thanked her with a smile, then stretched out along the rock rimming the larger pool to soak up the sun. That was *his* prescription for muscles aching from his unbalanced climbing last night. ''I think he may be trying to model himself off this Tadrith,'' he suggested. ''It's just a thought, but the way he Mindspoke the name suggested something of the sort to me last night.''

Nightwind unwound her hair from the knot at the back of her head, and shook it free; it fell in rippling waves to her waist. ''I can certainly think of worse examples, and gryphons that have tried to follow them. Well, for one thing, trying to model himself off Skandranon would be a very bad thing to do. We don't have *any* stories of Skandranon as a young, rash, and fallible gryphon, only those in which Skandranon succeeds beyond anyone's wildest dreams and pulls off another miraculous, heroic coup. By this time there is so much myth associated with the Black Gryphon that trying to emulate him would be impossible, and failing would be devastating. No, he could do a lot worse than try to copy Tadrith Wyrsabane; by the time Tadrith was growing up, White Gryphon was well established, and we have plenty of tales about how difficult it was for him to make a name for himself in his father's shadow.''

Snowfire rolled over on his stomach, and she began working on his back muscles without his having to ask. He sighed with content— and occasionally grunted in pain—as her hands worked out knots and sore spots. He decided to change the subject—he really wasn't in the mood to discuss gryphonic myth. ''About those little monsters—''

''Yip Dog and Attack Dog?'' she said; the terms were so strange he wasn't certain he'd heard her correctly, and craned his head around to give her a puzzled look. She giggled at his expression. ''That's what I thought of when Kel described them to me. The little one was like the small dogs one of the Haileigh peoples created. They've made pampered, spoiled pets out of a breed that was supposed to be alarm-dogs; very small, very fast, *very* annoying. When they see a stranger, they swarm him, yipping; we call them Yip Dogs, and when I reminded Kel of them, he agreed that the smaller creature was exactly like a Yip Dog.''

''Huh. Good enough name for it,'' he replied. ''So you think this Yip Dog was meant to raise alarms?''

''I'm sure of it—and I'm sure Kel was right. From his description, it detected the aura of magic that is a part of every gryphon." She sounded quite positive, and after a moment of thought, Snowfire was inclined to agree tentatively with that conclusion. He couldn't think of any other reason why it would have been able to find Kel in the heavy cover of the forest canopy.

"Do you think, perhaps, that it was intended to raise an alarm against people screening themselves magically, or using magic to disable sentries? Or was it set to catch mages trying to use magic to get past magical alarms?" he asked curiously.

"I can't think of a better reason to have them," she told him, as she bore down hard on the small of his back. "After all, *they* don't know that the mage-storms are over, and a mage-storm could disable a magical protection. Animals, on the other hand, sleep more lightly than humans, and they aren't disabled when mage-energy is disrupted. Fortunately, Kel followed his initial impulse, which was to go away from the place the Yip Dog was guarding. Otherwise, I think the whining might have escalated to something a lot louder. That's what the real Yip Dogs do; if you stay near what they consider to be their territory, or worse, try to approach it, they get positively hysterical."

"And the other—obviously the term *Attack Dog* suits it." Snowfire rested his chin on his folded hands to keep it off the hard rock beneath him. "In fact, that's probably why they were paired. If whatever the Yip Dog was warning about kept coming, the Attack Dog was to hold it where it was until the masters came." He grinned a little. "It must have been awfully puzzled about how to get at Kel!"

"Fortunately for us, the masters didn't consider a sortie by air." She kneaded his shoulders vigorously and he grunted. "Does that hurt?"

"Yes, but don't stop. No, you're right about that. They must not know there are Tayledras anywhere about, and they've never encountered Kaled'a'in before. All I can say is, it's a good thing we didn't have any human scouts on this one." The more he thought about it, the more grateful he was. Tayledras scouts would have sent birds in, seen nothing to worry about, and might perhaps have been tempted to come down out of the trees and go in afoot to recconoiter. They would *never* have been able to escape the fast-moving monsters—and only an eye-shot would have killed the beasts, given the way that Hweel's talons just skidded off the scales.

"The Yip Dog was probably alerted by physical attributes such as scent and sound as well as by magic," she agreed. "It wouldn't be very bright to have them sound alarms only for the presence of magic.''

I'm just glad there were only two of them. ''I saw them through Hweel's eyes, and the things *did* look like *wyrsa*,'' he told her, wondering if she had any more insights gleaned out of Kaled'a'in history for him. ''Or rather, it looked as if their ancestors could have been *wyrsa*. Now, that triggered a dream last night of all kinds of creatures that looked as if they also could have been bred from *wyrsa*, and that made me wonder when I woke up this morning if the being that Darian described as a 'demon' and the creature it was riding could have had *wyrsa* ancestors.'' He cocked an eye back at her.

''That must have been one hell of a dream,'' she observed. ''I'm glad *I* didn't share it. Still.'' She paused to work on a particularly bad knot in his neck, and he clenched his teeth to keep from yelping. ''The story says that the *wyrsa* Tadrith fought were definitely intelligent. And there is no reason whatsoever that there couldn't have been more of them created somewhere else. Or at least, more *wyrsa* Changed in different ways. The beasts aren't exactly stupid, so it's not that great a jump to significant intelligence.''

''Intelligence enough to realize that it would be to the monster's advantage to cooperate with a human?'' he hazarded. ''And given that we have a mage with these barbarians who, we assume, already knows how to make Changechildren—'' He took a deep breath as she let up on his shoulders a bit. ''You see where this is going.''

''Yes, and I don't like it. But it does make it all the more imperative that we concentrate on keeping Starfall safe rather than messing about with these people and alerting them to the fact that we're here.'' He felt her hands starting to tremble. Was the imperturbable Nightwind actually afraid?

She should be. Intelligent, humanlike versions of wyrsa! *That is a truly frightening thought.*

''How did Darian sleep last night?'' she asked, abruptly changing the subject herself.

''Wintersky says he had a couple of nightmares, but nothing that even woke him. That's enough, thanks.'' He rolled back over and let the sun work on his chest muscles. ''I don't know what tonight will bring, but so far—I'm going to assume that minor nightmares are good, but the ones that send him out of sleep screaming in hysterics are bad?''

''As a general rule; we don't want him assimilating too much, too fast.'' She stretched herself out on the rock beside him ''Ah, that feels good. He'll probably have a hysterical one in a few nights, though. That is, if what Tyrsell did fades out at the rate I think it will. It might go more quickly; he's a boy with a strong will, and that's likely to make him fight what we put in place."

Snowfire sighed. "Wonderful. Well, if he gets too hysterical for me to handle, remember your promise."

She laughed. "Big, brave Tayledras warrior worried about a little boy's nightmares?"

"Big, brave Tayledras warrior needs his sleep, or he isn't going to be much good at protecting annoying little Kaled'a'in *trondi'irn*," he growled, cracking open an eye to see which side of her was uppermost, and smacking her on the rump when he had a target.

That, of course, led to her rolling him into the water, and him pulling her in, and a conversation that had nothing whatsoever to do with Darian, Kelvren, or *wyrsa*.

Darian woke screaming from a nightmare of fire, to find a sleepy, yawning Snowfire kneeling at his pallet, shaking him gently. "Easy, Darian," the Hawkbrother was saying, as if he had been saying the words over and over for some time. "It's all right; you're just dreaming. Wake up, little brother—"

There was a lot of light around; where was it coming from? "I'm—awake," Darian said, feeling dazed and confused, and still full of a sourceless grief and fear. "I'm awake—"

"Good." Snowfire smiled, but he had to put up a hand to cover his mouth as it turned into a yawn. That was when Darian saw the source of the illumination, after Snowfire moved. There was a very dim globe of light hovering just at Snowfire's shoulder, and Darian stared at it, distracted for a moment. It startled him, but Snowfire didn't act as if it was something strange.

"What's that?" he asked, pointing to it.

"My mage-light," the Hawkbrother replied casually, as if he conjured such things all the time. Perhaps he did—and Darian just hadn't been awake at the right time to see them. He had been so exhausted these last couple of days that he went to sleep almost as soon as the sun went down. "Would you like it a little brighter?" A heartbeat later, the glow intensified a measurable degree.

"You can make those?" he said, staring at it. "Really? Justyn couldn't—"

Then all at once, as the sound of his own voice screaming Justyn's name echoed in his memory, his fear and grief had a source; his throat closed up, and he fought back tears. A man shouldn't cry; tears were useless. They hadn't brought back his parents, had they? "Justyn's dead, isn't he?'' he whispered, closing his eyes to hide the pain. "He's really dead."

"Yes, little brother, he is,'' Snowfire replied quietly, with an odd inflection in his voice. Darian opened his eyes, to see the Hawk-brother looking down at him with—what? Pity? Understanding? He couldn't tell; he hadn't seen anyone in Errold's Grove wearing either expression around him.

Just then, over on the other side of the hut, Wintersky snorted in his sleep, turned over, and mumbled. That seemed to make up Snow-fire's mind about something.

"Here," he said, getting to his feet, and holding out his hand. "We shouldn't wake Wintersky, and I don't think you'll be getting back to sleep soon, so let's go for a walk."

Darian hesitantly accepted the outstretched hand; Snowfire pulled him to his feet, then turned toward Hweel's perch and held out his arm to the huge owl. He wasn't wearing his arm-guard, and Darian gasped and winced as Hweel stepped onto the bare flesh—but the owl barely closed his feet around the arm and half-spread his wings to keep his balance instead of maintaining it by gripping the arm.

Snowfire turned to give him a reassuring smile. "Remember, Hweel isn't an ordinary owl; I'm only going to take him outside to let him step up onto the roof. He can be very soft-footed when he needs to be for me."

Yes, but if he gets unbalanced and can't save himself, he may forget what's under those talons— Mindful of that possibility, Darian stepped in front of Snowfire and held the curtain of vines aside so that the Hawkbrother wouldn't have to juggle vines and owl at the same time. With a nod of thanks, Snowfire stepped out into the night, with the mage-light trailing at his shoulder. Darian followed him.

Once outside, Snowfire raised his arm just enough that Hweel could move onto the end of an exposed roof-beam. Hweel stepped off his arm carefully, settled his feathers, looked all around, in that bizarre way only owls could. His head went nearly all the way around, then he settled on a direction, crouched down, and pushed off, flapping hard, vanishing silently into the darkness. Snowfire turned, just as silently, and after a backward glance at Darian, walked slowly along the path.

After a breath of hesitation, Darian caught up with him. Wintersky had given him what he called "sleeping clothes"—that was a new idea to Darian, who generally slept in that day's shirt and put on a clean one in the morning, but he'd obediently changed into the odd garments every night. He saw now that Snowfire wore very similar clothing; a draped, pullover shirt of some light, loosely-woven, cool material, and drawstring trousers gathered at the ankle made of the same stuff. Darian felt a little like a ghost, walking barefoot through the sleeping camp in the pale garments.

Ghosts . . . how many ghosts haunted Errold's Grove now? One, at least. Or would Justyn have stayed to haunt the place?

"What are you thinking?" Snowfire asked quietly, hardly above a whisper.

"I was thinking—about Justyn," he replied, feeling sorrow again rise to close his throat.

"I think that he must have been a very good and brave man," came the quiet reply. "People of his sort do not need to linger, haunting their old homes; ghosts are those who left things undone, and I cannot think he left anything undone that truly needed doing."

"Where—" He couldn't manage anything more.

But Snowfire must have guessed his question. "Having had no *personal* experience of one who has gone, I cannot give you firsthand evidence," he replied, as one hand somehow came to rest on Darian's shoulder as a comforting weight. "But—well, I know enough folk who *have*, whose word I trust, to make me certain that we do not simply cease to be. But as for the nature of the path he took, the faith we Tayledras profess tells us that each path is different, according to the belief and the nature of the one who takes it." He paused. "I am not certain what your people believe, but would you care to hear what one who had been a Herald supposedly told one of my people?"

"I—yes," Darian said, after a moment. *One who had been a Herald? But Heralds don't quit being Heralds, so—*

"He said, or so I was told," Snowfire replied, interrupting Darian's thoughts, "that when a Herald dies, he is given three choices. One is that he may return again as a Herald-to-be, the second that he return as a Companion, and the third is that he have some time in a place where all his desires are granted. I suspect that your teacher has been given the same choices."

Darian blinked as his eyes blurred, and felt tears coursing down his cheeks. "I hope—I hope whatever he picked, he got a *lot* of magic!" he choked.

Snowfire's hand closed briefly on his shoulder. "I think that he must," the Hawkbrother replied. "In fact, I cannot imagine anything else."

That was too much for Darian, and he lost his last shreds of control. He stumbled, and started to sob, and found Snowfire holding him just the same way as his father used to when some childish grief overcame him. Darian forgot that he was supposed to be a man, forgot that men didn't cry—forgot everything except that he had failed to help Justyn, he had failed to help his father and mother, and now they were all dead and he was utterly alone.

He cried silently as he had learned to do since his parents' death, sobs shaking his frame, leaning on Snowfire, who simply held him and rocked a little from side to side, saying nothing. And only when the worst of his terrible grief had passed, did it dawn dimly on him that he really wasn't alone after all. . . .

Finally, there were no more tears left, and Snowfire let him go at the exact instant when he thought of pulling away, more than a little embarrassed.

"Don't be ashamed for allowing yourself to feel, little brother," came the quiet words. "You should rather feel sorry for those who do not. They are either cripples—or very sick in soul."

As he stared at the Hawkbrother in astonishment, Snowfire patted his shoulder. "I think that a midnight swim might be a good thing for both of us," he said, and gave Darian a gentle push to start him moving again.

Darian was in a bit of a daze, and it seemed as if they only took a few steps farther before they came to the two ponds, their water reflecting the stars and a sliver of moon above them. Snowfire simply stripped off his garments and plunged in; after a moment of hesitation, Darian copied his example.

He had expected the water to feel cold, but he had been standing in the night air long enough that it was only pleasantly cool. He swam back and forth on his back, staring up at the stars, letting his mind empty of everything. He didn't stop until his arms and legs were tired and he was beginning to feel a little waterlogged. Only then did he stop to tread water, and saw Snowfire was back on the bank, putting on his clothing, the mage-light still hovering near him, but much brighter now.

He paddled back to the same place, and looked up at a towel being held out for him to take. He dried himself off, and started to look around for his discarded clothing, but it wasn't where he'd left it. Quickly, he wrapped the towel around his waist, wondering what had happened to it, when Snowfire noticed his confusion and pointed. There, neatly folded on a rock, was a fresh set of garments.

"*Hertasi,*" was all Snowfire said, as he turned his attention to carefully braiding his long hair. Quickly, Darian slipped into the clean clothes, and used the towel on his own hair to cover his uncertainty about what to do or say next.

"The sense of loss never leaves, little brother," Snowfire said in a perfectly normal tone of voice. "But it does grow less over time, as long as you permit yourself to feel. If you bottle it inside, it only eats at you, until you are hollow and full of nothing but grief."

"How do *you* know?" Darian blurted, feeling unaccountably angry—then he could have beaten his head against a tree for snapping at Snowfire so.

But Snowfire didn't snap back; he just finished braiding his hair and looked at Darian quizzically. "Who told you that Tayledras are immortal?" he asked. "Whoever he was, he was misinformed."

Darian hung his head, his cheeks burning. "I'm sorry," he mumbled. "I didn't mean. . . ."

"You didn't *think*," Snowfire corrected, with a kindly tone in his voice. "And given the hour and the circumstances, I can hardly fault you. You are tired, in every way. Much longer, and I will be snapping in an ill-tempered snarl myself."

Darian flushed even hotter, if that was possible. "I can't imagine *you* ever doing anything wrong!" he stammered.

To his surprise, Snowfire chuckled. "Oh, Darian, do not *ever* allow Nightwind to hear you, or she will fill your ears with the myriad ways and times in which I have transgressed!" He rolled his eyes skyward. "I cannot even tell you which is worse—that she never forgets, or that she is right far too often—or at least, thinks that she is!"

To his surprise, Darian found himself smiling a little, for he had certainly heard the men of Errold's Grove making the same complaints in the "tavern." "I guess all ladies are like that. The ones at home—"

He stopped in midsentence. There *wasn't* any "home" anymore. And as for the men who frequented the tavern, he had no idea where they were or what had happened to them. Were they even still alive? Shouldn't he be getting help for them? What was he thinking of, lolling about in ponds like this, when he should be helping the people of Errold's Grove? How had he managed to forget the rest of his people?

"What's the matter?" Snowfire asked, breaking into his silence.

"I should—what am I still doing here?" he asked, feeling a frantic urge to do *something*, and not knowing what he could do. He shifted his weight from one foot to the other in a nervous dance. "I've got to go somewhere, got to get help. Why am I still here? I should be out there, trying to get somebody to help us, not here, enjoying myself!"

Before he could yield to that urge and just run off into the darkness, Snowfire seized his elbow, and somehow the mere touch calmed him. "Darian, listen to me, and please believe me," the Hawkbrother said urgently. "Hweel and Kel and I have been to your village, the second night after you came to us—we saw no signs that your people had been killed, and none that they had been captured either. We are fairly sure they must have escaped completely. You can be at ease, for it seems likely that they have already found help!"

"But you're not *completely* sure?" Darian asked, wanting to believe, and not sure that he dared to. "You think they're all right, but you—"

"I could not be *completely* sure without going into the village and looking into all the houses," Snowfire interrupted, and added, "I think you will agree that this would not be a very wise course of action."

"Uh—probably not," Darian replied, trying to think where people could have escaped *to*.

"We think that they probably went down the river," Snowfire continued. "There is a place there with fortifications—some great lord's holding, we think?"

"Kelmskeep," Darian replied automatically, "Lord Breon's manor." And somehow, just being able to identify the place made him lose some of that feeling of frantic urgency. "What did you see when you went back? I have to know! What if they didn't get away, how would you know?"

"Then sit here, and I will tell you." Snowfire gestured at a rock that seemed perfectly sculpted to act as a chair, and took another like it. "I do not know if you have been told this, but a Tayledras can see through the eyes of his bondbird. I remained near where we found you, in the boughs, on the same line as the sentries. Hweel and Kelvren went on, since it would be far less likely they would be detected than a human, and it would be far easier for them to escape if they *were* sighted."

Darian nodded, leaning forward tensely to better hear Snowfire's soft voice.

"The bridge crossing the river had been repaired, and it appeared that few of the buildings had actually been burned, mostly a handful of sheds. There were livestock in crude enclosures in the fields, and many, many horses in better enclosures there also." Snowfire tilted his head and brushed a strand of hair out of his eyes, as Darian flinched at the thought of cows pastured in the young crops. "Why do you wince?"

"They're eating the crops," Darian explained, thinking with pain of all the work that the villagers had put into those fields, only to have those animals devouring the food that should have gone to feed the village over the winter. "There won't be anything to last until spring."

"The barbarians of the north—which is what I *believe* these are—do not farm much; they are mostly hunters. Crop growing is a task for women and thralls, and the men don't trouble themselves with where food other than meat comes from." Snowfire seemed lost in thought for a moment, then came to himself with a shake of his head. "This tells me that the barns are empty of livestock, and there must be something *else* in the barns. I count the horses, knowing that northern barbarians are not great horsemen, and that there will be a dozen men who fight afoot for every rider. I decided then that the barns must be full of those soldiers, and the houses are full of the riders, who are of higher rank. Guessing at the numbers by the number of horses, I would say that there was no room in the village for your own people, and there are no people sleeping out in the open. So, I think they must have escaped."

"And then?" Darian persisted. "Then what happened?"

"Then Kelvren was discovered, and he and Hweel had to leave." Snowfire shrugged eloquently. "So do you think I am right?"

Darian tried to think, but he could not imagine where the villagers could be—other than escaped—if they weren't in their own homes or in the barns. "I guess that must be right—" he said, and suddenly found himself yawning. "But why can't *you* attack these people? Aren't you supposed to be Valdemar's allies? Aren't you going to help?"

"If we thought that your people were in danger, we would, regardless of the danger to us," Snowfire said firmly, "But, Darian, just what do you propose we should do? You know how few of us there are, and you had a glimpse of how many the enemy has in his ranks."

"But magic—" Darian protested. "You can use magic—"

"Not as yet," Snowfire told him. "Not in any way that will balance our small numbers. First, we must see if your people summon their own aid; it would be foolish, wouldn't it, if we tried to attack and failed, only to see an army of your people come the next day?"

Having seen what the enemy could do, Darian had another word for it than "foolish." He gulped, thinking of what a *real* battle must look like. Not merely one man with a wounded arm, but many people hurt, even killed. And it wouldn't be strangers dying, it would be people he knew. The thought made him sick to his stomach. "I think that would be a bad idea," he replied weakly.

"On the other hand," Snowfire continued, in that same, reasonable tone of voice, "if we wait long enough, the enemy will relax and drop some of their defenses. Even if help from your land does not come at once, we may well have an opportunity to do them a great deal of harm—perhaps even enough to drive them away. That sort of fighting does tend to make the best use of our abilities."

"With magic?" Darian asked hopefully. Surely if even Snowfire, who said that he was inferior as a mage, could do things even Justyn couldn't—what could Starfall do?

"Well, you told us that there was a mage with these people," Snowfire began.

"I did?" Darian blurted.

Snowfire nodded. "When you told us of the creature riding the lizard—and the men with the aspects of bears. Only a mage can work such changes, which meant that there must be one among them. Well, you know what has befallen magic and you know that our task is to reestablish order in the patterns of magic. This means that Starfall *must*, before all else, seize control of the magic here."

"So that the *other* mage can't get it!" Darian exclaimed.

"Exactly so. Then, once *we* have control of the magic energy, he will be weaker. That is the good aspect." Snowfire frowned. "The bad aspect is that this means Starfall will be busy holding the power, and unable to do other things he would otherwise—such as watching the enemy from afar or protecting us from the enemy's magic. And in the meantime, the enemy mage is *not* having to hold the power-matrix, and he is free to act. None of the rest of us are his equal, and I do not know that we could be, even acting together. So—we will ensure that *some* message comes to your people, calling for help, and meanwhile we will wait to see what happens."

Wait and see. Wasn't that what Justyn was always harping about? Patience.

But this time, rushing into things is going to get people hurt and killed. He sighed, and nodded his head.

"I guess that's what you'll have to do," he said reluctantly. "But—"

Whatever he had intended to say was interrupted by an enormous yawn, and he found himself blinking hard, trying to keep his eyes open.

"Hold the thought, little brother," Snowfire said, and got up. "Whatever it is can wait until morning. For now, sleep is waiting."

Darian stumbled along in Snowfire's wake, trying to keep his thoughts in order. There was something about Starfall holding the magic—something important—

But whatever it was, it didn't last past putting his head down on the pillow.

When he woke up, his memories of last night and the nightmare that had awakened him were waiting for him. Snowfire, however, wasn't.

He went through most of the day, doing whatever chores the *hertasi* or Hawkbrothers asked him to, without once seeing his new mentor. He guessed that Snowfire must be out doing *his* job, scouting, and that made him feel a little better. *Something* was being done; it might not be obvious to him just what it was, but clearly the Hawkbrothers were not lounging about looking decorative.

He helped Nightwind groom Kelvren after the latter returned from his own scouting foray, making certain that the enemy wasn't getting too near their encampment. Kelvren told him more of the night-sortie, especially the combat with the two smaller monsters; it was exciting, but scary, too, when he thought how Kelvren could have been hurt. Now all those old stories about battles and fighting took on an entirely different complexion when he thought about these people he *knew* being in the middle of all the hewing and smiting and all.

The notion of seeing Kel sick with poison—of Wintersky with some terrible wound, bleeding into the dirt—it was horrible. Not that he hadn't seen nasty injuries, because obviously he *had*, but to think of such things being inflicted *by other people* on his friends, and on purpose, to hurt or kill them—well, it was just entirely different from seeing the results of an accident, and it was hard to wrap his mind around the idea. Not just hard—ugly. It made him feel horrible inside to realize that people could actually want to hurt other people. Oh, there were plenty of times when he'd wanted something nasty to happen to other people, but the wish was always vague and ill-defined, and what he'd wanted was for something to happen to them, not that he wanted to inflict a hurt.

But—I think I could have hurt those men who were chasing me. He considered it a little more. *I know I could have hurt them. I was ready to shoot them.* He recalled quite clearly how he had felt at the time—coldly calculating an eye-shot, as if the men were nothing more than tree-hares he was hunting for the pot.

But they were going to kill me and Snowfire. And they *attacked the village. And for no reason! Or, not for no reason, but not for any good reason.*

When he finished with Kel—who had really enjoyed being able to tell someone about his fight—Wintersky caught him before anyone else did.

"We need to get the hawk furniture in order," Wintersky told him, "and you're the only one free," without any explanations of what "hawk furniture" was, or how to get it in order. Instead, the youngest of the Hawkbrothers left him in the charge of a painfully shy *hertasi* in someone else's hut, the entire left side of which was full of—hawk furniture.

Which was not little chairs and tables for birds of prey, as his imagination had devised, but the bits and pieces of hawk *equipment* needed for the bondbirds.

For all their intelligence, bondbirds were still hawks, and a hood slipped over their heads would let them sleep in a noisy and brightly-lit room. "Darkness—makes them sleep," the little *hertasi* whispered, cupping her hands over her eyes by way of illustration. "If the bondmate needs to be awake, the bird must still sleep—to feel well, they must sleep from dawn to dusk."

She showed him how to clean the hoods, made of hard, but extremely thin leather, odd bulges over the areas of the eyes to keep from touching the lids. Then, when he had cleaned them, she showed him how to repair those that were damaged. Most often, it was the braces, the leather thongs that held the hoods shut at the back, that were damaged, broken, or worn out. That was easy to fix, once he saw the odd way in which they were laced, so that a Hawkbrother could tighten or loosen the hood with one hand and his teeth. But sometimes what was damaged was the welt of leather protecting the raw edge of the bottom of the hood, or the ornamental knot on top, which was supposed to be used to take the hood off and put it on. The *hertasi* let him repair the simplest of these, but for the really complicated repairs, such as restitching the eye-covers, she insisted on doing the work while he watched. It was fascinating, for he would not have thought that such stubby little fingers could take such delicate stitches.

Most of the bondbirds didn't need restraints, such as jesses, but all of them wore the bracelets on their ankles that the jesses fitted through. The bracelets were good for other things, for tying a light string onto, for instance, that a bird could carry up and over a high branch, so that a rope could be pulled up afterward. So the *hertasi* taught him how to cut and oil such bracelets—then how to make leather- or rope-wrapped and padded perches as well. Hawks took wall- or floor-perches of tree limbs wrapped in leather, while falcons, it seemed, required perches made of upthrust sections of stump, like upthrusting rocks, but padded so that the talons of a sleeping bird had something to grip. Care of the feet, it seemed, was all-important, and sharp talons were hard on wrapped perches. Perches had to be made to withstand hard use, but not made of things that would bruise or abrade the feet; bruised or cut feet could infect, leading to a state called "bumblefoot," which in turn could cripple a bird if not adequately treated.

He learned more about birds of prey in that morning than he had ever learned in his life, and when he and the little lizard were done, every bit of equipment that *could* be mended, had been.

Then it was time for lunch, and time to help clean pots for a bit.

It occurred to him after lunch, as he stood beside a half barrel with his arms up to the elbow in warm, slippery, soapy water, that he had seldom worked this hard with poor Justyn. But this didn't bother him at all, and that was the odd thing.

Maybe it's just—it's just that no one shouts at me, or tells me what a terrible, ungrateful child I am, he concluded. *It's not so bad to work when no one is scolding you.*

Of course, he'd never had such interesting work before, which might have been the reason. Ayshen always had funny or fascinating things to tell him while he scrubbed pots, and mending the hawk furniture had been something entirely different from anything he'd ever done before. It wasn't hard to get through a chore when someone was chatting to you and making jokes, and when the chore required concentration and delicacy, time just flew by.

And as for helping to tend Kelvren, well, he had felt positively *honored*. It had been an amazing thing, to touch the gryphon's huge feathers, and make sure the killing talons were pinprick sharp and immaculately clean.

Odd, he thought, as Ayshen left him alone for a moment, to tend to the bake ovens, *I thought Kelvren was so old, older than Snowfire, but it was almost as if he was my age. I wonder how old he really is?* There was no way of telling with a bird, of course. They didn't exactly show their age in any way that he could recognize.

I like it here, he thought, with yearning, as he watched Ayshen's back. *I wish I could stay.*

If only there was some way that he *could*! When things got back to normal, would anyone at Errold's Grove ever want him back? Was there the faintest chance that the Hawkbrothers would want him with them?

And what if things never got back to normal? What if no one wanted to go back to the village? Would the Hawkbrothers be willing to give him a home?

Last night Snowfire kept calling me "little brother." Is that just something he calls every boy, or—

"Dar'ian!" Wintersky popped up behind his back, and he yelped in startlement, dropping the bowl he'd been scrubbing back into the water. Wintersky jumped with amazing agility right out of the way, and didn't even get a single drop of water on himself. He laughed, and clapped Darian on the back. "Sorry! Didn't mean to creep up on you like that, it's just habit. Snowfire wants you for a moment, if Ayshen doesn't mind."

"Not at all," the *hertasi* said without turning. "He's done twice the work of any of *you* clumsy-handed louts. He can consider his work done for the day."

"Why, Ayshen, I am crushed!" Wintersky mocked, and threw Darian a towel to wipe himself down with. "Come on, this won't take long."

Wondering what Snowfire could want, Darian followed the younger Tayledras with increasing curiosity. He became even more puzzled, and a little uneasy, when Wintersky brought him down a very narrow path into a part of the encampment where he had never been before. It was heavily overgrown, cool, dim, and so quiet he could hear himself breathing. The path ended in a place completely overshadowed by the branches of the oldest and largest willow Darian had ever seen, with the usual log hut built right up against the trunk of the tree, which was easily as big around as the hut itself. No grass could possibly grow here, but that lack was more than made up for by the thick moss carpeting the area. Sitting on a bow perch beside the door was a handsome cooperi hawk, watching everything with alert, reddish-yellow eyes.

Waiting for Darian were Snowfire and Starfall. The Adept looked very tired, as if he had been working all night, and Darian wondered if he had gotten any rest at all. *They must be taking me seriously enough that Starfall is working himself as hard as he can to keep those people from getting at the magic.* That was oddly reassuring.

"Dar'ian, I understand you have been a great deal of help to us," Starfall said, by way of a greeting.

Caught off guard, Darian shrugged. "I guess so. Have to earn my keep, don't I?'' He winched a little, inwardly, for his words didn't sound very polite, but Starfall didn't seem offended.

''We do expect all of those in our own group to do their share if they are not disabled,'' the older man said gravely. ''We are not so well-equipped that we cannot use another pair of hands. In fact—'' he cast a glance at Snowfire, ''—we could use that pair of hands on a more permanent basis, if that would suit you.''

Darian stared at him, quite certain that his new-won ability to understand Tayledras must be faulty.

Starfall persisted, grave but earnest. ''Our impression is that you do not feel any truly strong ties to those of your people that remain. Is that impression true?''

He shook his head a little, hardly able to believe what he was hearing. Was Starfall making the offer that he *thought?*

Starfall was clearly waiting for an answer, and Darian was startled enough to give him stark, unvarnished truth. ''Uh, I'd say they'd probably be happy to see the last of me right now,'' he admitted, shamefaced. ''With no Master, I go back on the village to care for, and I don't think any of them would care to apprentice me now.''

Bet they could find all kinds of excuses not to, in fact, he thought with sudden bleakness, for how could Starfall take *that* as any kind of a recommendation?

''Then, would you care to remain with us?'' Starfall asked, watching his face intently. ''Snowfire has offered to take you as his younger sibling, and that is all that I need as Elder.''

''But there is a condition,'' Snowfire said warningly, before Darian could burst out with an astonished and immediate acceptance. ''You must agree to—to 'apprentice' to me, in the matter of magic, at least for as long as I have the ability to teach you. You may outstrip me; I do not yet know how strong your Gifts may be, and if that happens, you must go to a real teacher, Starfall, by preference.''

''And we shall be gone from our home Vale for some time, several years, perhaps, working to establish the ley-lines and nodes all through the northern part of Valdemar,'' Starfall added, watching him closely. ''So you will not actually *see* our Vale until our work is done. If you were hoping for exotic surroundings, well, our surroundings will be less and less exotic all the time that we are out. That is another reason for us to want you with us. It would be good to have someone who has a native's command of this tongue at our disposal.''

Darian stood rock-still, thinking furiously. So, that was to be the price of being given a place here—that he must continue the tedious study of magic. Of all the things he wanted to learn, surely that was the last on the list!

But perhaps he was doing Snowfire an injustice. Justyn was hardly the best teacher in the world, and as a practitioner, he was even worse. Maybe it wouldn't be so bad if he was studying with someone who actually knew something.

And even if it was just as tedious and boring as it had been with Justyn, well, wasn't that a small price to pay to be where he was actually *wanted?*

And Snowfire says he wants me for a brother? Me? *They want me to be a real Hawkbrother?*

He made a real effort to contain his excitement, but it surely showed. He stifled his urge to shout, and somehow managed to turn a grave face toward the Adept.

"I would like to stay, very much, Elder," he said at last, with a little bow to Starfall. "I am honored that you ask me, and I certainly accept! I promise that I will do all that I can to help everyone here, and I will try to be more patient in learning magic."

Starfall smiled, and motioned him closer. Taking his hand, the Adept placed a pendant into it. It was a hawk-talon, mounted in silver; the mounting was decorated with a blue moonstone and strung on a beaded chain. "Welcome to k'Vala, then, little brother," he said warmly, as he closed Darian's hand around the talon. "You must wear this as a token of your acceptance into the Clan, as Nightwind does. You both bear the talons of my father's great suntail hawk-eagle, Skyr, who shared my father's labors as a Healing Adept and went to white at the age of only four. I know that you will be worthy of the token, even as Nightwind is."

Snowfire took the talon from Darian's nerveless fingers and put it around his neck. Darian looked up at him, trying to find the right words to thank him, and failing completely—but Snowfire acted as if he had already said them.

"You have labored long and hard already, and I am *not* minded to begin your lessons with one today, little brother," the younger Hawkbrother said as he clasped and released Darian's shoulders. "Why not go out into the forest for a time? It will cool your mind and help you think."

If there was one thing that Darian agreed with, it was that he needed some time to think this over. He nodded. "But—do I need to have someone with me?" he asked, hoping that the answer would be "no."

Snowfire shook his head. "That horse that we stole is in need of exercise," he suggested. "Go take it about for a while. You will be safe enough, riding, and you won't have to worry about *dyheli* chatter in your mind." The corner of his mouth twitched a little, suggesting to Darian that although the remark was intended as amusement, Snowfire had suffered "*dyheli* chatter" in the past.

As he hesitated a moment, Starfall nodded at the entrance to his little sanctuary. "Off with you, young one. I am the one most needful of your elder brother's skills at the moment. We have some tricky work ahead of us before *we* can rest this day."

Perhaps yesterday such a dismissal would have made Darian sullen and resentful, suspecting that they were getting rid of him so that they could discuss him. But now—now he had no such feelings. If Starfall said they had work, then they had work, and *he* would only get in the way. He stammered his thanks to both of them, and turned and ran, his heart hammering with so many mixed feelings that he couldn't sort them out properly.

He already knew where the horse was; in the pasture, being guarded by the *dyheli* herd and kept from straying. He guessed that the tack would be in a hut he knew was used for storing things with no immediate use, and sure enough, it was. He hadn't saddled many horses in his life, but with the help of two amused *dyheli* who kept the nag from running off half-equipped, he managed to get all the gear on in the proper manner. It wasn't that the horse was at all ill-tempered, it was more as if it expected bad treatment; it didn't fight him, but if it could get away without being saddled and bridled, it would be very happy to do so.

The horse sighed with resignation as he clambered into the saddle, his stomach aching reflexively as he recalled the last time he'd ridden the beast. But it seemed tractable enough, and it moved out of the entrance to the valley at a calm walk.

Darian was used to finding his way in the forest, and had no fear that he was going to get lost. He set a general course southward, but otherwise let the horse have its head, and it ambled on beneath the trees while he let his own thoughts wander. They tended to stray into mere contemplation of his surroundings; it was so easy to let his mind go blank as he admired a golden shaft of sunlight piercing the green gloom, then saw with surprised delight a single flower basking in its warmth like a precious jewel displayed for his admiration. It was more comfortable to contemplate the majesty of the enormous tree trunks rising in a never-ending vista of columns all around him than to contemplate his own future. And the liquid notes of birdsong dropping tranquilly down through the boughs were infinitely preferable to the discords of his past.

Everywhere he looked, he saw things that his parents would have drawn his attention to, if they had been there. Summer was not a time to trap for furs, so his summers in the past had been spent in exploration. Here in the hills, wonderful and magical spots seemed hidden in every valley. Sometimes it was a sparkling stream burbling over a stone-filled bed. Sometimes the stream poured down the side of the hill in a series of exuberant waterfalls. He caught sight of a pair of does with their fawns, grazing in a tiny pocket of meadow, surrounded by moss-covered boulders. Once they passed a fallen tree that supported an entire community of plants and ferns on its decaying, moss-covered side.

All was well for some time; the horse, given no commands, chose to eat as much as he walked. He meandered from one sparse bit of grass to the next. The grass beneath the tree canopy was thin and tended to grow in widely-spaced, wispy clumps; thick growths of fern and moss were more common here than grasses, and the horse disdained both. Darian let the reins hang loose on the horse's neck, engrossed in his own increasingly troubled thoughts.

Those thoughts weren't really coherent; too much had happened to him for coherency. He had the vague feeling that perhaps this was the root of what bothered him—events had taken him so completely by surprise that he wasn't acting anymore, he was reacting.

At least before, when anything happened to me, it was generally because I'd already done something to make those things happen, he thought. *And it was usually something that I knew would make trouble.* It was true he hadn't had a lot of control over his own life, but at least he'd had some, and he'd had choices, even if it was only the choice to resist what other people had in mind for him.

But now—fate or chance was hitting him with one hammer blow after another, not even giving him the time to reel back from one blow before slamming him with the next. Being invited to join the Hawkbrothers was the first thing that had happened in days that involved any choice for *him.*

And now that he'd accepted he felt strange. There was a creeping sense that he had betrayed the people of Errold's Grove in some way, and yet at the same time he resented the fact that he felt that way. What right had they to claim his loyalty? Why should he chain his fate to theirs?

There was guilt, too, a great deal of it, and he wasn't at all sure what to do about it. What *had* happened to the folk of the village?

He hadn't made any real effort to find out. Surely he ought to at least do that. And no matter what Snowfire said, how could anyone be sure there was nothing that he could have done that would have saved Justyn? Maybe if he'd been beside his master on that bridge, the way any good apprentice would have been, the outcome would have been different. All right, so he didn't have any real magic yet, but he'd learned a lot at the side of his parents, and maybe he would have been able to do something that would have saved them both. *I could have jumped off the bridge when he set it afire, and dragged him along with me. I can swim, even if he couldn't. Or—* His mind buzzed with a hundred absurd things he might have done, or could have done, or *thought* he could have done, and all of them just made him feel guiltier.

He became so engrossed in his thoughts that he didn't realize that the horse had stopped eating and was sneaking through the forest at a fast, if furtive, walk, until he saw a landmark he recognized with a start. He knew then that they were getting far too close to Errold's Grove for comfort and made a grab for the reins.

But the horse was an older hand at this game than he was; with a flip of its head, it tossed the reins out of reach, and increased its pace. Darian didn't have to be able to read its thoughts to know what they were—the beast had scented its herdmates, and it was going to get back to them by whatever means it took. The blacksmith had explained once why all the horses in the village were kept in a single herd; horses weren't happy alone, and even though the Errold's Grove "herd" wasn't a breeding herd, the lack of a stallion was no impediment to the horses' comfort in each other.

This horse probably felt the same about the rest of the horses he was used to being with, and no dim memory of mistreatment was going to overwhelm the urgent need on his part to get back to the safety of the herd. Darian considered trying to throw himself out of the saddle, but the horse was going faster now, and suddenly the ground seemed very far away to a boy who'd never done more than steal rides on the innkeeper's old pony. With the horse moving, he didn't know how to get himself out of the saddle and onto the ground without breaking something. So he just held grimly to the saddle, gritted his teeth against the jolting, and prayed that they wouldn't run into any enemy sentries.

The trees cleared away up ahead, and Darian felt his heart stop with terror as he thought they were *almost* at the village. But the horse hesitated as the tree cover thinned, and Darian managed to seize the reins before the recalcitrant beast managed to bolt into the middle of town.

But then, Darian realized that the daylight ahead of them was *not* the daylight of the cleared fields. Somehow the horse had managed to come out of the forest at the top of the only bluff that overlooked the village. How it had managed that, Darian had no clue, but once he dismounted and led the horse cautiously to the edge of the bluff, he had as good a view of the village as if he'd been sitting in one of the trees.

But what he saw made his skin crawl, and filled him with the desperate feeling he had to *do* something, along with the knowledge that there was nothing he could do.

In the distant fields were people, people he recognized, toiling like beasts in the heat of midday. Hitched to plows like oxen were the biggest men of the village, sweating beneath the blows of a whip held in the hands of a stranger. Behind them, guiding the plows through the fields meant to be sown with late-ripening crops, were the women, who were also chained in their places. Others worked, chained at the waist in pairs, beneath the watchful eyes of more strangers. These men weren't wearing the armor that Darian remembered, but he knew they must be the same men who had invaded the village.

As to why men were being used to pull the plows instead of oxen, well, the smell of roasting beef coming up the bluff certainly provided a reasonable explanation. There were no oxen now, and the horses had probably been confiscated to serve the army.

How many of the villagers had been recaptured? Enough, evidently, to provide field-slaves for their conquerors.

Darian found his hands clenched on his bow without any memory of reaching for it. He *could* sneak in closer, get a position up in one of the trees, and start picking off guards. They weren't wearing armor; they'd be easy shots—

I could kill all the guards I see and they could escape, I could lead them to the Hawkbrothers—

Right. He could kill all the guards that he could see. How many more men were there that he couldn't see? If they'd gotten to the point this quickly of killing and eating the oxen—tough meat at best—

Anger flooded him next, anger at the Hawkbrothers. Why hadn't they told him the truth?

It faded as quickly as it came. They hadn't told him, perhaps, because they didn't know themselves. It was entirely possible that this was the first day the villagers had been put to work in the fields. Why *should* the enemy have put them out? It would have been more logical for them to take their captives away; sell them, perhaps, or put them to work in their own fields back in the northern mountains.

Unless, of course, they had decided to stay.

He couldn't do anything here, and this was information that the Hawkbrothers didn't have. He had to get back, as quickly as he could.

It's not cowardice to go. I can't do anything by myself, and Starfall and the rest need to know what's happened here.

Carefully, he backed the horse into the heavier cover before he mounted. He considered his next move carefully. He hadn't really been paying attention when the horse took off on its own. Somehow, if there were sentries (and there probably were) the horse had managed to thread its way past them without being spotted. So if he could retrace the horse's path, he could do the same.

Finally, *finally* something he *could* do right! He felt a grin stretch his mouth, an expression that had not been on his lips since his parents died. If? Say rather, *how quickly*. The day he could not track a shod horse in the soft earth of the forest floor would be a day when he renounced his heritage and asked to be apprenticed to a clerk!

He had to cast around a bit before he found the clear trail; it had gotten a little muddled when he finally got control of the reins back from the stubborn beast. But once he found the trail, the rest was easy.

He soon saw how the horse had gotten up onto the bluff without his realizing it; the beast had wound a zigzag course up the slope, taking the ascent so gradually that he hadn't known they were climbing. He was tempted to cut straight down, but reminded himself that the horse had managed to avoid the sentries this way; it wouldn't be a good idea to take what appeared to be a shorter path only to run into one of the enemy.

The horse didn't want to be ridden away from its mates, and fought him for a good long time, which didn't make finding the path more difficult, but did take up more valuable time. It was sunset by the time that Darian got to a point where he was fairly certain that there were no enemies to watch out for. By then, the horse was tired enough to stop fighting, which was just as well, because Darian's temper was frayed to a thin strand, and he was in no mood for further nonsense.

With a clear path ahead of them, Darian finally got some revenge; he smacked the horse's rump with his unstrung bow, startling it into a tired gallop, and headed for the Hawkbrother encampment as fast as the miserable beast would go.

Weary and aching, Darian found himself the center of another Council, but now he understood what was being said, which was certainly an improvement over the last time.

Hweel had met him outside the valley, and Snowfire at the entrance; Darian had feared anger or reproach for being gone so long, but to his surprise, Snowfire had been perfectly calm right up until the moment he had gotten within speaking distance and blurted, "I've been to Errold's Grove! They're all slaves!"

Snowfire's expression had changed completely in that moment, and Darian found himself swept off the horse and into the middle of a Council that was assembled so hastily that people actually came running to the clearing while pulling on tunics or holding half-braided hair in one hand. *Hertasi* simply appeared with boots, shirts, food, hair-thongs, or anything else that had been forgotten, and vanished again. One of them left a bowl of stew, bread, and tea at Darian's hand without him ever actually seeing the food left there, just the flash of a departing tailtip.

As firelight flickered on the concerned faces of his Hawkbrother hosts, he alternated bites of stew and gulps of tea with words of explanation.

The only person missing from this council session was Starfall, but although no one said anything, Darian guessed from what wasn't said that Starfall had more than enough problems of his own.

Finally the others stopped firing questions at him and began a worried discussion among themselves. Darian turned his own attention to the remains of his meal, too tired and hungry to really think of anything else. As he wiped the bowl with his bread, Wintersky came and sat on a rock beside him.

"I hope you don't think we deceived you, Dar'ian," the young man said, leaning forward earnestly. "After the way that Kel and Hweel were caught by those magic-sniffing creatures, we didn't want to risk anything or anyone that might set off more such guardians, and someone kept us from being able to use scrying to set a watch on the place magically. And it didn't seem advisable to risk being seen ourselves—the enemy doesn't *know* we're here, and if he did, he might decide to attack. We were certain that all the barbarians had were houses, some stock, but never people. If we'd had *any* idea that those barbarians had your people, we'd have risked more to find out for certain, then to do something for them—"

"I know!" Darian interrupted, just as earnestly. He scratched his head, and gave Wintersky an anxious smile. "I was mad at first, but, well, I had a lot of time to think on the ride back. I trust your word; I know that—if you say you would have done something, if you'd known what was going on, then you would have."

"We should have made sure."

Darian looked up, and saw Snowfire standing over him, his eyes expressionless and flat, shadows flitting over his face as the light from the fire shifted and changed. "We should have made sure," the Hawkbrother repeated harshly. "That was a mistake on our part. I'm sorry, Dar'ian."

Darian shrugged awkwardly. "Wintersky was explaining—and I'd kind of figured some of it out myself. You thought everything was all right. And you and Starfall were busy," he reminded his mentor shyly. "You told me yourself, you have to fix the magic so no one else can get at it—" Suddenly, the thought he'd set aside last night came back to him. "Snowfire, how are you doing that? Are you making just—uhm—what's the word—nodes the way they used to be?"

Snowfire's expression changed, and he looked down at Darian with speculation. "Not exactly. Why?"

Darian licked his lips, and wondered just how stupid he was going to sound. After all, compared to what the Hawkbrothers knew, he didn't know much of anything about magic, really. But still—

"There's definitely a mage with the enemy, right?" Darian asked. "I mean with them, at Errold's Grove, not just working with them or behind the attack."

Snowfire nodded. "I cannot imagine how they could be blocking our scrying if there wasn't."

"And the mage is going to want that power—he'd have to want to grab for it." He bit his lip, hoping that he wasn't going to make a total fool of himself. "And I guess if there was a *big* source of power, he'd try to get to it, right?" Before Snowfire could answer that, he asked another question. "And there are way too many of those enemy soldiers for us to fight, right?"

Snowfire looked both guilty and relieved. "Far too many for us to take in direct confrontation," he acknowledged. "Yet—I do not know how we are to free your people, otherwise."

"But what—what if you baited a big trap for them?" Darian asked. "What if you made a big source of magic, made it show up all of a sudden? Wouldn't the mage send out men, maybe a lot of them, to try and take it over?"

"Or loot it," Wintersky suggested, his sleepy eyes brightening. "If you moved it around a little, he might get the idea it's portable and send his fighters to loot it for him. He might think it was an artifact someone had found."

"And I know traps, *lots* of traps," Darian offered in eager triumph, holding out one hand as if he was offering his knowledge as a gift. "My parents and I, that's what we did. A lot of the animals we trapped were as big as humans, or bigger. We could take a lot of the enemy out with traps, without ever needing to send anybody closer than bowshot. You set a trap that blocks them from going back the way they came, then you make sure that they can't *get* back without having to go through all your other traps. That's called a channeling trap. Maybe we could even fix things up so that the enemy has to divide up into small groups. Why, if we did that, we could just have *one* bowman up in a tree near each trap, and what the trap didn't take care of, he could!"

Snowfire looked at him, and beamed with the most wonderful expression Darian had ever seen.

Respect.

And what was more, others among the Hawkbrothers, who had overheard the conversation, were looking at him in the same way—and those who had been too engrossed in their own conversation to hear were whispering questions to those who had. In another few moments, they were all looking at him that way, and silence replaced the murmur of voices in the clearing.

"Just how many traps do you mean, when you say *lots* of traps, Dar'ian?" asked Rainwind, a scout only a little older than most of the rest. He stood up and joined Snowfire, a man who was a little more weathered, a little shorter, and a little stockier than Darian's mentor. "We know some, obviously, but trapping is not the way we usually deal with things. We are more direct and, to be honest, more accustomed to having a superior force. What traps we do use are for snaring game, not stopping soldiers—" He shrugged.

Darian blinked, and made a quick mental survey of the traps he and his parents had used for large, dangerous, clever animals. "I know by heart maybe six or eight major different kinds that would work against a man—or several men at a time," he said finally. "Maybe more; we might be able to adapt others I know by disguising them, or we could combine some. I grew up making traps in this part of the Pelagirs. Some of what we caught were probably smarter than these barbarians."

Someone whistled through his teeth with admiration.

"So you'd already know how to adapt the designs to use the local cover!" Snowfire exclaimed, his whole body taking on a new animation.

Darian nodded. "Entirely using found materials, too," he said earnestly. "We only carried basic tools with us when we went out trapping, and adapted what we found at the different locations. The most we ever carried were some metal triggering devices and those were mostly just time savers. I can show you some examples of the traps I know if you can stand to watch. I'm not just talking about different kinds of pit-traps. I know how to set a pit-trap to get a *lot* of people instead of just one or two, I know of snares and drop-nets that will get more than one, a couple kinds of channeling-traps, deadfalls with wood, deadfalls with rock, ankle-traps, leg-breakers, foot-piercers—" He began rattling off the kinds of traps that could be set in such a way that wary enemy soldiers wouldn't see them until it was far too late, and the eyes of his listeners either widened or narrowed according to the nature of the listener. The others rose to stand around him, until once again he was the center of a circle of listeners. "Trapping is just a different kind of hunting. My father said that it was hunting while absent, using the ultimate in disguise—not actually being there!"

"If we can do this—if we could lure a good number of their people out—" Snowfire murmured to himself, as his eyes widened.

"If you can lure them out and we can channel them past the bluff, or through a couple of other places where there's only one way to go, *I* can show you where and how to rig a deadfall that will block their way back!" Darian assured him. "There is one place where the river is very deep and dangerous and the path beside it is narrow, and if you can weaken one of the overhangs, we can drop a large piece of the bluff just behind them at that point. Then they'll *have* to go the way we channel them."

"And that will be a gauntlet of further traps." Snowfire's lips thinned with satisfaction. "It is cruel, perhaps, but have they not earned such an ordeal?"

"Yes!" Darian responded fiercely. Nodding heads showed that the others agreed with him.

"Show us!" demanded one of the others; paper and a charcoal stick appeared when Rainwind left the group and returned with them in his hands, and Snowfire conjured a mage-light to give Darian brighter and steadier illumination than firelight. Darian hunched over the first sheet, drawing a map.

"Here, here's the village, and here's the bluff, and here's where the bluff goes up to the riverbed; far enough from the village that they just can't call for help.'' He sketched in the landmarks with a careful hand. ''Now, if we rig a deadfall *here*, when it's triggered, it'll completely block the way back. It's all sandstone through there; too dangerous to climb the rockpile, or at least that's what they'll think. Their only choice will be to climb the cliff, swim the river, or keep going.''

''What's to stop them from swimming the river?'' Wintersky asked. ''Some of them did that when they attacked your village and the bridge burned.''

''Us,'' said Ayshen, as he strolled into the firelight, his sharp teeth set in a grim smile. He had one of his enormous cooking knives in one hand. ''Forgive me, Snowfire, but this may be the first time in *my* memory that there has been a combat where *hertasi* might be of service. *We* can swim like fish—how do you think we catch them, so big and so fresh?—and any clumsy human foolish enough to be in the same water with us will not live to learn his mistake.''

''Or if he does, it will not be for long,'' added another *hertasi* in his shadow, who then ducked shyly out of sight.

''If they stay out of sight, the enemy won't even know what's attacking the swimmers,'' Rainwind pointed out. ''They've never been here before, for all they know, that part of the river could be inhabited by gigantic, man-killing Changed fish. They'll have no reason to think of traps at that point.''

:I fancy we can be of service in the woods.: Tyrsell was nowhere in sight, but it was obvious he had been listening to the Council talk. *:Exactly how, I am not yet sure, but certainly we will be useful in some capacity. I will have to see the territory, first.:*

''If nothing else, perhaps the *dyheli* could drive the enemy into further traps,'' offered Daystorm, a female scout. ''It would be useful to have them in a panic, fleeing from the sound of many hooves. And again—it would just look like animals. It seems to me—''

''Go on,'' Snowfire urged, when the other hesitated.

''Well,'' she said. ''It seems to me that we ought to keep things looking like it's accident or Changed animals as long as possible. If we do that, they won't actually be *looking* for traps for a while.''

''Eventually—'' Snowfire began.

''Oh, eventually, a trap will *look* like a trap, of course,'' she admitted. ''But it would be very useful to have them thinking that fate—or the Forest—has suddenly turned against them.''

''And therrre isss, of courrrrssse, myssself,'' Kel put in gravely, sounding quite calm—but the pinning of his eyes gave away his excitement. His wings were extended a little, as if he wanted badly to be in the air at this very moment.

"*Not* if they have bows," Snowfire replied sternly. "You are hardly arrow-proof. And in the air you are a very large target, especially in the day. So was Skandranon."

Kel's only reply was a snort, but it was obvious that Snowfire was going to stand firm. "I am the scout-leader, and you are tacitly working under my command, Kel," he reminded the gryphon. He didn't add anything else, but Kel sighed.

"Verrry well," the gryphon said, giving in. "Commanderrr."

"We have an advantage," Snowfire continued. "Many of us are Master-level mages; we can help create these traps with magic at a low enough level that working this magic will not immediately attract the attention of the enemy, especially if we shield what we are doing. So we can work quickly, much more quickly than if we did this with hands alone."

Darian studied his crude map. "I wish we could get them all with a single deadfall here," he muttered, and looked up hopefully. "Could you bring down that much rock?"

Snowfire sighed. "Before the Storms, it would have been possible, with a waiting crack-spell, which would create a split at an angle that would cause a slide, when it was triggered. Now—no. That kind of spell, on that scale, wouldn't remain stable long enough with the way mage-energy is in flux—it depends upon tension through its length. We will probably be able to catch the tailmost rank with what crack-spells we can set, but no more." Now the Hawkbrother joined Darian in close examination of the map. "It might even be worthwhile to do nothing *more* than block their way. As Daystorm pointed out, so long as they think the fall of rock is accidental, they will simply carry on with their original mission, and worry about finding a new way back when they've obtained what they were sent after. We don't want them swimming the river, of course, but other than that, we could leave them alone for a while. We could lead them quite a merry chase before we start eliminating them with traps and tricks."

Kel laughed, a deep, rumble. "In fact, my frrriendsss, we could let them marrrch unhinderrred and make a night-camp—and rrremove theirrr sssentrrriesss one by one. Sssilently, if posssible." He examined his talons critically, and held them up, shining redly in the firelight. "Think of the consssterrrnation when the next watch came up, but the onesss to be rrrelieved werrre—poof! Gone!"

Snowfire looked up at him sharply, with one brow raised. "You," he said severely, "are an evil creature."

:I like it,: Tyrsell countered. *:That would be a place where we could be useful. It is no difficult thing for one of us to come upon a man silently and unseen.:*

"I like it, too," seconded Ayshen. "We might be able to help there, if we aren't too tired from swimming. Three or four of us could swarm a sentry, and he'd never hear or see us coming."

"If we did that," Windshadow pointed out. "If we triggered the deadfall, set up the traps, and left the harrying to our *hertasi* and *dyheli* allies, *we* could go in that same night and get the villagers out. Even if the barbarians have a way to get messages back and forth, it won't do them any good. The leader in the village is going to be preoccupied with clearing the blockage, not watching his back, and the leader in the expedition is going to be busy with shadow-fiends picking off his men one by one."

"That would also be dividing our forces," Snowfire objected, then sighed, and scratched his head. "No, it wouldn't really," he corrected himself. "The *hertasi* would be of limited use in a raid on the village, and the *dyheli* would serve only as targets."

:True, and I would refuse that assignment if you were to give it to me,: Tyrsell replied calmly. *:This plan plays to all our strengths. Perhaps Kel could come with us?:*

"I can go along as well," Nightwind offered. "Tyrsell ought to command the group, but I'm not bad with a bow, you know. Kel and I could work together."

Snowfire looked as if he was thinking about the proposition very hard, and finally nodded. "It's the best division of labor," he agreed. "And the best use of the limited number of fighters we have. Dar'ian can tell us and show us what to do, and once the traps are all in place, we can set the plan in motion." As Darian looked up at him anxiously, Snowfire patted his shoulder reassuringly. "That will take no more than half a week. Surely your friends can hold out for a few days, can't they? I know they were being mistreated, but they weren't in any danger of being handled brutally, were they?"

Darian wasn't certain, but he nodded anyway. *It won't do any good to rush in there before we're ready,* he reminded himself. *A few more beatings aren't going to make that much of a difference. Even if it does make a difference—this is better than their alternatives.*

"It's settled, then." Snowfire said decisively, then shook his head. "I wish there were another way, but there doesn't seem to be." He pointed to Wintersky and Windshadow. "You two go scout with your birds and make us some good maps of the area tomorrow; figure the best direction to herd the barbarians, and where to get them to make a camp, after we block their path behind them."

The Hawkbrothers nodded, and Snowfire turned his attention back to Darian. "Now," he said. "About those traps. . . ."

Hours later, hands still smudged with charcoal, Darian stumbled back to the *ekele*, thinking longingly of bed. He stopped just long enough to wash his hands and face before stripping off clothing that still smelled of horse, getting into a clean set of night clothes, and lying down on the pallet. He was keyed up enough that he didn't really think he'd be able to fall asleep quickly, but he was either better at relaxing or much more tired than he thought, because he didn't even remember closing his eyes.

He woke as Snowfire and Wintersky came in, whispering about something, and propped himself up on one elbow to blink at them. "I'm awake," he called softly. "Anything I should know about?"

"We just worked out tentative placing for your traps, and ways for the *hertasi* to trigger them," Snowfire told him, raising his voice to a more normal level. "I didn't expect you to be awake, but I'm glad you are. You made all the right choices, today, and you deserve credit for doing so."

"Right choices?" Darian repeated, puzzled.

"Oh, you could have gone charging right into the village, thinking you could free your friends, but you didn't," Snowfire said, his voice muffled in the folds of his shirt as he pulled it over his head. "You stayed long enough to make detailed observations, then you came straight back here. You didn't waste time with accusations and carrying on when you got here, you simply told us what you knew and then offered constructive suggestions. In short, Dar'ian, you behaved in every way as a man and a warrior, and I am very proud of you. We all are."

Darian felt his neck heating up and averted his eyes. "Ah," he stammered, "thank you. I—I don't want anything bad to happen to anybody, and—" He gulped, and decided to tell the rest of the truth. "The horse brought me out on the top of the bluff, not down at the edge of the village. If I'd been closer, I probably would have done something stupid. But there was no direct way down from there, and, well—that's probably why I stopped to think."

"You still made the right choices." Snowfire sat down on his pallet, blinking at him with eyes that looked as large and dark as Hweel's. "That is an important thing for you to know."

"Heyla—it's going to be an early day tomorrow, and the night is only getting shorter for all your talking," Wintersky pointed out, a little crossly. "We do not *all* fly owls, here." He was already lying on his sleeping pad, and he glared pointedly at the mage-light above Snowfire's head.

Snowfire chuckled, and the light blinked out. "Good night, Wintersky," he said. "And good night, Dar'ian."

"Hmph," Wintersky replied, mollified. "Good night."

"Good night," Darian said softly. He lowered himself back down onto his pillow, and the next thing he knew, Wintersky was shaking his shoulder, and it was morning.

The day wore on, filled with explanations and examples of trap placement and construction. Around him, there were the sounds of wood being chopped, branches split, and snippets of conversation in Tayledras. Darian caught himself feeling like he was playing, once, while he bent and notched saplings for lashing-traps. He felt a pang of guilt, since after all he was engaged in acts of war, to cause pain and even death to those who had done the same to his village.

My village? I suppose they are, when all is counted up. They weren't the people I would have chosen to be with, but they were better than—alternatives.

Yet, making traps was at least something familiar, from a better time in his childhood. It brought back wistful memories of his parents.

He sighed, thinking about them while he tied off his fourth or fifth lasher, then hacked away steadily at a branch as thick as his upper arm. Things would have been so much better if they were here with him now. His mother always seemed to know the right things to say, or how to touch in just the perfect way to put him at ease. His father was always so strong and capable, with a quick smile.

"Dar'ian?" a timid voice asked from below a bush. Two small, pebble-scaled hands held out a cup of water from under the cover, and nothing else of the *hertasi* could be seen. He wiped his brow and murmured a thanks to his largely-unseen benefactor, then drank the cup dry. In a blink, after setting the cup down, it was gone, and a second *hertasi* voice spoke from behind another bush.

"Dar'ian, the stakes you requested are stacked on the east side of the red boulder. We hope they will be enough. We go now to prepare the vines."

Then there was the slightest rustle of leaves and the sound of scuttling through underbrush, and Darian was alone again.

Well, I'd better see how many they managed to get done. I'm getting nowhere on this branch, and my arms hurt. If we can't have enough of these traps ready to stop the soldiers, we might only wind up injuring them enough to enrage them, not discourage them. Darian sheathed his knife and started off toward the place the *hertasi* had told him of. *Hertasi* were amazing to him—shy ghosts with astonishing speed and industriousness. What were *their* parents like? He found it hard to imagine them having families like his, or the Tayledras. And what about the . . . ?

At that moment, a large shape detached itself from the shadows of the thicket surrounding the red boulder. Darian froze in place and then relaxed, exhaling sharply when he saw the shape resolve itself into golden-tipped feathers, the hook of an aquiline beak, and the flip and flash of a huge wing refolding against a feathered body. The gryphon stalked out, looking directly at Darian. He seemed impossibly huge even at this distance, yet Darian knew that was only a trick of the mind.

He caught himself blushing, wondering how long he'd been under the creature's scrutiny. Kelvren looked down, picked from several clear spots for the most comfortable, and sat down, waiting for Darian to approach. The gryphon's chest rose and fell quickly as he apparently recovered from some physical effort or other, and his gaze appeared to soften the closer Darian came to him.

"Grrreetingsss, Darrr'ian," Kelvren rumbled as he dipped his beak in a nod. "I have jussst completed brrringing the ssstakesss the *herrrtasssi* have made. They arrre behind the rrred blouderrr."

Darian nodded self-consciously. "I heard. I mean, one of the *hertasi* told me that's where they were—I didn't know you'd brought them, though. I hope there's enough of them."

Kelvren's eyes sparkled and a moment later he wryly said, "I think therrre will be—enough." Then he raised his head, flicking a tufted ear, and blinked a few times before opening his beak. Kelvren paused, roused his feathers, and bluntly asked Darian, "What trrroublesss you?"

Darian frowned. "Was it obvious?"

Kelvren clucked. "If you werrre not trrroubled, I would ssssusss-pect you of not being human. But you arrre trrroubled, ssso, Changechild you arrre not. Ssspeak."

"All right. Do—you have parents?" Darian asked the gryphon.

"Chah!" Kelvren barked. "No, I wasss borrrn ssspontaneousssly of an arrrtisssst'sss drrream and a villain'sss nightmarrre."

Darian blushed. "I'm sorry. It was a stupid question. Of course you had parents."

Kelvren raised his beak up to point at the sky, then looked back to Darian. "If you mean, do I know my parrrentsss and rrressspect them? Yesss. Verrry much ssso. And do I misss them now? Yesss. Verrry much ssso." He took a step toward the red boulder, and Darian followed. "One doesss not outgrrrow the feelingsss of fledging, jussst the intensssity of the feelingsss. It isss the way of thingsss."

Darian was incredulous, and stopped in his tracks. "You? You miss your—mama and papa?"

The gryphon walked on without pause and rumbled only, "Don't you?"

Darian caught up. "Well, yes, but you're a gryphon—"

"And you arrre a human, and we werrre crrreated by humansss, and live with humansss, and learrrn frrrom humansss, and we arrre farrr morrre like you than you know. Why ssshould humansss have exsssclusssive rightsss to any anxsssiety?"

Darian had to laugh at that. "I guess you're right. You probably share your gryphon anxieties with us humans, too!"

The gryphon nodded firmly and winked, stopped a few steps after reaching the boulder. "It isss only fairrr, afterrr all." He pointed his beak, and Darian was astonished at what he saw.

Stacked in bound bundles of twenty or more were sharpened stakes, in different thicknesses, piled as high as he was tall. There must have been hundreds of them, if not thousands.

Maybe this plan would work after all.

Snowfire had always considered himself to be in fine shape, but the need to favor his wounded arm was throwing everything off a little, including his balance, and as a result, he ached with unaccustomed strain. A full day of work on man-traps had been more than enough to show him that he probably ought to be in better condition than he was. He was stretching and twisting his good arm as he approached Starfall's clearing and *ekele*, hoping to ease some of the aches.

Hweel was already ahead of him, waiting on a spare perch beside Starfall's cooperi hawk. Snowfire carried a rough meal of cold sliced meat, flatbread, and wild berries wrapped in a napkin. Ayshen was not cooking today, for he was needed to help set the traps, and although he would not have complained had he been asked to cook a supper as well, no one wanted to place that double burden on his too-willing shoulders.

Nevertheless, they all had to eat; it would be cold meat, greens, and flatbread for as long as those lasted, and after that, each of them would be in charge of his own food. That was not exactly a hardship for a Hawkbrother; rabbits and tree-hares were plentiful and the birds more than willing to share a catch with a bondmate. Snowfire had already decided that *he* would see that Starfall ate and drank; if Starfall's young bird failed to make a kill out of inexperience, Hweel was such a fine hunter that he could have supplied the needs of six people, not just three.

He found Starfall sitting cross-legged in the center of a containment shield in the clearing beneath the willow branches. The Adept's eyes were closed, but he sensed Snowfire's presence as soon as the scout arrived, for he motioned to his visitor to sit and wait without ever taking his attention off what occupied him. Obediently, Snowfire did just that, taking weary pleasure in watching the way the light filtering down through the branches changed from pure gold, to reddish gold, to dark red, and finally to the blue of dusk. The clearing could have been in the heart of the deep forest, it was so quiet and peaceful here, and Snowfire was content merely to rest both mind and body while he waited for the Adept to complete his current task.

He did not even conjure a mage-light; he didn't want to disturb either Starfall's concentration or the delicate balances of power within the containment shield. So the ball of blue light that appeared above his head was the Adept's, not his, and was Starfall's way of telling him that the work was over for now. There was no outward change to the figure within the shield, but a few moments later the shield dropped away and Starfall stood up, stretching.

"Here," Snowfire said, handing him the meal. "Ayshen said I was responsible for making sure you eat. So what sort of progress have you made?"

"The enemy mage *is* trying to consolidate power for himself, and he's trying to work his way through all of the locks I put on the lines," Starfall confirmed. "From the way he's working, trying to bludgeon his way through, I think he's under the impression that it's crude work, possibly done by that master of young Dar'ian. I don't think he realizes that there is still an active worker about, and I know he isn't aware of me."

"As long as he keeps thinking that, I'll be pleased," Snowfire replied, helping himself to some of the berries.

"I have the bare hint of a power-point out along the river," Starfall continued, laying a slice of meat neatly on a slice of bread, and rolling them up together. "I'll strengthen it gradually, as you are setting up the traps; he'll notice, but it won't be enough to tempt him. But once the traps are done, I'll remove it and put it on a *dyheli*; then I'll pour enough energy into it that it will look tasty, and I'll have the *dyheli* move it farther down the river along the river path. At the same time, I'll build an illusion around it of a heavily armed caravan moving away. I want to create the impression that the river has uncovered a talisman or artifact, and that someone found it and is carrying it off.''

"Even if that isn't what he thinks, he'll still assume the caravan has something tasty and send his fighters." Snowfire nodded with satisfaction. "It's a good ruse. Just make sure your illusion won't be broken."

"It shouldn't be; I've gotten a *dyheli* doe to volunteer to carry it." Starfall applied himself to the food. "I'm linking the power-point to her once she gets into position, but not before. I don't want to have a moving power-point to attract his attention until then. And once we're done, of course, I'll gather it back in and use it as the core of the Heartstone."

Snowfire swallowed, and raised his eyebrows. "So you *are* going to make a Heartstone here?"

"A small one," Starfall confirmed, as he finished his first meat roll and built a second. "Not powerful enough for a Clan Vale, and at any rate, it will take a long time before it has accumulated enough energy to be useful. It will be four or five years before anyone could use it to create even a small Vale."

Snowfire was not at all sure he liked the idea. He'd thought of several objections when Starfall broached the plan, and those objections hadn't changed. "Still. A Heartstone out here? Why? And who are you going to link into it, besides yourself?"

"Why? Why not?" Starfall responded, apparently surprised that Snowfire would object at all. "Sooner or later the k'Valdemar will produce a mage that can use a Heartstone—or we will want an outpost here. You have all complained at one point or another about the lack of civilizing amenities here; well, a Heartstone will make those things possible, eventually."

Snowfire grimaced. "And meanwhile? Wouldn't it attract unwanted attention?"

Starfall shook his head and took on a little of that arrogance that seemed to come with being an Adept. "Oh, do trust me to know my business, Snowfire; by the time I am finished with concealing it, only another Tayledras Adept who knew that it was there would be able to find it."

"I hope you're right," Snowfire replied. "Never mind; what more can you tell me about this enemy mage?"

"He's certainly strong enough to be an Adept, or whatever these barbarians call such a thing.'' Starfall folded and refolded the napkin pensively. ''If it came to a fight, he's not a match for me, but he would exhaust a great deal of my resources in defeating him. I don't want to have to do that, and to keep from coming into direct conflict, I will have to be subtle. Subtlety requires time and concentration, rather than power. He's powerful enough that it is going to take all my attention to keep him from breaking the illusion, finding our encampment, and tapping into the new matrix of ley-lines and nodes.''

''Which means when we move against the village, you stay here.'' Snowfire nodded. ''I rather thought you'd say that. I can leave someone here on guard, if you like.''

''Why not Nightwind and Kel?'' Starfall suggested. ''She's a good shot, and he's worth five fighters in intimidation alone.''

''And it would keep him out of close combat; now that is a good idea.'' Snowfire felt a bit more cheered. He'd been trying to think of a way to keep the gryphon from flinging himself into situations where he'd be a target rather than an asset, and this was perfect. Put him in the air and Nightwind at the valley entrance—put a couple of *hertasi* and *dyheli* in the valley right here, around Starfall's *ekele*, acting as bodyguards—that would work very well. No matter how clever enemy fighters were, they wouldn't get past the combined senses of a gryphon, *hertasi*, and *dyheli*. If somehow there was a concerted attack by a formidable group instead of an incursion of one or two fighters, Starfall would have warning, covering fire, and time to escape.

And Kel would rightly see this as a trust and an important assignment—which it was—rather than an attempt to keep him out of combat—which it also was.

''How are the traps coming?'' Starfall asked, as Snowfire ran through his mental roster of hertasi and dyheli and made some tentative selections.

''Not so badly that anyone is getting frustrated, and not so well that anyone is nervous, thinking that things are going *too* well. The *hertasi* are approaching it with their usual zeal, and they've been making enough trap parts that Kel's had to struggle to keep up with carrying, even with *dyheli* helping,'' Snowfire told him, and picked up a small twig to draw in the dirt with. ''Here's where the main deadfall will be, along the river. We got that done first, before sunrise this morning. We found a place where a flood undermined the sandstone of the bluff and cut under it a little farther; if there wasn't a magical prop holding it up now, it would be down in an instant. There is going to be more than enough stone blocking the path that they aren't going to want to go back that way. This morning, we cut a path and aged it, then made things so difficult on either side that they aren't going to want to leave it.'' He sketched in the path, leading away from the river. ''We put in a log bridge over this ravine *here* that is going to fall apart as soon as anyone puts a foot on it. They'll either have to rebuild the bridge or make a strenuous climb down and back up; in either case, they'll be tired, and it'll be dusk by the time they reach this clearing.'' He made a circle and tapped it with the twig.

''Then that is where they'll stop,'' Starfall eyed it with interest. ''And that is when the *hertasi* and *dyheli* begin removing sentries and other woods-wanderers?''

''And while some of them are doing that, the rest of the *hertasi* will be setting the traps we set up today along the trail they came up from the river on.'' Snowfire grinned at Starfall's look of surprise. ''Exactly. No matter which way they try to go in the morning, they'll run into man-traps. I didn't see any reason to give them an unhindered path in any direction. By that time, they'll already know they're under attack, so there's no point in putting a lot of effort into making traps that will look like accidents. When they trigger *these* traps, they'll know it's something left for them by an enemy.''

''Good so far,'' Starfall mused. ''But you can't get all of them with traps. So?''

''So the man-traps themselves form a channeling-trap. Tomorrow when we set everything up, we'll be leaving one easier direction— here.'' He drew a sweeping arrow toward a patch of green moss. ''They'll come out into the clear, with no place to go for cover and a ravine at their back. It ought to be no difficult thing for the *hertasi* to pick them off with bows.''

''And at any rate, by the time the survivors struggle back to the village, the rescue should be long over. I like it.'' Starfall nodded decisively.

''Even if the mage at the village can communicate with the fighters out here, they won't be able to get back in time to do him any good. It'll be the middle of the night, and the woods will be full of *hertasi* with knives and traps just waiting to be sprung.'' Snowfire nodded, feeling very pleased with himself. ''And to avoid leaving a trail back here to the encampment, we're going to try to get the villagers across the bridge and take them downriver to that Kelmskeep place Dar'ian told us of. I think if anyone follows us, it will be that way, and I hope there will be a force to meet us from the Valdemarans.''

''I have sent a message to Lord Breon of Kelmskeep, that reached the place today,'' Starfall confirmed, but then frowned. ''The thing is, I do not know if it will be heeded or even seen by the man himself.''

''How did you send it?'' Snowfire asked.

''A written message, delivered by raven to the gatekeeper this morning; Raindance saw it through the bird's eyes. She said he seemed startled.'' Starfall shrugged. ''It took the bird this long to reach Kelmskeep; the best we can hope for, I think, is that an escorting force meet you on the way.''

Snowfire sighed, well aware that the Adept was right. Best to count on what they had, not what they *hoped* they would have.

''Well, I leave all the magic doings in your capable hands,'' he said.

''And I will leave the rest in yours.'' Starfall stood up and stretched, and walked back into the center of the clearing, where he took his seat again and closed his eyes. A moment later, the containment shield had sprung up around him. Snowfire whistled to Hweel, who was still gossiping with the cooperi, and the great owl launched himself into the air to follow him back to the main encampment.

:*What were you two chattering about?*: he asked his bird. :*You don't usually have that much to say to the daybirds.*:

:*Mates,*: Hweel said shortly, then elaborated. :*He may be young, but he has a mate. He has two fledges this year, now flying strong.*:

Snowfire sensed that there was more. :*And?*: he persisted.

:*They come, all five. His mate, mine, three fledges.*: Hweel's mind-voice was tentative, as if he was afraid that Snowfire would object to the arrival of his mate and young.

That was the last thing on Snowfire's mind. Although he wasn't bonded to Hweel's mate Huur, she worked with Hweel so effectively when she wasn't tending youngsters that he might just as well have been. And having a clumsy fledgling around wasn't a bad thing as long as you could keep the youngster close to the camp.

:*I'll be glad to see them,*: he replied, and sensed the relief in Hweel's mind. :*It was clever of you to have his mate come with yours; the fledges will have protection by day and night on the journey.*:

Hweel *huured*, a contented little sound of pleasure from which his mate got her name. He liked being praised, and he had greatly missed his mate, so knowing that Snowfire would welcome her arrival made him doubly happy.

It would be no bad thing to have a couple of unbonded birds along with the expedition either. They would make excellent camp guards, and if the unthinkable happened and someone lost a bird, there would be possible replacements at hand.

Enough; concentrate on the immediate problem, he reminded himself. He needed to collect Darian and some paper and a charcoal stick; it was time to make a detailed plan of how to get into and out of the village.

He'd left Darian about to take his turn in the bathing pool; by now the boy should be clean and ready for something to eat. Snowfire was terribly proud of him, for Darian had worked as hard as any of them, and had mastered his frustration admirably when someone didn't quite understand what it was he wanted for a trap. The boy had matured a great deal in the last week, though it was clear every so often that he *was* still a boy.

When this is over—he needs some time to play and be young, Snowfire concluded to himself. But right now, well, none of them could afford to be anything other than mature and responsible.

He collected more meat and bread from the stores; the berries were gone, but when Ayshen heard who this next meal was going to, he pulled Snowfire aside and passed him a honeycake surreptitiously. "The hatchling didn't get enough the last time I made them," Ayshen said, as if daring him to challenge the statement. Since Snowfire had seen Darian stuffing himself with the coveted sweets, and knew Ayshen knew he had, it was clear that the *hertasi* had taken very strongly to the boy.

"I'll make sure he knows who sent it," Snowfire replied, and carried the treasure off. He'd seen Ayshen watching the boy out of the corner of his long eye; evidently this was the *hertasi*'s way of rewarding hard work.

He met Darian on the path, hair damp, dressed in fresh clothing. "Here, I brought you something to eat," Snowfire said, holding the napkin out to him. "There's a honeycake in there from Ayshen."

"There is?" Darian looked as pleased as if it had been a lump of amber. "I love Ayshen's honeycakes! Where can we go so I can eat, and help you with those maps of the village you wanted at the same time?"

"Let's try the council clearing," Snowfire suggested. "There's a game place there that no one is going to be using tonight. We'll have a drawing surface there."

Darian nodded, his mouth already full of bread and meat. He followed Snowfire to the clearing and at the far side Snowfire took over the game place, a flat sheet of rock balanced on a stump that served as a table, and two more stumps, one on either side of it. He took the taller of the two, and Darian took the shorter, as he spread out the first sheet of paper and took out a scribing rod. "All right," he said, making a diagonal line for the bank of the river. "Here is the riverbank. Let's start there."

"Put one edge of the forest here, and one here," Darian suggested, pointing with a sticky finger. "And the bridge would be here." He devoured the last crumb of his cake and licked his fingers clean while Snowfire sketched. "Right, now put the back edge of the forest there. The road goes from the bridge to the center of town, and stops there. Here's the mill, with the waterwheel there. There's the forge."

Snowfire was agreeably surprised at the lad's clear and precise ability to remember and place everything in the village, but there just weren't enough adequate areas of cover to sneak a number of people in without getting caught.

"... and here's where the aqueduct starts," Darian was saying, and the words brought him out of his thoughts with a jolt.

"Aqueduct?" he said, suddenly interested. "What aqueduct?"

"We use it to bring river water to the fields in summer," Darian explained. "See, it goes around through the middle of the planted fields, then to the cistern house and the watering trough in the center of town."

"And where does it stop?" Snowfire demanded. "What's it made of?"

"It stops at the river, I guess," Darian said, confused by the sudden barrage of urgent questions. "There's a water-lifting wheel beside the mill that brings water up to the aqueduct and that brings the water out of the river down to the fields because it's always sloping down from where it starts. As for what it's made of—hollow tree trunk, mostly. It's covered to keep trash out of it."

"Is it big enough for a man to crawl in?" Snowfire persisted.

"Oh, certainly—and I see what you want to do!" Suddenly Darian was all smiles. "It's absolutely big enough for a man to crawl inside. What's more, even though we use it all summer, I doubt that anyone's tending to it now. I can't imagine a bunch of barbarians thinking to irrigate the fields, and I doubt that anyone in the village is inclined to help them by telling them that the fields need water."

"So it starts at the river?" Snowfire asked. "Where, precisely?"

Now Darian's face fell. "I don't exactly know," he confessed. "It's all overgrown there; I know it's *somewhere* near the mill, but not exactly. At least, I don't know what the place looks like at night. It's real tall, though, because otherwise it wouldn't be able to slope down to the fields."

"But if we can find it, we can get right into the heart of the village undetected." This was exactly the sort of thing Snowfire was looking for. "Darian, your memory is so good, *surely* you can remember where the aqueduct starts!"

But Darian shook his head unhappily. "I know what it looks like, but I can't tell you where to find it," he confessed. "I only remember that it's near the mill, not in it." He looked up at Snowfire hopefully. "I could guide you, though."

Snowfire frowned. "I don't want you anywhere near possible fighting," he objected.

"But if you won't let me guide you, how do you expect to convince people you aren't a different kind of enemy?" Darian asked shrewdly. "None of them have ever seen a Hawkbrother, and they'll probably be frightened of you!"

That was something else Snowfire hadn't thought of, and he hated to admit it, but the boy was probably right. Still, it went against the grain to permit someone as young as Darian anywhere near combat.

He argued with the boy for some time, and in the end Darian had more good, sound reasons why he should go than Snowfire had counters for them.

"All right," Snowfire sighed. "You can guide us. But just to a place of safety, mind! You aren't to rush in and try to help if there's fighting. You'll only get in the way, and you might make someone lose his concentration and his life."

"I promise!" Darian agreed, his eyes shining.

Snowfire only hoped that both of them—and ultimately, the village and the Hawkbrothers—would not regret this decision.

Lord Breon

Seven

Now, in some ways, came the worst part. All of the traps were constructed and set, and now came the waiting. Daystorm had her birds over the village, while Starfall created his "bait," and the nagging question was, *would their foe take it?*

If he closed his own eyes, Snowfire could picture the scene as clearly as if he himself were there. A flock of five crows perched in a tree above the rooftops of Errold's Grove, an unusually silent gathering, but no one in the village seemed to notice either their presence or their silence. Through their eyes, Daystorm watched the activity in the village below. Two of the crows were bonded to her, the rest were the offspring of her original pair, but all were willing to lend her their eyes and wings, especially when the activity at hand promised to be entertaining. Snowfire occasionally envied the Tayledras who bonded to crows and ravens; the birds had tremendous senses of humor, and as a matter of course, when the original bird took a mate, the mate also became his or her bondbird. Sometimes Hweel's sober dignity was a little wearing, and he would have welcomed the raucous hooliganism of a band of crows; he would also have welcomed having both halves of a pair as his bondbirds. He sometimes worried that having an unbonded mate gave Hweel divided loyalties.

Last night the *dyheli* doe Pyreen had taken her place upriver, carrying the double burden of an illusion of a heavily guarded caravan and the newly-strengthened power-point. She had remained stationary until daybreak, then moved slowly southward, mimicking the plodding pace of heavily-laden mules. By then Daystorm's birds had already been in place to see if the mage somewhere below would take the bait. Tentative experiments had proven that either the mage could not sense anything different about the bondbirds, or that there was enough magical energy in the form of his own Changed fighters to mask the magic of the birds and their links to their bondmates. To Snowfire's mind, that only confirmed his impression that it had been Kelvren that the "watchdogs" had reacted to, and not Hweel.

Daystorm was simply sitting quietly with her back braced against a tree at the side of the Council circle, with an eager audience waiting around her. She took it all in stride, including the audience; there was very little that rattled this experienced scout. She sat so quietly that she could have been a painted statue, for her chest rose and fell so slowly that it would be very difficult to tell that she was breathing. Her hair, shorn short on the sides, cut into a stiff crest on the top, and braided in a long tail down her back, never moved in the fitful breeze that came with sunrise, contributing to the statuelike illusion.

Finally she broke the silence. "There's some activity around the Lutters' house," Daystorm announced. "Someone just dashed out. Now—he's going around to all the houses of the village at a run. He's pounding on the doors and shouting something at each house. Now there are men coming out of the houses, one out of each, walking fast toward the Lutter house."

Well, that confirmed the guess that whomever was in command of this force had taken over the Lutter house, which—although it was not the largest—was definitely the finest house in the village, according to Darian. Lutter had been one of the dye-merchants, was still the only merchant in the village, and was possibly the wealthiest man in Errold's Grove before the Storms. By now, of course, his store of ready cash was used up, but his house and the contents were still the finest in the village.

So, naturally, the place would be taken by the most powerful person in the invading forces, and that person appeared to be the mage. That was good to know, but it did leave several questions unanswered. There was a question of who was in absolute control—was the mage the definitive leader, or did he serve a military leader? Was there more than one mage, and if so, how powerful were the others? So far, no recognizable mage had come within view of any of the birds.

"Just the usual, now," Daystorm announced. Snowfire sighed; after several days of observation, they had a good idea of the usual daily schedule. Once the sun rose, the villagers were roused from sleep by the slavemasters—they had all been crammed into the threshing barn, which was the least weathertight of all of the village buildings, serving merely to keep rain and damp away from grain while it was being threshed from the stalk. Men, women, and children were all housed together, and at a rough guess, the barbarians had managed to round up and take most of the villagers prisoner. Everyone, old and young, regardless of physical condition, was expected to work in the fields or do menial tasks. The numbers didn't add up exactly, but there were probably a few "special" slaves in the houses, serving the barbarian leaders and elite fighters, and thus exempt from field work.

"The fighters are coming out to practice." Every morning the fighters had limbering and practice sessions before they ate. The fighters were mostly housed in the barns, though some of them had taken over the houses that those of higher rank didn't want, cramming two and three times as many people into each dwelling as the houses had been intended to hold. But, from all Snowfire knew of their way of life, they were used to cramming themselves together like wolves in a winter den, and probably didn't think they were suffering from overcrowding. After the practice sessions were over, and the morning meal distributed and eaten, the leaders would pick out men for hunting parties and fishing parties, and the rest would be drilled in formation-combat. *That* was quite unlike the barbarians Snowfire knew of, who fought as individuals rather than groups. This signified a new and disturbing development, and something that would have to be looked into when he had the time.

If I ever have the time. Well, he'd made notes on all of this, and if everything went wrong, Starfall would take those notes with him as he escaped to safety.

Daystorm collected more of an audience as the morning passed; after all the preparations, the Tayledras were on edge and eager to get into action. Ayshen had somehow found the time to bake more flatbread, and *hertasi* were passing around rounds of the stuff wrapped around bits of honeycomb. Snowfire took one and munched it without ever taking his eyes off Daystorm's face.

She took one without ever opening her eyes, but then, she had always had an extra sense where sweets were concerned. "They're calling the fighters in to eat. Still nothing from the Lutter house."

"I wish we dared send a bird down to the roof to see if it could overhear anything," Wintersky muttered to him. Snowfire nodded agreement; he would have given a great deal for a set of ears in— or on—that house.

In no way would he have ever endangered a bird by putting one there, however. Some of the barbarians knew what Tayledras birds looked like, for there had been conflict along the northern ranges with barbarians before this. Even if it somehow escaped notice that the bird in question was much larger than normal, well, bored barbarians with bows tended to make targets out of anything that moved.

Including each other—they seemed to find it howlingly funny to shoot blunted arrows at each other, with the intended target trying to dodge and the bowman trying to hit in an embarrassing and potentially excruciatingly painful place. Snowfire had spent a great deal of time in the past few days, watching their antics through Hweel's eyes.

He had noted that they seemed to have done a pretty thorough job of looting the village, not that there was much to take. Clothing that didn't fit or that was for a child or a female was either cut up or put to other purposes. Tools that weren't needed for immediate field work had already gone to the forge, presumably to be remade into weapons. Food and drink were gone, of course, and there were rapid inroads being made on the ripe stuff in the fields; any objects of metal had been melted down, either to be made into ingots or into arrowheads. Livestock had either been eaten or would be soon, except for horses, which had been taken for the mounted fighters. Anything valuable was presumably in the hands of the leaders by now. There wouldn't be a great deal for the villagers to salvage when this was over. Hopefully they would be grateful just to escape with their lives.

"Ah! We're getting some activity!" Daystorm exclaimed. "The leaders are coming out of the house—now they're heading for the fighters. They're shouting orders. Most of the fighters are running back to the barns, except for a couple who are going to the houses. Oh, they're coming back with the leaders' armor, and here come the rest of the fighters with theirs. Everyone is getting into armor. No, that's not quite right. Everyone except the mounted fighters is getting into armor—they're getting ready to send out a raiding force. I think it's working, Snowfire. He's taking the bait."

"Sounds to me that since your illusion only shows pack-animals, he's keeping his mounted troops behind," Rainwind observed shrewdly to Snowfire, leaning over and speaking in a low voice to avoid disturbing Daystorm.

"That would make sense," Snowfire agreed. "It would be best not to risk them on this. He knows that his foot troops can easily overtake a pack-train, and why take the chance of losing a mounted fighter who is much more expensive to replace than a foot soldier? It's what I'd do."

"Right, they're all getting into formation, strapping on their armor," Daystorm reported. "And packs. They're taking light overnight packs. So the mage has a pretty good idea of how far the target is likely to get before they reach it."

Snowfire nodded with satisfaction. That was good; it meant that the mage wouldn't think anything of it when his troops didn't make it back by nightfall.

Daystorm continued to report on preparations, and then finally said the words he had been waiting for. "This is it. They're moving out, and they're taking the river road, exactly as we wanted them to."

"Excellent!" he exclaimed. It was time for the next stage, but he didn't have to tell the others that. Daystorm would leave her crows standing sentry at the village, but Wintersky's bird would pick up the departing troops as they reached the river. Hweel had already passed word of the departure to Sunstone (or rather, Sunstone's falcon); Sunstone was stationed at the bluff and would trigger the avalanche blocking the road. Wintersky would count them and pass the number on to Sunstone. Sunstone would wait until the last ranks were in view, then let the stone bluff fall. They had agreed that, although it would be a fine thing if they actually caught some of the enemy under the rockfall, they wouldn't actually *try* for anything more complicated than blocking the path behind them all. It would be a disaster to have even one of the enemy fighters left on the village side of the blockage, for he would return to get help, and the mage would detect the telltale traces of magic in the fallen stone.

So, the rock would fall, the enemy force would be whittled down. They would soon find that the riverside path that had been so easy to follow deteriorated into a hellish nightmare of washouts, slippery rockslides, and narrow ledges where only one man at a time could pass. The river itself was swift and deep there, and anyone who fell in would fall prey to Ayshen and his friends. Nor would bodies bob to the surface with obvious knife wounds, for Ayshen had weighted ropes to keep them on the river bottom. All that anyone above would know was that those who fell or jumped in were pulled under and never reappeared. That should thoroughly discourage would-be swimmers.

When a path leading inland appeared, it would be welcomed with relief, and the steep ravine with its derelict bridge would seem no great obstacle until the men tried to cross it. Only then would they learn that the sides of the ravine were crumbling clay and gravel, and the bottom was a morass of sticky muck as deep as a man was tall, or perhaps even deeper. It hadn't always been that way, but ever since Snowfire opened up a spring at the bottom, it was. As difficult as it was to climb down, it was even harder to climb up. They probably wouldn't lose any men to the climb, but they'd be wet, filthy, and exhausted before it was over.

Meanwhile, the rest of the *hertasi* and the *dyheli* were all in place, waiting for the exhausted and demoralized enemy troops to get to the spot chosen for the ambush. The *hertasi* were making the place look very attractive without making it look like a trap. Signs of old camp-fires and just enough deadfall wood piled up would leave the impression that others—perhaps the very caravan they were following—had camped here before. There was a clear, cold spring near enough to the campsite that someone should stumble over it, and between that ready source of water and the wood already at hand, the situation should be too tempting to resist.

But that would be for later tonight. Now it would be another long wait until the enemy troops marched past Sunstone, late this afternoon.

Now that everyone knew the enemy was on the move, the group waiting around Daystorm broke up. Snowfire looked up to find Darian at his elbow, waiting patiently for the scout to notice him.

"What is it, little brother?" Snowfire asked. "Do you wish to change the plan for tonight?"

"No!" Darian exclaimed. "No—I mean, I—I *am* afraid. I'm scared, but I don't want to back out or anything. I just—I just need something to do."

Snowfire understood only too well the need to have "something to do" before a planned engagement, but he was at a loss to think of anything. Finally he had an inspiration. "Please—practice those exercises in magic I have shown you," he said earnestly, "and try to think of ways in which they could be used tonight. We will need every weapon at our disposal; remember what I said about the way that a small application of magic can be used to a great effect."

Darian grimaced a little, but nodded and trailed off to find a quiet place in which to practice.

Hweel, Hweel's mate Huur, and their young fledgling watched him move off with unblinking gazes. Then Huur yawned hugely, her youngster did the same a moment later, and both of them shut their eyes and hunched their heads down to sleep. They had arrived last night, and were probably exhausted. They had certainly eaten hugely of the bounty that an excited Hweel had provided for them.

Hweel practically radiated contentment as he sat beside his mate and their bumbling youngster. Huur was considerably larger than Hweel, as was usually the case with birds of prey, and Snowfire paused to consider whether he really *wanted* Huur to bond with him. After all, Hweel was quite a burden; Huur would be worse.

Well, it wasn't within his power to decide one way or another. It

was the bird's decision, not his. And meanwhile, Hweel was over-
joyed to have her beside him and that was no bad thing.

Snowfire had his own ritual of preparation to begin. He had things
timed to a nicety, so that his hours would be occupied and his mind
would not be idle to make up scenarios of disaster.

First, he ran through his own magic practice, though he didn't have
to think of ways in which small magics would be useful in tonight's
raid, for he had plenty of experience along those lines. All the while
he practiced, he sat across from Daystorm, with one ear cocked in
case she said anything about activity in the village. He put himself
through his paces, pushing to speed up the time it took for him to
work a particular piece of magic, by even a fraction of a breath. That
was always what he worked toward; it would be useless to try for
more power, for he had reached the limits of his ability there—but
it was always possible to try for more speed.

By the time he was done, it was about noon; he left Daystorm's
side just long enough to collect food for himself, Daystorm, and
Starfall. He left Starfall's ration just outside the containment shield,
though Starfall was so deep in concentration that the Adept never
noticed he was there. That was all right; the food was covered and
would keep, and Starfall's bird would keep pests from carrying it off.
Then he took Daystorm's ration to her, and the scout accepted it with
thanks.

"There's nothing unusual going on at all," she said, tearing off a
strip of dried meat with her strong, white teeth. She looked very much
like a fox when she did that, and Snowfire wondered if she knew it.
"The only thing going on is that the mounted fighters are all practicing, mostly on each other. I think they're pleased that the foot
soldiers are gone; it gives them more space to practice in."

"That's probably true," he agreed, and grinned. "Let's hope they
forget it's practice and take out a few of their own."

She laughed, and he turned his attention to his bondbird. :How
close are they to the trap?: he asked Hweel, who was in contact with
all of the bondbirds.

:Close,: Hweel told him, and showed him what Rainwind's falcon
saw from high above, so high that the men below her would not see
even a speck in the sky overhead. It would not be long now until the
first of the troops reached the undermined section of bluff.

"They're getting close," he said aloud to Daystorm. "Keep a close
eye on the Lutter house; if this mage has any way of communicating
with the other troops, we'll find out about it soon."

He held to the vision of the river road as seen through the eyes of the circling falcon, watching as the antlike, foreshortened figures crept along at a maddeningly slow pace. The falcon knew exactly where the fall was to take place, and centered her circle on that part of the bluff. There was no way to communicate with Sunstone, but part of Snowfire ached with tension, hoping he would not drop the rockfall too soon. The tiny figures crawled onward, completely unaware of what waited for them. Half of them were past the bluff now, with most of the rest beneath the area where the rock would come down. *Most* of the rest—

Not yet, Sunstone, not yet. Let them pass—

Now they were either past the fall area, or within it, but there was always the chance that the rock would not fall as they thought, letting one or two escape.

Not yet, not yet—

There! The last of them was past the halfway point!

A little puff of dust at the base of the bluff was all the warning Snowfire had; Sunstone had released the fall.

It began slowly, as these things always did; a trickle of rock from the top, a rumbling sound, then the first signs of the slide. Most of the enemy fighters reacted immediately; they looked up, and ran downriver, away from the village. Three hesitated, started to run *toward* the village as Snowfire bit off a curse. Suddenly, as a few rocks hit the trail in front of them, they paused, and reversed themselves. But that hesitation was fatal; in the next instant, they were buried beneath a cascade of dirt and rock that ran out into the river. A huge cloud of dust rose and obscured everything, even for a falcon's sharp eyes, and Snowfire waited impatiently for it to clear.

Finally the strong breeze from upriver cleared it away, and he saw that there would be no passage back across that fall for anyone. They had managed to drop far more than he had estimated across the roadway; until it all settled, it would be insane to try and climb it. The enemy fighters milled around the edge, as if wondering whether they should make some attempt to rescue their three companions. Evidently they decided against it, or their leaders did, for after a bit more confused meandering, they formed back up into ranks, and moved out along the river again.

Snowfire broke contact with the falcon with a feeling of fierce pleasure. "The first stage worked perfectly!" he told Daystorm. "Any sign from the mage that he knows what happened?"

She shook her head. "Nothing at all out of the ordinary," she reported. "You ought to check with Starfall, though. He might have noticed something."

That was an excellent idea, and he was not at all loath to follow it. He brushed the dust off his trews and loped up the trail to Starfall's *ekele*, hoping that the Adept was not too lost in his work to speak to him.

As it happened, Starfall was just finishing the last of his rations, and greeted Snowfire with a wave of his hand. "We've dropped the bluff; it worked perfectly, and they lost three in the rockfall," Snowfire reported. "Have you noticed anything from the mage?"

"Only that he's trying harder than before to take control of the lines and nodes from me," Starfall replied. "He's getting aggressive; I think he's getting extra energy from his fighters. Are they doing anything unusual?"

"Only the mounted ones are left; Daystorm says they're practicing against each other, and that's unusual, because there isn't a lot of room for them to practice ordinarily." Snowfire cocked his head to the side. "From what I saw, the mounted fighters are the least disciplined. Would that be enough to generate extra energy for him?"

"Probably; it isn't a lot, but these days, when there isn't a lot of energy to be had, a mage would grasp at anything." Starfall blinked, and rubbed his eyes. "At least he isn't practicing blood-sacrifice."

"I'll say this much for the barbarians; so far as I know, they don't tend to stoop to that. They'll use the power generated by slaughter on a battlefield, but they won't practice blood-sacrifice. Or at least, not of humans." He grimaced. "Let's hope this lot runs true to form."

"Dar'ian would never forgive us if anything like that happened," Starfall muttered, and shook his head. "Well, he's due for another try, and I need to be on guard; keep me informed if you can."

Starfall raised the containment shield again, and sank back into his trance. Snowfire left him with his falcon standing watch and returned to Daystorm.

"I think you can drop the close watch on the village," he told her. "Starfall says the mage hasn't reacted to what we did at all."

She sighed with relief. "Oh, good. If I don't get myself stretched out, I won't be any use for the raid. I'll leave the hooligans in place; I don't need them here, and they'll call me if something catches their attention."

"Good plan," he said approvingly, and went to check on the others.

Wintersky had taken charge of building their packs; each of them would carry an identical load of climbing staff, short bow, arrows, and throwing darts. The idea was *not* to get into combat, if they could avoid it; the idea was to free the slaves and guard their backtrail. Snowfire wished he had some other sort of magic than the type he had; it would have been so useful to be able to turn water into drugged brandywine and arrange for the remaining barbarians to find it!

Seventeen Tayledras and one adopted boy would be the whole of their army; Nightwind and Kel would remain behind to guard Starfall, with five *dyheli* and three of the most timid of the *hertasi*. Wintersky had finished seven of the packs, with ten more to go; he was checking each and every weapon with utmost care as he packed it, and there was a small pile of rejected arrows beside him. Snowfire didn't interrupt; he had the job well in hand.

Seventeen against how many? We must be mad. Yet if they could just avoid rousing anything or anyone, the odds of pulling this off were good. Or at least, they weren't *insurmountable.*

Time to check on someone whose optimism more than equals my pessimism. He left Wintersky and took the path that led to the pools and Kelvren.

The only quiet place to practice was beside the bathing pools, and Darian was more than tired of repeating his tiny magics over and over when Kelvren provided a welcome interruption.

"What passsessss, brrrancherrr?" the gryphon called, as he flew low over the pool, craning his neck to the side to keep his eyes on Darian. When Darian waved at him, the gryphon executed a slow and graceful gliding turn, then backwinged to a perfect one-claw landing on the rock edge of the pool beside Darian. Darian had to duck his head and shield his eyes against the dust storm kicked up by the gryphon's wingbeats, but he grinned a greeting anyway.

"Nothing much passes except time, and that's passing too slowly!" he complained, as the gryphon settled himself with a couple of crisp wing-flicks. He noticed that Kel had a bundle in his right front talon, which he placed on the ground behind the rocks, just out of sight. "I want to *do* something, not just sit here!"

"I agrrree," Kel responded readily. "But I happen to have sssomething you can do. Do you sssupposse you could give me a hand with grrrrooming? Nightwind isss bussy prreparring herr weaponsss, the *herrrtasssi* arrre all gone orrrr busssy, and I am no grrry-falcon, to have handsss that hold toolsss well."

Help Kelvren? In a heartbeat! Darian was absolutely thrilled to be asked, and jumped to his feet, prepared to do anything that Kel requested. "Do I need to get anything special?" he asked anxiously. "The feather-oil or anything?"

"Not featherrr-oilsss," the gryphon replied, "I have everrrything we'll need. Thisss will be battle preparrrationsss."

With his foreclaw the gryphon picked up the bag which he put down in front of Darian. He opened it and spread out the contents on the ground. It contained the usual brushes and combs, but also held files, a thin and flexible chest protector that was clearly made to fit over the chestplate on Kel's harness, and a set of sharp metal claw-sheaths. "Thesssse fit overrr the talonsssr," Kel said, indicating the metal sheaths. "You'll have to file my talonsss to fit; they arrre a bit longerrr than they werrre when I wasss fitted with thessse."

Darian picked up the set of three files and the right-side set of sheaths and went to work, as Kel advised and corrected what he was doing. He found that if he sat just under the gryphon's chin with his back against Kel's chest, they were both able to see what was going on clearly and were more comfortable. It was very pleasant, sitting there with his back against the feathery warmth of his friend, working diligently with the files on the shining black talons. He could almost forget why they were making these preparations. He couldn't help thinking what the other boys of Errold's Grove would say if they saw what he was doing now. *Wouldn't their eyes just pop! They wouldn't believe what they were seeing! Imagine, me, helping take care of a real, live gryphon! Why, next thing, I'll be helping trap a snow-drake or something.*

The talon-sheaths fit over each claw and were held in place with a glovelike web of fine, strong leather straps. The workmanship was really ingenious, and the articulation was perfect. The sheaths didn't really extend the length of the talons all that much, so Kel would still be able to walk, land, and pick things up. When Darian finished fitting the whole contraption to Kel's right leg, the gryphon had what was effectively a set of four single-edged knives on the end of his leg. Not only did each sheath taper to a point as sharp as a needle, but the first third of each had a real sharpened edge for slashing.

Kel flexed his foot, and looked at it with a mixture of pride and chagrin, his huge golden eyes blinking slowly as he admired the shining metal now covering each talon. "Harrrd to walk in, thessse, becausssse of all the damage. You don't want me anywherrre nearrr a tent, forrr insssstancsse. Sssstill. They prrrotect my rrreal talonsss; metal won't brrreak the way a talon can. And obviousssly, a weapon can't chop one off."

Darian nodded soberly, and set to work on the left-side set. *I'd hate to see how awful it would be if a talon did get chopped off. He could bleed to death!* Much better to have the sheaths, even if they were a bit awkward to wear. When he finished, Kelvren reared up on his hindquarters and made a few experimental slashes in the air. "Perrrfect!" he said with a gleeful sparkle in his eyes. "You may be my *trrrondi'irrrn* any time!"

"Oh, I don't know about that," Darian replied, blushing with awkward pleasure. "I don't know a fraction of what Nightwind knows, and anyway, any of the *hertasi* could have helped you just as well. Let's get this chest thing on you, all right?"

"Sssurrrely," Kel agreed, dropping back down to all fours. "It goesss onto the harnessss—ssssee the bucklesss? Then the neck-piecssse wrrrapsss arrrround the thrrroat."

The protective armor would never withstand the blows of a sword or ax, but it would protect against arrows; it was made of overlapping articulated plates of a light, strong metal totally unfamiliar to Darian, backed with a thin leather that was the toughest such substance Darian had ever seen. Unlike the talons, which were a satin finished, highly-polished silver, the chest protector was a matte black and would not betray Kel by reflecting light. The whole thing didn't even weigh as much as a single ordinary breastplate for a smallish human—but then, it would have to be light if Kel was going to fly while wearing it.

When Darian finished buckling it onto the harness, Kel gave himself a tremendous shake to settle it, and had him tighten two or three straps, then shook himself again.

"Urrrr," he said, clicking his beak meditatively. "Not the mossst comforrrtable thing to wearrr. But then, I have hearrrd the human Sssilverrrsss sssay the sssame of theirrr arrrmorrr."

"It could be worse, you could have a helmet and a stomach plate and things," Darian pointed out. Kel shook his head comically.

"I think not!" the gryphon exclaimed. "I would not be able to walk, much lessss fly! Thisss isss bad enough, and I would not wearr it had Nightwind not insssssissted. I fearrr it looksss rrridiculousss."

"Well, you look tremendously warlike to me," Darian told him, stepping back to admire him from a little distance. "Very impressive. Terrifying, in fact."

"Oh, do I?" Kel exclaimed, ingenuously pleased. "Terrrifying? Trrruly?"

"Truly," Darian told him. "If I were the enemy, I'd take one look at you and run, I wouldn't stick around to find out what you could do to me."

And the gryphon did make a daunting sight, with the metal breast-plate and neck guard forming what appeared to be a seamless black shell over his chest and neck, one claw upraised, and the metal talons gleaming wickedly in the sun. It was no exaggeration to say that Kel would probably have frightened any of the Errold's Grove militia members into scuttling back to the village, metaphorical tail between his legs.

But would he have the same effect on the barbarians? The plain truth was, virtually *anything* the militia thought of as a "monster" had sent them scuttling back to the safety of the village. What did *he* know about fighting? Only what he'd heard and read in books.

I just hope we never find out, Darian thought, keeping his doubts to himself. *I'd rather not know than have those barbarians turn up here.*

"I think if I was Starfall, I would feel completely secure with you on watch," he said aloud. "I wouldn't need anybody else."

"Rrreally?" Kel arched his neck, and his eyes pinned with ex-citement. "You arrre too kind. I am only a verrrry juniorrr Sssilverrr."

"I agree with him," Nightwind said, emerging from the shadows of the path. "You look quite formidable, Kel. Starfall will feel quite secure with you on guard, and rightly so. You're going to do a fine job."

Kel's neck arched a little more, and he practically purred. "Thank you," he said. "I hope yourrr confidencssse is jussstified."

Nightwind smiled. "I'm a *trondi'irn*, remember? I've served quite a few gryphons in the past. I have no doubt of it."

In Darian's opinion, Nightwind herself looked just as formidable as the gryphon; she had a breastplate made much like his, with gaunt-lets to match, a light helm, and a bow that Darian would never dream of being able to string, much less draw. He couldn't see the business-end of the arrows she carried in a quiver at her belt, but he had no doubt that they were more of the nasty, man-killing type that the Tayledras were using tonight.

Her hair had been braided back tightly into a no-nonsense knot at the nape of her neck, and there wasn't a single extraneous bead or feather on her spare, uniformlike costume. Like Kel, her breastplate had a badge embossed on it, and he peered at it curiously.

She noted where his eyes went, and smiled. "This is the badge of the Silver Gryphons," she told him, the fingers of one hand lightly caressing the edge of the emblem. "Kel and I are both Silvers, the only ones in the group. I don't think they quite realize yet what that means."

"Why isn't anyone else?" he asked.

She chuckled. "Because we are the only two *Kaled'a'in* here," she told him. "We aren't Tayledras at all—or rather, the Tayledras *used* to be Kaled'a'in, but—"

The gryphon waved a claw, interrupting her. "You arrre confusss-ing him," Kel chided. "Darrr'ian, it isss sssimple. Long ago therrre wasss one people, the Kaled'a'in. When the Cataclysssssm wasss overrr, that people wasss sssunderrred. The Kaled'a'in Clan k'Lessshya wasss farrr seperrrated frrrom the otherrrsss, and thossse within it did not even know if the rrresst had ssssurrrvived, sssso they went to sssaferrr landsss, wessst and sssouth, and became the allliesss of the Black Kingsss. Forrr the otherrr Clansss it was differrrent. Theirrr homelandsss werrre desssstrrroyed, ssso they found when they went to look. The otherrrsss quarrrelled overrr the ussse of magic—thossse who wanted to continue the ussse of it became the Tayle-drrrasss, and thossse who wisssshed to ssshun it became the Sssshin'a'in.''

"But—because your people weren't fighting over whether or not to use magic, you stayed Kaled'a'in?" Darian asked, scratching his head. "But if your people went so far away, why are you here?"

"Because we decided that the moment was right to come back north and see what time had made of the lands we left," Nightwind told him, and smiled ruefully. "Little did we guess that we'd end up being here at the beginning of another Cataclysm! At least some of us managed to prevent this one, anyway. Kel's version is a *very* abbreviated one, and at some point, you'll have to hear the whole story."

"Prrrobably frrrom one of the *kyrrree* hissstorrry-keeperrrs," Kel said, meditatively examining his steel-sheathed talons. "Becaussse asss sssoon asss they learrrn you do *not* know the tale, you will have no choicsse but to hearrr it!''

Nightwind burst out laughing as if Kel had said something terribly funny. Darian couldn't make out just what the joke was, but laughed politely anyway.

"Well, the point is that only the Kaled'a'in have the Silver Gryph-ons," Nightwind continued, wiping her eyes with the back of her hand. "They serve a lot of the same functions that your Heralds do; peacekeepers, border guards, and as the Kaled'a'in militia. Some day I'll tell you why things turned out that way, but the fact is that of all the people on this expedition, Kel and I are the only true *warriors*. Mind you, some of the others, Snowfire in particular, have seen com-bat—but we're the only ones actually trained as warriors." One corner of her mouth quirked in an ironic smile. "To tell you the truth, I don't think Snowfire quite realizes that about me. He still thinks I'm just an Empath and Kel's attendant. We haven't had to get our battle gear out before this."

"Not that it matterrrsss," Kel added. "Thisss isss what we prrrrobably would have volunteerrred forrr if he hadn't asssked usss. I am a bit larrrge to hide in a waterrrr-courrrrse."

"And we are the best sort of guards he could have on Starfall," Nightwind finished. "That's one of the things we're trained for; there is always a set of gryphons acting as bodyguards to our chief ally among the Black Kings."

But a new set of dazzling possibilities had opened up to Darian. "Could *I* be a Silver some day?" he asked breathlessly.

"Now that is an interesting thought," Nightwind replied, looking at him with surprise. "I never considered that possibility. Yes, I suppose you could; you're far too young right now, but once you're at the age where we accept candidates, you could train as a Silver, if you still want to be one."

"Being a mage would be an advantage," Kel added, his eartufts pricked forward with interest. "Magessss in the Sssilverrrsss learrrn combat-magicsss; verrry ssspecializssed ssstuff. It would mean anotherrr ssseverrral yearrrs of ssschooling."

Now that was a daunting thought. *More* training? But it might be worth it.

"You certainly don't have to make up your mind right now," Nightwind said, before he could even begin to consider the ramifications of the offer. "Let's get through this, then finish up this expedition. By the time we get back to Tayledras territory, you'll have a better idea of what you want to do. And if that includes joining the Silvers, Kel and I will see that you get a chance to apply and train."

He stammered his thanks, and helped Nightwind pack up the grooming utensils, aware in a dazzled fashion that he had gone in the past few days from having *no* choice in his future life to having a bewildering array of choices.

He did not remain dazzled for long. *First we have to get through this. Then I have to make sure that no one in Errold's Grove thinks he still has any claims on me. Then—then I have to learn how to be a mage and a Hawkbrother.* The enormity of the tasks still ahead of him sobered him quickly.

He glanced up at the sun, and judged that someone would probably come looking for him shortly. "I ought to go find Snowfire," he began.

"Snowfire has already found you," Nightwind chuckled, and pointed over his shoulder. He turned and saw the senior scout coming out into the sunlight by the side of the pool.

The Hawkbrother's eyes widened in surprise at the sight of Kel and Nightwind, though his lips curved in a slow smile. "Welladay!" he said, with appreciation in his voice. "I find all three of the folk I needed to gather, and all in one spot. Very efficient."

"Pure coincidence," Nightwind pointed out. "But as you can see, *we* are ready to take our posts."

"Whenever you're ready," Snowfire told her, with a little salute. "Unless you can think of anything you need to know, I'll leave you to handle the business of guarding Starfall as you see fit."

Darian had the feeling that Snowfire had *intended* to give Kel and Nightwind some careful instructions, and on being confronted by a pair of properly equipped professionals, had quickly revised his plans.

"Thank you for your confidence, Snowfire," Nightwind said, without a hint of her usual irony. "I hope we will prove worthy of it. Now, I take it that you have come to fetch your guide?"

"I have," he said, and turned his attention to Darian. "I hope you are ready, little brother, because we need to set off soon if we are to be in place after dark."

Darian nodded, unable to trust his voice, for he knew that the fear rising within him would make it shake. Even if he wasn't brave, he didn't want Snowfire to guess. *I have to go through with this. I let Justyn down; I'm not going to do that to Snowfire.*

"Come, then," the Hawkbrother said. "Nightwind, Kelvren, wind to thy wings."

"Good hunting," Kel said, as Nightwind sketched a salute to both of them, with a sly wink to Darian. That made him feel a little better; he managed to get out a proper farewell and followed in Snowfire's wake to where the rest of the Hawkbrothers were gathered. His heart was in his mouth, and he felt queasy, but what needed to be done would be done.

For the most part, the journey was a blur to Darian; the Hawkbrothers set a pace he would never have been able to match if he had not been riding the horse stolen from the barbarians. He could not for a moment imagine how they managed to keep up that steady lope for furlong after furlong. With Hweel and Huur providing "eyes ahead," they kept up the grueling trek long after sunset, and finally came to a halt somewhere in the deep woods after full darkness fell.

"Dar'ian, you must get off the horse now," whispered Wintersky, who had been holding the beast by a lead rope to prevent it from bolting off the way it had the last time. "We will turn the beast loose here, for we are now going down to the river."

Darian dismounted stiffly; the horse's trot had not been a comfortable gait, especially not for someone who never had been much of a rider. Wintersky untied the rope from the horse's bridle, and used it to flick the beast on the flank. With an indignant squeal, it trotted off into the darkness, leaving them all standing beside one of the enormous trees. Beneath the whisper of wind in the leaves above, Darian heard the sound of the river; it couldn't be too far off, then. They were very near their goal, the end of the aqueduct that carried water to the village.

"Come," Snowfire whispered; somehow he had replaced Wintersky at Darian's side. "Do not fear to keep up; we must go slowly now, avoiding the sentries."

As gruelingly swift as the pace had been before, it was now just as agonizingly slow. The Hawkbrothers moved from cover to cover, slipping in and out of the shadows like silent shadows themselves, and far quieter than Darian was. Darian winced every time he stepped on a rock or a twig, for the sounds he made sounded as loud as shouts in the relative peace of the forest.

But there were other things making sounds out here; he was amazed to realize how loud deer were, as they came across a pair of does and a fawn, feeding. He'd always thought that deer moved silently, but they tramped through the sparse underbrush as noisily as he.

At last they reached the river itself, with no signs of sentries that Darian could see. But then, what did he know? Hweel, Huur, and Snowfire were probably the only ones who would know where sentries were, and the point was to avoid them.

The brush along the rocky riverbank was much thicker than under the heavy shade of the great trees; they had more cover to hide in, but there were more branches to snap, leaves to rustle, and rocks to trip over. Wintersky found a game trail that wound in and out of the bushes, often requiring that they go on all fours to keep their heads below the covering undergrowth; Darian discovered that he had his hands and mind full just following in his wake without making too terrible a noise. The river here did not make enough sound to mask their passage; though swift and deep, there were no rocks or deep bends to cause even a ripple along its tranquil surface. A chilling, damp breeze rose from its surface, penetrating Darian's clothing.

It seemed to Darian that they had been moving so long that it must surely be dawn, and yet by the stars it could not possibly have been much later than midnight when he felt Snowfire stop and crouch under the shadow of a bush. He stopped as well, then felt Snowfire's hand reach back and tug at his shoulder. Obedient to the signal, he crept forward to peer out at whatever it was that Snowfire was looking at.

"Is this the place?" the scout breathed into his ear. He squinted, and peered out into the darkness, straining his ears as well as his eyes when the dark bulk ahead of him failed to resolve into anything he recognized.

It was his ears that told him they had reached their goal; a rhythmic splashing, the creaking of wet wood, the steady trickle of water. They had reached the aqueduct, and the water wheel that fed it.

He put his mouth to Snowfire's ear. "This is the place," he whispered.

Snowfire nodded, and motioned to him to be silent. He froze where he was, and tried to ignore the three or four insects that decided to negotiate the new piece of territory—his legs—that had suddenly appeared in front of them. He was just glad that Snowfire had given him a handful of aromatic herbs to rub all over himself before they left, for *most* of the insects had left him alone tonight.

Finally, after what seemed far too long a time, Snowfire motioned him forward, and slipped out into the open himself.

Now, for the first time in days, Darian found himself on totally familiar ground. The wooden aqueduct hung above their heads, dripping fairly steadily; he followed the sounds of dripping until his outstretched hands encountered the ladder that led to the first clean-out door up above.

He took a chance that one word wouldn't betray them. "Here!" he whispered harshly, and was suddenly surrounded by seventeen Hawkbrothers.

He scrambled up the ladder and felt for the catch that released the door. The aqueduct wouldn't have worked for a week if it hadn't been covered to keep leaves and trash out; nevertheless, things did manage to get in, and moss and algae grew in the trough. Hatches had to be made to permit occasional cleaners—usually older, more responsible children—to scrub the troughs. To avoid accidents with overcurious or adventurous younger children, the catches were reasonably tricky. Darian had already served one stint as a cleaner; that was how he knew where the catches were and how to open them.

He had a moment of panic when the mechanism jammed and refused to open, but after some desperate prying and jiggling, it broke loose and let him lift the hatch up. With a sigh of relief, he lifted the heavy hatch off to the side. Darian listened for a moment to the cold water running inside, and permitting himself a shiver, climbed in.

He was immediately soaked to mid-calf in very cold water, but he knew that before they reached the village, he'd be soaked clear through. He dropped to his hands and knees and crawled into the tunnel formed by the trough of the aqueduct and the arch of the roof above it. As he crawled forward into the darkness, he felt someone immediately behind him.

Now they were all relying on him to pick the right branching. The right one would bring them out in the village, to the village cistern house right beside the horse trough. The wrong one would send them out into the fields somewhere.

None of the left-hand branchings, he reminded himself. *Those all go out to the fields.* As he crawled, he tried not to think about his surroundings. It was so dark in here that he couldn't see even a glimmer of light. It was cold, there was water up to his chest and the roof of the aqueduct pressing into the back of his head. And someone hadn't done his job, because the floor was slimy with algae. He tried to remind himself that it could have been worse things, but as he started to shiver, that thought wasn't at all comforting.

It's the second right-hand branching. I'm sure of it. But the longer he crawled, the less sure he became. *Was* it the second? He'd been crawling an awfully long time, and he'd only come to one place where the aqueduct opened up to the right. What if he'd missed it? What if he'd gone too far? What if they were already crawling off over the fields of barley and turnips?

Then, just as he was beginning to panic and thinking about trying to get everyone to crawl backward so he could recheck where they'd been, his hand encountered emptiness and water where the wooden wall had been. He stopped, and reached back with his foot to signal that they'd come to the turning.

He felt a hand grab his foot and squeeze; he moved into the right branch, and continued the crawl forward.

Here, at least, the cleaners had done their job. Slime gave way to clean wood under his palms, and he sighed with relief. This must be the correct branch; it was the only one that got scoured religiously, for it not only fed the horse trough but was the main water supply for the whole village.

But now he had new worries. He froze; suddenly they were no longer alone.

He heard the guards before he saw signs of them; heard their voices echoing toward him down the hollow wooden tube. He froze in place, afraid that they had already caught the sounds of hands and knees shuffling through the water above their heads. In another moment, he saw little flickering bits of light reflected in the water, coming through cracks and crevices in the aqueduct cover. *They're going to hear us. They have some magic, or another Yip Dog, that will sense the Hawk-brothers. They have a* real *dog that will smell us up here!* It was all he could do to keep from shouting in panic as the lights drew nearer, as he felt the walls pressing in on him. He began to shiver even harder, and clenched his teeth tightly to keep them from chattering.

Then, miraculously, the lights and voices passed right on by.

He hardly believed it at first, and only a sharp prod from behind got him going again. Twice more, lights and voices approached and passed, and twice more they all froze in place, waiting, shivering in the cold water.

At long last, his hand encountered the end of the aqueduct. They were in the cistern house, where the aqueduct spilled into a storage cistern which in turn led to the horse trough outside the cistern house. He hung onto the end of the trough, and lowered himself down into the cistern, being careful not to make more of a splash than the water pouring into the cistern already made.

One by one, the rest of the Hawkbrothers followed, first into the cistern, then, shivering and chilled, onto the floor of the cistern house beside him.

"I want you to stay here," Snowfire said in his ear. "Keep out of sight. You've done all you need to."

He nodded, his teeth clenched to keep them from chattering. He couldn't have replied if he'd wanted to, for he was shivering too hard, and not just with cold.

"He shouldn't stay here," hissed someone else. "There's no place to hide and only one way in or out, and if anyone comes in here after water, they're going to find him!"

Snowfire growled, but reluctantly agreed. "Let me have Hweel check the stable."

Silence then, except for the sound of falling water and occasional voices outside the cistern house. Darian was in a constant state of terror lest some drunkard stumble in to douse his head and find them all there. At long last, Snowfire spoke again.

"Dar'ian, go to the stable," he ordered. "Hweel says that there are no humans quartered in there, nothing but horses. You should be safe enough at this time of night, and it's halfway between the threshing barn and here. We can get you on our way out of the village.''

Darian just nodded, and waited while the others slipped out, two and three at a time, his gut clenched tight all the while.

How am I going to get out of here? he asked himself, once the last of them were gone. *I can't move and hide like they can! Somebody is going to see me for sure!*

As if to underscore that fear, he heard precisely what he had feared most to hear—the sound of three or four drunken men approaching the cistern house, talking loudly in some foreign babble.

Were they coming here? Where could he hide? Could he get inside the cistern? Would they see him if he did? As he felt blindly about for the edge of the cistern, his hand encountered a bucket that had been left behind, and suddenly a plan burst in on his mind in a blaze of illumination. Quickly, he grabbed the bucket, filled it at the cistern, and just as the men reached the door, he opened it, trudging openly out into the square with his heavy, sloshing bucket.

Exactly as he had hoped, the men ignored him. He was just another slave, and a child at that, insignificant and unworthy of a moment's thought. They shoved past him, and as he trudged away, he heard them splashing and choking in the water, trying to sober themselves up.

Ugh. It's a good thing that from there, the water goes to the horse trough. But if I was a horse, I wouldn't want to drink it after they'd had their dirty heads in it.

He continued to trudge toward the stable, carrying the bucket-handle in both hands, hoping that no one would notice his long knife at his side, the only weapon he had with him. Snowfire wouldn't let him have anything else, and at the time he had thought it a pitiful excuse for a weapon, but he rather doubted that these people allowed their slaves to have anything as dangerous as a knife.

At last he reached the shelter of the stable. He put down the bucket, opened the door, picked the bucket back up and slipped inside. Just in case Hweel had been mistaken, he wanted an excuse to be here, and a bucket of water was a perfectly good excuse.

But it was black in there, without even a night-lamp. That meant that there was nothing, and no one waiting, except for horses.

He waited for his eyes to adjust to the dark, listening to them stamping and blowing, breathing in the scent of horse sweat and hay. Once he could see a little, he walked up to the nearest stall. Each of the stalls had an outside half-door, so that the upper half could be left open for ventilation, and in this weather the upper doors were left open all night so the horses got air. The beast on the other side of the stall door seemed far too large for the stall he'd been put in. Darian stared at him in awe; he was huge, bigger than any horse he'd ever seen before, and a true war-horse. Every stall in the small stable was full, and it was quite clear why the barbarians had put their beasts here instead of using the place to quarter more fighters. These horses must easily have been worth a small fortune apiece. They were certainly worth more than a simple foot soldier, or even a squad of them.

Darian put his bucket down and closed the door, then felt for the ladder built into the wall beside him and climbed up into the loft where the hay was stored, moving carefully and feeling for each rung to keep from making any noise. He would have a good vantage point and a comfortable place to wait as well.

Both loft doors were open to the night air, and he got down on his stomach and wormed his way over to the one that pointed in the direction of the threshing barn. Loose hay covered the floor to the depth of his knees in the middle, and his neck on either side. Mice skittered about in the hay; in the silence he heard two of them fighting, voicing their anger in tiny squeaks.

He settled in with his nose barely poking up above the sill of the door, and strained eyes and ears, trying to penetrate the night. The plan called for the Hawkbrothers to get to the threshing barn, remove any guards that were there, and free the villagers. Wintersky and Raindance would lead them through the village, across the bridge to the road on the other side of the river, and upriver to Kelmskeep; Snowfire and the others would form a rear guard to deal with pursuit.

Nothing in the plan called for actually attacking the barbarians, except in the person of the guards watching the captives. At the time, Darian had been disappointed, but now he was relieved. Trapped inside the cistern house, he had suddenly become aware that he was one young boy surrounded by many, many, strange, hostile men who would not think twice about killing him. Once again, he felt his insides go to water, felt the fear he had experienced when the barbarian army attacked. This was *not* the time or place for a confrontation, and now he was glad that Snowfire had already made up his mind about that.

I just wish someone could have told the enemy so we'd be sure that they would leave us alone—

Suddenly, the peaceful night was split by flashes of red, orange, and green light and a roar as deafening as the worst thunderstorm he'd ever lived through. Darian stifled a yelp and winced away from the door, but immediately reversed himself and peeked back over the top of the sill. Something awful must have happened out there—

It was all coming from the direction of the threshing barn, and he knew with a thrill of dread that the enemy had not gone along with the plan of avoiding confrontation.

More brilliant flashes of light lit the village below, followed by more thundering noises, and men boiled out of the nearby houses like so many angry hornets streaming from a disturbed hive.

His heart pounded, and there was a metallic taste in the back of his mouth. He began to sweat, and had to clench his hands on the sill to keep from jumping up and running out there. *What do I do? Where do I go?* Nothing in the plan told him what to do *now*—

Don't panic. Think of something! He didn't dare move from where he was, and yet there must be something he could do! *If I can stop some of these men, delay them—if only I had a sling, or a rope to trip them with!* What had he learned? How to raise things—how to heat water and call fire—how to sense magic and—

Wait a minute; if I can raise things, can I keep them down? Too late to guess, he just had to *try*; spurred by fear and excitement, he reached out with his tiny spark of magic toward one of the barbarians running below him, and momentarily glued his toe to the ground.

The man tripped and fell heavily, taken too much by surprise to fall properly, and Darian heard something break with a dry *crack*— though whether it was a bone or a weapon, he couldn't tell. The man staggered to his feet, dazed, and stumbled off; he was clearly not in a condition to fight now, and might not be for a while.

Encouraged, Darian did it again, and once again, it worked, sending the man crashing headlong into the ground and driving all the breath from his body. This one was stunned, and only moved feebly rather than trying to get up. It took him a long time to get to his feet and lurch away.

Darian tried the trick again, and yet again, with equal or better success. It was working! He was doing something!

If only he knew what was going on out there—

There was more light, real fire this time, rising above the roofs of the nearest buildings, the harsh smell of smoke, and the sounds of shouts and screams in the distance where the barn stood. He could not tell what was going on, except that the quiet raid had become a full-scale confrontation, and that was not good.

There were no more barbarians where Darian could see them, and he realized belatedly just how exposed his position was. He wormed his way back into the loose hay, pulling it up over himself until there was hay all around him to the depth of a pitchfork's tines; he could still see out the loft door, but now he was peeking out from under the hay like a mouse in a burrow.

He got under cover just in time; someone with a mage-light following him ran toward the stable, and by the long robes the man was wearing, he was *not* one of the Hawkbrothers, nor one of the barbarian fighters.

The stable door slammed open as Darian lost sight of the man, then slammed shut again. He heard a *thud*, the creak of wood and a voice uttering what sounded like curses, and heavy steps on the ladder. He was shudderingly grateful for the cover of the hay, as the mage-light popped over the side of the loft, and the entire loft lit up as brightly as day.

More heavy steps, a shadow passed over Darian's hiding place, and the man stepped into Darian's line-of-sight. He blocked about half of Darian's view, but Darian had a very good view of *him*. Tall, a bit less muscular than the barbarian fighters, but just as shaggy and bearded, he wore an outlandish reddish-brown robe, with a design pieced into it in dark brown leather. It appeared to be the stylized head and forequarters of some beast, but what, Darian couldn't tell. There was a pendant around his neck that swung into view as he turned; a sun-disk, with the rays in metal but the disk in black. An eclipse?

All his attention was centered outside, which was a very good thing, as Darian was in plain sight from where he stood if he chose to look in that direction.

Is this the mage? It must be. What's that pendant mean? Is it magic? Darian tentatively stretched his new "magic-sense" toward the man.

And he was all but "blinded." He shielded himself again, as he'd been taught, and lay there, dazed. *I think this is the mage, all right.*

And the man was doing something; he had his hands cupped in front of him, and he was muttering. And from a point just below them, Darian heard an ominous, deep sound of growling, and the noise of very heavy feet shuffling away.

He's—he's got monsters! He's turning monsters loose! The Hawkbrothers had no warning of *this*—bad enough that they were facing half an army, but no one had thought about facing monsters, too!

He had to do something. He had to! He couldn't let Snowfire down, the way he'd failed Justyn! The man was still muttering, probably calling up another monster. Darian couldn't wait any longer.

With a yell, he leaped out of the hay, pulling his knife at the same time.

The man turned, quick as a thought, but only in time to keep from getting knocked out of the loft door. Darian hit him with a shock, his right shoulder nearly wrenched out of its socket as the man deflected it. They both went down in the hay, with Darian on top; he tried to bring up his knife to finish things, but the man seized his wrist, and rolled to the right. Now Darian was underneath; the man tried to get the knife away from him, bashing his hand down uselessly into the soft hay, his knees digging into Darian's stomach. Darian squirmed, trying to break his hold and get away, and the man held off Darian's knife hand with his right and got his left around Darian's throat and began to squeeze.

He couldn't breathe. His throat was agony, his chest felt as if it were going to burst, his blood pounded in his ears. He writhed and twisted, clawed for the man with his free hand, kicked and thrashed, while the man held him down and throttled him.

Darian's mouth opened, but nothing came out; his eyes felt as if they were going to pop out of his head, his ears and face burned, and he couldn't hear anything but a roaring. His vision went red, then began to tunnel, until all he could see was the man's impassive, bearded face, and that was starting to black out.

Then, with no warning, the man let him go and flung himself backward.

Darian rolled out of the way, coughing and gasping, and looked up to see Huur attached to the man's scalp, flapping her wings furiously and digging bloody furrows along his forehead with her talons.

She must have come in the hayloft door—she saved me!

The man was screaming at the top of his lungs and flailing at the bird with his fists; she in her turn battered him with powerful strokes of her wings, disorienting him. Belatedly, Darian realized he had to get out of there. She hadn't managed a killing hold, she couldn't hang onto him forever, and once she let go, he was free to go after Darian again. Darian scrambled for the ladder and slid down it, with his feet braced on the outside of the uprights and his hands slowing him. He had lost his knife somewhere—he didn't know where, but right now all he wanted was to get away.

But the door was closed, and the bar was down across it. The mage-light dropped down into the stable, and the man stopped screaming; Huur must have let him go.

Please, please, don't let her be hurt!

The horses were all frantically stomping and neighing, upset by the commotion and wanting to take their agitation out on something or someone. The mage would be down there any moment—

Where can I hide that he can't find me?

There wasn't much room in the tiny stable—and with the horses ready to kick anything that stood in their path—

The horses! Yes!

He darted along the center aisle, throwing open the doors to the stalls as he went. The horses hadn't been tied, and once they felt space behind them, they kicked and backed out into the aisle, then proceeded to fight with each other, milling and squealing, and providing a barrier of large and angry bodies between Darian and the ladder. Just as he opened the last stall, he spotted the mage's feet on the ladder, and he saw a pitchfork leaning against the back wall. He seized it, and darted into the last stall, dangerously close to the horse that was vacating it. Fortunately, the horse was more interested in getting a piece of one of his rivals than in stomping Darian into the straw.

This stall had no half-door at the back, and neither did the one opposite it. There would be no escape that way.

As he cowered in the back of the stall, pitchfork clutched in his trembling hands, he heard the mage's voice roaring over the squealing and bugling of the fighting horses, and the *thud* of hooves on wood. He heard the louder sound of the stable doors slamming open, and then the noise of a riding whip on flesh and the thunder of hooves receding. The mage had opened the stable doors and was driving out the horses. Soon he would come looking for Darian.

I'll only get one chance at this— Darian broke out into a cold sweat, shaking all over, but his mind seemed strangely sharp and clear, and as he watched the lighted space of the open stall door, he saw the last of the bulky shadows vanish, leaving only the long shadow of a man.

The mage-light's behind him.

He watched the shadow, and listened to the footsteps, waiting for the moment when the mage would be just around the corner of his stall.

The man was thorough; he checked every stall, while Darian's heart pounded and his gut churned. *He's looking at the opposite ones first. When he first gets up here, I'll have just that long while he checks the other one*—

He saw the shadow's legs, the body silhouetted on the wall; he braced himself, and with the next step, the mage himself appeared framed in the stall door.

Darian charged, screaming.

This time he caught the mage entirely by surprise, driving him into the wall and pinning him there. He looked terrible, with great gouges bleeding down into his face and his robe wet with his own blood—but he was obviously far from finished. One tine of the pitchfork held an arm pinned between it and the next tine, one pierced the man's clothing at his side, although Darian couldn't tell if it had caught flesh, and one was buried in the wood of the back of the stall.

But the mage wasn't dead—and he wasn't done with Darian yet.

There was an insane rage in the man's eyes; he foamed at the mouth, and he clawed at Darian with his free hand. Failing to reach Darian, he grappled with the shaft of the pitchfork, and tried to wrench it away, while at the same time, he pushed away from the wall. There was blood seeping into the mage's clothing, but this was obviously not a fatal wound.

If he could get off the wall, he could free himself.

Darian panted, bracing his feet in the dirt of the stall floor, and hung on with the strength of desperation. Why wouldn't this man *die*?

Bit by bit, the mage pushed Darian back, struggling in eerie silence. Bit by bit, Darian's feet slipped, and he scrambled to reestablish his hold.

If the mage got loose, he'd kill Darian—then he'd kill Snowfire and all the others. Then he'd go after Nightwind and Starfall and Kelvren. And all because Darian had failed.

"No!" he screamed at the top of his lungs. *"Not—this—time!"*

With a last burst of energy, he drove the mage back, and felt a surge of elation.

But the madness left the man's eyes for a moment, and the mage screamed something guttural. The handle of the pitchfork burst into flame, splintered, then crumbled away, leaving Darian standing with a handful of kindling and ash. The mage plucked the metal tine out, and cast it to the ground contemptuously.

Darian stared, frozen.

The mage laughed, and reached out, his fingers curling into a claw.

Darian ducked and rolled to the side. He came up running, or trying to, heading for the open stable door.

Behind him, the mage screamed something else, and the door slammed shut in his face; he hit it, unable to stop in time, and dropped to the floor.

The mage laughed again, and Darian rolled over, his back to the door, and his hand fell on the bar that had held it shut. He didn't even think; he just grabbed it, and came up swinging.

He caught the mage on the side of the head, once again catching him by surprise. The man reeled back, and Darian swung again.

This time the mage caught the wooden bar and wrenched it out of Darian's hands, throwing it aside.

Darian dove underneath the man's grasping hands, gambling that the wound in his side was too painful for him to move easily. He somersaulted and came up on his feet on the other side; the mage was between him and the door again. He looked frantically about for a weapon, any weapon.

His eye fell on the forged tines of the pitchfork as the mage turned.

This time he didn't dare fail. It didn't matter if *he* died; he couldn't fail the others.

He snatched up the tines, braced the rounded end against his chest, and charged again, but this time with every last bit of strength, and every bit of his weight, holding back nothing.

He drove the larger man back against the closed door; felt the tines hit flesh that yielded, resisted, then gave with a wet *pop*. The man screamed horribly; he flailed at Darian and a terrible blow to the side of his head knocked him away, stunning him; he fell to the ground as everything went dark.

He couldn't move, couldn't see anything.

Am I blind? With a convulsive shudder, he managed to move, to get to his knees, but he still couldn't see anything. Everything was dark.

Then, with a creak, one of the stable doors swung open, and vague and flickering red light outside proved that he *wasn't* blind after all. It was the mage-light that was gone.

But the mage was still moving. In a moment, he might get up again. He was hurt, but by no means dead yet.

Darian's right hand was wet, as was his sleeve, and as he moved it, his fingers touched his abandoned bucket. He grabbed it and lurched to his feet, staggering over to the mage who stared up at him in the changing light, spittle at the corner of his mouth.

He gave the man no chance to act; he brought the bucket down on his head as hard as he could. If the man wouldn't die, at least he wasn't going to stay awake for long!

He hit the mage a couple more times for good measure, then left the bucket upturned over his face and staggered, exhausted, out into the open. He didn't care who or what saw him at this point. He stood in the middle of the dirt path, swaying on his feet, wondering where he should go next. The shouting had decreased; who was winning?

Then he sensed something gathering at his back; something oddly familiar. Magic—but—where and when had he sensed something like this before?

Magic—like— For some reason the sensation called up a memory of Justyn, but Justyn had never had enough magic for him to sense like this—

Except the day he destroyed the bridge!

Fear gave him energy he thought he didn't have; he sprinted for shelter, any shelter, heading for the nearest building as fast as his feet would carry him. He reached it just as the stable behind him exploded into flame, the shock of the blast knocking him into the side of the cottage. He saw fireworks behind his eyes for a moment, and had all the wind knocked out of him. He struggled to breathe, lying on his side, trying to make his lungs work again.

He didn't stay that way for long; when his eyes cleared and he got a few good breaths, he picked himself gingerly out of the remains of a flower garden. He looked around, and things were pretty much the same as they had been. With a single exception, that is. What was left of the stable blazed fiercely, as if it had been soaked in oil.

Darian went looking for Snowfire and the others, but didn't have to go far to find them. No sooner did he round the corner of the house than he saw the entire cavalcade approaching—the Hawk-brothers, battered and injured, but all still alive, followed by the villagers.

The villagers of Errold's Grove were a far different group of people than they had been a half moon ago. They had clearly been kept on short rations by their captors, and just as clearly had been worked to exhaustion. They were filthy, unkempt—precisely the kind of folk that they themselves would have turned away from the village as vagabonds. Clothing, dirty, torn and tattered in the course of hard labor, had not been changed, cleaned or mended in all the time they'd been captives. Some of the men showed signs of beatings; all looked as wary and spooked as the horses running freely among the houses.

But Darian had no eyes for them; with a joyful shout, he ran to Snowfire and the others, who answered his shout and surrounded him, babbling questions, while the villagers stared at him with wide eyes. The villagers recognized him, yes, but this was not the same Darian that they had scorned and disregarded before.

"One at a time!" Snowfire ordered, and some of the babble subsided. "Dar'ian, we were surprised by a group coming to claim some of your people. We were attacked. We took shelter in the barn, and were promptly put under siege. What saved us was that the elite fighters that were left here had been drinking, and simply didn't fight *together* at all well. We were holding our own, until we were attacked by a—a bear-creature. It must have been summoned and controlled by their mage. It broke through our defenses and killed three of your people and injured several of us. We are sorry—there was just nothing we could have done to save them, though we tried. Then, the creature suddenly went berserk, as if it was no longer under control, and turned on the barbarians! They had to fight us and it at the same time; they killed it, but seemed to lose heart and retreated—then there was a tremendous roar and flames shot into the sky, and their retreat turned into a rout! What happened here?"

"It was the mage," Darian said, too tired to feel even a flicker of pride in his deed. "I saw him making magic and I knew I had to do something. I think he's dead; I think he did what Justyn did at the bridge."

He told the tale as quickly as he could, in as few words as possible. He was a little afraid that Snowfire and the rest might not believe him. After all, who was *he* to claim to have destroyed a powerful mage?—but they accepted his tale at face value. And the results were there for all to see, so perhaps it was not as difficult to believe as he had feared.

"You were one thing he would not have been concerned about," Snowfire said thoughtfully. "He would never have believed that a single young boy could be a threat to him, not even when he had the evidence of that threat slashed into his own body. He should have known better. We all know that the smallest creature can become dangerous when driven to desperation."

"I couldn't have done it if it hadn't been for Huur," Darian said hastily. "She *is* all right, isn't she?"

"One broken feather, and a ruffled temper, which she has flown off to cool," Snowfire assured him, and looked around at the wide-eyed group of villagers surrounding them. He switched to stilted Valdemaran.

"I believe we hold Errold's Grove, and need not fear the return of the barbarians tonight," he said, raising his voice. "I believe it is safe enough to stay and sleep, and in the morning, begin to rebuild. If you will go to your houses, we allies of Valdemar will secure the place against intruders."

Still shocked and bewildered, ready to listen to anyone who offered a voice of authority, they trailed back to their houses by twos and threes. Snowfire divided the Hawkbrothers into three groups of five, leaving out the two worst wounded, to take night-watches. "Is there anyplace you can go to rest?" he asked Darian, with a hand resting lightly on his shoulder. "Would anyone give you bed space? You have done more than enough for one night!"

Darian felt each and every separate bruise aching, thought longingly of Justyn's little cottage, once despised, and nodded.

"Go then," Snowfire said, giving him a gentle shove. "I will see that you are awakened in the morning."

Already those not on the first watch were putting out the fire in the blazing stable; soon concealing darkness hid the signs of battle, leaving only the acrid scent of smoke in the air. Darian trudged toward Justyn's cottage, wondering what he would find there.

What he found in the light of a single lantern was signs of recent occupation; the furniture was gone, probably broken up for firewood. The contents of the shelves lay piled in a corner, discarded as worthless, including all the bad paintings of famous mages, and there were bedrolls spread across every available bit of floor. He wrinkled his nose at the smell of sweat, burned food, and unwashed bedding; he took the time to throw all the bedrolls out the door and open the windows. The fireplace hadn't been swept in ages, and it seemed that when the barbarians finished eating, they tended to pitch what was left into the fire, for it was littered with bones and burned crusts— hence the odor of burned food. Darian climbed the ladder to his loft bed, and discovered it was the one corner of the house that hadn't been touched, probably because his little bed was too short for any of the barbarians.

With a weary sigh, he tumbled into bed, leaving the lantern to burn itself out.

It was the sound of horses and men's voices that woke him in the gray light of dawn, and before he was even properly awake, he tumbled down out of the loft and emerged from the cottage with a poker in one hand, ready to do battle all over again.

But it wasn't the barbarians who had returned; the noise was the arrival of a rescue expedition. Men on horses milled around the square, all of them wearing Lord Breon's colors and badge; more men afoot were rounding up loose livestock and confining it in hastily-built corrals. Darian put down his poker and scratched his head, watching all the activity with a sense of bleary bemusement.

After another moment, he quietly got himself a bucket of water and used it to clean himself up, wincing as he scrubbed a body that was black and blue from neck to knee. Once clean and marginally presentable, he went back out and joined the milling people, picking up what had happened this morning by listening to fragments of conversation.

Lord Breon had gotten Starfall's message and had gathered his men to respond to it—but on the way, he had encountered the thoroughly demoralized barbarian foot soldiers, and had fought an unequal battle with them. Then, having defeated the barbarians, he had been stopped by the rockfall, and had been forced to find a place to ford the river to get to the road on the other side. By this time, of course, they were certain that they would find Errold's Grove occupied by a hostile force, and had only hoped to catch the remaining barbarians by surprise. Ready for battle, they had clattered over the bridge a little before dawn only to encounter the sentries; after learning that the town was in friendly hands, they had made enough noise to wake up most of those who were sleeping.

When Darian wandered in, rubbing his eyes with the back of his hand, Lord Breon himself was in earnest consultation with Snowfire, with townsfolk standing awkwardly about, still looking dazed and bewildered, though most of them had cleaned themselves up and found more presentable clothing. They formed a sad contrast with their once-respectable selves, however, and looked rather as if they had grabbed whatever would fit with little regard for the sex or size their garments were originally intended for.

Snowfire spotted him and hailed him with relief. "Here! Little brother! Your command of the tongue is better than mine, come and help me with this!"

Not at all reluctant, Darian ignored his bruises and aching bones, and trotted to Snowfire's side, feeling flushed with pride. When Snowfire was at a loss for words, he translated. Lord Breon, a neat and handsome gentleman of middling age and height, clothed in a businesslike suit of riveted armor, brown of hair and eyes and beard, took the Hawkbrothers completely in stride. But Darian's fellow villagers started every time any one of them moved suddenly, and kept circling warily around the birds. To Darian's relief, he caught sight of Huur, Hweel, and an awkward-looking youngster dozing on the rooftree nearest Snowfire, where they had evidently been most of the night, with Daystorm's bondbird corbies keeping the natives at a respectful distance.

"My Lord Snowfire," Lord Breon said when they were finished, a look of profound respect in his eyes, "you have certainly kept things well in hand here. I am sure that the Queen herself will want to thank you eventually."

Snowfire shrugged. "We are allies, are we not?" he pointed out. "And if you had not intercepted the foot troops before they returned, we should probably have been forced to defend ourselves from them as we marched these folk toward your holding and safety. Now they need no longer seek shelter among your people."

"Beggin' your pardon!" Lutter spoke up, interrupting him. "But we need to know what we're to do now."

The man was a far cry from his former, prosperous self. He had changed his clothing, but it hung on him loosely, and his middle-aged face bore signs of both fresh and not-so-recent bruises in purple, black, green, and yellow.

"What are you to do?" Lord Breon looked at him askance. "Why, pick up your lives, man, what else?"

"Pick up our lives?" he replied, aghast. "What are you talking about? How can we pick up our lives? There's nothing left here! The barbarians took it all—what they didn't eat, they destroyed! We've no crops, no food, no herds or flocks, how are we to get through the winter?"

Darian snorted with contempt, and all eyes turned toward him. Snowfire looked at him curiously, Lord Breon with surprise, and Lutter with astonishment turning to anger at having been interrupted by the village scapegrace.

"I'll tell you what you've got!" Darian said hotly, amazed at their stupidity. "You've got your homes back, you've got a *pile* of weapons and armor that ought to be worth *something*. You've got a dozen or more real warhorses that are each worth the price of a good house, and you've got a whole lot more regular horses, too! You've got mules and two wagons, whatever was in those wagons, and you've got the *whole Peligiris Forest* to hunt dye-fungus in. You can *buy* food again, you don't have to grow it! What are you complaining about?"

"And you've got this." Lilly, the barmaid, came up dragging someone's once-fine coverlet, made into a crude bag, across the ground. She let the corners fall, revealing a mixed pile of coins and jewelry. "I couldn't tell whose was whose," she continued. "So I just piled them all together, but I *know* that most of this didn't come from Errold's Grove."

It certainly couldn't have, since a great deal of the jewelry was of gold. No wonder the bundle had been too heavy to carry!

"Shkar had all this in his room," she continued. "And I thought that when you get done picking out the bits that belong to you, Lord Breon could arrange to sell the rest and buy new stock for everybody who lost beasts and fowl."

"What about the stuff you're wearing?" asked a woman, shrilly, and only then did Darian look up to see that Lilly was bedecked with several heavy gold bracelets, chains, and odd-looking pendants.

Lilly flushed, but looked angry. "This is *mine*," she replied fiercely. "I earned every bit of it!"

"Oh, *earned* it, did you?" the woman snarled. "At your ease, in comfort, while the rest of us sweated out in the fields? Earned it, did you?"

For once, Lilly stood up for herself, pulling herself up tall and staring the woman down. "Yes, *earned* it! Earned it by waiting on Shkar day and night, doing things I don't even like to think about, keeping him and his bullies looking at *me* and thinking about *me* instead of you, making sure that every time their eyes started wandering toward your pretty little daughter, Stella Harthon, that they got pulled back toward *me*. How did you think it happened? By magic? I fought for all our sakes with the only weapon that I knew would work against them! And now I'm *keeping* what I earned from them, I'm taking it, and I'm going to go and buy a real inn someplace else where nobody is going to look down her long petty nose at me again!"

Darian flushed with anger as he saw sour and angry faces among the women still, in spite of the fact that the pile of loot in the coverlet was vastly more valuable than what Lilly wore. *How greedy can they be?* he wondered.

But Lutter coughed, and said to Lilly, red-faced, "You're right, girl. You've earned it. And you've earned the right to take it and yourself someplace else if you want to. But if we're going to get the dye-trade going again, we're going to need a real inn—"

Lilly interrupted him, shaking her head, though her demeanor softened. "No. If I go elsewhere, I'll be Lilly, the respectable innkeeper. I can never be that if I stay here. I'm leaving. Besides," she chuckled weakly, "when I leave, it'll give your wives a bad example to show their girl-children."

"I would like to ask you some questions about your time among those men," Lord Breon said with delicate tact. "You knew the name of one of the leaders, for instance."

"Shkar," she said, and shrugged. "I didn't learn much of their tongue. They didn't need me for language lessons, and what they wanted they could get by pointing.''

"Nevertheless, you may know more than you think you do," Lord Breon persisted. "If you'd care to come back with me, after I've learned what I can from you, I'll gladly provide an escort to wherever you choose.''

"That suits me." She turned abruptly and went to stand among Lord Breon's men, who, after a stern look from Lord Breon, did not leer or make suggestive comments but simply made a place for her.

"In the meantime, the woman is right," the Lord continued, surveying the pile. "Between the loot there, and the horses, you will have more than enough to rebuild what was lost. I'll trade ten cattle or twenty adult hogs for each warhorse this minute, sight unseen, for instance. Or you can take them to the horsemarket and try your luck there." He raked his eyes over the crowd. "You'll have to agree on equal shares, as you all suffered equally, so far as I can see. It will take a great deal of work, but in the end, Errold's Grove will be as prosperous as it was before.''

There was some muttering, especially among those who had been the most well-off before the invasion, but finally everyone agreed.

"Now, as for Darian," Lord Breon began.

Snowfire interrupted him this time. "With all respect, we have already taken him into our clan," the Tayledras said, and Darian's heart leaped. "*We* do not consider him a burden.''

But evidently some word of what Darian had done had gotten to the villagers, for there was an immediate protest. "But he's our mage! We are going to *need* a mage!" exclaimed Lutter in dismay. "What if someone like these barbarians comes back?''

"You need a trained mage, which Dar'ian is not," Snowfire replied sternly. "He must be trained, and you have no adequate teachers. Nor are you likely to get any, considering how long it took to get you the first one.''

"But he can heal—''

"As I believe, some of you once pointed out, any of your young people could learn to do, apprenticing for six months with a Healer.'' Snowfire's mouth twitched at the dismay on certain faces; Darian had to hide his face lest his own expression give him away. "I suggest you do that. Perhaps, if at some time, a *generous* offer is made, you may tempt another mage to come and take residence here. Until that time, I fear you shall have to learn to watch your own borders and defend yourselves.''

But Darian felt a twinge of guilt as he looked at the real fear in the eyes of some of them. Terrible things had happened here, things that people would never speak of, but which would shadow their dreams for the rest of their lives. They would never feel truly secure again.

"What is it, lad?" Lord Breon asked, seeing the doubt in his own eyes. "What is it to be? Do you go with the Hawkbrothers, or do you remain here?"

He looked from Snowfire's calm eyes, to Lord Breon's worried ones, and back again. "I—I *have* to be trained, first," he said, echoing Snowfire's words. "And I'd rather it was with my friends than anyone else. But—" He shook his head, and tried to put into words the idea he'd had. "But—this place is right on the border, right on the edge of Hawkbrother lands and Valdemar, right? Shouldn't there be someone who was as much a Hawkbrother as a Valdemaran, right here all the time, to make sure that there are never any misunderstandings?"

Lord Breon looked astounded, and Snowfire impressed and pleased. He hurried on. "And Lutter is right. Errold's Grove is going to need a real mage, sooner or later. The Peligirs haven't gotten less strange, even after the Storms; if there was a mage here, he could look at stuff that was brought out and tell if it was good for anything besides dyeing. Other things, too. So—couldn't I do both?" He turned pleading eyes to Snowfire. "Couldn't I go with you, learn to be a mage and one of the Clan, then come back here and maybe make a little Vale where Tayledras would always be able to come?"

"It would be a hard life, and often lonely, being neither of this world nor that," Snowfire said softly in the Hawkbrother tongue. "But you are correct, that there is a need for such a person. Especially here, where there is—scope for a great deal of misunderstanding."

"Then that's what I'd like," he sighed. Then he laughed a little and shook his head. "Hellfires, I never *could* take the easy way with anything!"

"I am glad that you made that choice, little brother," the scout replied, and switched to Valdemaran. "That is a good plan, and a generous one. You shall come with us and be trained, and when you are ready, you shall return here and be a living example of the Alliance. You shall make for us a haven for our kind, and a place where those of Valdemar will find help when it is needed."

Sighs and smiles all around, but Snowfire wasn't finished yet.

"And since it is a plan that shows wisdom beyond your years, I shall do as Hweel and Huur asked me, though you are not quite yet of an age for such a joy and a responsibility." He smiled. "After all, usually in matters of this sort, our winged ones are far too wise to be bound by convention."

He whistled and held up his gauntletted arm—but instead of Hweel coming in to land on it, the youngster woke up, hooted loudly, and blundered in to his fist. Before Darian had a moment to think, Wintersky grabbed his left hand and slipped a shoulder-length glove over it, then held it up. The youngster made a clumsy hop from Snowfire's fist to Darian's, and looked deeply into Darian's dazzled eyes as Snowfire laughed with delight at his expression.

"H–hello," Darian stammered, beside himself with so much joy and excitement that he shook. "What's your name?"

:*Kuari,*: the bird said solemnly in his mind. :*I am Kuari. I like you. We'll be bondmates. Yes?* They *want it, too:* The owl didn't move his head, but Darian knew that *they* meant Hweel and Huur, sitting side-by-side up on the rooftree. :*I like mice. I want to hunt mice. Bring you some, too?:*

"I have the feeling that Hweel and Huur have decided that this will ensure your place within the clan, little brother," Snowfire said in Tayledras, with suppressed laughter in his voice.

Darian didn't care; the trust he sensed in Kuari's "voice" won his heart as nothing else could have. With gentle care, he reached up and scratched the youngster's head at the eartufts, as he had seen Snowfire do for Hweel.

:*Oh, I like that. I like that better than mice. Do that a lot.:*

Kuari closed his eyes in ecstasy, all but melting under the caress, and butted his head into Darian's hand.

"I told you," Daystorm muttered to Snowfire, in a whisper Darian probably wasn't supposed to overhear. "The boy's a natural with the birds. He'll be fine."

Yes, I will be fine, he thought, his heart so brimming with joy and contentment that there was no room in it anymore for anger, resentment, or grief. *Yes, I will. I've got a family, adventure, a worthy goal. I'm home. I'm finally making my own home.*

Darian looked up, and out at the villagers, who were conspicuously silent. "One last thing," he said boldly. "I won't even consider returning until there is a portrait of the great mage Justyn displayed in a place of honor in Errold's Grove."

He paused a moment, then added, just to make sure, "A *good* portrait."

Then Darian, Hawkbrother of Valdemar, turned his full attention to his new bondmate's soft feathers, and the shared bliss that came from being with each other.

Maybe the young owl's flight was not all that graceful at the moment, but in time, with support and guidance, he would be a master at whatever he tried. In time, so too would Darian, and he would be at home wherever he went.